THE MAGI'S MAN

A SHEPHERD'S STORY

A.I. Wexler & Mark Cardona

2020 Library of Congress (ECO) System 1-9888950811

Certificate of Registration Number TXu 2-235-048

ISBN 9798742180906

The Magi's Man is a work of fiction. Characters, names and the story were created by the authors. Historical people and events are seen from the perspective of those individuals. Descriptions of historical places and actions are from the imagination of the authors.

Table of Contents

Preface · · · · · · · · · · ix

Abba—Father · · · · · · · · · · 1

Chapter 1 The Night · · · · · · · · · · 3
Chapter 2 The Grotto · · · · · · · · · · 11
Chapter 3 The Road · · · · · · · · · · 17
Chapter 4 The Secret · · · · · · · · · · 23
Chapter 5 The Aleph · · · · · · · · · · 29
Chapter 6 The Favor · · · · · · · · · · 37
Chapter 7 The Oranges · · · · · · · · · · 41
Chapter 8 The Reconnect · · · · · · · · · · 45
Chapter 9 The Arrival · · · · · · · · · · 53
Chapter 10 The Concerns · · · · · · · · · · 59
Chapter 11 The Covenant · · · · · · · · · · 63
Chapter 12 The Massacre · · · · · · · · · · 69
Chapter 13 The Porch · · · · · · · · · · 73
Chapter 14 The Baby · · · · · · · · · · 79
Chapter 15 The Meeting · · · · · · · · · · 83

Ben—Son · · · · · · · · · · 91

Chapter 16 The Decade · · · · · · · · · · 93
Chapter 17 The Amazement · · · · · · · · · · 103
Chapter 18 The Family · · · · · · · · · · 111
Chapter 19 The Dispatch · · · · · · · · · · 115
Chapter 20 The Pondering · · · · · · · · · · 119
Chapter 21 The Wedding · · · · · · · · · · 123
Chapter 22 The Decision · · · · · · · · · · 133
Chapter 23 The Walk · · · · · · · · · · 137
Chapter 24 The Story · · · · · · · · · · 141
Chapter 25 The Doubter · · · · · · · · · · 147

Chapter 26 The Fishermen · · · 151
Chapter 27 The Daughter · · · 155
Chapter 28 The Witness · · · 161
Chapter 29 The Centurion · · · 167
Chapter 30 The Tables · · · 175
Chapter 31 The Immerser · · · 183
Chapter 32 The Passover · · · 189
Chapter 33 The Mentor · · · 197
Chapter 34 The Zealot · · · 205
Chapter 35 The Baton · · · 213
Chapter 36 The Son · · · 217
Chapter 37 The Shawl · · · 223
Chapter 38 The Madman · · · 231
Chapter 39 The Mother-in-Law · · · 237
Chapter 40 The Innkeeper · · · 243
Chapter 41 The Curse · · · 247
Chapter 42 The Honor · · · 255
Chapter 43 The Aide · · · 261
Chapter 44 The Guest · · · 267
Chapter 45 The Blessings · · · 271
Chapter 46 The Breakfast · · · 277
Chapter 47 The Sandals · · · 283
Chapter 48 The Roof · · · 291
***Ruach HaKodesh*—Holy Spirit** · · · **299**
Chapter 49 The Pool · · · 301
Chapter 50 The Sleep · · · 305
Chapter 51 The Divide · · · 309
Chapter 52 The Breeze · · · 315
Chapter 53 The Well · · · 319
Chapter 54 The Scrolls · · · 325
Chapter 55 The Beggar · · · 329
Chapter 56 The Perfume · · · 333
Chapter 57 The Colt · · · 337
Chapter 58 The Ride · · · 341

Chapter 59 The Tent ··· 345
Chapter 60 The Children ··· 351
Chapter 61 The Teaching ··· 355
Chapter 62 The Courtyard ··· 359
Chapter 63 The Pet ··· 363
Chapter 64 The Darkness ··· 367
Chapter 65 The Path ··· 373
Chapter 66 The Curtain ··· 377
Chapter 67 The Silence ··· 381
Chapter 68 The Eviction ··· 385
Chapter 69 The News ··· 389
Chapter 70 The Smile ··· 393
Chapter 71 The Fire ··· 397
Chapter 72 The Cylinder ··· 401
Chapter 73 The Parchments ··· 405
Chapter 74 The Decision ··· 413
Chapter 75 The Preparation ··· 417
Chapter 76 The Beginning ··· 421
Names ··· 425
Glossary ··· 429
Acknowledgements ··· 435

PREFACE

HAS GOD EVER spoken to you, not in a thundering voice on a mountaintop but through the voice of a friend? Perhaps something you heard or read? Music? Art? He speaks to us in countless ways we may not immediately recognize.

As a twelve-year-old, I was chased by a man for being a "Jew boy." I had come out of synagogue after studying for my bar mitzvah and ran three blocks before hiding in the fold of a glass doorway. My pursuer looked right at me. He stared, paused, lit a cigarette, scanned the street, then walked away. I didn't know it then, but God made me invisible, protecting me so that someday, many years later, I could write this book.

A friend introduced me to Messiah, but I ran away. Ed Goetze did not stop until I understood, and I was freed from lifelong fears and struggles. Ed gave me a complete Bible and challenged me to open my mind. Many years later Mark Cardona asked me to cowrite the book he had notes on and a few chapters, but business pressures would not let him. This is what Mark says:

"The idea for this book came while I was reading the story of the Magi at Christmas. It occurred to me that these *kings* from Persia traveled far to see the promised Messiah, then rode off without knowing what happened. I would have wanted to know!

Our country was at war at the time and embedded reporters were sending dispatches from the front lines, critical information. Why not have a shepherd meet the Magi before they leave to escape Herod's rage and become their reporter? He would find the Messiah then document his life and times. The mission would be to meet with one of their men each year and pass those accounts to be taken to the Magi.

My purpose was to glorify the God of the universe and His Son in the same way Francine Rivers built a wonderful and inspiring novel about Jesus and the widow of Nain. I sought to do something similar with a shepherd and several miracles. I wanted to make it known that the Savior came through ordinary people like Mary and Joseph, was humbly born, lived an austere life and died an ugly death on a cross; all for us!

Often, we lose the human side of the Gospel message. Think of it; Jesus is the only King we will ever speak with and he the only one we will ever need. I tried staying true to the facts in the Bible while trying to make it come alive.

Mark Cardona"

I declined Mark's offer until the *aha* moment, the denouement to build the story prompting me to weave this work. *The Magi's Man* is the result of that yearlong effort.

Each chapter is a short, short story. Events and words from scripture are paraphrased. Hebrew names and words are transliterated. The Shepherd Academy was created to elevate the significance of a lowly but critical profession. The presentations of the Magi's gifts are imagined, as are many other events. An angel told Joseph to give his son the same name as the high priest of the temple in Jerusalem; that's in the Bible!

There are times I read these pages and know it was not my hands alone on the keyboard. Night and day for a year, the *Ruach HaKodesh* (Holy Spirit) fed me ideas, courage, and stamina to complete a book I pray will be compelling. As I was challenged to seek the truth, please do the same. Read the *Tanakh* (Old Testament) and the New Testament; they are one book!

In some ways my journey with this manuscript is my testimony. It is me reaching out to you, my beloved family, to understand who I am and why I believe that *Yeshua* (Jesus) is *Mashiach* (Messiah)!

Come along with me on a journey. Read the story and see what could have happened.

Arnie Wexler

To the discoverer of this scroll:

I write these words for my children, grandchildren, and any future family, for I am about to set out on a journey to a land far away. Therefore, I leave this record behind should I not return. My life has been quite a long road with, I believe, more to come. I started out as a boy without cares, tending sheep for my father. Only Adonai knew what he had in store for me when my odyssey began over thirty years ago.

Abba—Father

CHAPTER 1

THE NIGHT

THE WOLVES WERE getting closer; I could smell them. All the hair on my body was bristling with fear and excitement! There were four of them. They had a lamb isolated away from the flock, and it was bleating in terror. Lying flat on the ground, I was able to see their images against the canopy of stars on that clear, moonless night. Slowly I rose to one knee, keeping an eye on the largest of the pack. With a practiced motion, I placed a large, smooth stone in my sling and began rotating my arm as I stood. Taking one quick step forward, I snapped the sling toward the large male and released the missile. My efforts were rewarded with a smack, a crack, and a howl. The wolves bolted away, following their whimpering leader, and I was able to calm myself and the flock.

I am a shepherd, a Levite, one among many in our country. I come from a long line of shepherds that go back to when my people settled at the place the prophet *Moshe* (Moses) declared was filled with milk and honey. As Levites we were not given land like the other tribes. Instead we were to be servants of the temple in villages throughout the land. I am descended from shepherds serving the temple providing sheep and lambs for wool, milk, and sacrifice. They are much needed and important commodities of the people.

All shepherds are adept with slings and have been since well before the time of *Melech Dav'ed* (King David). As small boys we were taught how to load, wind, and release carefully chosen stones. To learn, we start with small pebbles that are as round as possible so that their flight is true. As we grow in stature, the slings and stones get larger, and the skill is practiced daily. We become excellent marksmen rivalling the tribe of *Binyamin* (Benjamin), renowned for their prowess as left-handed sling marksmen; they were experts. Our oral history tells us that the stone that slew the giant Philistine *Golyat* (Goliath) was as big as the young shepherd David's fist.

The line of shepherds I was about to become part of had the special assignment of traveling from village to village in Judea to inspect sheep and find spotless specimens that would be perfect for the *Pesach* (Passover) sacrifice. The *Kohen HaGadol* (high priest) in Jerusalem had an academy that trained and certified Levites who tended the flocks and journeyed to villages throughout the land. I was about to become one of those shepherds entering the academy in *Yerushalayim* (Jerusalem) for training.

The wolves were the second attack of the night, but the first was even more frightening for me personally. I was leaning against a tree on the western edge of the flock when I was startled by an alarming bleat. It sounded like the cry of a ewe calling in desperation to a missing lamb. I jumped up, grabbed my hooked staff, and ran toward the recognizable sound.

Even though it was a moonless night, I was able to see two images stumbling at the edge of the herd. Being sure-footed on the hillside from having grown up on these uneven grounds, I kept a good pace and wrapped my hand around the rod fastened to my sash. At the same time, I started growling, a sound the flock was familiar with when I was on the hunt for a predator. They knew I was there to protect them, so there was no cause for severe alarm and stampede.

What I came upon were two men carrying a lamb that had a large cloth over its head; they were fleeing. The rod I carry has pieces of flint hammered into the knob at the end—a formidable weapon. I dropped the staff and looped the leather band attached to the rod, securing it to my wrist, then ran at them. I started swinging the rod at the nearest thief and caught the edge of his garment, ripping it and causing him to stumble.

As he fell, he dropped his end of the lamb, causing his partner in crime to fall and drop the lamb completely. They scrambled away as I stopped to see about the lamb. My heart was pounding from the run, the fear, and, in some respect, the excitement of the confrontation. I had never before encountered thieves by myself, and I was alone against two grown men. Even though I was young, I was quite big and strong. Years of practice with the rod and sling had paid off.

My first concern at that point was the precious lamb. It was lying still, with the burlap rag wrapped around its head; I was afraid it was dead! I knelt down and touched its side, felt it breathing; it stirred from my touch. I started humming as I unwrapped its head, and it began to struggle to its feet. I picked it up and started back toward the flock, carrying the one that was not lost.

The night I dissuaded the wolves with a stone about the size of a ripe fig was just like almost every other night during the long summer as it came to an end—clear, dark, and utterly still. The land had gone months without rain, with almost no clouds in the sky. Our banked campfire had burned down to embers, a dull red glow, and the only other light was in the heavens. The stars were so bright, so radiant, it seemed that if I reached up, I could touch them.

I spend most of my time outdoors with the sheep and goats. These animals are totally defenseless against a predator, so we become their only protectors. Sheep are the animals of choice for our worship and sacrifice, and there is always a huge demand for an almost endless supply.

But for all the needs we meet, shepherds are usually looked down on by most of society as odd and peculiar, even though the group of which I was becoming a part was educated and well trained. We are a section of a spiritual leadership team, and many of us are judges in our villages. Perhaps it is the rough-hewn garments that we wear, clothing made for a life outdoors that causes others to look down on us. Of course the smell of sheep and goats that soaks into what we wear does manage to keep us at arm's length from others.

I am called *Eliyahu ben Etzrah* (Elijah, son of Ezra)—known as Eli by most. That night there were four of us bringing a flock of sheep from *Kanah* (Cana) in Galilee to the hills near Jerusalem. The demand for lambs was very high that season as the cold weather would soon be upon us. It was wise and good business for small flock owners to take advantage of the Roman census decree to take them there since so many in Israel were originally from *Beit Lehem* (Bethlehem) of King David and forced to go there to register.

When I was a child, my *sabba* (grandfather) and *abba* (father) told me stories of when the Romans became our conquerors. Our proud people were a great nation until unity eluded our leaders and we became subject to a host of tyrants. At least the Romans allowed us to practice our faith under their appointed King Herod. But we were subject to two oppressors at the same time.

The Romans were elegant savages. Everything they did was dressed in finery, but underneath their costumes, they were a greedy, bloodthirsty lot. Their power had always been their military. Roman soldiers were there to keep us oppressed and squeeze us for more taxes year after year. That is why at that time the whole of our nation was afoot and on the road; the governor Quirinius, at the demand of Caesar, ordered a census to extort more tax money from our people. It was a constant, growing burden on all.

Often being in the way of a Roman was akin to a crime. With impunity any Roman in uniform could beat us for the slightest provocation. Usually no provocation was necessary, and they seemed to be everywhere. And yet for some reason, during that trip there was an air of excitement, an unexplainable sense of anticipation despite the Roman oppression.

Our route was from Cana in the north. The flock was a cooperative effort of the local small farms to get their sheep to market. Each owner had sent thirty sheep and a shepherd to form a crew. In all we were four men and a flock of 120 sheep. We had argued as to which route to take. I was only sixteen years old and, as one of the younger shepherds, had little say. Besides this was my first long working trip away from my village, even though I had been working officially as a shepherd three years since my confirmation as a man into the tribe, becoming a *bar mitzvah* (son of the commandment). Growing up in the community of shepherds made it an easy transition into my adult occupation. I was also being groomed as a judge, to take my father's place at some future date.

After the wolves I was exhausted, but it was the middle of my watch, so movement was necessary. To lighten my heart as I walked, I started thinking about the love of my life, my betrothed, *Rahel* (Rachel). That scrawny, little, raven-haired firebrand had grown up. I don't remember when the child I knew all my life became an almond-eyed, olive-skinned beauty; what a woman she had become! Adorable, smart, and so full of life. We had grown up together in Cana, and we were to be married in less than two months. I could not wait to get back to her. Thinking of her deep brown eyes and radiant smile helped pass the seemingly endless hours of my watch.

It amuses me to think about the changes in my feelings for her. When we were children, she would tease me for being big, slow, and clumsy. She was so agile, so fleet of foot, and would run circles around me during our free time with the other children. She would get her work done quickly then come to our house and sweetly taunt me about being so oafish. I found myself smiling as I stood imagining Rachel in my arms.

Then, in a moment of time, the world changed! The most brilliant light shattered the inky blackness. It was like a hundred suns in a cloudless sky blazing at noontime. Total darkness exploded into white light in an instant. I fell trembling, face to the ground in total terror. The light was so bright I could see it with my eyes squeezed closed. The brilliance showed through my eyelids even with my face pressed into the grass. It was as if my body and the world around me had become illuminated so intensely that everything had become part of the light itself. Bright as the light was, there was no heat!

As the light grew even more intense, I heard words that were a musical melody of thunder telling us not to be afraid, that there was good news that would bring great joy to all people. The sound was that of a chorus of countless voices, powerful yet soft. The world was vibrating like the strings of a thousand lyres being strummed by giant hands, a sound so complete my body became part of the lyrical music. Words cannot aptly describe the event.

I felt as if I were drifting in the air, and slowly, with no effort, I turned over. My eyes were opening and being drawn skyward by some force as if my chin were in a powerful hand. I could not help but look up. I saw what could only be an angel of *Adonai* (the Lord), a gigantic warrior. And yet the image was, at the same time, kindly looking, endearing, and inviting.

The flock was on its feet but standing stock-still. I thought later that they must have heard the angel too, saying not to fear, because they did not run. But my fellow shepherds were as terrified as me. The loud, all-consuming voice continued saying that *Mashiach* (Messiah) had been born and he was in Bethlehem, the city of David. The angel told us that we would recognize him when we found a baby wrapped snugly in strips of cloth, lying in a manger.

No one had time to blink before an even greater light burst around us and the angel was joined by a vast chorus of others, the host of heaven praising Adonai and saying, “Glory to the one in highest heaven! Peace will be in all the lands to those with whom Adonai is pleased.”

At that moment it was as if my entire body turned into a soft cloud of vapor and absorbed the sound instead of my hearing the heavenly chorus with my ears.

In the next moment, the immense host of angels rolled up like a sheet and vanished. It seemed to take forever for my eyes to adjust and allow me to see again. Back was the total, stunning blackness of the Judean night. The flock began to lie back down and settle. They seemed totally calm despite the extraordinary light and absorbing sounds; the night became amazingly quiet. For a moment I thought I had gone deaf from the experience; I could hear nothing—not a bleat, not a rustle, not a whisper of air. I could not even hear myself breathe.

Breaking the quiet was a growing noise from our little encampment. My three shepherd partners were jumping about like little children and shouting. “We must go to Bethlehem! Let us see what has happened, what has been foretold!" Time seemed to stand still as we tried to absorb what had occurred; the sheep appeared frozen, motionless. At last we regained our senses and settled down.

Then and there we decided to go to Bethlehem. The youngest, barely a year younger than me, my best friend, *Ya'acov* (Jacob), met the decision with howls of protest because he was ordered to stay with the flock. Someone needed to stay with the sheep. On this night paralleled by no other in anyone's memory, his protests fell on deaf ears as we began the short journey.

It was in the middle of the night watch, the darkest of the posts, when without doubt we became part of the greatest event in our peoples history. Since we had seen angels and were humbled by their glory and might, we all agreed that young Jacob would be safe.

Besides, at the age of fifteen, he did have almost three years of experience. Off we went. After centuries and so many generations of anticipation, Messiah had finally arrived and had come as a baby.

CHAPTER 2

THE GROTTO

AFTER THE ANGELS departed, we regained our composure and left at a run for the caves outside Bethlehem. *Avram* (Abram), the oldest, who had been to Bethlehem many times, said, "I know a grotto where there are rabbis who could know where Messiah might be! There are a number of small caves that have been at the foot of a certain hill forever. It is near the tomb of our patriarch Jacob's beloved wife, Rachel, called *Migdal Eder* (Tower of the Flock). I saw it just last year. It is the largest of the caves that dot the hillside, where the Levitical shepherds care for the flocks used for the Passover offering. Let us go there first and tell the head rabbi what we have witnessed."

That made sense to us; since they were the authority of the temple out in the field, they should know what to do. With all the travelers on the road, we had to move carefully and quietly so as not to make a disturbance and awaken sleeping pilgrims and their animals.

The sun was just coming up, and the lighter it became, the faster we ran, even though none in our little troop had had much rest. It was as if an energy far beyond what we were capable of on our own was pushing and guiding us through the fields, up and down the hills. Though it was not a long distance to the smattering of caves, the rugged landscape slowed our progress. We were diligent in not startling or scaring the other flocks of sheep we passed.

"There it is!" Abram panted. We burst into the cave like crazy men coming to a sudden halt, bumping into one another, grunting as a result.

At first we saw nothing as our eyes adjusted to the semidarkness after running toward the rising sun on our way. What a strange sight it was. The mouth of the cave was about as wide as the four of us standing shoulder to shoulder, but after about three strides, it opened up into a wondrous sight. When we did stop, we stood in awe, dumfounded, seeing a village-sized area.

The first thing I noticed was how well lit the huge cave was. Circling the entire cavern were *menorahs* (oil-burning lamps), fashioned after the ones in the temple. They were not on stands since they were mounted to the rock walls. They were the seven cupped ends of bronze branches, almond shaped, resembling the temple fixtures. Instead of standing on the smooth dirt floor of the cave, the trunks were bent to an angle and attached to the cave wall. The tops of the cups were tapered, allowing the wicks to stand almost upright, with an opening large enough to accommodate fresh oil.

There was a man dressed like a shepherd whose clothes were of a fairly fine fabric, wearing a striped shawl, bound at the neck, fastened as a hood. He was placing a thick, cord-like wick in one of the many cups around the enclosure. The menorahs were way above his head and reach, so he stood on a stepped stool, moving from one cup to another.

To our left were dozens of small pens housing ewes and one or two little lambs. The enclosures were made of wooden slats, and the dirt floors were covered with fine wood shavings. Each pen had two wooden buckets: one for water and one for food. All the ewes and lambs were pure white and looked like perfect mirror images of each other. The animals seemed content since none of them looked restless or made much sound. The gated front of each pen had a round wood placard with a strange symbol etched on it.

Continuing my gaze toward the back of the cave, I saw fresh water trickling down the wall into a shallow pool large enough to accommodate at least ten grown men and an equal number of sheep. Coming out of the water was a man wearing a *michnasayim* (priestly undergarment) of fine linen. He was carrying what appeared to be a freshly bathed newborn lamb, a shepherd priest carrying a lamb.

He walked to a large waist-high table laden with stacks of cloth strips and a huge bowl of salt. Gently setting the lamb on the table, he reached into the salt, scooped a small fistful of the crystals, and began sprinkling the lamb. He then carefully rubbed the salt on the bleating baby. When he was done with the salt, he wrapped the lamb in a cloth strip then took it to a pen where a ewe was waiting to nurse her newborn. We stood there openmouthed, slack-jawed at the sight.

Near the pool were large clay casks, filled with the fresh water that gently cascaded down the cave wall. Near the casks stood a huge wooden pen enclosing a mound of salt taller than most men and as long as a camel from one end to the other. The pen next to the salt was fully twice the size of the salt pile and latticed with a wooden structure of long pegs on which were hanging hundreds of strips of linen. Some of the linen strips were drying, having just been washed, supplies for the cleansing table.

To our right was the mouth of a huge open area bustling with activity, which we later found out housed a kitchen and all manner of food. The aroma of cooking teased my nose; that signaled my stomach I was famished. My partners were looking in that direction, and I saw my friend Benji licking his lips in anticipation of a meal.

Startled gasps came from across the cave and directed our attention to a young couple who were now wide awake, thanks to all the noise we had made. There was a newborn baby wrapped in swaddling made of the same material as the strips on the table and pegs we were just looking at. The baby was lying in a feeding trough, a manger, with the young couple, obviously the baby's parents, at its side.

The young man, who seemed to be about my age, was sitting on a pile of blankets, and a young girl was leaning into his embrace, presumably resting after the night's events. Standing near them were two old, wizened men who were dressed in shepherd's garb similar to ours. I noticed the difference immediately; their turbans were purple, and there was a jeweled pin just over their foreheads. The tunics they wore were finely woven and had ornamental designs stitched on the chest. The sandals they wore covered their feet; the strapping was tightly braided leather. The leather of the soft sandals shone with oil and looked brand new.

Even though these men were obviously shepherds, their clothing was immaculate. These two were not only shepherds but also priests from the temple in Jerusalem! They were in charge of the most revered, perfect flock of sheep. Looking at the baby with the couple then at the shepherds, I knew they had helped with the birth. Shepherds very often assist farm families with the birth of children, so adept are they at delivery, though only in emergencies when a *meyaladet* (midwife) cannot be found.

Breaking our silence, Abram whispered in awe, "Is this *Mashiach* our long-awaited savior?" We were staring at the startled couple.

Looking at the baby, I said, "We just saw what seemed to be all the angels in heaven. They just appeared to us in the field and told us that the savior of the world was born, and we would find him lying in a manger here in Bethlehem! Is he the Chosen One?"

The young man seemed to stare into the middle distance for some time then slowly smiled and answered, "I am *Yosef ben Heli* (Joseph, son of Heli), from Nazareth in Galilee. This is my wife, *Maryam bas Yoachim* (Mary, daughter of Joachim). This is our newborn son, whom we have been told to give the name *Yeshua*. It is the same name as the high priest who now presides in the temple in Jerusalem. This is our son, *Yeshua ben Yosef* (Jesus, son of Joseph), of the line of David. We are here to register for the census."

"How can this be?" I asked. "How did you arrive at the name?"

With a knowing look on his face, the young man humbly said, "Please don't think me mad when I tell you that what you have witnessed, so have we." The young man, Joseph, looked at his radiant wife, took a deep breath, looked around at all our faces, and began in a slow, steady voice, "The angel *Gavri'el* (Gabriel) appeared to her by name many months ago and said, '*Shalom* (Hail), highly favored one. Adonai is with you! Do not be afraid. You are blessed for you have favor with Adonai. You will bear a son, and you will call him Yeshua. He will be great and called *HaElyon* (Son of the Highest). Adonai will give him the throne of his forefather David. He will rule the house of Jacob forever.'"

The young father said it as though he had said it a hundred times to himself but still could not believe it. He was married to the mother of the savior of all mankind! Mary picked up the baby for us to see. The child lying in Mary's arms next to him was Messiah. Praise *Elohim* (God Most High)! He then said, "When I was deep in doubt, Adonai told me in a dream to take her as my wife and that she was with the child of the *Ruach HaKodesh* (Holy Spirit)! I obeyed, and after quite a journey, here we are."

As we talked into the early hours of the day, I realized they did not see or hear the angels' announcement to us in the field. They already knew from Adonai and Gabriel directly what we were told. At that moment I knew that only they and a few shepherds were aware that Messiah, savior of Israel and the world, was born!

I had no idea where this all was going and how what I had seen and heard would so drastically change my life. Messiah was a baby born in Bethlehem of David. I was there—a young shepherd in the fields nearby, keeping watch over a flock of sheep that wonderful night.

CHAPTER 3

THE ROAD

A PRIEST CAME to us, handed Abram a large loaf of bread and a skin of wine, and said it was time for us to leave. Abram took the bread, broke it into four sections, said blessings, and washed the bread down with wine, and we left the cave. We worked our way back to the flock and found Jacob playing his flute and dancing about, the sheep watching him closely. It looked as if the animals were keeping time with the music and even looked to be smiling. Smiling sheep—perhaps my imagination was running wild.

"Jacob, Messiah is here!" Abram yelled, startling Jacob and the sheep.

"You have seen him?" his voice was giddy with delight.

"Yes, he is a beautiful child."

My best friend continued to dance around, hugging the nearest lambs he could find and kept repeating, "He is here! He is here! We are saved!"

"All right, men"—Abram sighed with a grin on his face—"gather your things. We have a herd to deliver."

By midday we had completed the drive to the market. Abram collected payment, and we set off for home. The trip back to Cana with no sheep was supposed to be quicker and uneventful, but it was strange. There was no way we could keep what we had seen to ourselves. The expectation of the coming of Messiah permeated our society, and everyone was anxious to see him come and throw off the Roman yoke, just like our heroes, the judges and kings of the past.

It had been over seven hundred years of oppression and domination, first by the Assyrians, then the Babylonians, Persians, Greeks, and now the iron fist of Rome. Messiah would come to our rescue! The Romans would be vanquished. Jerusalem would be our center of worship and national capitol once more and forever. We heard what the angels had said, Messiah had been born! We heard what Joseph and Mary related from the angel Gabriel. We were intoxicated with delight.

Everywhere we went on the road, we talked nonstop about the angels and told everyone we met about seeing the baby Yeshua with his parents, Joseph and Mary. "He is here!" we almost shouted to everyone we saw. "Messiah is born in Bethlehem of Judea! We saw him! We saw and heard angels announce his birth!"

Most of the people we talked to just stared as if we shepherds were crazy and talking nonsense. As excited as we were, we must have looked wild-eyed, even possessed. It was no surprise many shrank from us in fear.

Sadly it became obvious that we were the only ones who saw the angels. How could that be with the sounds so loud and the lights so bright? Even Joseph and Mary did not see what we saw; they were in a cave. Why were we, shepherds, the only ones to hear the heavenly announcement?

As we walked along, we became quiet with this realization. Jacob grabbed my arm and, with a sob in his voice, said, "Eli, did this event really happen? Was it something we all ate? Are we all suffering the same dream, some illusion—the light, the angels, the baby you saw?" We thought the heavenly hosts would have been everywhere, certainly visible for miles and that everyone in the country had seen the image, as bright, loud, and all-consuming as it was!

"How could those we told not understand what we said? Is it because we are just shepherds?" Jacob said with an even louder sob in his voice. Even though the nation silently anticipated Messiah, it seemed no one else could grasp the fact that it had happened. Was it because Adonai had been silent for so long?

Then, without notice or warning, Roman soldiers on horseback came thundering down the road toward us. For some reason we had not heard them coming at a distance, and Jacob just stood in the middle of the road staring straight ahead, not moving. It was as if he was in a trance. I grabbed his arm to pull him to the side of the road to make way for the horsemen, but he would not move.

"Jacob, come with me! Run!" I screamed. But he just gazed at me with a look so vacant it was as if his senses had departed.

As I ran to the side of the road, Jacob turned toward the oncoming horsemen, raised his staff in one hand and his rod in the other, faced the soldiers, and started screaming, "Messiah has come! Messiah has come! He is here, and you are doomed!"

The lead soldier must have thought Jacob was going to attack because he spurred his mount, leaned forward, drew his gladius, and in one smooth motion slashed at Jacob's neck near his upraised staff arm. The swift cut separated Jacob's shoulder from his neck, and he spun from the blow, collapsing sideways away from the other horsemen toward the side of the road. The riders continued forward at a gallop, leaving my friend behind like a pile of rubbish.

In disbelief I ran to Jacob, who was moving, trying to get up, but could not. I skidded to a stop beside him, dropping to my knees as he turned toward me. In disbelief I saw blood pumping out of the raw wound created by the sharp blade. I grabbed his hanging arm and drew it up, trying to close the gash near his neck as if that would fix it. I knew he was mortally injured as the blood kept coming in a torrent. His eyes were glazing as he looked at me smiling and said, "Messiah is here. Messiah is among us. We must..." He seemed to relax, his life departing, and he stared at me with a smile on his lips.

"Elohim, Elohim, what has happened? Why have you forsaken my friend?" Clutching Jacob, I looked around and saw Abram standing over me tearing at his heavy woven cloak to rend it, signifying a death. Unable to tear his garment, the horrified shepherd unsheathed the short flint knife we all carried and sliced the outer robe over his heart, allowing it to tear. Falling to his knees, he sobbed while reciting the *Shema*, "Hear, O Israel, the Lord our God, the Lord is One." Unable to control himself, he rocked back and forth, moaning, "Shalom, *Ya'akov ben Zavi* (Jacob son of Zvi), shalom, shalom…"

Looking at Abram, I could not believe this giant of a man who had always been a pillar of strength and courage was mourning so deeply. With tear-flooded eyes, I reached out to him, laid my hand on his shoulder, and asked, "Abram, what do we do? What do we do now?"

Looking at me with his tear-stained beard, he took a deep breath and rumbled in a voice I knew well, "We must carry him home for burial immediately."

Abram stood, handed me his staff, and said, "Gather the others, and we shall fashion a litter out of our garments and carry him to his parents' home, where they will prepare him for burial. Do it quickly." He wiped his face with his hands. That seemed to transform him back to the leader of our little troop.

I laid Jacob's head down on his *skyt* (all-purpose carry bag) and started removing his *simlah* (heavy outer garment) to be used as a sling between the staffs to make the carrying device. Benjamin, the fourth of us, obeyed quickly. I laid two staffs end to end on either side of Jacob's garment and started taking strips of cloth to tie the staffs together. Benji then took off his cloak and laid it over and across Jacob to make a sling long and large enough to hold his lifeless body.

Quickly, as if he had done it many times before, Benji slit four holes, one in each corner of the overlaid garments, and slid the staffs through the openings. With similar speed he took his heavy hook needle from the bag at his feet and started sewing the garments together, forming the litter.

When Benjamin finished, Abram gently but firmly said, "Eli, lift Jacob's feet, and I will get his shoulders." Together we shifted Jacob to the litter. Removing my own cloak, I laid it over my friend, covering his serene face. Abram said, "Benji, you and Eli each grab the staffs at his feet. I shall take the other end." Without another word we hoisted Jacob and started the journey home.

What was to be a two-day trip stretched into three. All along the trail, people stopped, allowing us to pass. We were never sure if clearance was made out of respect or fear of accidentally touching us or Jacob's body and thus becoming ritually unclean. I like to believe it was respect due a man slain by a Roman soldier in an unprovoked attack.

When we arrived back in Cana, a crowd started gathering on the outside of the village and began following us, creating a procession. Solemnly we made our way toward the house of Jacob's family. News had already reached his parents as they stumbled toward us, his mother keening and his father, *Matityah* (Matthias), pounding his chest over his rent cloak.

Jacob's father stood before us, stammering, "Take him directly to the burial site. We will prepare him there."

After setting Jacob down on the ground at the village cemetery, I walked to my parents' home, where they were standing outside, waiting for me. My father, seeing me covered with Jacob's dried blood, wore a grief-stricken look. In a somber voice, he said, "Son, go to the stream to begin the cleansing ritual. I will set up a tent outside the village and bring you clean clothes, food, and see that the same is done by the families of Abram and Benjamin. I will have the rabbi contacted to perform *mikvah* (ritual purification / baptism)."

We left the house and were led to an area outside the village boundaries where traditionally the *tumah* (unclean) would stay until purified. On the way there, I could only glance at my beloved Rachel since we could not speak, let alone touch. Hearts heavy with loss we made our way to the area of cleansing.

For seven days the three of us who carried the body camped by the stream and entered the water in the morning, and the rabbi poured water over us, conforming to the purification ritual. It was a sad, lonely week with no visitors. Our fathers brought food, leaving supplies outside the tents. Neither one of us could enter the village or touch anyone for fear of making them unclean as well. We prayed, sang the songs we knew, and each one of us had a small musical instrument to play, the ones we used to call and calm the sheep in our care. Both Benji and I had small flutes, and Abram played his lyre after the fashion of King David.

On the seventh day, I first went to see my parents out of loyalty and respect. Benji left to return to his little settlement, and Abram walked to the other side of the village. My father, with gritty voice, greeted me at the door. "Shalom, my son. Welcome home." He was standing in the doorway with a weak smile on his rugged face. He looked much older than he did when I left, as I felt much older.

It had barely been a week since my first experience with violent death so close and so personal. That Roman soldier changed my life—sadly in a dark way. Bubbles of anger with overwhelming grief kept surfacing regularly. The anger grew with frequency and intensity at each surfacing. I touched the *mezuzah* (encased prayer) on the door-frame with three fingers of my right hand, kissed them, and entered our home, saying, "Shalom, *Eema* (Mother)."

My dear mother was stirring something in a pot at the fireplace when she looked up, set the wooden spoon aside, and walked quickly into my embrace. "Elijah, my beloved son, welcome home. My child, you left a little boy and returned to us a man. I can see the innocence of youth has fled your face and am looking at a new, older creation."

Releasing her grip on me, she turned and sat on a low stool next to my father, who had taken his place at the low table in the large master room of our house. Looking up at me, she said, "Go, see your Rachel, then return to us so that we may speak of your change." She knew I was not the same.

CHAPTER 4

THE SECRET

I EXCUSED MYSELF and ran to Rachel's house to call on her. Greeting her widowed mother, I was told that Rachel was drawing water at the well. I ran out the door and made it to one of the wells outside the village in record time. Being away from her for over three weeks had seemed like an eternity. I felt my spirits lifting as I made my way north of the village near a little rivulet that fed the stream that I had used to be made clean.

Drawing water from a deep well takes concentration, strength, and patience. Most of the time, women do that work for their families while the men farm or tend the flocks. I saw her, but she did not see me since she was hefting a skin of water from the depths of the well. I carefully kept behind her with a playful heart and began to sneak up to her.

How beautiful was her form, her coal-black hair flowing with every movement. Closer I came. "Rachel," I whispered. Startled by my voice, she spun around with the full skin of water and fell right into me. In a moment both of us were drenched; we fell to the ground in joy-filled laughter.

"Thank you for the bath. After a week in the river, all you can do is throw water on me?" She laughed even louder.

"After time on the trail, you always smell just like the sheep! One skin of water is usually not nearly enough! You always need a real bath on your returns!" With that she stood, reached down, and poured a bit of the contents of the second skin on my head. "Now you are presentable to me." That was my playful Rachel; it was one of the things I loved about her.

Standing there with her in the warm sun, at home in familiar surroundings with my loved ones, Bethlehem and the appearance of the angels seemed like a dream. Did all the things that had taken place since I last saw her really happen? Shaking myself, I turned to her and said seriously, "We need to talk. I have a very important matter to share with you."

Then it was her turn to be serious when she saw the intensity in my eyes and heard the tone of my somber voice. "Oh, Eli," she murmured, the smile disappearing from her lovely face, tears welling in her eyes, "I am so sorry about Jacob." She touched my cheek with a dainty but leathered hand. "Let us sit down in the shade of the fig tree here," she said, motioning to a small bench.

Taking hold of her hands, so tiny in mine, I had her sit, but I needed to move while I talked. "We will speak of Jacob later, but first another matter." In an instant my thoughts changed to the greatest moments of my life, and my broken, mourning heart was rapidly filling with joy. "Rachel, have I ever lied or misspoken to you?" I asked, looking into her eyes as I sought her answer.

"Never, Eli. You always speak the truth. I trust what you say. You are a man of great honesty and integrity. Even when we were young children at play, you were not like the other boys. So pure of thought and always knowing right from wrong—it was as if you always had an adult heart and mind masquerading in a child's body. So, my love, great is my trust in you."

I knelt in front of her, taking her hands. "Future wife of Elijah ben Ezra, please listen carefully to what I am about to say. My words may test what you have just spoken. While we were in Bethlehem, the very night we arrived, we bedded down the flock, made camp, and ate our evening meal. I was chosen by lot to have the midnight watch, so I slept for a bit and then was out in the field. Thinking of nothing else but you to pass the otherwise dreary hours, I walked around and around the flock." A smile lit up her face.

"When I was around the side of the flock farthest from camp, the most brilliant light burst into the blackness of night all around. It was like the sun had exploded right above our heads without making a sound—radiance as a hundred suns at noon! Blinding light completely surrounded everything that instant. I threw myself to the ground, shaking and terrified, having no sense of anything else. The light was so bright it was as if I had no eyelids, and I started burrowing my face into the grass and dirt beneath me. The light grew brighter and more intense, and at that moment I thought I must have been struck by lightning. I believed I was dying. The next words I heard were absorbed into my very being." I told her everything I had seen and heard that night, starting with the angel's words. Her eyes grew wide with the meaning of what I said.

With giant tears of joy running down her cheeks, she said, "You and the others heard the announcement of Messiah?"

"Yes!" I shouted. "But that is not all! The angels said that Messiah had been born in Bethlehem, the city of David! We would recognize him as a baby wrapped snugly in strips of cloth, lying in a manger.

"Rachel, we were right there in the cave just outside Bethlehem. We were told how to recognize him, as if the angel knew we would want to know and go, which we did! We all ran to find him. Abram knew where to look, the caves at Migdal Eder. We made our way there, went to the largest cave, and we came upon a young couple with a baby. Just as we had been told, there was a baby in a manger wrapped in swaddling." Rachel was still wide-eyed, pouring tears and trembling at the impact of my words.

"I have told no one else here at home but you. We tried telling everyone we saw and met coming back from Bethlehem, but they all thought we were crazy or possessed. Rachel, you believe me, don't you?" I groaned.

At that she stood, squeezed my hands, looked into my eyes, and said, "I believe you. I know what you say is true. But what does it mean? How will a baby deliver us?"

"I do not know. I know what I saw and heard while there was true." With that I continued in detail about meeting Joseph and Mary, seeing Yeshua in the manger, describing the contents of the wondrous cave and the shepherd priests, the expressions on her face showing even more astonishment.

I told her the words of Gabriel and Joseph's dream. Tears continued rolling down her beautiful cheeks toward her big smile.

"This is wonderful news," she said, but immediately her smile faded. "I can understand why, after all these years of hope and waiting, the people you encountered would not believe the great news that Messiah has come. Who can you and the others tell? Who will believe what you have witnessed?"

We stood there looking at each other, considering what she had just said; who would listen and understand? Suddenly we realized the sun was setting, and we had to get back to the village. I helped her pull up two fresh skins of water, and we headed home. Together we agreed to keep what I had told her to ourselves for a time until we decided the best way to share the story. I was encouraged that my beloved Rachel believed me and felt relief.

I assisted pouring the water from the skins into the clay pots at her home, and we set out together to the house of Jacob's parents, who were at the end of the seven days of *shiva* (ritual mourning period). Before entering the little home, we each took a pinch of ash from a small bowl at the door and sprinkled it over our heads as a signal that we joined them in their loss and grief. "Shalom," we said in unison as if we were already a married couple, so attached were our hearts.

"Father Matthias and Mother Anna, our hearts are torn with you, and we came to share your grief. I only regret that I could not be here this past week to help comfort you. Your son Jacob and I shared a friendship that we thought as deep as the one between David and Jonathan. We were as close as brothers." With those words my voice started to crack as tears poured from my eyes. "There was no reason for his death!" I sobbed, my tears a torrent. "That wretched Roman, may he be cast into *Sheol* (Darkness) for an eternity of torture!" I fell to my knees, and

Rachel lowered herself, wrapping her arms around me as I shuddered with each mournful sob.

Matthias came to me and Rachel to lift us to our feet. In a steady voice, he said, "Elijah ben Ezra, our mourning period in ashes is not over. We must continue to live and be part of our community, our family. We have work to do. For the remainder of a year, we must wear our torn clothing, remembering our Jacob. But now we have flocks to attend, and you, both of you, must prepare for your wedding. Eli, you must also prepare for your first tour of duty at the temple in Jerusalem." As I stood looking directly at him, I realized for the first time my childhood had indeed withered, and I was considered a peer among men.

What a busy time it was, completing the addition to my father's house for me and Rachel to begin our wedded lives together. How quickly the time passed, and how diligently we all worked to prepare for the upcoming wedding. As excited as I was about becoming one with Rachel, I was really nervous thinking about my first stay in Jerusalem at the temple, living there for a month with the other Levite shepherd trainees, called *Alephs* (A's/Firsts).

The weeks passed quickly, the work on the house was completed, and the day of the wedding had finally come. How happy I was to become the head of my own family, and how sad I was that Jacob would not be standing with me as part of the required *minyan* (ten men of age), the quorum needed to begin the wedding service. As I stood under the *chuppah* (covered alter), under which we would be united, I looked over at my father, standing next to Matthias. What a contrast of faces. My father, *Ezra*, was beaming with delight, and Jacob's father wore a mournfully sad look. His face sagged with grief, and he appeared to have aged ten years in the weeks since our return with his slain son.

The village rabbi walked up to the cloth-covered altar, looked at me to one side and Rachel to the other, and began chanting, "*Baruch atah Adonai*" (Blessed are you, O Lord). He recited and sang as we approached the canopy to say our vows, neither one of us really paying much attention to anything or anyone except each other.

Focusing, I paid strict adherence to the rabbi when he prompted us each to recite the words *"Ani ledodi vedodi li"* (I am my beloved's, and my beloved is mine).

We were then pronounced husband and wife, and I had my first opportunity to kiss my beautiful bride in the presence of others.

I remember a little food, some wine, dancing, and each of us being lifted by our friends and villagers. The men carried me while the women carried Rachel to the new addition on my parents' home. It was our first night to unite as a couple—awkward, clumsy, and yes, divine!

We had three weeks adjusting as a wedded couple before I had to make the first of many monthlong sojourns to Jerusalem as an Aleph. I was almost as nervous going to the grand temple as I was the first night with Rachel in our own home. I knew there would be strange surroundings and hard work that waited for my arrival. Yet with all the heady elements of newly married life, the burning in my soul about Messiah smoldered.

CHAPTER 5

THE ALEPH

We shepherds are a hearty lot. Living out of doors, constantly on the move, eating meager yet substantial foods, we tend to be lean and tough, able to withstand all weather conditions. I am an exception to the presumed look of a shepherd, being rather tall and large, with a generous amount of muscle. My body is shaped very much like my father and his father before him, who were blessed with great physical strength. The walk to the grand temple that Herod Antipas lorded over was fairly easy for me, though I missed the newfound comfort and delight of my wife and wedded life.

As the sun was setting on the fourth day of my walk to Jerusalem, the temple looked larger than ever. Sitting at the top of the city, the walls surrounding the temple area seemed to stretch all the way into the far horizon. Having to make my way to the northeast part of the structure was not easy after the long walk up the steep road and curved walkway. I was breathless with effort, but the view of the city at sundown made me gasp. Never had I seen such a magnificent vista. The sky was red, fading to orange and yellow before yielding to the deepening starlit blue overhead. I stood there enjoying the view, thinking how much Rachel would love the look of this place.

"You, Aleph Eighteen, have you been lost?" I spun at the sound of the loud voice and was startled to see that it came from a very small man. He was dressed in a simple tunic of deep blue with a matching turban. Wrapped around his waist was a braided belt that looked like it was spun out of silver. Hanging from a silver chain around his neck was a simple silver amulet holding a brilliant amber stone. "Are you mute or stupid or both?" he spat. His face looked like a shriveled apple, wrinkle upon wrinkle, with a wry smile under a tiny nose and light brown eyes that sparkled like the gem on his chest.

"I am Elijah ben Ezra, here to report for my first lesson," I stuttered.

"Silent!" was his rapid and loud response. "If you are as slow-witted as you are slow to travel and respond, I fear your stay with us will be brief and painful! Follow me." The little man walked quickly for someone I thought to be about a hundred years old.

I had a hard time keeping up with him even with my long strides. As he walked he spoke. "You will listen and speak only if you are asked a direct question. You are the last to arrive. Therefore, you will be rewarded with the simplest and dirtiest of jobs while you are here. I am your teacher, your leader, and the one who will determine whether you will survive your training."

"But I am already an experienced shepherd—" the words were barely out of my mouth when he turned around and, with lightning speed, hit my shoulder with a short rod that seemed to appear out of nowhere.

"Did I ask a question, Eighteen?" I was hesitating, not sure how to answer, when the rod struck my other shoulder in the exact mirror spot of the first blow.

"You are slow, Eighteen, so I will speak clearly, in a cadence you can comprehend. The only name that you and the seventeen other Alephs are to call me is *chazzen* (servant leader). I am not a rabbi. I am a servant. Your responses to me will be swift and obedient. There will be others involved in your training, and you will respect them and their positions. But I and I alone am responsible for you and your shepherd brothers. Do you understand?"

"Yes, chazzen!" My reply was quick and loud. The impish smile never left his face.

He turned, and I followed closely behind him down a long corridor to a large open room. He stepped in and to the side, motioning me to pass him. The room was at the end of the temple enclosure wall and was like nothing I had ever seen before. It wasn't a room at all; it was a courtyard. Laid out in three rows of six were eighteen pallets for sleeping. Each pallet had a brand-new staff, rod, and carry bag laid next to a pile of new garments. At the foot of each pallet was a young man standing ramrod straight with all eyes on the little man, the chazzen. He looked at me, the smile disappearing, and said, "Eighteen, take your place at the empty pallet, and stand just like the others, straight and silent, until I return."

I found the empty spot, laid my belongings down, stood at the foot of the pallet, and looked around. Seventeen young men wearing worn clothes similar to mine stood silently watching the door the little man had exited. Turning to the closest man to me, in a low voice, I said, "Shalom. I am Eli."

In a low whisper, not looking at me, only at the door, he responded, "Say nothing, or you will feel the sting of his rod or a stone." As I turned toward the door, he said, "I am *Tevyeh*."

What am I doing? I thought. *Why am I here? I should be home with my new wife! I should be running around the countryside telling everyone about Messiah's arrival.* As I stood there, the whirlwind of events that I lived through these past months spun in my head, and I felt so tired. My only thought at that moment was to lie down and go to sleep. As I was turning toward the pallet that was to be my bed for the next month, a sharp pain stabbed my left thigh, and I heard, "Eighteen, what are you doing?" It was the voice of the little man, from across the room.

I snapped straight, looked at him across the opening, and said, "I just wanted to rest from my journey, sir."

The thin smile was back on his face. "I am not a *sir*, Eighteen—I am nothing." It was then I noticed a small sling in his left hand. My thigh was throbbing, and I realized he had hit me from across the room on the meat side of my leg with a small missile. This was no ordinary little man; this chazzen was a warrior, and all eighteen Alephs were his captives! "There will be no sleep for any of you just yet. Form a line, two by two, and follow me."

He led us to a large dining hall, similar in size to the open area we had just left, filled with tables and benches, most of which were occupied by men eating. Hunger hit me, and we were led to a huge kitchen area filled with all manner of food. There were breads in all shapes and sizes, fruits and vegetables of many colors, some I could not recognize. But the best thing I saw was meat, huge mounds of roasted meats, the smell of which filled the room and triggered all our mouths to fill with the wet of anticipation.

The boy Tevyeh who had spoken to me in a whisper was my two-by-two partner, and he handed me a large plate made of polished tin and said, "Take as much food as you want, but make sure you eat all of it, or you will suffer blows from that rod the chazzen carries." I filled my plate and ate every morsel, thinking it the best food I had ever eaten. The varieties were all delicious, and in a short while, I was fully satisfied, finishing my meal with a sweet orange. While I was eating the orange, the memory of the cave where Messiah was born came flooding into my mind, and I had to control the burning impulse to jump on to the table and shout, "He has come! Messiah is here!"

The month was a blur, and every day was the same except *Shabbat* (Sabbath). Each morning before sunrise, the chazzen, standing at the entrance to our area, would awaken us with a blast from a small *shofar* (ram's horn) he had tucked in his sash. We would all rise immediately, roll up our pallets, follow him to a pool somewhere in the building, bathe quickly, and clothe in fresh linen undergarments supplied by the temple laundry. We would eat a spare meal then head to another large room filled with tables and benches. On the table were scrolls, styluses, papyrus, and ink. Mornings were crammed with lessons by different teachers, and we were required to write a brief synopsis of what each rabbi would teach.

Most shepherds are illiterate farmhands, but we, the Alephs, were Levites who could trace our heritage back to Aaron and his offspring, charged with serving the temple in a variety of tasks. The Levites were trained as builders, maintainers, teachers, judges, and in many other vocations. My father was our village judge as well as the owner of a large flock of sheep. As his firstborn and only child, I was pledged to the temple in Jerusalem to serve as a Levitical shepherd. I was educated and loved learning. My father and mother taught me how to read and write, starting when I was three years of age. As much as I loved education, I loved the outdoors, the joy of freedom with the sheep and the other animals in the field, even more.

My punishment for being late on the day of my arrival lasted a full week. Each morning, a full hour before the chazzen would awaken us with his shofar, he would show up at my pallet and tap one of my ankles, never gently, to get me started. I would then stumble, half-awake, to the common waste room, where I was responsible for cleaning it completely.

Thankfully the room was small, all stone with seven openings in the floor to receive our water and excrement. Waiting for me were two large buckets of water, both laden with strong-smelling herbs and two large sticks with bunches of hyssop at the ends. The first bucket was to swab the room then the openings. The second bucket was to follow up, making sure the room was, in fact, clean. The hyssop was pried off and dropped down one of the holes; the large sticks and buckets were placed back where I found them.

Gladly I had this duty for only seven days, at which point other servants resumed the task.

Afternoons the chazzen led us to a field northwest of the great walled city, where we practiced with slings, rods, and staffs. The slings were used to perfect our aim and help us choose the proper stones for the appropriate targets; we learned different techniques for differently made slings. The old man had to have been a descendant of the tribe of Benjamin as he used his left hand with accuracy that was astonishing. Then he switched to his right hand, with which he was equally proficient. Tevyeh nudged me during one of these lessons and said, "Who is this little fellow that can best the lot of us at anything we try? He always looks like he is wearing freshly laundered clothes no matter the time, day or night, and he never seems to tire or sleep. Where is a man like this fashioned?"

When sling practice was over, a cadre of temple and palace guards came marching to a sandpit adjacent to the sling range. We were taught and practiced new fighting skills with our staffs, rods, and *cherevs* (flint knives). But the most valuable time for me personally was unarmed combat. Every Aleph was paired off with an equally sized guard, and we were taught secrets of how to fight barehanded.

To my chagrin the very first time we entered the pit, we all learned a lesson at my expense. Rather than pair me with a guard of equal size, the chazzen stepped into the center of the pit wearing only his linen undergarment. The first thing I noticed was that the body of the man looked much younger than his weathered, wrinkled face. He was still in his turban, and his lips wore that twisted smile, and he beckoned me with empty hands to join him in the sand.

"Come, Eighteen, show me how strong you are, and throw me down." I must have had a puzzled look on my face when he said, "Can you not beat an old, small man? Surely you have wrestled and been intimate with goats larger than me." Insult and anger bested me, so I strode willfully toward the tormenter of all the Alephs.

My intent was to wrap my large arms around him and lift and throw him to the ground as I had done so many times with both sheep and goats for shearing as well as slaughtering. When I was within arm's length of the imp, who was showing all in attendance his agility, he stepped to his right, grabbed my left wrist, and with incredible strength twisted it back and at the same time swept my feet out from under me with his small leg; it felt like I had been struck with an iron poker across my ankles.

Facedown into the sand I landed, and in an instant, I felt his knees on my back. One of his hands grabbed a handful of my hair and pulled my face out of the sand, and I felt that ever-present rod that always appeared out of nowhere slide across my throat. "You are dead, number eighteen. Go meet your maker!"

Anger boiled in me as laughter boomed around the pit. I jumped up, faced the little man, and was about to charge when I realized that anything I tried would be in vain. I stood erect and motionless and said, "Teach me." He smiled broadly for the first time that any of us had seen, revealing a mouthful of brilliant white teeth. "You are not so stupid after all, Eighteen." With that the laughter died, and our real training began.

The weeks dissolved quickly, and on our last Sabbath night, we had a farewell meal brought into the open area we, the Alephs, had lived in for the last month. The food was simple, hearty, and fresh. New leather *skyts* (shepherd bags) and supplies for the road were set at each of our billets. At the end of the meal, the chazzen said, "Stand!" and we all jumped to our feet and stood at the foot of our sleep areas. Through the door strode a man we had never seen before, dressed in a purple tunic and turban of the same color, with a braided gold belt and sash.

"Shalom, Alephs. You did well, all of you. As of today you are committed to be part of the most important brotherhood of shepherds anywhere. As Levites attached to the temple in Jerusalem, you now have the lifelong responsibility to secure herds for the Passover sacrifice. These pins that the chazzen will apply to your garments are to be worn always as a sign to everyone that you serve the temple and the high priest. Wear them with pride and protect them for their value and significance. Shalom." He turned and left as the chazzen began pinning badges on all the Alephs as he dismissed them.

Since I was the last to arrive for training, I was left alone with the chazzen as one by one the other Alephs departed to go to their respective villages after receiving their insignias. The little man approached me and looked up while pinning the silver badge, the Aleph, over my heart.

"Eighteen, my boy, you may have been last to arrive and start your training, but you are first in ability, and you have won my respect." With a slight bow, he raised his left hand and gave me the little rod, the baton that disciplined his latest class of Alephs. "Remember your training, remain true, and you will make a name for yourself. Shalom. Go in peace, my boy." Another slight bow and he left me alone in the open area that had helped transform me into a servant of the temple. Time to go home.

CHAPTER 6

THE FAVOR

IT HAD BEEN over a year since that unforgettable, world-changing trip to Bethlehem. Life had settled into a rhythm in Cana of Galilee for us as newlyweds with our firstborn on the way. I was still a shepherd but was now focused on building my own flocks, not just looking after someone else's. My father started us out with a wedding gift of six ewes and a ram, advising me on how to build strong livestock. The first lambs of my own had been born as Rachel and I were excited with the prospect of building our own family.

But I had the added burden of spending three months out of the year in Jerusalem with the other Levite shepherds as well as traveling to other villages to find unblemished lambs. Becoming an Aleph was not only a source of training and pride; each month served in Jerusalem earned me a better education plus a nice stipend. Life was good for us in Cana, yet through the patterns of life, there were always the woven thoughts of what I had seen and heard in Bethlehem; it was never far from my mind.

Yeshua was now more than thirteen months old, and certainly no toddling child could be savior of the world. There were times that I thought I was losing my mind and all that I had experienced was a dream, just as Jacob had questioned. Rachel believed me, but we still kept our secret, and it seemed there was never any hint of Messiah. Abram never spoke of it, becoming sullen and withdrawn even when I approached him. Benji drifted away from his settlement and did not return. Of course the absence of Jacob and the sight of his rapidly aging, mourning parents were a constant reminder of what had happened. Not a word was heard from the south, from Judea, nothing about a Messiah.

While I was in the market the day after a Shabbat, Jacob's father greeted me. "Eli, how do you fare?" he asked.

"Being the master of my own house and husband of Rachel, I could fare no better," I answered. "And you?" I asked cautiously.

"I am well for an old man!" His voice was more of a squeak as he spoke.

"You are all of what, forty years, and you say you are old?" I retorted, smiling.

"Yes, sometimes I feel old, too old. When Jacob died, his mother and I lost our future. We have aged. He was our only son. We miss him beyond reason. The emptiness in our life with him gone is unbearable. Jacob loved being out in the fields with you and the flocks and would have died happily among your little brotherhood. Instead he died not doing what he loved but at the hand of a ruthless Roman—may he perish in pain with all of the multigod barbarians who are now our oppressors." Matthias's face twisted into an angry scowl as he spoke.

It was still a fresh memory to all in our village, but especially hard on Matthias and his wife. She had become very frail and reclusive since our return with her murdered son. We stood there for a few moments, then Matthias shook himself, straightened his stance, threw his shoulders back, and in a firmer yet inquiring voice said, "Elijah ben Ezra, I have actually come here to the marketplace to seek you out and ask a favor of you. This meeting is not as chance as you might think. As you are Jacob's dearest friend, I would ask this of no one else but you."

"What is it, Father Matthias?" I asked, curious at his sincerity and intensity. I was also honored to be thought of this way, to be considered a family member, not just a neighbor.

"As you know, Jacob had a small flock of sheep that I had given him at his bar mitzvah and have been tending this past year. The flock had flourished and was ready for the southern market when he died, and now those sheep are getting older by the day and will soon start losing value, as you know. I have been able to contract for a buyer in Bethlehem, but I feel too old and weary to take them or even make the trip."

Matthias paused and, taking a long breath, asked with a sigh, "If I were to hire on three helpers, would you take them for me? I would give you a third of the contract as your wages. You would be the lead shepherd, having been trained as an Aleph."

My heart sped for a moment; I was thinking, *Bethlehem, the lead shepherd, a third of the profits, a chance to see Messiah!* I had often wondered when the next opportunity would present itself. Bethlehem, birthplace of Messiah, where the angels announced Savior and also the birthplace of King David. Was Yeshua still there? Could I find him and his parents again if I went? Those and a thousand other thoughts raced through my mind as I stood there.

"Eli, my son! Are you all right?" A tap on my arm brought me back as I heard Matthias's words.

"Yes, Father Matthias. I was just thinking about Jacob and the honor that you have placed before me," I answered, not knowing quite what to say. "I was thinking about my last trip to Bethlehem when Jacob was with us, and now you, calling me son, allowing me responsibility in your household, I am humbled."

"Yes, Eli, you will actually honor me and Jacob by taking his place and leading his sheep. He was a good friend to you and always spoke highly of your way with the animals, your strength, honesty, and integrity. So you will do it?"

"Yes, I will take Jacob's sheep to Bethlehem," I answered with an excitement in my soul that could not be denied. I tried to act as if the request was not as large a favor and opportunity as it was.

In response Matthias smiled knowingly. "The honor is mine, my son."

CHAPTER 7

THE ORANGES

THAT EVENING I told Rachel of my meeting. "Today Matthias sought me out in the market and asked a great favor of me."

"What would Matthias ask of you?" As I explained, I could see her reaction was the same as mine. "Bethlehem...," she stammered. "Bethlehem...," her voice trailed off to a whisper. Regaining her composure, she said, "You said yes, did you not?"

"What else could I say to the father of my best friend? It wasn't just anyone who asked. It was Matthias." And it was Bethlehem of Judea. But a flood of doubts drenched my enthusiasm as I looked at Rachel. "What of you and our baby you are carrying? I can't just run off and leave you alone! Who will look after you?"

"My silly oaf," she said, smiling. "We live as part of your parents' household. My mother practically lives with us. And now you have apparently been adopted as a son of Matthias." Her smile widened to a grin. "You will be missed, but I will not be alone." With that we were agreed—a new adventure awaited me in Bethlehem!

Within a week we left for the City of David with Jacob's sheep. I was now the lead shepherd of three older, experienced men from nearby villages. Our combined flock was similar in size to the one of that extraordinary night. It was not my height or strength that made them listen to me and obey; it was the silver Aleph that I wore over my heart. I was a servant and worker of the temple in Jerusalem; that was my authority over three shepherds and one hundred prime sheep for the southern market to be delivered. Rachel and I agreed that I should take a day or two, after delivering the sheep, to see if I could find Joseph, Mary, and Yeshua. I just had to look for them!

The trip was fairly easy as there were no crowds on the road. The weather held, and thankfully we had no wild animals or brigands to defend against or other major issues. The flock was delivered, and I accepted the payment for Jacob's flock from the buyer on behalf of Matthias. The helpers were paid off, and they left to return to their home villages the very next morning.

Having earned a tidy sum for my leadership role on this trip, I stayed at a roadside inn and ate well, an unusual luxury for a shepherd. Hiding my coin pouch, stowing my skyt and tent in a corner of the room, I went to sleep with my flint-laden rod handy next to me in the not-so-luxurious bed. How independent I felt, a true adult, an accomplished man.

I awoke before dawn with the sole purpose of finding Joseph and Mary and to see the little boy Yeshua, the angel-announced Messiah. Emotions flooded me as I recalled that night more than a year ago, ready to be overjoyed if and when I found them. It had rained during the night, and the day dawned with low clouds—cool, if not cold. It was a windy and gloomy morning, yet despite the weather, I felt alive with anticipation.

After my morning meal, I set out along the trail through the village toward the marketplace, a great location to gather information on the possible whereabouts of the little family. The market was almost abandoned as the cold, wind, and rain had kept most people in their houses. I had been cold before, and I had been in the wind before—no real hardships for shepherds, who live outdoors. The weather would not dampen my plan. I was going to find Messiah, if he was here.

The merchants were all huddled with their wares as I tried to find a little gift to bring to the family. Off to my right, I saw an orange peeking out of the bottom of a skin tent, so I approached the seller of fruit, who was wrapped in several blankets. I asked him about the little family I described, but he could barely speak. I was able to purchase three oranges from the old man huddled with his meager supply of fruit. Putting the bright oranges in my bag, off I went, continuing my quest.

Asking the remaining few vendors in the market, who had braved the elements, I posed the question: "Is there a Yosef ben Heli and family living here in the village?" In my home in Cana, everyone knew everyone else, as well as everybody's business. If someone like Joseph and Mary had moved in and lived in the area, they would surely be known.

I politely inquired at most of the booths or tents, one by one. The last vendor I asked, who was hunkered in his stall, was the most helpful.

"Yes, they are near here, a young man Joseph. He has a lovely wife, Mary, and a charming little boy. Joseph is a carpenter and often sells his wooden goods here in the market. I remember him because his work is beautiful, simple yet almost always perfect. I believe their house is just up the road toward Bethany. It is to the right, on the first turn of the trail as you go. I remember him, this Joseph, since we had a delightful conversation one afternoon about what a well-behaved child he had with him. The little fellow watched as his father and I talked. His gaze was steady, and even though he was little more than a baby, it was as if he understood every word we spoke."

As I left his tent and turned into the wind and misting rain, I stopped. Even though I should have been elated knowing they were near, trickles of doubt and fear crept over me, and I was paralyzed. Standing there, I was stiff as a wooden statue as the chill wind swept over me. Was this a wild chase for nothing? What if it was not them? A thousand other thoughts assailed me.

Finally a thought came unbidden into my mind, as if an inner voice were speaking, like the whisper of an angel. "This journey you have taken is not an accident. Stay true to your course, and you will see him." I shook off my doubt and fear with little further thought and tucked my head into the wind. I started on my way to the house, the dwelling place of Yeshua, the long-awaited Messiah.

CHAPTER 8

THE RECONNECT

THE TRIP, WITH the cold wind in my face, seemed to take half the day, but soon I rounded the bend in the road the vendor had mentioned and saw the house. It was made of stone with wood-trimmed windows and a solid wooden door. Above the door there seemed to be enough height to accommodate additional living space with a small cutout window covered by a wood panel. Off to the left side of the small house, there was a slatted wood enclosure about chest high that was a caged area for livestock.

A small tendril of smoke came from the draft, and I could smell bread baking, which made me realize I was quite hungry. Slowly I made my way off the road to the house. Mustering my last bit of courage, I tapped softly on the door with my staff. Within a few moments, it was drawn open; there stood the young man Joseph.

He recognized me instantly, and I realized that the earthly father of Messiah and I were about the same age! Standing there transfixed, I was almost startled by his greeting.

"Eli! Praise Elohim and all of his minions, it is you! Come in, come in. Let me have your cloak. It is soaked, and so are you. Inside it is warm and dry."

He put his arm on my shoulder, turned, and stepped into the house, saying, "Mary! We have a visitor!"

As we passed through the threshold, Mary walked into the light of the doorway. She was radiant and seemed pleased to have a visitor despite the surprise. In the warmest, most composed voice of a teenager I had ever heard, she exclaimed, "Eli, what a pleasant surprise! It is so good to see you again! You look every bit the man you are growing into. Shalom. Welcome to our home."

The house was larger than I expected. I entered a warm, well-lit room that had a stone fireplace blazing away at the far end. The dirt floor was cleanly swept and solidly pounded down from years of countless footsteps. The low table in the center of the room was large enough to accommodate at least four adults. It was simple but beautifully crafted, as the fruit seller had predicted. A stool with a seat fashioned on top to accommodate a child stood near one end. I spotted at least eight well-made, adult-sized stools stacked against the wall to my left, apparently for guests or perhaps selling in the market. In front of the stools were a dozen good-sized, well-worn pillows.

As I looked around the room, which had wooden stairs on the right side leading to a loft area with a solid railing surrounding it, I thought, *This is a room familiar to the savior of Israel.* I started feeling lightheaded at the thought and was quickly brought about by Joseph's voice.

"You must be hungry from your journey." As he handed me two of the pillows I had just been looking at, he said, "Please sit while I fetch some water to wash your feet." He disappeared under the stairs, where there was a door I had not noticed before.

While I was taking off my heavy outer garment, Mary approached with a neatly carved goblet of the darkest wood I had ever seen. "Here, Eli, a little wine to warm you while you recline and rest while Joseph brings the water and some towels." I placed the pillows next to the table, lowered myself into a reclining position, and realized that I was both famished and exhausted. I could have put my head down and slept, feeling as comfortable and safe as ever before in my life.

Joseph reentered the room carrying a basin, with towels draped over his arm. He knelt at my feet, setting the bowl down, and said, "Here, let me take your sandals." Although it was customary to accept travelers and wash their feet, this was the first time anyone had offered it to me. I had never felt so humble in my life. The earthly father of Messiah was about to wash my dirty feet! My eyes welled with tears, and I could not speak; there was a huge lump in my throat.

Joseph asked, "How have you been this past year, my friend? Although you look weary, you appear to be well, in good health."

Clearing my throat, I was able to mutter "It has been quite a year." I launched into a little summary of Jacob's murder, life in Cana, the wedding, and my pending fatherhood.

"*B'hatzlacha* (with fortune)! Married and soon to become a father, how wonderful indeed. I am so sorry to hear about your friend Jacob. Such little regard the Romans have for the lives of their oppressed. Someday the sins and atrocities they pour out upon their subjects will exact a huge penalty, and like all repressive kingdoms, they will fall."

As we talked Mary began setting out some food for the midday meal while Joseph handed me back my sandals after drying my feet. He gave me a small bowl with water and clean towels. "Here, refresh. You must be hungry after your journey in the cold. Please, let us enjoy what my lovely wife has prepared." When Joseph said that, I washed my hands then pulled the three oranges I had purchased out of my skyt and laid them on the table.

Mary had placed a platter of warm bread down with some olives, dates, and a small wedge of cheese. A beautifully crafted wood wine jug and a bowl of sliced figs completed the meal. Joseph gave thanks as he broke bread, chanting the blessing and added praise to Adonai for the bounty, for me as a traveler, and for the opportunity to extend their hospitality.

With that we picked up where we had left off over a year before as if we were neighbors bumping into each other in the local marketplace; how easily we talked. Smiling, Mary said, "Speak of your wife and child, Elijah."

My face cracked into a smile. "We were childhood neighbors and antagonists, actually, but we were friends from birth. My Rachel, she's a little bit of a thing but strong, quick, and always with a smile on her beautiful face. She has slowed down a bit since our child she is carrying has made her chores a bit ponderous. I pray that our child will carry her good looks, for she is the most beautiful of women."

I must have been grinning broadly when Mary said, "You appear happy."

"I am delighted with married life and look forward to holding my forthcoming son or daughter, however Adonai chooses to bless us. Sadly the cloud of Jacob's death at the hand of Rome is always there to wipe away a smile."

"Such a burden to carry," Joseph replied. "What brings you to Bethlehem and out in this rain to bless us with your visit?"

"I brought a flock of sheep to town under contract, hoping to find that you were still here. I was told by a vendor at the market where I might find you. This is a lot different than the last time we met, the night that changed everything!" I then dug into the food that Mary had placed on the table.

Joseph looked at Mary; they exchanged brief smiles. "It surely is. And speaking of different, it appears that you have made quite a move in stature, Aleph Eli." I forgot the silver pin on my tunic and was a little uncomfortable at his recognition of my status. Here was the father of the Son of Heaven complimenting me for being an employee of the temple.

"Tell us of your homelife, friend," he added.

I had to take a few moments to finish chewing and swallowing the fresh bread and cheese I had stuffed in my mouth because of my hunger. After a sip of the sweet wine Mary had brought, I was able to elaborate on Jacob's assassination on the way home then spoke of the Aleph training. Then most important of all, being married to the love of my life. Their faces changed from horror to delight as I spoke. Their joy was evident when I talked about Rachel and the baby she was carrying. "What of you?" I asked. "I never really knew how you wound up in that cave and what has life been since your blessed event when we unwashed shepherds crashed in on you in the grotto."

Joseph smiled again, and Mary nodded as he spoke. "Let me tell you of the miracle upon miracle of our trip after we set out for Bethlehem from Nazareth. We expected it to take four to five days because Mary felt strong and wanted to walk, saving our wedding gift money by foregoing the purchase of a pack animal. Not long after we left Nazareth, a merchant caravan came up beside us and offered us passage riding in one of their carts. They were cloth merchants from Damascus, and it was the wife that noticed Mary's condition since she had two young of her own. We rode with them for two days and at night slept in the back of their wagon that trailed their main cart.

"When we arrived at the north edge of Bethlehem, the merchant stopped at the caravansary for us to seek a room for the night. The inn was crowded to overflowing, so they decided to camp while we went to register for the census. We planned to seek shelter in the center of the town. Before we set out, the merchant's wife gave Mary a gift of the scarf she was wearing, saying, 'Here, child, the night may bring a chill, and you must be warm. Be safe on your journey.' As it turned out, Mary needed the scarf—the night was a long one.

"We made it to the town gate where the Roman census takers had set up their tents. They were not alone. They had a centurion with his soldiers and an additional dozen horsemen as part of their marching camp, roaming the city to keep order. The appointed magistrate of the census was flanked by four weapon-bedecked soldiers on each side of his booth. It seemed as if they were expecting trouble, but there was none that we were aware of. There was a bit of murmuring when each family was charged a tax of a small copper. We doubt that it was a decree from Caesar but rather the Romans and magistrate on the spot taking advantage of us."

I nodded. "They did the same in Cana, and some of my cousins from the high hill country were so outraged I thought that rebellion was just a moment away. But my father, the village judge, was able to talk sense to the zealots. Actually I think he paid the census 'tax' himself for the protesters in our family just to keep the peace. Knowing what happened with Jacob, my father bore the expense that probably saved lives. What did you do after signing and registering?"

"The streets were very crowded, and it was hard to walk without being constantly bumped. I was concerned for Mary and the jostling she was subjected to, so we turned off the main thoroughfare to seek a small house where a family might accept payment for us to rest near their fire until morning. We walked down the narrow street that ran straight through to the edge of town and knocked on every door that had a light burning in the house."

Joseph paused to sip some wine. "Before long we were out of the town and on a trail with no hope of shelter. We stopped and sat at the base of a pine tree, where I gathered the fallen needles to make a soft place for Mary to sit, wrapped in the gifted scarf. We sat together for a few minutes, then a voice, deep and calm, coming out of the darkening path, said, 'Do you intend to spend the night here, my children?'

"Startled, we looked up to see a tall man dressed in a white shepherd's garb standing on the path. In one hand he had a staff. The other held the lead to a donkey laden with supplies. 'You need shelter, and there will be none in town. Please, children, come with me.' He lowered his staff and offered me the crook, helping me to stand. 'I am called *Peleg*. Please let me help you.'

"Mary looked at me with a smile on her face, turned to the stranger, and said, 'Peleg of ancient name, thank you. Yes, we accept your help. You are a gift from Adonai.' The shepherd handed me the rope to his animal, fashioned a sitting space on the supplies, stepped over to Mary, lifted her with ease, and set her on top of the pack. We then set off to the cave in which you found us."

Smiling at the irony of Joseph's comment, I said, "So that is how you made your way to the cave, a shepherd took you? I know it must have been quite a time for you since we left you in the care of the shepherds. How did you come to settle here rather than returning to Nazareth? I thought I might have been on an empty errand trying to find you here in Bethlehem, but I needed to start my search in town before going to Migdal Eder and the grotto where we met."

The young father smiled in response. "The two days while Mary was resting, I worked with the shepherds in the cave repairing the feeding troughs and containment pens for the sheep. With some extra wood, I fashioned some stools for Peleg to take to the market to try and have a vendor sell them for us. He made daily trips, bringing fresh bread baked overnight in the grotto ovens to a merchant that relies on the shepherds for a big portion of his product. The vendor supplied the ground barley and wheat, some of which were in the sacks Mary rode on as we traveled to the cave where our son was born. That is how we got started in Bethlehem, and the kindness of the Levite shepherds is why we have stayed."

CHAPTER 9

THE ARRIVAL

"How did you get this house? It seems as if you have lived here for ages."

I must have had a puzzled look on my face because Joseph's smile broadened. "Obviously, how could we afford a place such as this, coming here with practically nothing? This house does not belong to us. It is owned by a relative of Peleg, who is the senior shepherd, the one with the purple turban whom you met in the cave. I pay him a portion of what I make and sell in the marketplace, where I share a booth with others, including the cloth vendors from Damascus.

"In addition I have steady work doing repairs to the homes in the village. We like the townspeople. Mary has made some friends, as have I, and it is close to Jerusalem. We took Yeshua there for his *brit milah* (circumcision ceremony). It was easy to get a minyan and find an experienced *mohel* (rabbi performing circumcision). There are many available around the temple grounds."

At that moment, as if on cue, a sleepy-eyed, beautiful little boy walked into the room. It was obvious that he had just awoken and was a little surprised yet smiled to see a visitor in his house. "Give him a few moments, and he will be in your lap," Mary said. "He knows no strangers!"

Yeshua toddled to the oranges, picked one up, smelled it, and then looked at me and grinned. Surely enough, within a few minutes, he was on my lap, laughing and giggling. I thought of a soon-to-come firstborn at home, how much Rachel and I loved children. Yeshua was certainly easy to love. For a moment I was breathless when the thought that *El Elyon* (Son of the Most High) was in my embrace. Realizing that Mary had said something, all I could muster in response was "No, no stranger."

We talked late into the afternoon until I felt it was time to start the journey back to Cana. I had done what I had come to do—deliver the herd, find Joseph and Mary, and see the growing Messiah. As I was preparing to say goodbye, a distant noise that sounded like horses and camels came from the road, grabbing our attention. The wind had died down, and we could hear the sound clearly. Men on horseback were rare in these village roads and usually meant one thing—Roman soldiers on the move. If they stopped, there was no telling what might happen.

The sound grew louder then stopped. Animated conversation could be heard coming from the road. We were stock-still, holding our breath while the toddler looked at the door, awaiting a surprise; he appeared to be smiling. Moments later there was a soft tap on the door, and we all relaxed. Romans would not tap; they would just kick the door down and barge into the house. Joseph got up slowly and, somewhat tentatively, made his way to the door, opened it, and just stood there.

When he did not move or speak, I stepped up alongside him and was stunned at the sight. There was a strangely dressed man in the doorway, and behind him was a grouping of other oddly garbed men, some on horses, some on camels. Twelve men to be exact, appearing like none I had ever seen. Just a glance told us that these were not ordinary travelers or a merchant caravan and certainly not Romans.

Before we could speak, one standing next to a magnificent nut-brown horse bowed slightly and addressed us in a heavily accented voice. "We have come from the east, far off lands, to meet Messiah, sent by the One of All Creation who has fulfilled prophecy. We have traveled far to worship him. His star rose and led us to this place."

Mary came up between us and said softly to Joseph, "Invite them in. Surely Adonai has brought them to us!"

Nodding, Joseph said, "Please enter. You are welcome in our home."

Four other men dismounted and entered the house, which suddenly felt quite small to accommodate such richly clad visitors. The others who remained outside we later learned were servants and bodyguards; they stayed with the camels and horses. Mary picked up her son, who was smiling, looking at the strange visitors.

The very instant they noticed Yeshua, all five men fell to their knees and bowed in worship! With faces on the floor, each one was chanting in languages as strange as their garments, words strange yet familiar. We stood there in total amazement for a moment, realizing the import and gravity of the event. Joseph took the boy from Mary, seated him on a stool atop the table, and sat at his feet.

At that moment I realized that the stool was a throne, and I joined the men in worship. I fell to my knees and began reciting a song of King David I had learned as a child, ending with "HaShem (the Name), we are exalted in your strength. We sing and praise your might!" I looked up at Yeshua, who was bathed in a halo of light from within, and I knew he was heaven-sent.

Even though the young Messiah was worthy of worship, it took a group of strangers from the east to reveal his majesty. The look on Mary's face told us she knew more than she was letting on. Her look confirmed her son was indeed Messiah! The young king sat still with a peaceful look on his face as one by one the men ended their chants.

At last they rose to their feet, as did I, all of us with smiles and tears adorning our faces. Joseph stood and held out his hands to his son, who responded with extended arms, finishing with a gentle embrace. The first visitor bowed to the little group of father, mother, and son; stood erect and said, "I am called Il Gadsparim, trail leader of this group of seekers. Please excuse us for a moment. We have each brought gifts for your son, our king."

He went to the door, opened it, and nodded. While the five visitors stayed in the house, servants outside went to the camels and horses, returning with ornate boxes: three small, two fairly large. Each richly dressed visitor in turn opened his gift and honored the young Messiah with their treasures, one after the other.

The first gift was a hand carved box filled with gold coins bearing odd stampings. Il Gadsparim bowed low, saying, "The world and all of its gold is yours, O king. Please accept this example of the world's treasure that I bring from the mountains of my home across the eastern horizon."

The second gift was a beautiful chest loaded with yellow crystals that filled the room with the most heavenly fragrance as another of the strangers stepped forward. The visitor said, "O king, I am Melech bin Yissachiore from the land near the Purple Sea. Please accept these crystals as a fragrant offering to celebrate your arrival."

The third gift I recognized as the valuable medicinal myrrh that was presented with a bow, the giver claiming, "I, your majesty, am Balthea de Salzari. I have traveled from our home, an island country very far east and south of here called Sea Land. May your life be filled with perfect health, and may this pure medicine be an aid to you and your family." The presenter fell to his knees and placed his forehead to the floor. He rose and backed away from Yeshua, making room for the next visitor.

"My king, I, Heshben Nebo of Susa in Persia, humble myself before you. I have come to present you my gift to clothe you in the finest silks, as befits majesty." He bowed low, sweeping his arms, with hands open, in a wide gesture, and stepped back. The long chest he presented held the most brilliantly colored bolts of the finest silks.

The last and largest gift had animal skins that bore patterns and colors I had never seen before—blacks, yellows, browns, and different shades of orange. As I stood there stunned at the sight, a very tall, thin man with skin color so dark it looked like the purple tint on the horizon at sunset, bowed low. "I am Tizra Ebali from a land eighteen moons' journey from here. These hides are from the animals I have hunted and present as a sacrifice to you, my chief." The tall man raised his head, closed his eyes, and chanted in a tongue so foreign it sounded like humming and clicking at the same time. The sound was harsh yet beautiful.

The looks on the faces of the men were pure joy as they presented their offerings! We learned that the Magi, as they called themselves, were from different areas and countries east and south of us. While the caravan was twelve in number, five were Magi, and of the others, three were servants, and the remaining four were well-armed soldiers, security for their travel. We had no idea how large the caravan they were a part of might have been.

Il Gadsparim said, "Over one year ago, we all saw a star arise in the west in each of our own lands. We knew from the prophecies of old that they forecasted the Chosen One. Most of us fill a role in our country much like your priests but with greater influence. Our roots and heritage are in the wise men of old, our forerunners, the prophets of history. The prophecies given told of future rulers, kingdoms, and of a king who will rise from the descendants of Abraham and reign from Jerusalem. We were drawn by a mighty hand to come to worship him. The star led us to this house. And we, who are called men of wisdom, are witnesses of this wonderful event! This child is a gift from *He Who Brings to Existence What Exists*, and he now resides with us!"

With that the four men fell facedown again before Yeshua.

CHAPTER 10

THE CONCERNS

After the men ended their renewed chanting, they all rose and looked at their leader, who said, "We came seven days ago after meeting at an oasis south of Jerusalem. Each of us knew in our hearts to wait and gather information, another sign from above. We had purchased local clothing and entered the city on foot, asking everyone we saw where Messiah was born. All we encountered appeared confused, even ignorant, about our inquiries! We have scouts that speak most languages that are heard in Jerusalem, yet none seemed to understand us or were willing to help. Some were in fear of us even though we were unarmed and peaceful in our approach.

"One of our men reported back to our camp that word of our inquiry was carried to Herod. Things started to stir when he heard that we were asking about a newly born king, Messiah. Apparently we were followed back to the oasis, and Herod summoned us to his palace in secret. He questioned us and asked very directly when we had first seen the star. We felt ill at ease in his presence; an essence of evil came from the man. We do not trust him. Every word from his mouth was spoken sweetly yet seemed dripping with deceit and venom.

"In each of our countries, we are sometimes known as kingmakers. No one can ascend to a throne unless filled with knowledge and wisdom of the ages necessary to rule the people. We would never support one like Herod to be king. He may seem wise, but he is a fox, and he is evil! We must take care, my friends. Walls have ears!"

I nodded in agreement, looking at Joseph.

"Herod bid us, 'Find this child, this Messiah, and bring me word of his whereabouts that I may honor and worship him.' Herod was not interested in worshiping. His smile could not conceal the look in his eyes. He is called king and wants no other to rule where he reigns."

Taking a deep breath and looking at each of us, he continued. "We know that Herod is ruthless, having killed members of his own family he considered a challenge to his rule. It has been said that it is better to be Herod's swine than to be Herod's sons. His reputation has spread far and wide."

Bowing, he added, "We must leave before we draw too much attention to this home and Messiah. We know it is not time for his rule to begin. We are camped in the valley south of here and will remain for another day before we depart for our homelands. Please visit us if you so desire." With that he bowed once again as he turned to lead the others out the door.

Mary said to the guests, "Please wait. My husband made these stools for the marketplace. Will you do us honor and each receive one?"

"It honors us beyond measure, my lady" was the reply.

Mary handed each stool to Yeshua, who, in turn, pushed them toward each of the visitors. One by one the Magi bowed and received the wood seats presented by their avowed king. The men received the gift crafted by Joseph as it was the most priceless treasure.

With a broad grin and a deep bow, the leader said, "Now we can return to our own countries in peace, knowing these things are true, and tell of this wondrous event. The prophecies have been fulfilled! Praise the One of All Creation!"

Joseph, the host of the house, said, "Sirs, the night is upon us. It is getting dark. As you have said, our neighbors will talk, and much attention will be drawn to all of us. Let us continue our conversation with our visit to your camp at morning light." It was agreed to meet the next day and bid them safe travels. With that the visiting Magi, servants, and guards mounted and took leave.

"Shalom," we all said in unison as they departed. They left as quickly as they had appeared, leaving the four of us alone in the center of the room looking at the treasures they had presented. We stood silently for some time, alone with our own thoughts.

Images raced through my mind. Five strangely garbed men from the "east," presenting treasures to the young Yeshua, their king. Joseph and Mary standing in rapt amazement, and the toddler Messiah presenting wooden stools crafted by his earthly father in return. And I, Elijah ben Ezra, a shepherd from Galilee, servant of the temple in Jerusalem, was witness to all that occurred. And all I could think at that moment was that all I had brought as a gift were three oranges!

What was I doing in this house at this momentous time in history? How had all these things occurred? These questions buzzed through my head, and the answer came as a whisper to my soul. "It is the hand of Adonai."

It was almost too much for me to take in; I was so insignificant in the event. The visage of the little warrior chazzen came to mind, and as he had taught, I realized that so much in life, while we experience it, is quite different than it appears. The thought calmed me, and I was thankful for that tough little man who disciplined me and helped me learn so much.

Joseph broke the silence. "Eli, it is too late to begin your journey home. Please stay the night."

The thought of being in the same house as Messiah was intoxicating. I nodded and said, "I am humbled by your request. Yes, I cannot refuse such an offer."

After a light meal, they made a pallet of pillows and took a magnificent, soft hide from the chest given to Yeshua by the visitor named Tizra for me to use as a blanket. After saying good night and a short prayer, I fell into a deep, peaceful sleep, thinking of the smiling young Messiah.

CHAPTER 11

THE COVENANT

It was well before dawn, and I was fully dressed, rekindling the embers in the fireplace to heat water for the small family. I was bending toward the building flames when I felt a tug at my leg. I turned and there was the young Messiah, smiling and holding up his hands for me to lift him. I picked him up; he wrapped his arms around my neck and in the sweetest child's voice whispered, "Shalom."

At that moment I felt weightless and as if I were a streak of lightning soaring across the sky. My eyes then focused on Joseph, wearing a smile, who said, "Come, let us eat and go visit the camp of our new friends." Mary entered the room and started heating some barley cakes when there was a soft tap on the door, just like one the prior evening.

I was closest to the door, still holding Yeshua. I looked at Joseph, who nodded, allowing me to open it. Standing there was a man I recognized from the day before as one who had carried a gift. "I am Arsham, sworn protector of the men who have traveled so far," he said with a slight bow. He looked at Yeshua. They exchanged smiles as Joseph came up beside us and invited him.

Joseph asked, "Are you here to guide us? We were preparing to visit your camp as invited."

Shaking his head, Arsham in a near whisper replied, "I am here as an alarm, my young friends. Heaven warned all five of my masters with the same dream last night to go back to our countries by a different route and not return to Herod. There is grave danger for all. We have packed our camp and are preparing to depart immediately." Looking at me, the man said, "I have a very important matter to discuss with you, master shepherd."

Slightly confused by his words, I handed Yeshua back to Joseph. We stepped outside over to the camels and the others dressed as pilgrims, who were commonplace throughout the land. "These are our finest scout-warriors. I have trained them, and they report to me. This honored family will be safe with them," he said, looking at Mary, who stood in the doorway, now holding her son.

Addressing the mother of Messiah, Arsham bowed, saying, "They will pack your belongings and lead you to safety. Herod will not be idle to end any threat to his crown. You must flee! My men will take you and your belongings to safety. As soon as you depart, there are others who will come behind and empty the house, leaving no clue as to your whereabouts."

My elation of the morning dissolved as the looks on the faces of the young couple changed, not to fear but to concern.

"We shall prepare and be ready in short order," Joseph responded and turned, going back inside to gather items to pack. The men Arsham referred to as warriors entered the house and moved about, loading the gifts and all the personal belongings Joseph and Mary had gathered while their son sat quietly on one of the stools Joseph had crafted. I went to the fire, dousing it with the water I had started heating for morning tea. It was to be a rapid, quiet departure. Dawn would break, and the village would awaken. We wanted to be gone before anyone could observe the direction of our departure.

Arsham took me aside, away from the hearing of anyone else who might have been awake and listening. In a quiet voice, he said, "As all five masters had the exact same dream warning them to leave and go a different way, heaven is telling them that Yeshua is in danger from Herod. Now that we have had time to warn, protect, and send them to safe hiding, you need to do that as well. Our caravan is already prepared to leave. What you did not see were the scores of others camped outside of the city: pack animals, servants, and more warriors. Every armed man in the caravan is pledged to give his life for the safety of his charges. But with the numbers of palace guards Herod and his Roman allies could advance against us, stealth is the most important asset we possess. You must leave first. If you see the path we take, Herod may look for you, as you may have been seen with us. Your life will be in danger as well. He is a monster, and you would never stand against his torture, or what he might do to your family to get information!" I inwardly cringed at the thought of Rachel and any of my family in the hands of Herod's men.

"However, before you take your leave, my masters have talked and have decided to ask you to make a covenant with them." His voice fell to a near whisper; he leaned toward me as he spoke. "All have agreed that they desire that you be their agent in Galilee and Judea, to follow the life and activity of Yeshua as he grows. We know he will be the king someday, perhaps sooner than we can imagine. My masters cannot return to your land to see for themselves. Herod would surely hear of their coming, and they would be subjected to his wrath." I nodded, his reasoning true.

"In our countries we are safe but cut off from the one we came to find. You see, we all believe he is Messiah. We are asking that you be our eyes, ears, and sandals on the ground as he becomes king. We want to know how the prophecies of old are fulfilled. Will you honor us and accept this task, binding yourself with our quest?"

The proposal caught me totally unprepared as to what to say. All I could blurt out was "Of course!"

Arsham sharply whispered, "Speak softly!" With a slight smile, he continued. "We knew you would agree, for you are just as devoted as the ones who have traveled so far. This is our counsel and commission on how to proceed. First, you will be provided with funds to travel as you need. Every year when you go to the Feast of Passover and Feast of Tabernacles in Jerusalem, one of my trusted men will meet you at one of the holidays to get your report and replenish your funds. They require the reports to be written. You can write, can you not?"

I nodded, answering humbly, "My father is a judge in our village, and I have been educated. Someday I will replace him as judge, as will my son, should Adonai so bless me. Recently I have become a member of the temple shepherds called Alephs, so I have free movement and passage in most areas."

Reaching under my cloak, I showed Arsham my Aleph pin, and he broke into a wide grin, whispering up to the sky, "The hand of the Almighty One is with us! He has chosen the perfect man with whom to cut covenant. This is excellent beyond our planning.

"We ask that you provide our man a complete and written report. You seem to have a keen eye for detail and are a chosen shepherd able to move about without raising suspicion. You and your fellow shepherds were first on the scene at his birth. But you, you are the one who came to seek him. We are sure that the Great Hand brought you back not only to see the Holy One of Israel but also for service to my masters!"

With that he led me into the shadows. Arsham had been carrying a worn leather bag. Reaching into it, he pulled out a small purse. "Eli, these coins are your local currency, which we exchanged at the temple in Jerusalem. If you only had our original coins, suspicion may have been aroused." With that he handed me a leather pouch containing one hundred denarii, worth about an equal number of days of common labor.

"This will get you started and finance your first trip to Jerusalem for the next Feast of Tabernacles as well as cover other costs you may incur. My man will meet you by the Pool of Siloam on the second full day of the festival. He will have a bag with a seal clearly displayed on its side." He gestured toward an insignia of a star on his saddle. "Meet him there at the fourth hour after sunrise. He will know who you are. Take this pouch with this matching symbol, wear it on your belt, and our man will spot you should you not see him first."

Accepting the bag, I asked, "What if I cannot find Joseph, Mary, and Yeshua? They are here now, but I must return to Cana. They are leaving and may not return to Bethlehem or Judea." Thinking about the very real possibility of not being able to find them worried me, and I did not want to fail in my suddenly accepted mission.

"Elijah ben Ezra, all we can expect is that you do your best. We trust that you will want to know where he is, just as my master does, and that desire will help with your quest. Return to Jerusalem this coming fall at the festival, and we will declare if we want you to continue your obligation."

I replied, "Yes, my friend, you are correct. I do desire to know everything he does. He is Messiah! At some time he will make himself public, and I will find him!"

With that word, and a firm handclasp, we said our goodbyes. "Shepherd, you leave first and head home. Leave immediately. We may have taken too long already. Make haste, and do not look back!"

I was handed my gear by another scout then headed out of the village toward home, keeping my eyes straight ahead. As much as I wanted to see the family and the caravan that brought the Magi, I knew Arsham was correct. "Adonai, speed their trip!" I prayed softly.

I walked as fast as possible down the dark road, anxious to return home with first light coming fast. Passing through the village, I saw no one and was gripped by a fear that I had not said a proper farewell to Messiah and his family. I spun around, quickly returning to the house where I had spent the night.

All was still and quiet, with no movement. I hesitated only briefly; with the importance my mission and my desire to get home set aside, I tapped lightly on the door and waited for a short time. Receiving no answer, I pushed the door open, and amazingly the house was completely empty. It appeared as if it had not been lived in recently. What mystical abilities these Magi seemed to possess. Smiling to myself, keeping my head down, I walked at quick step out of the village.

As I moved, the whisper into my soul returned. "Eli, fear not! Adonai sent those angels you saw and spoke through Gabriel to Mary then gifted all five Magi with the same dream at the same time. He is the Ever-Living, Everlasting One, and he will not forsake you. He will protect his chosen." I felt light and strong as my trip home became burden-free!

CHAPTER 12

THE MASSACRE

HOW EXCITED I was to arrive in Cana after my time in Bethlehem. I was full of energy, even though the journey on foot home was long and the road hard. The little addition to my parents' home was a beautiful sight. We had our own door through which to enter, our own garden, and our own pens for chickens and goats. What a generous community we were part of, giving gifts to start our own household.

It was noon, hot and quiet in the village, as I touched our very own mezuzah and entered our rooms, our castle. "Rachel, *isha* (wife)!" I shouted. "Your beloved returns," I said with a smile in my voice. Silence greeted me. Still smiling, I went to the door attached to my parents' home, tapped, and entered, calling, "Father, Mother, where is everyone?"

The quiet was unnerving; even the animals outside were still. I went back to our addition, set my gear down, and started toward the village square. Once again I was met with emptiness and silence; how strange. Walking toward the square, I started hearing a commotion, so I picked up the pace and started running toward the source of the growing noise.

The closer I got, the louder the sounds became. I recognized wailing, weeping, and shouting! Oh, Adonai, what now? I spotted one of the town elders sitting on a wooden bench in front of our little *shul* (synagogue). With a prayer shawl over his head, he was rocking back and forth in the traditional *davening* (praying) mode. With growing panic, I sat down next to him, setting a hand gently on his shoulder to gain his attention. Slowly he raised his face toward me and with a cracked voice said, "Elijah, my boy, you have come home to terrible news."

My heart sank as I asked, "My family—have I come home to a tragedy? My wife, my parents—tell me!" My voice was harsher than it should have been.

"Not your immediate family, son. Our family of the faith is suffering terrible news from Jerusalem."

"What news?" I moaned. "I have just come from Bethlehem, and there is no news to report."

With an unsteady voice, he continued. "In the center of that crowd gathered there, where your family stands, hale and well, is a messenger from the capitol with news of a massacre."

"What massacre?" I yelled, bolting upright, jostling the old man.

He slowly looked up with a face so sad it broke my heart. His rheumy eyes were tearing. "Herod the Great has ordered the slaying of all male children under the age of two years in and around Bethlehem. It is said he fears that there have been signs that Messiah has come and has been born in Bethlehem in line with prophecies in our ancient writings. With the fear that his kingship will be challenged someday, he is eliminating all possible usurpers."

Another flash of panic clenched me as I wondered whether Arsham and the caravan had fled in time to elude the slaughter. Knowing Messiah had indeed arrived, I said with a sob, "He is insane, and with the Roman legions behind him, there is no stopping this madness." Remembering the whispered voice I had heard while leaving Bethlehem, I calmed at once.

As I sat down next to the old man who was tearing at his garment, I put my arm around him and in a soft voice asked, "Would the One, who saved Moses, who crumbled the walls of Jericho, who has brought us to this time and place, abandon us now? I think not, my old friend. We shall mourn for the innocents but not Messiah."

With a much calmer demeanor, he looked at me, removed his fringe-laden tallit (prayer shawl), and said, "You are right, Eli, we are not abandoned." He stood, took two unsteady steps, turned back to me, and in a stronger voice said, "Come, let us reassure our people." Holding his walking stick, he set out toward the crowd with a stronger gait than I could have imagined.

Helping him move through the crowd to the center of our village, I saw my father rocking back and forth, weeping. Making way for me and the elder, the crowd parted, and I saw Rachel and others pouring tears as well. "Eli, you made it home safely. Have you heard the news?" Rachel asked with a broken heart.

"Yes, just now. Let us hear from our elder. He has some reassuring words."

As Rachel threw her arms around me, the old man spoke words similar to ones I had spoken in our recent exchange. The crowd quieted with his authority. He ended by saying, "Messiah will be revealed. He will not succumb to the whims of a madman. Let us mourn and pray for the families that are grieving loss." We each quietly recited prayers known from childhood, and they brought comfort. What none of us realized at the time was another prophecy had been fulfilled.

Over the next weeks, we heard awful reports from Bethlehem, and the pall of mourning settled over all of Judea. Sooner than I would have liked, it was time again for me to return to Jerusalem and the temple training. Rachel was growing large and uncomfortable with the baby, but I had to leave.

CHAPTER 13

THE PORCH

JERUSALEM WAS DIFFERENT upon my return. The city was tense with fear and loathing because of Herod's decree and the slaughter of innocent children. The Romans, however, seemed more relaxed knowing that death could be meted out so easily. Even the chazzen was changed; he seemed softer in his treatment on our return for additional training.

"Aleph Eighteen, step forward," he said at our first assembly.

I took a long stride forward, two steps to the side, and, looking down at the face that seemed even older, said, "Yes, chazzen."

"Eighteen, the last session you showed the most promise in all areas of training. As a result, you now have responsibility as the leader of this class of Alephs." His statement for all to hear brought audible gasps from some of the others behind me. "It is now your job to assist me to make sure that the rest of your brothers in this class respond to every order, every command, and only excellence will be accepted. Understand?"

I couldn't hesitate in my response, shouting, "Yes, chazzen!"

"Very well. Turn around and address your charges."

My mind was swimming, but I had to speak with little hesitation. Thinking about my father the judge, trying to imagine what he would have said in this circumstance, I began. "My brothers, I feel unworthy of this honor and responsibility. I seek your assistance and at the same time challenge us, all of us, to be the class of Alephs that sets the standard for all classes to come."

The training started the same way as before, with instruction, then a meal. We practiced briefly with our slings, rods, and staff then were taken to a room in the temple compound that staggered me. There were eighteen high tables, each one fitted with knives of all shapes and sizes; it was a butchery! Experienced shepherds slay, prepare, and eat a wide variety of game and of course sheep and goats. What we were in for was a lesson on mass preparation of daily and holiday sacrifices.

Standing at each table was a priest wearing a small, tight-fitting turban and a hide apron that covered neck to feet. Sandals were replaced with laced-up leather boots, and the only other garment we were able to see was a woven linen tunic that exposed the arms. Stacked next to the tables were slatted wooden crates filled with pigeons.

The priest at the first table nearest to us when we entered the room said, "Eighteen, put on this apron and stand to my left." Pointing to a spot between me and the crates, he said, "Open the crate, and hand me one."

With a slow motion, I lifted the lid, reached in, and handed him the small bird. He said, "This is an example of the sacrifices that will be performed for sins such as those of omission. The draining of all animal blood complies with all laws of *kashruth* (kosher practice)."

With hand speed hard to imagine, he grasped the body of the bird. One finger bent the head back, and at the same time he drew a short knife from his waistband. He slit the bird's neck over an opening at the end of the table, replaced the knife, and with the same hand wrapped a string around the legs, dropping the bird into the opening. At the other end of the string was an iron hook that held the bird upside down to drain all the blood. He repeated, "Atonement for sins of omission, demanded by the law of kashruth." The rabbi had the class repeat that phrase as the afternoon was spent practicing the routine we were shown.

Tevyeh, the brother Aleph I had befriended during the previous training, was at the table next to mine and in a low voice said, "I hope this is not tonight's dinner."

We were covered with blood after the slaughtering and made our way to the baths to wash the aprons and ourselves, glad knowing there were servants cleaning up the area we had just used.

After we dressed for the evening meal, a voice bellowed from behind, "Hey, big man!" Turning I was face-to-face with an Aleph from Hebron, south of the city. He was about as big as me and had a ratlike face that spoke trouble.

"Ah, Eleven, did you enjoy the day's training?" I asked.

"Not as much as I will when we get to slaughtering bulls. Now that will be fun!" he said, taking a threatening step toward me.

"Have I offended you in some manner, Eleven?" I asked.

"Just the sight of you offends me," he growled, tensing up to strike.

With a practiced stroke, I pulled the little rod the chazzen had given me at the end of our first month and poked him in the belly hard enough to take his breath and double him over. Bending down, I spoke quietly in his ear, "We will get along and finish this month with no conflict."

Tevyeh and I walked to the dining hall and had a great meal of fruits, vegetables, and breads. With a mouth full of apple, he asked, "Do you think Eleven is going to give you trouble, Eli?"

As I was peeling an orange, I said, "I hope not, for his sake." I was in a somber mood. "Working with the pigeons made me feel like we were the birds. It seems Herod and the Romans can slaughter us any time they choose. In class the more we cut the birds, the more I thought about Jacob, and I imagined the birds were Roman soldiers. I must put away my anger." The last words I barely mumbled, almost adding, "For the sake of Messiah," but I caught myself, not wanting to bring Tevyeh into a possible snare.

Unlike the first month of training earlier in the year, we had two free days to explore the temple and the city this time. This gave me an opportunity to find and get acquainted with the Pool of Siloam. In less than half a year, I was going to have my first visit with a messenger from the Magi. But first I wanted to explore Solomon's Porch. I grabbed Tevyeh on our first free day, and off we went. The times I had been in Jerusalem in the past were always focused on some business or holiday; this was freedom.

When we rounded the corner on the eastern side of the temple grounds, I stopped and gaped at the sight—162 columns as tall as eight men on shoulders and as round as the eight grouped together. I touched one, and it was the smoothest marble I had ever felt. The colonnade was truly a wonder to behold. As I was turning to speak to Tevyeh, something struck in the middle of my back. It was a ripe pomegranate that exploded on my tunic and made a mess. It had been thrown by number Eleven. He and two other Alephs stood there laughing as I approached them furious and boiling with destructive intent.

"Boy!" a booming voice shouted, stopping me and Tevyeh in our tracks. It was a huge soldier, one of the temple guards, walking toward our little cluster. He got to us and grabbed the rat-faced Eleven by the front of his tunic and, with his face inches from Eleven's, said, "Scum, you just broke the law." With his other hand, he drew a brass knife and held it to the chest of Eleven.

"Sir," I said, "please let him be. We have been training hard at the Shepherd Academy, and we were just trying to let off some steam. We will clean the stain the fruit has left and be on our way." Lowering my head, I added, "Please, sir."

He released Eleven and, still nose-to-nose with him, sheathed his knife while asking, "What is your name, boy?"

With a shaky reply, he said, "Shabach, sir."

In a growl the guard said to Eleven, "You know I could stick you and add your blood to the floor of this sacred area if I so desired."

Shabach, trembling, said, "Please do not. I am sorry."

The guard grabbed Shabach's tunic. "Give this boy your garment and wipe up the mess with the dirty one. Put it on then leave!"

"Yes, sir" was the meek reply.

We exchanged tunics. Eleven, whom I then knew as Shabach, cleaned up the mess and put on the dirty tunic, and we all left.

"Thank you, Eighteen, you saved me from harm and the possibility of dismissal."

"We are a brotherhood," I said, and without further comment we walked down to the huge marketplace.

Since I carried a pouch with some coins, I purchased five oranges and gave one to each of my classmates and said, "I am going to roam about on my own for a while. See you all at evening meal." With that I set off to find the pool on the south slope of the city.

Jerusalem was the biggest, noisiest city I had ever seen, but it had such grandeur, such history it was easy to ignore its shortcomings. I found the pool, which by itself was a wonder—fresh water brought by an aqueduct from the spring at Gihon. Standing there I watched comings and goings until the sun was near setting, and then I started back to the temple; I knew where to meet the Magi's messenger.

The rest of the month was pure drudgery because of the butchering lessons. By the time we were at bulls, the last week of training, I asked the chazzen a question that we all were thinking. "Why are we doing this? We are shepherds, not butchers, even though dressing meats in the field is necessary."

"Elijah, when this city welcomes pilgrims for the major festivals, there are never enough *kohanim* (priests) to keep up with the demand for *korbanot* (sacrificial animals). Therefore, you, other Levites, and I are pressed into duty to perform these rituals. We receive special ordinations to carry out sacrifice, but mostly we are needed to keep pace with demands and do the butchering. In the future you may receive a message to come to the temple in advance of the ceremonies, another honor of being a Levite," he said with a sly smile.

The time at the training academy was done, and I was off again to home and my beloved.

CHAPTER 14

THE BABY

By the time I arrived back in Cana, Rachel was ready to give birth. One of the village midwives had visited every day and reassured me upon my homecoming that things looked good for an easy birth. I was concerned because Rachel was tiny, and the baby she was carrying seemed enormous.

Three days after my return, her pouch water was released, and the pains began. I was sent off to the fields near *Har Ta'avar* (Mount Tabor) to find wild fennel that was to be made into a calming tea to aid Rachel during birth. I am sure the midwives had plenty on hand; they just wanted me out of the village.

My father and cousin Ira set out with me on the journey to bring back an *ephah* (large basket) of the herb. We were happy to break away from the sounds of childbirth; plus we had the added fortune of fresh fennel to boil with our meal of salted fish and oatcakes. Ira was an expert with the sling and that afternoon hit a plump swamp hen that provided a great feast.

Ira was also a scholar. His knowledge of so many facts about the land, its history, flora, and fauna kept us amused all the time we were gone. A large skin of wine added to the relaxed atmosphere of the day. Yet I could not put worry about Rachel and the baby too far away from my thoughts.

We had collected more than enough to fill the requirements of the midwives and made it back to the village before dusk. All seemed quite normal when we approached our home and were greeted by Ira's wife, Simcha.

With hesitation in her steps, she walked toward us and said, "Eli, *mazel tov* (good fortune has occurred), you have a beautiful little girl—"

Interrupting her, I begged, "What is wrong? Tell me."

Lowering her head and with a soft voice, Simcha answered, "Your Sarah is a beautiful, healthy girl. But it was a difficult time for your Rachel. She lost a lot of blood, and there was some injury, tearing when Sarah arrived."

"Will she be well again?" I asked with a shaky voice.

"She should be in a few weeks, but there may be problems with bearing other children. Do not concern yourself with that now. She needs you and your strength. Go see her and meet your daughter."

Walking into the darkened room, I could feel the bile of fear rising in my throat but had to put on a brave face. "Where are my girls? Where is my beautiful Rachel, and where is little Sarah? Come meet your abba, little one."

There was my Rachel, in the middle of the bed, looking so small and so pale. Trying to look brave for me, she smiled a weak smile. "My sweet man, come see the blessing Adonai has given us." Peeling back the cover, she showed me this oh-so-small version of my wonderful wife. I sat on the edge of the low bed, leaned over, and kissed Rachel's forehead.

"My, my, you have given me a girl almost as big as you." My words were said with as much of a smile as I could muster. "We are agreed this is Sarah," I stated, more as a question.

"We are agreed," she whispered with her wan smile fading. Her eyes closed as she drifted off to sleep.

I looked at the two *saftim* (grandmothers) in the room and in a near panicked voice asked, "Mother, what is happening?"

In a strong but quiet voice, my mother said, "Son, your wife has had a very difficult time. She needs rest more than anything right now."

Straining, I asked, "What about my little girl, what of her health?"

Tenderly my mother added, "She is perfect and strong. What we need for her now is to find a *menekes* (wet nurse). I am afraid that Rachel is too weak to provide enough milk for your Sarah. But at this moment, pick her up and hold her. Get to know your little girl."

My heart was heavy as I lifted the little package of life. But the wonder of fatherhood was a flood giving me a joy I had never known before. Looking at the angelic little face then gazing at her mother, I realized my mounting responsibilities. These arms that were cradling my own child had held Messiah.

CHAPTER 15

THE MEETING

Rachel was recovering slowly, as predicted, and Sarah was growing fast. The combination of wet nurses and goat milk was a good formula. How rapidly the time seemed to pass. The summer was over, and the excitement of the harvest festival season was everywhere. Rachel and I were making plans and counting the days until we left for Jerusalem. Sarah was old enough to travel; it would be our first trip as a family.

A good number of the townsfolk were going, so we were traveling as a fair-sized troupe. Our family had an old, good large cart that made it easier for Rachel and the baby to ride in comfort. The village maintains a small group of *cha'mohrs* (donkeys) that were commonly shared and maintained by a farmer paid with funds collected at the synagogue. We were able to harness one for our trip.

Other villagers from Cana had wagons, allowing us the ability, with my fellow shepherds, to set up a large camp. Other families from nearby villages joined us on the way. We were a big group of well-behaved sojourners destined to a festival celebration in the center of our faith, beautiful Jerusalem.

Even in Rachel's weakened condition, she was excited to be on the road. The fact that I had confided in her about that night of nights made her not only a trusted confidant but also a true believer. She was unique among women in our village and culture, being highly educated. Her father was a rabbi and held the belief that women deserved and needed educating every bit as much as men in our society. The fact that Rachel was extremely bright and loved learning set her completely apart, atop the pedestal of my heart.

Sadly she had to keep her knowledge a secret, even among her friends at home. An educated woman was not only an oddity but also even, according to some, a sin. Her father, may he rest in peace, taught her and treated her like a man, as an equal. That was one of the treasures of my Rachel, her mind. She had access to scrolls and writings, with knowledge of the prophecies of Messiah. Rachel was my partner in planning to locate and report about Messiah to the Magi.

We heard nothing of Yeshua's whereabouts. My trips for Aleph training in Jerusalem had produced not one clue or shred of evidence of his existence. I had asked various merchants and caravan members passing through if they had heard any word of Messiah. Since our area of Galilee was on a major caravan route, I questioned many. Most of the time, I was met with blank stares.

Finally we were on our way to the capitol as a family! With the ever-growing crowds heading toward Jerusalem, my anticipation of meeting Arsham's man at the festival was always in my mind. Since I had absolutely no news or word to give him, could he tell me to stop my mission? Regardless of his message, my need to know was all-consuming.

It was hard to describe the chaos of thousands of men, women, and children, some with flocks and herds, converging on the city of Jerusalem for the fall harvest festivals. *Rosh Hashanah* (Feast of Trumpets), *Yom Kippur* (Day of Atonement), and then the eight days of *Sukkot* (Feast of Tabernacles) were all celebrated in the fall. Adonai told Moses that all males were to go to Jerusalem three times a year, and his writings were sacred. The spring festivals were *Pesach* (Passover), followed in fifty days with *Shavuot* (Feast of Weeks), which was in the late spring.

In the fall many pilgrims stayed for the whole month, swelling the city to many times its usual size. People were everywhere! This was the biggest festival of all because of the construction of the little huts. It was custom to build small *sukkot* (temporary dwellings) made of palm branches to camp in. We brought our Levite tithes to pay for the trip. My Aleph stipend and the coins saved from the Magi made travel much easier. It was a joyous time. With our wagons herded together just outside the walls of the great city, we were able to build a sukkot for each family. We constructed a great camp.

On the first full day of the festival, I was in turmoil. Exhaustion from travel and the preparation of camp had me fatigued but excited to meet the liaison from the Magi the next morning. I had no idea what to do or say. The past year had been one of constant vigilance for the slightest whisper of Messiah and the name Yeshua. I kept thinking of all the events leading up to this day: the light, the angel, the cave, the baby, the toddler, the star, the Magi, the covenant, my training, my baby. I was to face one of the Magi's emissaries chosen by Arsham with nothing to report!

Noticing my distress, my wonderful Rachel brought me back as my mind wandered. "We know what happened is true. You have been chosen for an important task, and you will not waver or fail."

After a deep sleep and a warm embrace from Rachel, I kissed Sarah's head and left camp, winding my way through the crowds toward the Pool of Siloam. Thoughts raged back and forth through my restless mind as I wondered what I would say and how this would take place.

The pool was a landmark in Jerusalem. Our history told us it was carved out of solid rock by workers during King Hezekiah's time to bring water from the spring of Gihon under the city walls during a war siege. It was located near the Temple Mount, inside the present city walls. I was to be there at the fourth hour after sunrise. I had no idea whom to look for or what he looked like. All I knew was that he would be carrying the sign of a star on a pouch like mine.

The walk from camp was short enough, but the crowds made it longer. People were everywhere, with throngs at the markets, the money changers, the hated tax collectors, and the ever-present Roman soldiers keeping order. Winding my way through the crowds was challenging, but I made good time. While it was impossible to know the exact time, the sun said I was hours early when I arrived.

The Pool of Siloam was about fifty feet long, bordered on one side with a series of four sets of five steps down to the water. It seemed that the water level went up and down a little as I watched. Living in the country, I knew that springs were variable and the water flow erratic at times.

Pilgrims stood in small groups around the pool. I estimated at least two hundred men and women within a hundred feet of the pool. Some sat on the walls and steps, talking while washing hands and faces in the water. I posted myself on high step, alert like I was watching for wolves, full Aleph mode. Slowly I scanned the area and paths to the pool for any sign of the emissary, noticing anyone looking at me or anyone who looked out of place.

After a few minutes, I gave up and resigned myself to waiting. The fact there were pilgrims from all over the Roman world in totally different dress convinced me that the only way I would know the man was the pouch with the star. A few minutes after I arrived, I slowly and carefully pulled the leather purse from my waistcoat. I was now committed to the meeting. I continued scanning the crowd, slowly looking for the same symbol we shared in Bethlehem.

No one seemed to notice me or even glance my way. Still, I was early, so there was no need to be concerned just yet. As I waited I wondered if I should walk about or remain seated and still. I positioned the pouch, making sure it was visible but not obvious. I sat on the highest step around the pool and started peeling an orange that I had picked up in the market on the way to Siloam. It seemed that the orange had become a symbol attaching me to Messiah, and I took comfort in every aspect of the fruit.

As I was sectioning it, I started to pray in a soft whisper. "Adonai, you showed by signs and wonders that the appointed savior of the world has come. You allowed me to see what only a few in this world have seen or heard. If this meeting is a part of your plan, please show me whom I am to meet and assure me that I am your servant in this matter."

No sooner had the last word left my mouth than a shepherd's crook touched my foot, and a familiar voice softly whispered my name. "Eli, let us walk." As he came alongside me, I saw it was indeed Arsham, the warrior scout himself! I know that I must have had a stunned look on my face because Arsham smiled and nodded.

"It is you!" I stammered.

"None other, young shepherd! You look like you are faring well, Elijah ben Ezra." There was humor in his manner.

Smiling, I said, "I am well, and much better now that we have made contact! It is good to see you." Arsham was almost unrecognizable, even up close. He looked like an average pilgrim shepherd with his beard trimmed in local fashion, and he wore the plain, simple clothing of the day. No one would have picked him out of the crowd, especially during the festival, with pilgrims from dozens of other nations present. "I arrived early just in case but never saw you."

"Well done. You have had excellent training as an Aleph shepherd, but I have spent my life learning my craft—to be invisible as necessary. I was in the shade past the pool and recognized you the moment you came into view. As for me, it would not bode well to be discovered by any of Herod's men. Even though the old fox is dead and the world better off, the danger from his son and loyal soldiers still abounds. I recognized many of them when I walked into the city. My decision to hide in plain sight is well served."

We began to walk north then west to avoid the congestion of the Temple Mount. Jerusalem was packed with worshippers from all over. I heard conversations in languages I could not understand, but it all added to the intrigue of our mission.

We spoke little as we walked; Arsham seemed intent on a particular destination, striding with purpose. Our journey through the city took us past Herod's palace, a huge, ornate building that dominated the west boundary of Jerusalem. The late Herod the Great—Herodes Magnus, as the Romans named him—had spent a fortune in taxes and human lives building the ostentatious structure.

As we made our way north again, the road paralleled the east side of the palace, the seat of the beast of Rome in Judea. I could not help but think that we were in the middle of two worlds—that of the hated and feared iron fist of Rome and that of the newly arrived king who would throw off their yoke! Heaven had visited his people again! Only a small group knew; Arsham and I were two of that blessed number.

We had gone through the northwest gate of the city on the road to Joppa, on the sea far to the west. Vendors had set up shops, and we had worked our way to a small food stall for the travelers coming and going from the festival. My thoughts were broken when he said, "We are here. Let us sit. I scouted this area when I arrived, and it seems good for a private conversation."

I wondered how long he had been in Jerusalem as he seemed to know the city well. We purchased food and drink. Arsham, with a mouthful of bread and wine, said, "Our trip back to Susa and beyond was uneventful. How was your journey home?"

I realized he was talking about Bethlehem and the urgent mission for Joseph and Mary to leave. I had not thought that he might not know about the empty house. I picked up the story for him, relating it with the same detail I had given Rachel—the empty house, my fears that the family was discovered, the reassurance from the voice in me that the hand of Adonai was in control. I remembered my prayer, and I related all that I observed and experienced.

He was quiet for a moment, lost in thought. Then he slowly said, "Adonai warned all of us the same night, blessed be he! The Messiah, Yeshua, lives, and Herod, who sought his life, is dead!"

It suddenly dawned on me that Arsham knew nothing of the edict to kill the little boys in and around Bethlehem. I pondered for a moment and decided I must relate that news, and it must come from me, not a stranger. I shuddered at the recollection of the killing of the innocents in Bethlehem and hesitantly told of that atrocity ordered by Herod.

His distress was evident as he sat weeping silently at the news. This experienced, hardened warrior was broken with despair at my words. He realized the unwitting role the Magi and their caravan had played in the death of so many children. In a bit he regained his composure, and our conversation continued.

I asked, "The questions I have are, where did they go, and where are they now? Are they back in Judea, in Galilee? I have been so concerned since I returned that morning and found the house completely deserted."

With a wry smile, Arsham took a swallow of wine. "My masters arranged for them to travel with an armed escort to a place I know not. Rest assured that they are well, and Messiah will return, making his presence known at some point. You must be ready when he does. Your mission is still ongoing, even though at this time we have no idea where he might be."

Arsham's confirmation that the sacred family had escaped filled me with such joy that I jumped up, throwing my hands in the air, and yelled, "Alleluia!" Food and wine flew from my lap, causing Arsham to nearly choke on his wine from my reaction. I looked around at the stares from the people about, and all I could do was smile, wave, and say, "Shalom." Meekly I sat down next to the Magi's emissary and said with joy, "Finally I know for sure he lives." With renewed determination, I declared, "I will be ready to report whenever any news of Messiah is heard."

Over the past year, I had been working on improving my reading and writing skills in the language of Rome, one of the secret lessons taught the Levites at the temple. I told Arsham that I had been growing a network of caravan captains in the area to glean news far and wide. They were my eyes and ears from Judea to Galilee and beyond. The group was small, but it was enlarging with every trip.

After a nod and a few moments of silence, Arsham stood and said, "I am leaving for Persia tomorrow. I am getting too old to make this long journey each year, and there are pressing issues to deal with in my own country. I will select and train a man I trust to be my agent, and he will make the trip next year. Since the method worked well, let us leave the way of making contact in place."

With that he handed me a pouch containing coins for the coming year. I felt some guilt accepting a fee for a mission that was so important to me personally but had to admit the extra funds were a comfort for unexpected expenses. He reached into his leather bag, which looked like the skyts shepherds carried, and removed a large clay cylinder that was about a cubit and a half long.

With the most serious of looks on his face, he handed me the cylinder and said, "This, my young friend, contains information about the men who came to visit Messiah. Take it with you, hide it, bury it, do not break it open until you get a sign or signal that the proper time has come."

I asked, "How will I know the time is right?"

With a penetrating gaze, Arsham said, "The men of wisdom I represent said you will know!" And with that comment, he handed me the clay cylinder, and I secured it in my bag.

"Eli, I regret that I will not be seeing you again." His comment saddened me more than I would have expected. I knew there would be changes in contact because of our age difference, but this would happen sooner than I had desired. "While the need to know more about our Messiah burns more intensely than ever within me, I will not be back to Judea. I am convinced that you, my friend, are on a divine mission and that the Sovereign One of Israel has brought us together. You will succeed, but unless I live a very long life, I will not be the one reading and passing on your dispatches. Know, my friend, your work is of immense value. It is time to take my leave."

He extended his arm to me, but instead of shaking it, I drew him to me in a friendly embrace.

"Shalom," I whispered and felt great loss as I hugged him farewell. The man, barely more than a stranger, was a friend and ally so deep as to defy explanation. "Shalom," I said again in a weak voice as he left. I returned to the Cana campsite wondering where Messiah was at that moment.

Ben—Son

CHAPTER 16

THE DECADE

FOR ANOTHER TEN years, I had been diligent, waiting and watching for any sign of Yeshua, Messiah. In my mind I had seen him growing up as I watched my own son, *Yehonatan* (Jonathan), develop. He was born three years after my precious Sarah, with Rachel faring better with his birth.

Messiah should have been about twelve years old, a very special time for Hebrew boys. This would be his last year as a child, for at thirteen years, he would be considered an adult in the eyes of the Torah, entering manhood with the ceremony of bar mitzvah. Each of those years, I was met by a new warrior scout only to report rumors that occasionally were heard on different caravan routes, none of any consequence.

Our history taught us that King Josiah was only the age of eight years when he was made king of Judah, the youngest ever to sit on the throne of David. Judah was still a sovereign nation before the Babylonians destroyed Jerusalem and Solomon's Temple. Josiah died before that happened, after ruling Judah more than thirty years. He was the last of the righteous kings of Judah.

That bit of knowledge made me wonder all the more when Messiah would make himself known. Josiah was the son of a man, Yeshua, Son of the Most High. He could do as he chose, but would he mount the throne of David at age twelve? Nothing so important, so significant as declaring a new king could happen without a fight, and what a fight that would be!

Our ancestors had tried repeatedly to throw off the yoke of foreign rulers. Some were successful for a time, the most recent being the Maccabees, led by the warrior Judah ben Mattathias, called *HaMakabi* (the Hammer). He and his army of zealots, completely outnumbered by the Seleucid army, retook the temple that had been defiled with the sacrificing of pigs and other abominations. And most importantly, there was the miracle from Adonai, who provided eight days of oil from a single cruse of pure olive pressings so the temple could be cleansed and rededicated.

But none were able to prevail against the iron fist of Rome, which often crucified whole families for rebellion. The tension of uprising hung in the air, especially during the festivals. Whispers of Messianic rule and revolt sometimes grew loud and boisterous. Roman soldiers were everywhere, and the garrisons were constantly reinforced because of the huge crowds of fervent worshippers. Bands of zealots still roamed the countryside, occasionally attacking Roman soldiers then disappearing without a trace of their existence.

The spring Passover festival that year was especially crowded. Rachel and I made the trip with our two children: Sarah, who was now eleven and as tall as her mother and also built small of frame, and Jonathan, who was nine, ruddy and lanky like I was at that age before I began adding great amounts of muscle. As usual we caravanned together by village. By the time we approached Jerusalem, we formed a column that stretched for miles. It was one huge mass of people, animals, and dust inching along toward the Holy City.

Kids, animal and human, ran in and out of the throng, somehow finding parents and families at day's end for food and sleep. My mother and father were getting too frail to make the trip and stayed home to preside over the villagers and servants left behind. Also, there were the growing flocks to attend.

While tensions were high throughout the land for the always awaited advent of the Messiah, nothing happened during the week of the festival. I was not pressed into service to assist in sacrifice nor butchery since

I was a judge in training to take over for my father at home as well as having been promoted in my temple shepherd leadership.

Each year I advanced in status at the temple based on my abilities to perform and lead. The pending judgeship at home in Cana added to my status. I now wore a brass *dalet* (ד) on my tunic, bringing me added income and ability to roam the land at my discretion.

My dear friend and mentor, the chazzen, had grown too old to provide all the training but remained as a fixture in the temple as an advisor to the new chazzen, Shabach. That rat-faced boy from Hebron I had had trouble with years earlier had developed into a man of high principles and was honored with title and residence in the temple house. Over the years since the incident on the porch, we had become good friends.

Every year our people would spend this festival time remembering the years of bondage in Egypt. We are chastened never to forget or take for granted the one who rescued us after over four hundred years as slaves. Each symbol of the feast—the salt of tears, the herbs of bitterness, the *charoset* of mortar—gained depth with each year as everlasting reminders. None as powerful as the blood of the sacrificial lamb that kept us safe from the *Malech HaMovet* (the Angel of Death).

After a week of celebration, we started the trip home. The rope of travelers heading north to Galilee again stretched out miles. The sun lowered at the end of the first day on the road, and the children found their way back to each family.

How festive and open our little family from Cana was at each festival. Tradition and law command us to invite others less fortunate to eat and share passages from the Torah. The few musicians and instruments in camp always made the evenings joy-filled. With Sarah and Jonathan tucked in for the night, it provided Rachel and me time to relax and share the highlights of the past week.

Rachel looked at me as we were reclining and said, "I am so happy that we had much to share this year. That little family from the hills certainly needed help and good food. I love you for the gift of the ewe you were able to get from the herd at the training center. It will change their lives." She smiled and laid her head on my chest.

I stroked her hair and replied, "With the growing population and demands of tribute to Caesar, they needed the help." Sleep came easy with all the activities of the week and the time on the road.

The next morning, before striking camp, Sarah, with a face flushed from running, sputtered, "There is a young boy who is not with his mother and father and nowhere to be found in the caravan. He has younger brothers, who are terrified that he has been captured by bandits. His whole family is worried sick, and no one knows where he is! His mother and father are going back to Jerusalem to look for him."

Rachel asked her, "How did you hear of this?"

Sarah continued excitedly, "I just heard it from my friend Tamra. The boy walked with us a few times on the way to the Holy City. He was really nice. You would like Yeshua. He is smart and funny." I perked up a bit when I heard the fairly common name. After ten years of empty searching, could it be he, Messiah? The time and trips over the years had taken an edge off my enthusiasm as I had not heard any word on possible whereabouts. Would it not be ironic for us to be at the same festival, on the same trail?

I looked questioningly at Sarah, asking, "What did he look like? Did you meet his parents?" My words came in a rush as one sentence. Their intensity startled Sarah, and she took a step back, not sure which question to answer first.

"Papa, are you all right? You seem almost mad at me for telling you this!"

I caught myself and replied, "No, sweet one, I am not angry, just really concerned for the boy and his family. So tell me, where did you last see him, and how old did you say he was?"

Relaxing a bit, Sarah answered, "He told me he was twelve years old when we talked on the way to the Jerusalem. Like us, he is from the hill country in Galilee. His father is a carpenter, and he works with wood too. He has brothers and sisters too, but I met only him."

"Tell me what he looks like, and I will go back to the city to assist with the search." The unexpected edge in my voice gave way to concern.

Smiling slightly, my lovely daughter said, "He looks much like every other boy our age. He is very nice and"—she blushed slightly—"very handsome." My heart leaped within me as I knew this was not a coincidence—a twelve-year-old boy whose father was a carpenter and his name Yeshua!

I smiled at my little girl. "Thank you, Sarah. This is important information. With my influence and contacts in Jerusalem, I can help find him. Come get something to drink and rest for a bit before we load the wagon. Today will be another long day of walking."

I turned to Rachel and whispered, "Is it even possible, or am I just trying to make something out of nothing? It must be him!" I spoke with an assurance I had not felt for years.

After ten years of watching and waiting for some sign of him, Rachel's anticipation had not waned. "You must find out! I can go on with the other villagers while you go back down the line to see if you can find him. Ask as you go. Surely someone will know the parents. What if it is Joseph and Mary?" With excitement and urgency in her voice, Rachel touched my cheek. "You must find out. Leave now! Adonai has prepared you for this time, my love. You know how to search, and your strength will keep you safe on the road."

With my beloved's assurance, I grabbed my gear and headed back toward Jerusalem. Thoughts raced through my head. What would he be like? What did the savior of the world look like at twelve years old? How would he act, talk, think? Why was he missing, and where would he go? Had someone in Herod's lineage found him? No, that was not possible, but the thought was there just the same. Was it even him? Like Rachel said, I had to know.

I made it back to the city that evening and, using my dalet as a pass, went to Shabach's quarters. I tapped on his door and in a few moments heard his familiar voice booming. "This better be a matter of importance to bother me—life or death, nothing less."

He had become a true chazzen! I smiled. “It is your friend Eli,” I stated firmly so that there would be no mistake.

“What is the trouble?” he said as the door opened, wearing a serious look that must have mirrored mine. “Is it your family?” He stepped aside, allowing me to enter.

Having never spoken to anyone at the temple about Messiah, I remained secretive even though I could have used the help of a powerful ally in the city. “One of my daughter’s friends traveling with us has turned up missing. A twelve-year-old boy never made it to camp.”

“I can alert the temple guards and pass along the word to the palace guards as well. Can you describe him for me so that I can send a dispatch?”

Feeling stupid and unprepared, I said, “My friend, all I know is that he is a young man of confirmation age that looks like any other child of Abraham and whose name is Yeshua. That is the best and only description I can give you, and it comes straight from my daughter. Oh, yes,” I added with a sly smile, “and she thinks he is handsome.”

Smiling in return, he said, “Not an easy task in a city that still has so many pilgrims camped and wandering about. Nonetheless I will set a search in motion. Now come in and rest for a few hours. You will need your strength to begin your search at daybreak.” He led me to a small room outfitted for guests and said, “I will have some light refreshments, water, and towels brought to you.” He turned and yelled, “Guards, we have a guest!” In a few moments, two young servants appeared and brought exactly what Shabach had mentioned into the little room. “I will see you before dawn’s first light, my friend,” he said then left.

After a short sleep, I was awake before dawn. Sitting outside the door to the little room was a bowl of dried fruit, some olives, a hard cheese slice, and a flat bread with a skin of water. I wrapped the food, dropped it all in my skyt, and was about to set out for the porch area that would have pilgrims camped nearby.

“Eli, vigilant as ever.” It was the friendly, taunting voice of Shabach. “I expected you would be up and out early, so I had one of my guards alert me when you stirred.”

I said with a mocking tone, "Who is the vigilant one?"

The chazzen nodded and said, "Be careful on the streets! As you are well aware, the Romans are always fatigued and quick to act after a week when the city is loaded with pilgrims."

As light began to wash away the dark sky, leaving the shepherd training compound, I could hear chatter from small groupings. Slowly working my way along the base of the column support wall, I could discern different accents and recognized the sound of fellow Galileans. Someone had to know something!

As I was passing by a campfire, I heard someone ask, "Have you heard anything of Joseph's son? Did they find him?"

I turned toward the voice like an eagle diving on prey. "Sir, did you just inquire about Joseph's son? The one named Yeshua?"

There was slight hesitation, but the answer came. "I did indeed. Who might be asking?"

Calmly responding, I said, "My name is Elijah ben Ezra of Cana. My daughter, Sarah, came into our camp yesterday with the tale of a lost boy. I just wondered if they had found him yet."

"We had heard that there was a young boy wandering around the booths outside of the temple asking questions of the vendors. He was annoying them, and they continued to chase him away with angry voices. He was still pestering them with questions at sunset as they were shutting down for the day." The information seemed of no value other than conveying that a boy was alone and near the temple.

By then it was full dawn, so I decided to go to the market booths that set up daily on the temple *azarah* (ledge) to question the vendors myself. Since this was not an official or sanctioned market, the vendors started appearing with small carts they pushed to the base of the colonnade where they would start hawking their wares.

The first to show up was an old woman who looked as old as the temple itself. She was small and bent over, as if she bore the weight of the columns that towered above us. Her long brown hair was hanging down, falling from under her thin hood. Her hair was not brown at all, just matted and dirty as it had not been washed in months. She was fussing with a small basket of not-so-fresh baked barley cakes. I came up to her and asked, "Dear lady, may I have a word?"

"Who are you? I paid my copper mite to be here. What do you want?" Her voice sounded like the whisper of an old, rusty gate dragged on cobblestones. She did not even raise her face to look at me, her fear accented by her trembling.

Taking a denarius from my pouch, I bent down and placed it on the edge of the ragged cloth she was starting to lay the cakes on. Her shaking increased as she finally looked up at me. "Sir, all I possess is not worth what you give." She started to weep. I did not believe I had ever seen such an old look on what was obviously a young face.

"Please, all I seek is a little information. Yesterday there was a young man asking questions and annoying the merchants here. Did you see him?"

Her shaking slowed, and she seemed to relax. "Sir, yes. There was a young man yesterday who went to each of us selling our goods. I do not know what he was saying to the others, but they were distracted by his words and did not want to talk to him. They yelled at him to leave. But to me he seemed very nice. He sat next to me and sang songs in a sweet voice. He asked how I made my beautiful cakes and said they looked like they were made with loving hands. After a while the boy stood, and just before he left, he touched my shoulder and said that my pain would disappear soon. It was an odd thing for him to say, but I felt relief at his touch and his words. After he walked away, I did not see him again."

I felt elation with each word she spoke. *It is him! Who but the son of Adonai at the age of twelve could bring peace to this poor soul?* "Sister, heaven has touched you, and you are blessed!" I said it with such authority she just looked at me and smiled.

Walking from her, I thought, *Where do I look now?* An inner voice prompted me to head to the temple and seek guards who might have heard something in response to the dispatch from Shabach.

The temple was unusually crowded for midweek after a festival. I stayed at the edge of the gathering and approached a guard at the entrance to the *Ezrat HaGoyim* (Court of Gentiles).

"Greetings, friend. I am here to inquire about a lost boy—you may have had news from a dispatch sent by the shepherd chazzen."

The young officer answered, "We did get notice to inform our chief there was a lost boy walking around. There was a child yesterday and earlier this morning walking about, but he did not seem lost, so there was nothing to report."

"What did he look like?" I asked with heart quickening at yet another report of a sighting.

"Just a boy like any other in the city," the guard reported. "He seemed intent on finding someone or something. He did not wander around as a lost child would."

"What was he wearing?" I asked, my voice reflecting the growing impatience with the lack of detail from anyone I had spoken with.

The guard laughed and asked, "Why do you ask, shepherd? Is he one of your lambs that escaped slaughter?"

Checking my anger at his comment but using my authoritarian voice, I said, "Do not trifle with me, guard! This child is important enough to the chazzen that you have been given orders to report!"

Snapping to attention, the guard responded, "Sir, there was nothing special about the boy. He was just average looking, wearing garments any child that age would wear."

The guard put his hand to his face and added thoughtfully, "Sir, the one thing I did notice about him was that even though he appeared intent on locating what he sought, he was not upset or frightened. No, he was calm, even peaceful, much more self-assured than any boy should be. Now that I think about it, he was probably more confident looking than most adults I know." The guard let out a little ironic laugh.

With those words I clasped his shoulder and said, "Thank you, son. I believe that is the boy we are looking for. In which direction was he walking?"

"I think he was headed for the *soreg* (boundary prohibiting gentiles from entering the temple)," he said, glancing to his left.

With those words hanging in the air, I headed to the temple grounds with purpose and the hope that I was about to find him!

CHAPTER 17

THE AMAZEMENT

THE DAY WAS getting lighter and my excitement stronger as I moved to the center of the temple grounds. The seven cupped menorahs were still aflame, providing additional light for the men in the courtyard near the *Sha'ar Nikanor* (Nicanor Gate), and I could see light as well in the *Ezrat HaNashim* (Court of Women).

My brother Levites who had other duties in the temple could always be seen tending to something or singing on the steps. The men at the lampstands were using special poles to extinguish the flames in each cup and remove the remnants of the wicks that were to be burned in a special crucible. The tools that had been designed over the years that served in the temple always fascinated me. The same poles that extinguished the lamps were used to clean and fill the cups using different attachments. By simply changing the apparatus at the end of the long rod, fresh oil provided the fuel for the next lighting. Then another would place a burning wick in the center of each freshly filled cup.

Every morning after sunrise, a minyan of at least ten men would gather for daily prayer. I approached a small grouping of about thirty shawl-covered men, some with traditional *tefillin* (phylacteries) wrapped around their arms and worn as frontlets on their heads. I stood at the edge of the group, set my staff atop my scrip, covered my head with my new shawl, and joined in prayer. The comfort of chanting prayers I had memorized from childhood brought me a peace yet also somehow a growing longing.

"*Adon Olom*" ("Eternal Master") was recited, and the group of men of all ages began to drift into smaller groups before departing the temple court to begin the day of activities. Stepping toward the nearest cluster of six, I greeted them. "Shalom, my friends."

Recognizing the dalet and my shepherd's uniform, they each said shalom in return, the oldest of them adding, "Good day to you, shepherd. What brings you into the temple this morning?" He seemed quite curious and not at all disrespectful. I had come to learn all responses when nearing strangers; his greeting was sincere.

"I am Elijah ben Ezra. I reside in the north, in Cana, when I am not serving here in the temple or tending the flocks at Migdal Eder. Perhaps you can help me find a young man, a boy about confirmation age that has been seen in the city and here on the temple grounds. He has been separated from his parents, and I am assisting them with their search."

"Welcome, Dalet Elijah, servant of the temple. I am Phineas ben Zev, one of the Greater Sanhedrin about to make my way to *Lishkat HaGazit* (the Hall of Hewn Stones) to begin hearing cases. Walk with me, and I will tell you of a young man that I met yesterday."

Surprised at the random chance of meeting one of the seventy-one judges who gathered in the great hall where justice was meted out daily, all I could say was "Shalom. Thank you." As soon as "shalom" left my lips, I felt that this was not a random meeting. "Please, any information you can share can help. Our children are so precious."

Phineas started walking toward the hall. "Two days ago one of my colleagues came to our afternoon session and told of this young man, a child really, that was discussing Torah and writings with rabbis and others in the court under the colonnades. It was a bit of news because the boy apparently knew Torah as well as any rabbi or scholar in the courtyard. I had to see this odd occurrence, so excusing myself from session, I went to observe."

He continued. "As I approached this cluster of men in front of the boy, I heard him say, 'As it is written.' The men were silent for a few moments. A senior rabbi then asked the boy, 'Again, I ask, who are you?' The young man faced the old rabbi and in a steady, composed voice replied, 'My name I have already given you, but it pleases you not. Therefore, I tell you I am the son of the one who knitted me together with bones and sinew, fearfully and wonderfully made, and above all else one who guards his heart, for it is the wellspring of life.'"

Phineas stopped walking, turned to me, and with a look of wonder on his face exclaimed, "I was stunned, thinking, who is this child that in one brief answer speaks the words of Job, David, and Solomon?" The look of amazement continued until Phineas snapped back to the moment. "The rabbis then started talking among themselves, and I watched them for a few moments and realized that the boy was gone. I looked around the court. He was nowhere to be seen. He must have wandered off while I was standing there watching these learned men pondering the words they had just heard. In amazement I returned to the council room."

"Did you hear the boy's name?" I asked, walking beside him, hoping to get the final confirmation that it was him.

"No, I am afraid not. However, if you come with me to the chamber where we meet, I will see if I recognize any of the members that were there when I approached the gathering." We walked past the Court of Women to the entrance of the Sanhedrin Council Room. I waited outside while Phineas entered the court that I was prohibited from entering.

Gazing about while waiting for Phineas to return, I felt a rekindled joy sensing that Messiah was near and was among us. Oh, how I wanted to see the young man I had held those years ago before he and his earthly parents escaped the wrath of Herod's jealousy. It was minutes that seemed much longer before his return, and he said, "None of the Sanhedrin that were witness to yesterday's conversations remember the boy's name. They can only remember that he was a Galilean. Odd they could not recall the name but the region. Also, the two who are rabbis in the group were not only amazed at the boy's knowledge and poise but were also perplexed by his disappearance." Feeling that this was confirmation enough for me, I thanked Phineas and continued my search.

I decided that I needed to roam the market and the temple areas until receiving word of Yeshua or finding him myself. Off to the main market in the center of Jerusalem I went, thinking that I would walk about all afternoon and then return to the temple area.

The main marketplace dominated the center of the walled city, and the number of vendors was staggering. Hunger started gnawing away at me, so I decided to purchase some dried dates and a barley cake with a strong tea from a strange-looking vendor. He was very tall, muscular, with deep brown skin and the greenest eyes I had ever seen. Dressed in a freshly laundered tunic, he wore nothing on his cleanly shaved head, which glistened with sweat in the sun.

Pointing to the items of choice, I reached into my purse for a coin and heard him say, "A meager meal, shepherd. You seem like a man in need of more nourishment than these morsels." He spoke clearly, with a slight singsong accent I could not recognize.

I smiled at him and said, "From where do you hail, friend?"

Returning my smile, he answered, "My people are from a region called Aksum, very south of this glorious city. Goats and sheep are very familiar to my people, as to you who wears the Levite symbol. I now live in a tent village outside the walls of the city." In all my travels, I had never met a man who looked and spoke as this vendor. He took my coin and said, "You have paid for more than you have chosen, and I have no smaller coins to exchange. Can you return another time for more tea to balance our transaction?"

His booth seemed to be permanent, so I replied, "Certainly. I will be around the market all day as I am looking for a lost boy. I will return before sundown to complete our trade with or without the one I seek. If you see a boy wandering about, ask his name. That way I might know for sure that he, Yeshua, is in the area."

He bowed and smiled, showing a mouthful of perfect teeth, and said, "I am Moses. My wife, Bidi, may be here when you return. I must leave to reach a standing appointment with a certain caravan and acquire more dates. She will know who you are by my description of you. She will be on the lookout for the child as well. May I know your name, sir?"

"I am Eli and look forward to meeting Bidi. Do you know that your name is the same as the prophet who is revered by my people?"

He smiled. "Of course. I am named after him. I am a follower of Adonai."

I must have looked dumfounded; he laughed in a deep, warm sound, saying, "Shepherd, have you never seen any of my people before? Have you never been to this market?"

Regaining my composure, I said, "I apologize, my friend and brother. I rarely visit the market. When I am here, I am usually working. I have never seen a man of your description before. Please excuse my ignorance. How did you come to settle here from such a faraway place?"

Still smiling, he said, "Years ago there was a rumor from a caravan passing through Aksum that said Messiah had been born near Jerusalem. For ages there has been a longing of our people to be near Messiah, to walk in his footsteps. We decided to make the pilgrimage and settle here in hopes of seeing him. There are others of my kind in the tent village south of here near the Salt Sea. We visit with them as often as possible."

I wanted to hear more of his story but was compelled to move on to try and find Yeshua. Excusing myself, I said, "I must continue my search but hope we can talk more at some time."

"Go about your task, and we will meet again." He bowed and smiled. With food and drink, I set about looking for a boy.

There were many boys and girls in the huge market, and I spent hours going back and forth without finding a twelve-year-old Galilean named Yeshua. As the sun was lowering in the western sky, I made my way back to the booth of Moses and found a woman as tall as any I had ever seen; her complexion matched that of the man I met earlier. She had black hair woven in an intricate pattern with beads and bangles dotting the entire length, which was to her waist. She was as tall as me, and her eyes were light brown.

Greeting me with a dazzling smile and a slight bow, she said, "Shalom, Eli."

I warmed to her instantly, saying, "Good evening, Bidi, and shalom!"

"I have your tea waiting." She handed me a small skin with the warm liquid. "I see you have not found your child."

"He is not my child but rather the son of friends. He has been missing since the day after the festival, and the fear among our train moving north is that he may have come to harm."

With a sad look, she said, "Along with Moses, I pray that your search will conclude successfully and the child be reunited with his family."

Bowing to her, I said, "Thank you, Bidi. I must be off to the temple in hopes of finding him there. The boy knows Torah, and I am confident that he will be there praying and in discourse with the elders. Please thank your husband for his kindness, and I trust I will see you again in the future." She smiled and returned my bow, and I headed for the main temple area.

As I reached the edge of the market, with the temple's *Sha'ar Yafe* (Beautiful Gate) in view, a voice behind me said softly, "Shalom, Eli."

I felt as if lightning had struck me from a cloudless sky, and I froze in place. Realizing that I had been holding my breath, I exhaled, deeply drew in a lungful of evening air, and turned slowly. There, not more than three paces before me, stood the boy I knew immediately was Yeshua! He was average size for a twelve-year-old and looked like any child of the time. Yet there was something about him that was so different from the average young man. Brown hair, brown eyes, tan skin—but a composure that had him standing rock steady as he looked at me.

Smiling as he spoke, he lifted his right hand, which was holding an orange, and said, "Here. I am returning a favor years in the making."

I wanted to drop down and worship him on the spot; instead I laughed with tears in my eyes and said, "Have you not eaten it yet?" That earned me a hearty laugh in return. "Yeshua, your parents and villagers are looking for you. Some are frantic with fear."

He took a step and motioned to me. "Come, Eli, let us go to the temple and find them."

Without hesitation he headed for the temple grounds, and there I was, following him.

As we were walking through the *Ezrat HaGoyim* (Court of Gentiles), Yeshua veered off to the left in front of me and bent down to say something to a little girl whose mother stood clutching the child in fear, trying to draw her little girl away from the Hebrew boy. After a moment Yeshua stood and started walking toward the Beautiful Gate, leaving the now smiling child behind. With purposeful stride he entered the temple grounds and sat on the steps outside the Nicanor Gate that led to the *Ezrat Kohanim* (Court of Priests) and stairs near the sanctuary.

As soon as he sat, several rabbis approached him, one of them asking, "What are you doing here, boy?"

"That is not the question you should be asking" was Yeshua's reply.

With a smirk the rabbi responded, "What then should my question be, child?"

Remaining seated, Yeshua said, "What would you attempt to learn here? That would have been a better question to ask." More rabbis came closer as I stood two paces from the young Messiah. "Perhaps you should have asked me, 'What do the writings tell us about lighting a fire on Shabbat?' or 'Why did David slice the hem of Saul's garment?' These are the questions you ask of a young man who may need to learn."

"I see you are here to instruct us," one of the rabbis said condescendingly.

"No, teacher, I am here to discuss." And with that a flurry of questions came flying at the young man. I stood there and listened to the exchanges; the expressions on their faces changed from consternation to amazement as thoughts and writings were discussed.

This went on for a while, then Yeshua calmly stood and said, "Friends, I must meet my mother, who is entering the Court of Women." Stepping out of the group, he walked a few paces. I heard a woman's voice say, "Son, why have you treated us in this manner? Your father and I have been anxiously searching for you."

"Why were you searching for me?" he responded. "Did you not know I had to be in my father's house?" With a puzzled look and a slight smile on her face, Mary embraced her son, Joseph standing beside her.

"Shalom, Eli," Joseph said to me. "Why am I not surprised to see you here with him?" He smiled, stepped up to me, and embraced me. "It is good to see you again. Let us all return home."

There I was walking and talking with none other than the family of the Son of Heaven. Yeshua had been here in Jerusalem among the people.

The past years they had been living in Nazareth of Galilee all along, and we had not met.

I was excited to get home and tell my Rachel all that had occurred. At long last I had something to report to the Magi. Messiah was here! A young man among us—and growing in stature!

CHAPTER 18

THE FAMILY

"DEAR FRIENDS, THE hour is getting late, and the road home will be dark and dangerous with just the four of us. There is a safe place here on the temple grounds where we can spend the night and start out in the morning for our home villages." I spoke those words to the family of three, knowing that Shabach would extend us the courtesy of his hospitality.

"A sound idea," Joseph said, nodding to Mary and his son.

"Where is this place?" asked Yeshua, showing curiosity that any young man about to enter teen years would display.

Smiling, I said, "The chazzen that oversees shepherd training has comfortable quarters near the training area for Levites in his charge."

As one they said, "We should go there," and turned to me to lead.

Word of our approach reached Shabach quickly, and he was waiting for our little party near the entrance to his quarters with two servants.

"Shalom, my friends. You are welcome to eat and rest in this harbor of safety." With a nod from the chazzen, the servants approached. One of them, an older lady, smiled at Mary and said, "Come, child, we have a private area for you to refresh." Taking Mary's hand, she led her to a small room just a few doors down the corridor.

Shabach said to the remaining three of us, "Sylva will take you to a common room for men where your feet will be washed. There will be temporary garments for you to wear while yours will be cleaned and returned by morning."

Yeshua looked at Shabach and said, "Perhaps it would be fitting if we washed the feet of your servants to honor them for the work they perform."

A questioning look appeared on the chazzen's face. After a short pause, Shabach replied, "That is a very kind and revolutionary idea, my young friend. Perhaps that is something we should consider for the future. However, this evening you all should be weary, in need of food and rest. Thank you for the thought. Let us continue with the traditional hospitality procedures." With a snap of his fingers, we were led to the rooms Shabach had prepared.

After washing and getting into clean linen clothes, we were escorted to a small dining area that had cold roasted chicken, fruits, vegetables, bread, wine, and fresh spring water. Sylva, setting down a pitcher of water, smiling, said, "A feast fit for a king." Joseph and Mary glanced at each other, and I had to suppress a knowing smile at the implications of the comment.

"My dear friends," I started, breaking into the moment, "where did you go when you left Bethlehem?"

Mary looked at me with a warm smile then, looking at Joseph, said, "That is quite a story. Joseph, please tell Eli how we started our journey." All this time Yeshua sat motionless, absorbing everything.

Joseph's tale began with him telling of a dream he had of an angel advising them to flee. Then of a warrior guide similar to Arsham who gave them a pouch of coins for incidentals along the way. The guide was adept at taking very small elements of the Magi's gifts and selling them in markets and caravans along the trail. The journey was long, and they wound up in the city of Memphis in Egypt, a huge city in which to remain anonymous. Joseph, assisted by the warrior guide, was able to set up a small shop and stall in a marketplace next to a stonemason by selling some small portion of the treasures.

Though strangers in the city, the little family was welcomed by a remnant of one of the tribes of Israel, and Joseph was able to learn secrets of working stone while teaching the mason how to craft wood.

The friendship grew, and all the time Yeshua was there learning both crafts and growing in knowledge of all things.

Mary added, "We have five other children, four boys and a girl, waiting for our return home. They are with cousins who traveled with us in the group from Nazareth, where we have settled."

With a pleasant expression on his face, Joseph said, "I am a builder of small homes using my mason skill, which I have added to my carpentry. Yeshua and his brothers are all learning the trade and are a great help even at their young ages."

Shabach entered the room, announcing, "Your sleeping quarters are ready. Food will be available at dawn to fuel your departure." He bowed to the group, looked at me to signal a meet, and left the room.

Standing, I said to Joseph, "I will meet you in the morning, and we will strike out together since we will all be heading north. We can stop at the market for additional provisions and be off."

Stepping out of the room, I met with Shabach, who said, "I am happy you have found the missing boy. It is only by the grace of *El Shaddai* (the Lord Almighty) that he survived in the city by himself for so long."

I nodded and had trouble not blurting out that the boy was Messiah and instead replied, "Yes, my friend, Adonai has been kind to his children." We bade each other good night and agreed to meet again at dawn.

Sleep came quickly, and dawn seemed but a moment after I had lain down. Arising, I dressed in my freshly laundered garments, which had appeared at the door, and grabbed my gear to return to the same room where we had eaten just a few short hours before.

Sylva had set up a small meal and was standing at the door, Shabach just inside the little room. "Shalom, Eli. Your friends are astir and should be here shortly. This family is important to you. Are they related?"

Answering briefly, I said, "No, not related, but Sarah was so upset finding out that her new friend was missing I felt compelled to join the search. You know how familiar I am with the road and parts of the city, so here I am. However, the boy actually found me in the marketplace."

Avoiding any detail as to the nature of my history with Yeshua, I added, "He must have seen me on the road to the festival when our villages met. I was wearing my dalet, so I was fairly easy to spot." Feeling that was enough explanation for the moment, I added, "I will escort them as far as the road to Nazareth then continue on to Cana."

After a quick meal of cheese, figs, bread, and goat's milk, Shabach escorted all of us to the outer wall of the temple enclosure. "My friends, thank you for honoring me with your visit. Go in peace and safety." Bowing before Mary, he said, "I am thankful before Adonai that you have been reunited with your son. Shalom." I embraced my chazzen friend, bade him farewell, and started leading our little group to the market to stock up on food for the journey home.

As we started walking, I said, "There is a merchant and his wife that I met who are from a faraway land. We will stop by their stall on our way to the road north." In a few minutes, we were in front of Moses and Bidi filling pouches with dates and barley cakes.

"Your search has been more than successful, I see. You have found an entire family," Moses said, smiling his brilliant smile.

With a laugh I responded, "Yes, fruitful indeed. However, in spite of all my looking about, they actually were able to find me. This is Joseph, Mary, and their son, Yeshua."

"You are a lovely family, and Adonai has smiled upon you favorably bringing you back together."

Yeshua looked up at the tall man and said, "You are very kind, sir. I pray the desires of your heart be met."

Bowing, Moses replied, "Thank you, young sir. Seeing Messiah when he appears will be the answer to our prayers."

Joseph said to Yeshua, "Son, take the parcels from this lovely couple so that we may be on the road."

Stepping forward next to his earthly father, Yeshua took a parcel from each Bidi and Moses, touching their hands as he did so. He smiled and said, "Shalom."

Taking the lead again and waving at the couple from Aksum, I said, "Shalom, friends. I will see you again." We headed for the road north.

CHAPTER 19

THE DISPATCH

DURING OUR TREK homeward, Joseph and Mary spoke of their time in Memphis and what they experienced in Egypt. I told them about my life as a lead shepherd and about the family. Yeshua was quiet with us, not so with other travelers. He would engage anyone in conversation that would take the time to share some words. At the end of every conversation, there were smiles and embraces.

On the second day of our journey, there was an old man sitting by the road on a bale of wool, just sitting with a vacant look on his face. Not an unusual sight for a shepherd to see since age and weariness are traveling partners. But somehow this man's look was different, not just vacant but forlorn.

I was going to approach the old man to see if I could be of assistance. But Yeshua, with a youthful stride, made his way to the man and sat beside him on the edge of the road. "My friend, why do you mourn?" Slowly the man looked at the boy and wept. Yeshua sat still and waited.

"For many years I had a gentle ox that carried my burdens from village to village. Last week we were here, a favorite resting stop on our way back home to *Yitzra'el* (Jezreel). A line of mounted Roman soldiers were heading east when our paths crossed. They had been drinking and were in a playful but evil mood. They wanted to buy my ox to practice their archery skills, and I, of course, declined their offer. They were part of the detail that roam about protecting all things Roman. Informing me that their buying was not to be denied, they threw a silver coin at me, dismounted, took the wool bale off my gentle ox Tobis, and set it down where I now sit. They walked him over to that sycamore tree and tied him up." I groaned, knowing what was coming.

"They continued drinking and wagering then practiced their archery skills on him. Old and helpless, I could do nothing but watch. For an hour they took turns shooting my Tobis with me standing here listening to his cries of pain. When they were done, the lowest ranking of the men slaughtered him to prepare their meal. They built a huge fire, ate to their hearts' content, then burned all they did not eat. The fire consumed enough to feed a family of four for months. They killed my poor Tobis, wasted good food, then laughed as they left me here."

Once again anger boiled in my chest against Rome and her legions. We were captives and outnumbered by their army. I, too, felt helpless. Oh, if only the young Messiah now holding the old man's hand were like a roaring lion and would free us from yet another age of bondage.

Yeshua, looking at the old man, said, "Sabba, all empires crumble. Please take some comfort in knowing that one day Rome will dissolve into ruins."

We had to leave and continue on home but did not want to abandon the old wool peddler. Mary stood in front of the old man and said, "My friend, allow us to help you. We are on the road to Nazareth, and Jezreel is on the way. Each of us can carry some of your wool and help you home."

A look of life came back to the man's face, and he questioned, "You would do that for a stranger?"

"Yes, my friend. What is your name?" asked Joseph.

"I am Havilah ben Paran," the old man said, nodding to Joseph.

"We are strangers no longer, Havilah. Come, let us walk together." The five of us divided the wool and continued our journey north, a small caravan.

Jezreel was a common-looking village, and we stayed the night with Havilah, who lived alone in a small hut. After a spare morning meal, we said farewell to our new friend and soon departed Jezreel.

Toward the end of the third day, I had to say goodbye to my road charges as we split to follow the paths to our home villages. I was excited to be heading home again to be with my family and compose a dispatch for the Magi's messenger. At long last there was news of contact with detail I could submit about Messiah!

Little did I know it would be a very long time until I could again report anything of value to the Magi.

CHAPTER 20

THE PONDERING

YEAR AFTER YEAR the dispatch was the same—I had not one thing to report. There were no meetings, no rumors, no contacts at all. It was if the idea of Messiah had faded, and life under Roman rule just grinded along. For eighteen years I had not encountered Yeshua or his parents at any festival. Every night for all those years, I would ponder why Messiah was unseen, unheard. Though we lived in the same hill country and celebrated the same festivals, life had intervened and removed chance meetings.

Every year the Magi's messenger would meet with me at the pool in Jerusalem, and I would deliver a very brief dispatch. There were many exchanges and many different couriers. I remember thinking and praying each time that perhaps the following year there would be news and joy to report.

I had gotten used to a busy but solitary life; it had changed since that time long ago, walking with Yeshua and his family. I had prospered as a wool merchant with a very large herd of my own, six hired shepherds in my employ herding hundreds of sheep. And I had become the local judge, having replaced my father years ago, after he passed away.

Much of my time was spent away from Cana. Having completed my training years earlier in Jerusalem as a Levite shepherd, I rose in the ranks as a trainer of shepherds tending their home flocks. I held an honored position in the Levite shepherd hierarchy; I was a *tav* (ת). My title bore the symbol of the last letter of our alphabet, meaning I had reached the last and highest level of training and authority in the field. What was learned in Jerusalem under the tutelage of the chazzens I reinforced in the field.

In the entire region of Galilee, all Levite shepherds were under my jurisdiction, and I was responsible for their training and for locating the perfect lambs to be brought for central evaluation at Migdal Eder. Only the very best and blemish free were separated and bred for the Passover sacrifice. Plus, with my own flocks flourishing, I had become independently wealthy.

The only thing filling my empty life and heart since my beloved Rachel passed away in childbirth a dozen years before was the desire to see Messiah again. Every night I would implore Adonai for news or a chance encounter with Yeshua.

With help from cousins and villagers, I was able to still be a father to my children, and our love for each other held us together after Rachel's departure. We grieved together for a long time, and that strengthened our bonds as a family. We mourned mother and son passing into eternity together at his birth. The children helped decide the name of their brother, who breathed for a bit before his rest. We went through a formal naming ceremony before burial and continued to treasure the thought of him. Jonathan carved a little staff, and Sarah knitted a tiny blanket for their brother's interment. I was granted a year of freedom from the academy to care for my children before returning to full duties.

My children matured quickly and made lives of their own. Sarah was married to a distant cousin from Capernaum, *Shmu'el ben Zev* (Samuel, son of Wolf), and moved there. Jonathan fell in love with a local girl, Marta, they were wed and soon after welcomed their son, moving into the house that Rachel and I had shared.

It was bittersweet to have Sarah move to another village. Though I treasured her dearly, it was painful to look at her at times because she was the image of Rachel. Slight, raven-haired, and so quick-witted, she was so much the vision of her mother that stabs of pain assaulted me with a movement or a word.

Jonathan was just the opposite; he was a young image of me. Though he was my son, he grew to be my best friend. We worked together, and I trained him to shepherd and groomed him to become a judge to replace me someday, as I had done with my father.

As a judge in Cana, I had to sign many legal documents, including *ketubah* (marriage certificates), the ornate contracts between families. Weddings would always bring me great memories of early married life with Rachel. How easily we had become one; we were a perfect balance. Without her and no word of Messiah, those years seemed tilted, just not quite right.

Focus on work and parenting were satisfying, but there was emptiness unfilled. Whenever the pit of despair would surround me, I would think of Rachel and talk to her memory. Yet there was always the hope of Messiah's emergence to bring light to my darkened world. The memory of the angels and the grotto always transformed my mood into one of happy expectation.

CHAPTER 21

THE WEDDING

WINTER HAD PASSED; it was springtime. The weather was clear and warm. All around the country, flowers and trees were bursting into bloom from the winter rains. What a fitting time for a wedding, the beginning of new life together. Weddings in the hill country of Galilee were generally grand celebrations. Although most of the families in the region were poor, when it came to weddings, they spent what they could afford to make it special. Any occasion that took the villagers away from the daily grind of living was attended by all. When Rachel and I married, the festivities lasted three full days. Some weddings lasted a whole week. All the relatives and most of the families in the village came to any and every wedding.

The bride and groom were betrothed for over a year and their wedding set for that early spring. Even though it was an arranged marriage between the parents who were neighbors, the children loved each other. But traditions, customs, and laws needed to be followed. The dowry from the bride's father, *Natan'el* (Nathaniel), was agreed upon a year ago; it was time for the ceremony. The couple was truly happy compared with some who were forced together, where there was no love at all.

My wonderful daughter, Sarah, with Samuel and their children, *Rivkah* (Rebekah) and *Sha'ul* (Saul), would attend. It had been a while since I had seen them. Jonathan was excited to see his elder sister; they had always gotten along famously. Their bond grew with the departure of their mother and younger brother. It would be good to see them. It was time I broke out of my self-imposed hermitage, so sharing in the joy of a wedding would help.

The local wedding was planned to last five days, and finally the big event had arrived. People from all over the hill country of Galilee attended. The village synagogue was not large enough for the wedding service, so a chuppah was strung between two houses, and benches lined the village square.

The first evening of the wedding, the groom was carried by his friends to the ceremony area near the canopy. He was wearing his best cloaks and had on a small crown fashioned by a local ironsmith. He stood with his friends, waiting for his bride.

The bride was wearing a beautiful new dress and carried a bouquet of local flowers. Atop her head she wore a crown of the same blooms. Her bridesmaids, ten of her friends, carried her on a litter festooned with the flora theme of her bouquet and crown. They brought her to the canopy, where she stepped down from the litter and stood facing the groom.

All the men stood on the same side as the groom and the women on the same side as the bride. The village rabbi stood under the cloth covering and nodded to the groom's friends, who began singing. "Who comes from the wilds like a cloud of smoke, bathed with myrrh and incense made from all the spices of the merchant?" The ladies responded. The rabbi said traditional blessings and pronounced the couple wed.

There was a meal and dancing and singing through the evening until the new couple was carried to their home attached to the house of the groom's parents, where they spent their first night as one.

The next day the festivities continued with games, music, dancing, food, and wine. In the evening the men and women separated to different sides again, and the gifts to the bride and groom were presented. Blessings were said, and there was responsive singing, more from the words of Solomon. Again, the bride and groom were carried to their new home.

The crowd of guests continued to celebrate in the town square. I was in a melancholy mood, thinking about Rachel and our wedding.

Rather than going to my empty room, I slept under heaven's blanket of stars with the sheep.

On the third day, it was apparent that many more had attended than had been planned for; additional food had to be brought in for the guests. The dancing, eating, and drinking continued; it was a joyous time of celebration all day long. The village was more crowded than I had seen in the past. There were times where people in the square were pressed together, yet everyone remained well-behaved and had fun.

Even though I was a man of standing, I was still a shepherd by trade. I felt more at ease among the servants and family members I knew and enjoyed being with them. So beginning the third day, I generally stayed in their company. My usual garments were set aside, and I put on simple tunics that a servant would commonly wear.

Guests came and went, and there was much I could do to help with the work: cooking, cleaning, fetching water, serving. I enjoyed helping and staying in the background with the servants and was welcomed as part of the group. My wealth and status were not stumbling blocks to my participation.

Toward the end of the third day, one of the servants nervously remarked that the wine supply was getting low since so many uninvited guests had come. Extra food had already been a brief concern, but not having wine was a huge problem. The groom and his family were responsible for providing more than enough wine to last the whole of the festivities. For some reason, that did not happen, and no one seemed to know what to do.

It was spring, and no new local wine would be made and available until fall. If no one knew of any that could be purchased or borrowed from surrounding villages, the wedding celebration would come to a halt. Not a good omen as it could cause problems between the two families.

The wedding festivities were a part of the gift from the groom's family to the bride, and no one wanted it to become an issue. None of us had any idea what to do to resolve the problem of no wine. If more food was needed, I could have my shepherds bring enough goats and sheep to feed everyone. But wine in Cana and the surrounding hill country was rare and scarce in any real quantity.

Only we servants knew about the rapidly dwindling supply of wine at that time. The chief steward came to the service area in a panic to announce that the wine would not last the night. It was a serious situation, a social, and possibly legal, disaster.

No sooner had the words left the steward's lips than we heard a commotion outside the service hall. Had some of the guests or the groom's father heard and were coming to confirm? It sounded like half of the wedding party was heading toward us. We were in a large walled room that was used for storage and had been set up to provide working space for assembling the items needed to keep the food and drink flowing. There were about ten of us waiting for the next course to be prepared. All eyes went to the sound, and we waited expectantly to see who was coming.

The chief servant was the village bakeshop owner, who left the preparation room to approach the murmuring group. I, as the local judge, followed behind him to make sure there was order. There was a circle of burly men who had obviously seen a lot of outdoor living; they were a tanned, tough-looking lot. If they were here to make trouble or cause a scene, they would be hard to handle.

Before any of us could say a word, from the center of the group, I heard a woman's voice state, "They have no more wine." I thought she was stating the obvious and was curious as to who she might be. Perhaps she knew where there were some supplies stored nearby and had come to ask us to get them.

The circle parted a bit, and I was able to see the backs of a man and a woman. He was bending toward her and was speaking to her as he gently took her by the elbow and moved her to the side, away from us. They began to converse in low, urgent tones. One of the five remaining men was only a few feet away from them but made no effort to go any closer. The rest of us just stood there waiting.

After a few moments of quiet discussion, the woman turned, approach the steward, and said, "Whatever he says to you, do it." I mentally started to wonder where we would go to get the new wine supply. Instead the man she had just spoken to stepped out and pointed to six large stone pots along one wall. He said, "Take the empty pots and fill them with water."

The air around me seemed energized at the sound of the man's voice. How many years had it been since I had had that same feeling? It had to be him! Eighteen years since we went our separate ways on the road home from Jerusalem. Never once during that time did I encounter the family again. So strange—to live so close, attend the same festivals, and not once find each other. Was that part of some greater plan?

I was still feeling the charge of excitement, and my look went to the area where the man pointed. There were big clay pots, each capable of holding twenty-five gallons of water. Four of the water pots were empty; that would total about one hundred gallons; the pots would take some time to fill. But he spoke with a certain authority, and his tone and demeanor told us he meant for the order to be followed. The air continued to be charged with a sense of expectation. I wondered if anyone else felt what I was feeling.

Thankfully the preparation area was not far from the village well, so we each took a bucket, formed a line, and passed the jugs back and forth. It took about half an hour to fill all four. Meanwhile the festivities in the town square continued, with the revelers oblivious as to the wine situation. Finally the clay pots were filled to the brim. When we were done, we remained in the service room. None of us knew what to do next; we just stood there watching. I was one of them, a servant awaiting orders. Meanwhile I was thinking that even though some of the guests might be drunk, no one would mistake water for wine!

Once the pots were filled, the man said, "Draw some out, and take it to the chief steward." I had the mounting sensation that I knew the man, although he did not look familiar; there was something in the voice.

The lead servant took a large ladle and filled the serving pitcher that just a few minutes earlier had poured out the last of the house wine. He then headed to the banquet area to find the chief steward. As he passed by, I knew immediately what had happened as the aroma of wine floated in the air.

Wine does not come from wells in the ground! I walked over to the nearest clay pot, leaned over, and inhaled; indeed it was wine! I had not had a sip of any wine since the blessing toast at the beginning of the wedding, but the fragrance was undeniable. To confirm my notion, I grabbed the ladle that had just been used by the lead servant, scooped up some of the liquid, and tasted it. Wine it was, and oh, what wine!

Excitement and alarms were going off in my head. A woman, a man, an obvious miracle. It was not a trick—the wine was extraordinary! While the steward was gone, my fellow servants, along with the new guests, became aware of the miracle that had just taken place. The fragrance in the air was unmistakable. They looked just as puzzled as we did, which intrigued me. Who were these visitors?

I decided I had to know for certain. After all these years of waiting, watching, and wondering, now was not the time to be timid. The man and woman appeared to have left the area, but a couple of their party were still there. The man who had been closest to the earlier conversation stood only a few feet away from me. While the others talked among themselves, I introduced myself.

"Shalom. I am Elijah ben Ezra," I said with a voice that must have seemed nervous. I was not; I was excited. Yet my voice sounded scratchy and hollow as I spoke.

"Shalom to you as well, my friend," he replied. "I am *Yochanan ben Zavadai* (John, son of Zebedee)."

"I hope you have enjoyed the wedding," I said in an effort to get a conversation started.

"We have indeed," he answered. "We were just invited a few days ago."

"Really? From where have you traveled?"

"Most of us are from Capernaum. We are fishermen by trade." That explained the tanned, lined faces and strong statures.

"How did you come to be here, if you don't mind me asking? Capernaum is quite a trip."

"The woman you saw earlier is Mary from Nazareth, and she is a relative of the bride. We just met her son some days ago, and he asked us to come with their family to the wedding."

The feeling of elation almost had me bursting. Before I could ask the next question blazing in my mind, the chief steward came racing through the door, mouth first. "Where is the new wine? I have been told there was a new supply of many gallons! It is the finest wine I have ever tasted! As I said to the groom, the best wine is always served first, and when the guests have drunk freely, the poorer wine can be served with little notice. But this time, not so!" All that in one breath!

With that one of the servants showed him the clay vessels brimming with wine. He seemed so relieved to see what he had been told about that he never thought to ask where it had come from! All of us knew. He ordered the servants to start pouring it immediately, turned, and left the room.

I looked back to John as it seemed the impact of the miracle was beginning to hit him too. He grabbed a small cup from a shelf and took a sip; a smile came to his face as he passed it to me. "Doesn't taste like any water I have ever had!" My mouth was so dry with excitement I could barely part my lips. As I took a sniff and a sip, my taste confirmed that it was the best wine I had ever tasted.

"Who is this friend of yours?" I asked John.

"His name is Yeshua ben Yosef."

At that moment time seemed to stop. My thoughts raced back over the thirty years since the angels in the night sky, the Magi, meeting Mary and Joseph. It took only a second to recount the memories, and I came back to the present as John was speaking.

"We met him by the Jordan, where we had gone to be with *Yochanan ben Zekria* (John, son of Zecheria), the immerser. We were some of John's followers, until we met Yeshua. Have you heard of this immerser?" he asked.

"No, I can't say that I have. News travels slowly to the hill country, where I spend much of my time. Who is he?" I asked. I remembered there had been some mumblings about a prophet in the wilderness when I was in Jerusalem, but there were always murmurings.

John continued. "At first he made it clear to the powers that be from Jerusalem, the *P'rushim* (Pharisees) and *Tz'dukim* (Sadducees), that he was not Messiah, but he knew Messiah. They asked him many questions, but he did not fall into their traps. Instead he rebuked them and called them a brood of vipers, cautioning them because of their actions." John's words were laced with admiration for the way the immerser had braced the authorities from Jerusalem.

"He said that to the Pharisees and Sadducees? Not many are willing to talk like that to the religious authorities, but they are my sentiments exactly!" I responded, knowing they were a stiff, arrogant, and surly lot.

Many times, over the years in Jerusalem, I witnessed encounters with the "select," as they were called. People from the north steered clear of many officials, especially the Pharisees and Sadducees. They made no attempt to hide the fact that they despised Galileans. They thumbed their self-righteous, imperious noses at those they considered lowborn. They lumped the *Shomroni* (Samaritans), Galileans, and foreigners into the same category and maintained a haughty attitude toward all. Vipers, he called them, a fitting comparison, tragic because the analogy was so appropriate.

John continued. "The immerser quoted from writings of the prophet Isaiah when they kept asking him who he was and by what authority he could make such statements. He said that he was 'the one crying out in the wilderness preparing the way of Adonai.'"

Excitedly he said, "The very next day, we saw this man coming to the immerser, who then turned to the crowd and said, 'Look! It is the lamb of Adonai who removes the sins of the world!'" My head spun at the reference to Messiah as a lamb. Why a lamb? "It was then that John bade us follow Yeshua."

Just then a man they called *Shi'mon* (Simon) hailed to John from outside. "Yeshua is preparing to leave, and it is time for us to depart." John turned to me as he left. "Shalom, my friend. Perhaps we will meet again."

Once more the thunderbolt of excitement hit me when I heard the name Yeshua. As I was turning, a voice met me head on. "Shalom, Eli. I could not leave here without greeting you." It was all I could do to breathe. I collapsed at his feet and began sobbing. All the years of tension and wondering came flooding out in a release that made me a limp pool at the feet of Messiah.

"Elijah ben Ezra, stand, you have work to do." The power in that soft, gentle voice seemed to lift me from the ground. I stood before him, face-to-face, the one whom I now recognized as the man the young boy had grown into over the past eighteen years. "Master...," I whispered.

He interrupted me and said, "Eli, my ministry has not yet begun, and neither has yours."

"What would you have me do?" I said with a surge of energy and a strengthening voice.

Yeshua replied, "You will know it when the time comes. For now, be who you are—Eli the judge, the father, the tav, the merchant, the man." He smiled at me, put his hand on my head, closed his eyes for a moment, removed his hand, turned, and walked away. I stood like a statue, rooted to the spot, until he was out of sight.

I stood there and felt weightless, just like on the night he was born, when the angel spoke. My mind was reeling as if I had had too much of the wine he had just created. It was impossible to take in all at once. He was here, and it appeared that it was indeed his time. My wait for a solid encounter, event, or meeting was over. I had no idea what to expect, but I was ready to face whatever was to come. I would write up the events for the Magi and prepare a detailed dispatch for my next meeting at the Pool of Siloam.

Finally I knew for certain what the adult Yeshua looked like: average of height and build for a man of his day, with looks and grooming that would make it hard to pick him out of a crowd. Yet when you looked more closely, there was a steadfastness in his eyes and a certain power that radiated from him, unmistakably. The wedding in Cana was all it took to know that Yeshua was no ordinary man. Heaven was walking among us!

CHAPTER 22

THE DECISION

THE WONDERFUL WINE was served; the party continued. I excused myself from the service area and went home as if in a dream. At last! He had begun revealing his divinity. How would his reign unfold? Though I was tired, I knew sleep would be hard to come by. My head was spinning, not from the wine, of which I had only had a taste, but with possibilities. What to do and where to go were the two questions battling in my brain.

I bathed then sat down at my desk to begin the next dispatch to the Magi. I closed my eyes to think of the first words to write. When I opened them, it was morning! I had slept at my desk with a blank parchment in front of me. Laughing, I stood stiffly, groaning at the attempt. The dispatch would wait for more details.

Sounds from the kitchen and the smell of baking bread drew me to the common area, where I was greeted with squeals of delight from my grandson *Ka'lev* (Caleb) and smiles from Jonathan and Marta, who said, "Pappa Eli, come, sit and break the night fast with us." She handed me a goblet of morning wine and sat.

Jonathan tore a piece of bread, handed me half, and recited the blessing. "Papa, how was the party last night after we left?" he asked.

With my mouth full, I mumbled, "Interesting." All at the table were quiet, eyes on me for more information. I swallowed. "They thought the wine had run out, causing a bit of concern, but there was plenty available, enough to last the rest of the celebration." It was too soon to elaborate, so the meal continued in relative silence.

Looking around the room, I asked, "Do you all remember when I said that there would come a day on which I would begin a mission requiring me to travel more?" Silent nodding and interested faces met my question. "Last night I received a message that my new duties have begun."

"What are these duties, Papa?" Jonathan asked, eyes wide with curiosity.

"Unfortunately I am not free to discuss the details with you now. But you need to know that I am happy with the obligations I must perform and will be able to tell you more in the future. For now there is some business we must conduct." Jonathan laid both hands on the table, looked at me with a questioning gaze, and nodded.

"We must complete a document that gives you full ownership and charge of the family business and property." My announcement was met with shock and total silence.

I smiled and said, "My duties will not put me in peril since I am just traveling to gather information and document what I have witnessed. More than that I cannot say." Looking at Jonathan, I added, "My son, you have earned this, and you are more than ready to lead this family and judge the village."

"When do you leave, Papa Eli?" asked Marta. "The wedding festivities are not complete." Her look was sweet and her voice curious.

"Very soon, my dear daughter," I said, still smiling.

Looking back at my son, I added, "Jonathan, let us take care of the details, then I will be free to begin my task. Marta, we should return soon, then I will decide the time to leave." I looked at my grandson. "Caleb, you and I will have a talk when we return." The little man puffed up with delight.

We went to the desk in my room and wrote a simple *khozeh* (contract) transferring all my possessions and legal family authority to Jonathan, with me receiving an annual tithe of the profits from the flocks and wool. We took the document to the synagogue and, in the presence of a quorum of elders, sealed the agreement.

Walking back to the house, I stopped, faced my son, and said, "This task I am on is a mission that had its origins thirty years ago. It is not labor but a dream come true." Before he could speak, I added, "The time will come, very soon, when I will explain. But for now please just accept the responsibilities I have vested in you and know that this is the most exciting venture of my life." I was smiling, and that brought the response of a nod and slight smile.

Back at the house, I announced, "Today we will spend time together as a family, and tomorrow I shall be off." Turning to Caleb, I asked, "Who wants to go on a short adventure with their sabba?" A yell of delight rang in the room, and I said, "Dress like a shepherd. We are going to hunt wolves!" Caleb ran to his room to change clothing. Looking at Jonathan and Marta, I said, "We shall not be long. Later we will rejoin the wedding party, drink some wine to celebrate new challenges and the future."

Caleb was a delight in the fields as we played hunters and used slings at targets we made of sticks and brush. He was a natural with the sling and aptly named for the brave Caleb who had accompanied Joshua into the land of plenty.

The afternoon was spent speaking of family memories, then we all dressed to join the wedding party, which was well underway. When we arrived at the festivities, the wine was flowing freely, and everyone was quite cheery.

The prior evening Yeshua, Mary, and their friends had left early, to where I knew not. Jonathan handed me a cup of wine, and the thought hit me that Yeshua had said that my ministry had not begun; what had he meant?

"Papa, are you ill?" I heard Jonathan's voice as though he was in a valley yelling up to the top of a hill. "You seem lost, Abba!" He touched my arm, forcing the cup of wine to my mouth, adding, "Take a sip."

I inhaled the distinct aroma and smiled at Jonathan. "My son, I was just considering the direction I must go." Taking a sip of the wine, I smiled broadly and said, "Remember the taste of this wine. It is heavenly. Let us find the new couple and wish them a good life."

After a short visit to the festivities, I found the bride's father and said, "Natie, my friend, I have duties to perform. Therefore I must leave in the morning."

"Eli, I understand. This has been a wonderful wedding, and I am happy that you have been able to stay. Before you go, let me give you a skin of our wonderful wine for your journey." *What a gift,* I thought, *to take the heavenly wine with me.*

I excused myself and returned home. Where to start? Where to go first? Having grown up as a descendent of Abraham, the only prayer life I knew and understood was that of repeated verses, the standards of which were to be recited daily. However, lately I had been petitioning Adonai directly, without the benefit of a rabbi presenting liturgical praises and requests each Shabbat.

In my room I covered my head with an old prayer shawl and said, "Adonai, forgive me for my direct appeal, but I cannot ask anyone to petition this of you. I know that your son Yeshua is Messiah, and I have a mission that began years ago. Please tell me where to go. I have no clear vision."

I closed my eyes, bent my knees, took a deep breath, and in an instant in my mind saw a fishing village by the sea. At that moment the decision had been made—Capernaum! It was Adonai's answer. Of course! The fishermen following Yeshua, they must have returned home. "*Todah, Adonai* (Thank you, Lord)!" I chanted over and over.

My little family returned from the wedding party; I embraced them all and said, "I shall leave in the morning." Surely there was a divine hand guiding me. Peaceful sleep followed.

CHAPTER 23

THE WALK

I WAS AWAKE before dawn, packed for my travels, and was ready to go. I needed more detail for my dispatch with the Magi's agent. I said goodbye to my little family after morning meal to begin my walk to Capernaum.

I dressed in my tav attire which would provide a measure of authority should I encounter Romans. The mere thought of a soldier revived the memory of Jacob's slaughter and brought bile to the back of my throat.

It turned out to be a beautiful spring morning, with a warming sun on my face. Before long I had to remove my outer cloak and was enjoying the trek. The world was ablaze with color from the soft blue of the cloudless sky, the vibrant green of new grass, and a profusion of wildflowers all around. Spring was truly in the air, with the faint but unmistakable aroma of buds opening everywhere. Olive and fig trees dotted the hillsides. Figs produce fruit ten months of the year, and I sampled many growing wild along the road.

What a glorious day it was to be on my mission at last! The time quickly passed as I walked along, keeping a good pace. Capernaum was less than a full day's walk from my home in Cana. The route was hilly, just like the country all around; there was no such thing as a straight road anywhere. Traveling with my usual gear, I would make it before sunset.

Having grown up wandering the countryside with the flocks I was charged with protecting, walking had become my best time to think. It was never my nature to sit and be still. I preferred to move about and make decisions. It often seemed ironic that I could not be still when the ancient writings of David in a song admonished us to "be still and know Adonai." Knowing at last Messiah was among us, it was impossible for me to be idle!

When my actions became clear, I knew I had to tell Samuel and Sarah what I had seen and heard, of the covenant with the Magi of long ago. Sarah and Samuel had left the wedding after the second day; they did not taste the wine. They would be surprised by my visit and delighted with the taste from my new wineskin.

I had planned for this day many times and sought heaven's answer; who to tell and how much to reveal? The plan was simple: tell the whole story, the truth. Rachel and I had never shared the details with anyone, not even the children. Though my beloved wife and I often talked about Yeshua, we never took anyone into our confidence. Speculation about Messiah with friends was a topic that came up regularly. It was a part of our Hebrew heritage and thought process, always in the minds of the people.

For the past twelve years, there had been nothing but the memory of Rachel. She was the only one I would speak with in times of need. But there was no substitute for a human contact, so many times at home I would speak as if Rachel were in the room, only to have Jonathan come into my quarters and ask, "Abba, who are you speaking with?" My standard response was that I was praying out loud. There were times I needed another person to talk with in confidence or I thought I would go insane.

Before long the setting sun was lowering in the sky, and the late afternoon was beginning to cool. I knew I would have to have the right words to say, *truth*. There were two anchors or pieces of my story that I knew would have an impact. First, Sarah would remember the incident of the lost boy years ago. She was so upset when he was missing and oh-so-relieved when she heard he had been found. The other was the changing of water into wine at the wedding. Now I had evidence of the miracle, and it was easy enough to verify with the servants who were there if more validation was needed.

I knew Sarah would not doubt me, though she might wonder why I had never said anything. Now, after all the years, the story was being revealed. The challenge was that the story of us shepherds in the field was so incredible it was hard even for me to believe. And I had lived it!

I was concerned about Samuel. His reaction could be a different matter. He was one of the leaders of the synagogue in Capernaum, a man of stature in the community, and he was a Pharisee. He kept the oral tradition and letter of the law very strictly. While I was his father-in-law, I could see his tendency to dismiss those whom he considered to be of lesser learning. Would he believe that somehow Adonai had chosen to reveal the birth of Messiah to shepherds? That his earthly parents were poor young pilgrims from Nazareth, of all places?

But there was no one else to confirm it since Jacob was dead and the other two shepherds I had not seen or heard from in over twenty-five years. I did not even know if they still lived. It was entirely possible that I might be the only survivor among those who had seen the angels that night. No one else had seen or talked to the Magi; I alone held that honor.

That made my story either a fantastic tall tale or, at the very least, hard to believe. I resolved that Adonai had brought me that far, and I would trust him for the right words. Hearts should resonate with the truth when I spoke.

I made good time. The sun was just below the hills in the west as I arrived at the village boundary. Sunset was radiant, with rays shooting into the sky, fiery streaks of red, orange, and just a hint of purple haze. I stood for a few minutes taking it in and fortifying myself with praise to heaven for what was about to happen. It reminded me of the first day as an Aleph in Jerusalem, the beginning of a wonderful education. I was now fully committed to the mission; there was no turning back. There was a breeze, and I began to smell the sea air. How different than fields of green and plentiful sheep droppings; it was a welcome sensation.

Capernaum, a fishing village on the north shore of the Sea of Galilee, had a robust trade of grain and olive oil in addition to the fish markets. Samuel, my son-in-law, was an olive oil merchant with his father, and they did quite well financially.

Sarah, Samuel, and their two children lived on the west side of the village, not far from the synagogue where Samuel was a prominent member. He also served on the village council, following in the footsteps of his father. He really had done well, respected by all who knew him. I was proud to have him as my son-in-law.

When Samuel's father had approached me to arrange the marriage with Sarah, I was surprised that a merchant from Capernaum would have an interest in the daughter of a shepherd from Cana. It was only after I learned that we were related through Rachel that a contract was considered.

It helped that Sarah and Samuel had met at a Passover *seder* (celebration meal) in Jerusalem when she was younger. Sarah's family was there in great numbers. The young couple remembered each other fondly, so arrangements were made. The hardest part of my decision was allowing Sarah to move to Capernaum; I could have insisted she stay in Cana while I arranged a marriage within our village.

It was time for truth, and how I missed Rachel. Her wise counsel and perspective were always perfect counterbalances to my thinking. I would speak truth, starting with that night of nights.

CHAPTER 24

THE STORY

TURNING NORTH OFF the road into the village, I came to their house. The unobstructed view of the sea was beautiful. Their home was larger than most in the village, nestled into a hill at the back with a large courtyard on the side. The smell of roasting lamb floating in the evening air made my stomach growl. While I carried provisions, I had not stopped along the way for a real meal, wanting to make good time to arrive before dark. While the journey tired me, I was exhilarated to be with family and focused on my mission.

I saw no one in the courtyard, so I made my way to the door. Tapping lightly on the doorframe, I looked once again at the glorious sunset and beautiful view of the Sea of Galilee; I thanked Adonai for my safe trip. Hearing nothing, I tapped harder. Soon I heard soft footsteps on the cobbled floor within, and the door opened.

"Eli," boomed Samuel. "What are you doing here? Is everything all right?" Questions I knew would come; I had answers at the ready.

"I am on a special assignment, and Capernaum is my first stop. I just found out yesterday that my mission was to commence."

Samuel cocked his head to the side and, with a quizzical look, said, "Mission? What mission? What are you talking about?"

With a smile I asked, "May I come in? I am here in part to make sure you and Sarah were the first to know. But I would rather talk inside."

Sheepishly he said, "I apologize for seeming rude, but your sudden appearance and statement took me off guard. Of course, please come in!"

The house is expansive, I thought as he went off to get Sarah and the children. I could hear the yell as Sarah's musical voice cut through the silence of the big house. "Papa is here? Why on earth? Children, your sabba is here. Come quickly!"

Bursting into the room, Sarah ran to my arms. "Are you all right? Is it something with Jonathan, Marta, or Caleb?" The words tumbled out almost as fast as her tongue could form them. Before I could answer, my two grandchildren charged between us with leg hugs and squeals of delight.

Pushing her back so I could see her face, I said, "No, my sweet child, all is well with me and everyone we love in Cana. That is not why I am here."

"Why then, Papa? It is always good to see you, but this is a total surprise for you to visit so soon," she stammered.

I whispered, "It is a long-kept secret, too long. Let us wait until after the evening meal and the children are in bed before we talk."

The inside of the house was beautifully aglow with ornate oil lamps in the style of the temple but small enough for a home. The flames flickered and shadows danced, giving the room a warm and welcoming light.

Sarah turned to Samuel. "Papa wants to wait until Rebekah and Saul are asleep before we talk!" Turning back to me, she added, "The suspense is almost more than I can bear, my dear papa. Can you just share a little morsel?" She said it with an impish look on her face, just like the one her mother wore when trying to pry things out of me.

"I must say I am curious too," Samuel added in a more measured tone. "But you must have your reasons, so we will wait."

"Yes, my precious ones, let us wait." With that said Sarah nodded, shrugged in submission, and went to see to the final preparations of the evening meal and set another place at the table.

The house was truly suited to a man of Samuel's stature as a successful merchant. I was grateful for his ability to take care of my daughter and grandchildren. Samuel had been a brilliant student as a child and had been sent to Jerusalem to study for two years before returning to join the family business. As a Pharisee he was a strict adherent to the law, the coming Messiah, and the immortality of the human soul. I had to be very careful about my account when I spoke.

Arriving for the evening meal allowed me time to visit Rebekah and Saul. I talked to them about the games they played as they would shortly be off to bed. While it had only been a few days since I had seen them at the wedding, they looked a hand taller and the very picture of health and happiness. Sarah and Samuel had trained them well, and it showed at the table.

Rebekah bore a strong resemblance to her mother, and that, again, invoked the melancholy loss of her grandmother, Rachel, the love of my life. She was brilliant like her father and questioned me about Jerusalem and the politics of the temple. She talked with great knowledge, showing that her parents were teaching her well.

Saul, though very bright in his own way, wanted to know about the dangers of being a shepherd and was more interested in the battles that I had fought with wild animals and bandits on the road. I regaled him with my prowess using sling, staff, rod and flint knife while he hung on every word. He pushed me to describe the blood and gore of my encounters, and I gave him just a hint of the danger and praised the hand of Adonai, which had protected me all my years. He seemed satisfied with my descriptions.

Fresh bread and wine accompanied some roasted lamb and simple seasonal vegetables. It was delicious and perfectly prepared. Samuel had Saul say the *Hamotzi* (Blessing of the Bread) and the *Hagafen* (Blessing of the Wine), both of which he recited perfectly. But Rebekah still teased Saul about the cadence of his prayers; how like her father she was.

Dinner conversation was about Samuel's trade, how the Romans in the area were overbearing with their garrison in the city. There were one hundred troops set up in tents outside the city. He spoke of the centurion Salvius, their leader, who was sympathetic to the synagogue. Perhaps in different circumstances, Samuel and Salvius could have been friends. There were some incidents of soldiers taking advantage of the merchants in the village, but the friendly centurion kept good control over his troops.

Capernaum was a market city and trade center, and there was always information not available in the hill country. Much of the talk at the table was fresh news for me. The children joined the conversation as much as possible, showing how adult and well-informed they were. Rebekah spoke of the caravans that passed as the village was on the trade route between Jerusalem and Damascus. Saul was more interested in the Roman soldiers, and he was able to describe their armor and weaponry down to the shape of the breastplate decorations.

There were a few references to the synagogue and how it fared. When Samuel started talking about local politics, the children asked for, and were given, permission to leave the table. They ventured out to the open courtyard, where we heard them playing with other children. Sarah said, "They are very friendly with all the children in the village. We want them to get perspective into how all elements of society live." Sarah sounded just like her mother. Again, a pang of loss.

At dinner's end I produced the skin of wine I had brought, the creation of heaven. Pouring some for each of us, I said, "The bride's father gave me this skin to show that the best wine was served last, a special treat for all. The wine was a gift from one of the guests." Raising our cups, I toasted *l'chaim* (to life). Without mentioning its origin, I chose to venture a question. "Is there much talk or rumor about Messiah here in the city?"

Samuel was quick to reply. "Talk of the Messiah's coming is everywhere, and nowhere. He is here. He is there. He was seen in Jerusalem or in Gaza. He is Goliath's size or looks just like every other man in the country. There is so much talk that even the Romans are nervous."

"Nervous?" I asked. "Why would they be nervous?"

Samuel was contemplative when he replied, "The rumors are more intense coming from a variety of areas and many different sources. Even the rulers of the synagogue are in tune with the fervor. There is a building expectation that something is going to happen with Passover coming soon."

Before I could reply, Samuel turned to me excitedly and said, "Speaking of the Passover, we are leaving in a couple of days for Jerusalem. If the mission you spoke of allows, why not travel with us? I know you usually travel with the Cana family, but you are here now."

While I noticed a slight emphasis on the word "mission," I let it pass and instead instantly agreed. At that time my task was indistinct as to timing and direction. So Jerusalem it would be. While every Hebrew desired pilgrimage for the three appointed festivals in the year, it was rare one made it to Jerusalem for one, let alone all three. We made small talk for a bit and kept the conversation light.

Sarah called the children in to say good night, and Samuel announced that I would be accompanying them to Jerusalem for the Passover festival. Rebekah and Saul danced a little happy circle at the news then were off to bed. "Good night, Sabba Eli," they said in unison as they trundled off.

It was time. I was surprised how nervous and excited I was to finally tell another human being what I had experienced.

"I know you are curious about my being here, and the word 'mission' is really making you wonder, correct?"

"I have known you for many years, Eli, and have never known you to do or say something without purpose. Yes, I am curious!" Samuel said in a questioning tone.

"I have known you all my life," Sarah added, "and I agree. I am more than curious. What is your mission, and what brings you here to us?"

Gently I began. "I know what I am about to tell you may seem so bizarre you might think I have taken leave of my mind. Please allow me to say everything before you come to any conclusion!" My words were an earnest plea to them to hear the whole of the story.

As I began my narrative for the first time in so many years, the reality of what I saw that night of nights flooded into my mind, and my Rachel's young face seemed to appear before me. It was like I was a young, newly minted shepherd again, telling my betrothed the extraordinary events I had witnessed.

"Thirty years ago I, along with three other shepherds, took a flock of sheep to Bethlehem for market. It was the year of the useless census ordered by Caesar, and the roads and inns were jammed because everyone was traveling to their birth town to register. I can still see the throngs of people going and coming in my mind's eye, and there was strain on everyone's face."

As I began to tell the details of what I experienced that night, it was like I went into a trance. Even though I seemed to be reciting every detail, my voice seemed to be coming from far away. I do not know how long the telling took, but I remember the look on Sarah's and Samuel's faces. They started looking at me with slight smiles on their faces that quickly turned to wrinkled, puzzled brows. By the time I finished my story of that night of nights, their mouths were open, eyes wide as saucers. As I paused in wonder at my own words, there was total silence in the room.

CHAPTER 25

THE DOUBTER

I COULD BARELY hear a breath as the quiet was crushing. We just sat in the dim light of the lamplit room, trying to absorb what had been said. Though I was there thirty years before, the events sounded so incredible, even I had difficulty with their reality. Not that I doubted, especially after the affirmation in Cana with the wine and his touch. The enormity of my story was difficult for them to digest. I sat and waited.

Finally Samuel, his voice barely a whisper, seething with imperious contempt, pointed at my chest and said, "How can this be? That Adonai would reveal this to you? Where is it written that He of All Creation would choose a shepherd from a village in the hill country of Galilee to receive the announcement of the most anticipated event in the history of our people?"

I sat calmly as my daughter's husband fumed. The most common image in the minds and hearts of all Hebrews, from the time of the prophet *Mal'akhi* (Malachi), was that the king of Israel of the line of David would be born in a palace, a powerful warrior, and ride to the rescue of his chosen people on a valiant steed carrying a glimmering double-edged sword!

I could almost read Samuel's mind, for those would have been my questions too, before that fateful night in Bethlehem thirty years ago. What I had seen and heard that glorious night was etched into my heart and mind. Why Adonai would reveal his announcement to shepherds had been an unanswered question all my life since. I could not answer that question, though I had pondered it every day.

I replied with the only words I could. "I do not know. All I know is what I saw and heard. Every word I have spoken is true."

Sarah's eyes were locked on Samuel as he spoke, but he seemed not to notice as he frowned. I could not discern her mind but somehow sensed that his reaction and words did not surprise her. She did not try to counter him. Instead, while still looking directly at her husband, she reached across the table and took my hand as she began to recall some of the events from her childhood. One stood out in her mind as she began to speak firmly but gently.

"When I was eleven, there was a lost boy in our caravan returning from the Passover in Jerusalem. Papa, I remember your reaction when I came rushing into our camp that evening with the news. When I said the name Yeshua, you startled. I thought that you were angry with me for being late to come home, but it was not that, was it? Then the next day you went south while we went north without you."

She continued to look at Samuel. "I was almost asleep but overheard you and Mama talking about going back down the caravan to see if it was him. You asked her if you were making too much of it. She said that you had to go look for him, and you did. That I know. When you returned home, I was so happy he was found. You never again said another thing about that event, at least to me."

Her grip on my hand tightened as she looked back at me. "All the mysterious trips in the Holy City every year—you would leave us for several hours at a time. When you returned, you and Mama would talk quietly away from us, which you never did at home. You were looking for him, weren't you?"

"Yes and no. I kept my eyes and ears open for him for sure, but there were times I was actually meeting a messenger from the east." My answer brought a quizzical look to her face. I was totally engaged with Sarah and not aware of what reaction Samuel had to her remarks. I knew when I brought up the Magi and my covenant, he would have more doubts about my fantastic story. How much should I say, and when should I say it?

Samuel broke his silence. He turned to me with a deep frown and look of consternation, brows furrowed and eyes narrowed. "Why on earth would any messenger from the 'east' come all the way to Jerusalem to meet you? Your story is all too much! Talk of Messiah born to a couple from Galilee in a dirty cave somewhere in Bethlehem and revealed only to you and a few other shepherds. Then secret meetings at the holy festivals of all places with a pagan from the east? No wonder you warned us to hear you out and not think you had lost your mind because it seems you have!" With each word his tone moved from skeptical to sarcastic then angry.

Sarah winced at the disrespectful tone of his remarks but held her tongue. She knew Samuel well enough to know that any words from her in my defense would only make matters worse.

In a soft, conciliatory voice, looking at him intently, I said, "Samuel, dear *mek'hutan* (son-in-law), I have no answer to your question of 'Why shepherds?' All I can say is that what I have spoken is truth. I must point out to you again that this was no ordinary cave. It was and is a place of history, a sanctioned location run by Levites ordained by the high priest in Jerusalem. Must I remind you that I am one of their temple-trained emissaries, not a simple shepherd and goat herder from the hills of *Shomron* (Samaria)."

His retort was heated as he looked at Sarah then stabbed his finger at me. "You want me, us, just to take your word about the most important event prophesied in our nation's history? That is twice I have asked you why, and twice you have brushed off my questions with an answer that is no answer! I simply do not believe what you have said. *Sifrei Torah* (Holy Scrolls) tells us that a matter may only be established with two or three witnesses. You speak of this as one, with no other to testify the truth of what you have said. Where are your fellow shepherds from that night if it really happened at all? Where are the parents of this cave-born Messiah you speak of? For a man on a mission, you have no credentials!"

His angry words hung in the air for a moment as he glared at me. I realized that with mere words, I would never convince him of my story. I regretted telling him, although I felt at first I had to. Words failed me as I struggled to gather my thoughts. There I was, on the verge of arguing with a Pharisee, so I kept silent and prayed for wisdom as to how to close this conversation.

Before I could say more, Samuel abruptly stood, knocking over the stool on which he was sitting. "I will listen to no more of this. What you speak is not found in the Holy Scrolls, and you cannot substantiate your claims. You border on blasphemy with your words." Leaning toward me across the table, he hissed, "Heed my caution, speak no more of this to anyone lest you find yourself shunned!" Standing up tall, he stiffly said, "It is late, and I have had a long day of it." He glared at me, turned quickly, and walked off without another word.

"I am sorry, my angel. That did not go well. I have not told this story to anyone in years and should have known better than to speak of it first with a Pharisee," I said softly to Sarah.

"Samuel is a good man and very versed in the law and prophets. Every word must make sense, or he will not agree with anyone, not just you." There was a pained expression on her face.

"Papa, I believe what you have said is truly what you saw and heard, but I do not understand either. The experience you speak of is incredible, but I trust you. More than that, if Adonai chose you and showed all of this to you, I trust him to make our paths straight. Let us talk more of your mission tomorrow while Samuel is away on business."

"Yes, as I have much more to say," I replied with a voice soft, full of regret, and fatigue.

With that we called the seemingly disastrous night to a close with a father-daughter hug, hoping the morning light would bring clarity.

CHAPTER 26

THE FISHERMEN

THE NEXT MORNING, to avoid a confrontation with Samuel, I left the house before dawn. As I walked out the front door toward the lightening sky, my heart was heavy with the thought of bringing dissention into my daughter's home. The sun was just peeking over the Sea of Galilee, its light sparkling like morning stars winking at me.

I could see motion in the misty light of morning, fishermen bringing in their catch. Despite my somber mood, the sight enthralled me, erasing melancholy and frustration.

I walked the empty cobbled street toward the rising sun. I had no particular destination in mind, just to walk and think. Hill people are fascinated with large bodies of water, so the shore drew me like a magnet. I remembered being awed by a storm on my first visit to Capernaum many years ago. The only recent storm was the one raging in my head last night.

While I was not a religious man by the standards of the Pharisees, my family lineage was made up of synagogue-attending Levite servants. My parents instilled in me that Adonai was real and everlasting, the children of Israel his chosen people. Tradition taught us that Messiah would one day come to rescue and restore his people. The additional formal law training I received in Jerusalem to earn my status as a tav prepared me to engage Samuel but not enough to argue with a brilliant Pharisee.

While walking the streets, the thought kept recurring that it had been over four hundred years since a prophet spoke to our people. Why would Samuel, or anybody else for that matter, listen to me? I was no prophet! I was a shepherd! Though I was educated and of standing, it was not an occupation generally held in high esteem. There was no one to confirm my story. I knew what I had seen and heard that night three decades ago in Bethlehem. Perhaps I was naive to think that anyone else would believe my narrative.

My wandering brought me to the water, where fishing huts dotted the shore. Small boats were pulled alongside the huts, and nets were draped over crosshatched riggings to dry. The smell of morning, water, and fish accented the scene. It was strikingly different from Cana, where it was grassy pasture, wildflowers, and the musky odor of sheep that drifted in the air. I sat down on the bow of one of the idle boats next to one of the huts, pondering my dilemma.

While I was sitting there, Sarah's words came to mind. She believed me but did not understand, yet she trusted that Adonai would provide a path. It dawned on me like the rising of the sun that I should not dare to expect that anyone would instantly believe and accept what I said. Even my daughter wondered about me, and only her love and trust in my integrity and in Adonai held her doubts in check.

Peace came as I realized I was part of an enormous story, a divine plan. My task was clear—to find, follow, watch, and report the doings of the Messiah. As I stood to return to the house, a fishing boat came toward the hut near where I was sitting.

The men in the boat had their backs to me as they rowed with practiced skill and beached their craft. Four of them got out, moving a little stiffly. Though they were a distance away, some looked familiar, one in particular. It took but a moment to realize the familiar images of the men I had seen in Cana at the wedding. It was the one called John with whom I spoke and tasted the wine. They were the friends with Yeshua! I was immediately energized realizing that I had no idea when I left the house earlier this morning that my steps would take me to this place. Coincidence or divine appointment?

They struggled taking a net full of fish to a wagon then walked toward me. John walked in front with a tall, muscular man. He was taller than John by half a head and stood out not only because of his height. His long hair and beard were a deep orange, wiry, and in wild disarray. As they came closer, the tall one was talking excitedly to John. "Yeshua talked yesterday of going to Jerusalem for the Passover. I have spoken with my wife as you should talk to your father so that you and your brother can be with us. Give him some notice. He will have to make arrangements for help while you are gone."

I stood smiling, and John recognized me as they came closer to the hut. "Eli, from Cana, is that you? Shalom! It is good to see you. What a surprise to see you here in Capernaum."

The tall one looked at me then at John with a surprised look and asked, "You know this man?"

John pointed at me and said, "*Shi'mon*, this is Eli. I met him at the wedding feast where he was serving, the night Yeshua turned the water into wine. We shared a sip of the new wine together."

"Shalom, Eli. I am *Shi'mon ben Yonah* (Simon, son of Jonah) from *Beit' Tzaida* (Bethsaida), working here with my fellow fishermen and friends. You are welcome here as any friend of John is a friend of mine." He smiled, nodded, slapped John on the back, and with that he was off to help the others.

John looked intently at me and asked, "What brings you to Capernaum?"

Measuring my response, I answered, "My daughter and son-in-law live here with two of my grandchildren. Since they left the wedding early, I wanted to visit and spend more time with them."

"You are very welcome here. This is a wonderful place to live. I have been here all of my life and come from a long line of fishermen. *Zvadyah* (Zebedee), my father, still works the boats, as does most of my family. It is a hard but a good life. We have some family that are traders and merchants working the caravans, but most of us fish."

Still smiling at seeing these men, I said, "Our family has a long tradition of hard work, as does yours. Instead of water and fish, we work the land and herd sheep."

John stopped and asked, "Are you not a servant of the family who hosted the wedding?"

Laughing in response, I said, "No, my friend, I was just helping the servants that night. They were quite overwhelmed, so I decided to assist them serving the food and wine."

Slapping me on the back like Simon did to him, he said, "Well, old friend, any man that works hard is welcome to our brotherhood." Though I was probably twice John's age, I felt a kindred spirit with him. Men who labor hard and long usually have an immediate bond.

John started walking toward the house on the water, asking, "Have you eaten yet this morning? Come join us if you are hungry. By now the fish will be ready."

I suddenly realized I was ravenous and accepted his invitation. The new friendship felt quite natural. It did not occur to me immediately, but as we walked, I knew that I was being guided into the circle of Yeshua's friends.

Once again a divine hand at work.

CHAPTER 27

THE DAUGHTER

JOHN AND I walked to the house that he, his brother *Ya'akov* (James), and their parents occupied. It was a small stone structure, the house of Zebedee. The walls were of natural stone, the roof thatched palm fronds atop slats of wood. The homes in the hill country were built much the same way, with a few variations based on local materials.

When we arrived, the house was empty, the fish breakfast warm and waiting. Fried fish, bread, and morning wine were on the table. As we ate, John said that others of the crew had gone to Simon's house to finish preparing their catch for sale at the market. I asked John questions about Yeshua. It was over the course of but a few short weeks he and some of the others became his followers, believing he was a divine gift from Adonai.

John said Yeshua was staying in Capernaum for a few days then going to Jerusalem for the Passover festival just as I had overheard him and Simon discussing. It suddenly dawned on John to find his father to let him know he and his brother would be traveling to Jerusalem.

"Eli, I must be off. There is much to do before we leave and little time. Please, walk with me to the boats and fish exchange. I must find my father and brother."

Nodding, I walked for a short distance, then I realized that Sarah had no idea where I was or if I had left their hospitality because of conflict with Samuel. "Excuse me, John," I said, smiling. "I must let my daughter know that I am still among the living since I disappeared before the rest of the household was awake."

"Shalom. Until we meet again, my friend," John replied as we parted ways.

It was time to return and revisit the events of the previous night. My hope was to bring some level of acceptance with Samuel. Above all else it was necessary to restore peace in the household I had disrupted. There was no way to know what kind of reception I could expect when I arrived.

Sarah was waiting at the front door when I arrived. "Papa, I have been so worried about you since you left. I was afraid that Samuel's reaction might have chased you away. He can be quite assertive when his views are challenged or met with some possible alternative. Are you well?"

"Yes, my lovely child, I am quite well," I said, smiling as we walked into the empty house.

"The children are with a neighbor, and Samuel has gone to a nearby village to arrange a shipment of freshly pressed olive oil." All was quiet, and I sensed the perfect time to tell her all.

"I walked down to the shore at dawn to rethink the events of last night and get clarity on my direction. I just needed to walk and think. While I did not set out for the shore, I was drawn to the water, and it is where I wandered. I walked the shoreline a bit then sat down on an old boat next to one of the huts overlooking the water. I kept rehashing words from last night after Samuel left us. Your trust in me and Adonai, my sweet daughter, have brought me peace."

She looked at me with tender and expectant eyes as I continued. "I realized that I have had many years to think about the events that changed me. Time made the incredible familiar, at least to me. Your mother and I talked about it often, and I yearned to tell it to you before now. That said, I should have been more careful in the telling. I will hold it more closely from now on."

We sat at the table, and she took my hands. "I understand you have held this for over thirty years, but why tell it now? Why wait so long?" she asked.

"Do you really want to know, after last night?" I asked with a little skepticism in my voice and a wry smile.

Expectantly she said, "More than ever. My curiosity is hungry, and I want to know it all, if there is more!"

"Oh yes, there is more, much more. In fact, what happened only days ago in Cana at the wedding triggered my journey to you here in Capernaum. When you hear the rest of the story, you must keep it to yourself. Do not tell a word of it to Samuel and the children. Let what Samuel heard last night be the end of what he hears for now. The children for certain, as they will not be able to contain anything they hear, no matter how well they are prepared. What I am about to tell you must be our secret until such a time that we choose as appropriate. Agreed?"

"Papa, you are a man of unquestioned integrity and have always imparted the value of truth in everything you do and think." Without another moment of hesitation or thought, Sarah smiled and said, "Agreed!"

"Good, let us sit outside on the bench, where I can enjoy the view of the lake while we talk. It is a treat to see another landscape of Our Creator!" We went to the side garden with a view of the water and sat.

"There are several pieces of this story, but let me begin with what occurred after what I shared last night.

"Following the events in the grotto, we had to deliver the flock and make preparations for the return trip. We left Joseph, Mary, and the baby Yeshua in the care of the Levite shepherds and did not see them again for over a year. In fact, until a week ago, I had no idea where they were. But I get ahead of myself. Do you remember hearing stories about my friend Jacob being killed by a Roman soldier?"

She thought for a moment. "Yes, I do. There was occasional conversation over the years about the incident, especially when his parents died. There was always talk in the village that Jacob's death killed them."

"That is probably true. With his murder, it was as if that Roman blade slashed the life out of them as well. When we returned home with

Jacob's body, that was all we could think about and concern ourselves with. The wonderful events we experienced with the birth of Messiah were somehow temporarily buried with Jacob. I could not speak to or touch your mother for seven days until I became ritually clean, having carried Jacob's remains.

"When I finally had the opportunity to see and speak with your dear mother, I told her of the miraculous events. I remember standing in the warm sun looking at her beautiful face, thinking how blessed I was to love and be loved."

As I spoke of my conversation with Rachel, I was flooded with emotions. First anger at the Romans for the lives changed by what that soldier did to Jacob. Then despair hit me with the loss of my best friend, my beloved wife. Slowly as I spoke about the astonishing light, the sound, the angels, my spirits began to lift. By the time I was telling of the race to the cave, the other shepherds, the young couple, and the newborn baby, I was up pacing about arms flailing with excitement at the memories.

"Your mother believed every word of my story, and I never varied in the telling; every detail was etched in my mind. We decided to keep it to ourselves for that time. As it turns out, we never spoke of it to another person in all the years we were together. But that is only the beginning of the story."

I realized how crazy I must have looked not only to Sarah but also to others who were passing on the street. I sat down again next to her and in a much calmer tone started to tell her about the following year. "I had no idea Jacob had any sheep of his own, let alone a flock large enough to warrant a trip to market. Do you remember our neighbor Matthias, Jacob's father? You were young when he died, but I know you saw him around the village from time to time."

"Yes, I do remember him, Papa. What a tragic figure he was, and I barely remember his wife." Sarah looked sad as she spoke.

I touched her face, and she smiled in return. "Many events occur in a year, and what a year it was. Shortly after returning home and burying Jacob, I had to go and spend a month in Jerusalem to be initiated into the Brotherhood of Levite Shepherds. It was the beginning of my training. Shortly after my return home, your mother and I were married, and before the year was out, you came along as the wonderful blessing you are. A really great year!

"A short while before you were born, Matthias sought me in the market. He asked me if I would do him a favor for the sake of Jacob's memory and take Jacob's sheep to, of all places, can you guess?"

"Bethlehem!" Sarah squealed.

"Yes, Bethlehem! Oh, beautiful city of David, so close to Jerusalem, the staging area at the Tower of the Flock for the festival animals. I was going back to Bethlehem as a lead shepherd. Me, a mere child, returning to the place where Messiah was born! Your mother and I continued to wonder if he was still there.

"That arrangement made the possibility of seeing Yeshua again exciting and intoxicating! The opportunity of seeing Messiah, who would be a boy more than a year old, made us so happy." Sarah listened in rapt attention.

"What I am about to tell you changed my life forever in ways I could have never imagined." I paused, breathed deeply, and said, "Sarah, again I caution you to speak of this to no one."

"Papa, I hold to my affirmation of last night. Please, go on, tell me!"

"With your mother's encouragement, realizing that Messiah and his parents could be anywhere, I left for Bethlehem. There were times I thought the whole thing was a puff of smoke, a chasing after the wind."

Then while standing, sitting, pacing about, I related all the events of how I found the house where the little family settled. With every minute detail, I described the visit of the strangers from the east and their gifts. Sarah was giddy with delight when I described the Magi and their offerings.

It was then I sat, took my daughter's hands again, and told her of the covenant with the noble visitors and what motivated me—that I, Elijah ben Ezra, was the Magi's Man.

CHAPTER 28

THE WITNESS

TELLING MY FAVORITE story with all the details, I lost track of time and was not sure when the children would be home for midday meal. Sarah made some tea, and we sat at the table continuing to discuss my memories. When I told her of my returning to an empty house, she, as a mother, found the disappearance of the family quite troubling. Her facial expression slid from smile to worry to fear as she wondered if they had escaped or Herod's hoard had found them. She shared my delight in the Magi's people having cleaned up so quickly. Sarah agreed it was our mutual trust in Adonai that there was no way he would allow his son, the Promised Messiah, to perish. When I told Sarah about the comforting voice I had heard on that day, her eyes filled with tears.

She laughed with glee at the recounting of Yeshua in the temple years later teaching the older men and amazing them. Then I told her about the years that passed, my meeting Moses and Bidi and hearing his voice in the marketplace when offering me an orange.

Recounting the events took most of the morning. She now knew the essence of the last thirty years, the trips to Jerusalem, the meetings with the Magi's messengers, the frustration of almost thirty years of nothing until the wine at the wedding.

"Remember last night I said something had happened recently at the wedding in Cana that triggered my coming here to Capernaum?" I asked.

"Yes, Papa, I do. You said you would come back to that part of the story." She was jumping in anticipation.

"It is time to come to the end of the thirty-year wait and the beginning of my active mission as the Magi's Man. I saw Yeshua at the wedding in Cana, the day after you and Samuel left for home. Something so wonderful happened. It was a miracle!" Remembering the wine, I stood and went to my room.

A startled Sara asked, "Papa, what is wrong?"

I was back with the skin of wine from Natie and grabbed a goblet. As I related the details of the miracle of turning of water into wine with just the sound of his voice, I poured her a taste. "I was there, and it happened right in front of me. I drew the water, and then I tasted it as wine, wonderful wine. Here, taste." I handed her the goblet.

My daughter took a sip. "Who could do such a thing except a man who is from Adonai?" Sarah sat still, wide-eyed. "Oh my! This is a taste of heaven. Samuel must drink of this!"

We sat in silence, enjoying the moment. Then I related the conversation with John, his telling me they met Yeshua only a short time prior to that night when they were in Bethany to hear the immerser.

"He told me that this wild man looked up at Yeshua as he approached and cried out that he was the *Seh HaAdonai* (Lamb of God) and would take away the world's sin! John was there at the purification of Yeshua. I know he is the Son of Adonai!" My voice trailed into a whisper.

"Oh, Papa, this must be the time. Finally he is here!" Her voice was trembling with excitement. "What are you going to do now? You must be very careful. He will have many enemies."

"Yes, my sweet child, I will take care of myself and not take part in any activities that will stir the authorities. I am now just a scribe to relate what I observe. Being a tav gives freedom to roam about and follow him.

"Come, walk with me to the place I saw John earlier. I would like you to meet him and see the men that Messiah has chosen to lead." We stood, and I took her hand in mine and said to her, "My darling child, the world is about to change, and you will meet some of the people firsthand."

As we headed toward the fishing huts, I said, "Sarah, I have repeated this story in my mind so often and now will write it down for my first real report to the Magi. What a thrill it will be to give it to their messenger in Jerusalem! There is no telling how much more I will add now that I know him and he is so near." The joy in my voice was infectious, and my darling daughter skipped a few steps like a child.

"Sarah, one more thing. Yeshua, along with a few others, are going to the Passover in Jerusalem. There has never been a Passover festival that I have wanted to attend more!"

As we were approaching the area of the small fishing boats and huts, we saw a cluster of familiar men. John waved at us. "Eli, come here, let me introduce you to my brother and our friends."

The little circle opened up as we neared. In the middle was Yeshua, who looked at Sarah then at me, smiled broadly, and said, "Hello, Eli. Have you brought me another orange?" I stopped still in my tracks as Sarah squeezed my hand and looked at me in wonder.

John looked at Yeshua, confused. "Rabbi, you know this man?"

Yeshua took a step toward me as he looked at John and said, "We found each other in a market in Jerusalem about eighteen years ago." You could hear the gasps of surprise from the group, and my own was louder than all.

I wanted to fall on my knees at his feet and weep with joy. Instead I smiled and said, "Master, I bring with me a treasure of my life, my daughter, Sarah."

Yeshua stepped right up to Sarah, took her hands in his, and said, smiling, "Your father is a special friend and my favorite shepherd."

Sarah said, "Rabbi, my father told me about your meetings, and I am filled with joy beyond measure." She raised Yeshua's hands to her cheek, and a tear touched him. When Yeshua released Sarah's hands, she spun, embracing me with a hug that almost took my breath away. "Papa!" Sarah buried her head in my return embrace and was crying as she looked up at me and said, "My wonderful papa."

The moment was broken when John's brother James said, "Rabbi, the Roman centurion approaches."

We all looked at the powerful-looking soldier as he neared our gathering. I was filled with rage remembering the killing of Jacob and started shaking. The next few moments were astounding as the centurion spoke directly to Yeshua.

The Roman officer placed his right hand over his heart, bowed his head slightly, looked directly at Messiah, and told him that his trusted servant was home paralyzed and suffering greatly. Yeshua offered to go to the servant and heal him. The officer's response was astonishing. He declared himself unfit for the rabbi to visit his home and said that he was a man who followed orders and all Yeshua had to do was say the words and his servant would be healed.

We all stood breathless at the exchange. Yeshua looked at each one of us and said that he had not heard of such trust in all the land. Looking back at the Roman, who still stood with head bowed, Yeshua told him to go home and that as a reward for his faith his servant would be healed. At the rabbi's words, the centurion dropped to one knee, stood, nodded, turned, and walked away.

We were all stunned, standing rigid with amazement. I looked at Sarah and asked, "Did I just see a Roman soldier, a centurion no less, approach Messiah, the man who is going to free us, and ask him for favor?"

Sarah said, "Papa, that is Salvius, the centurion that Samuel mentioned last night." While our exchange took place, Yeshua said something to his followers. When we looked back at the gathering, they were all quiet.

Sarah clutched my arm again and said, "Papa, your mission is just beginning, and I do not know why, but I am full of joy and dread at the same time. I must go home and see to the children and absorb what we just observed. I am witness to a Roman bowing to Messiah."

I kissed her head and said, "Go. I will be along shortly. Let me speak to these men for a few moments." She hugged me again and left for home.

I took a few steps to join the circle of men who were still and somber after the exchange between Yeshua and Salvius. I looked directly at Yeshua and asked, "May I join your group and follow you?" He stepped over to me, put his hand on my shoulder, and led me away from the other men.

"Eli, my friend, you have known me longer than any of these men here, and your path is not the same as theirs. You may follow me, but you cannot be part of this group I am gathering." With those words my heart sank. He knew what I was feeling because he said, as he added pressure to my shoulder, "Do not despair, my friend. The road you will travel for me is different than that of these men I have chosen. Go. Be with your daughter and her children, and tell your son-in-law, Samuel, to broaden his thinking." He stopped, released me, smiled, and said, "Look for me in Jerusalem." Back to his group he went.

It took a few moments for his words to sink into my mind. I heard them but did not quite understand their meaning. I sighed and reluctantly walked away.

CHAPTER 29

THE CENTURION

WANDERING AROUND FOR a bit, I found myself in the village marketplace, where I bought an orange to lighten my mood. The disappointment of learning that I was not going to be part of Yeshua's inner circle was starting to fade as I realized there was something else he needed of me. Perhaps he wanted information to get to the Magi after their long years of waiting. That was to be my focus because, I reasoned, that was his plan all along.

Eating the orange did help, and my mood lifted dramatically. Browsing through the little market, looking for some small gifts for the children, I heard someone yell, "Shepherd, over here!" I turned to the voice and saw an old man standing next to a bent-over, ancient-looking woman. He was holding a rope tied to an aging goat.

"Come here, shepherd, and value my goat. That way all in the market will know I am asking a fair price." No matter where I went as a tav, people were always asking for pricing, advice, anything that could help them value their livestock.

Walking over to the couple, I asked, "What have we here, old friend?"

"Why, it is a prized goat in his prime that we bring to the market." The words certainly did not match the evidence.

Trying to be as pleasant as possible, I asked, "How long have you had this valuable goat?"

"We just purchased him from a passing caravan and sought to make a profit today." As I got close to the old couple, I saw it was desperation at work. The bent-over woman was wheezing so hard she could barely breathe. At a close look, the old man was suffering from a bone ailment so severe his hands looked like gnarled tree roots, and his feet were obviously clubbed.

Politely I asked, "My old friend, do you live nearby where you may have other prized livestock that I might value?"

"I am afraid this is the only animal we have for market, and I will appreciate a good appraisal."

Knowing full well that no one would even consider buying the goat, I said, "Let me have a closer look."

The old woman raised her head and looked directly at me. "Whatever we can sell him for, we will use to buy food to take home, prepare a meal, and Adonai willing, we will both rest in his arms tonight." Her plea broke my heart.

"Well, I can see that this prize has had some years and probably sired offspring of value. If you would allow me, I would like to purchase your goat for myself."

"And what price would you give for him?" the man said, standing a little straighter.

"Perhaps a silver shekel would be a fair value for your prized goat," I said this, knowing the old animal was probably worth a few coppers, at best, to be used in a stew. His eyes grew a little wider; his wife looked at me slightly puzzled.

"That would be a fair price indeed, sir."

Nodding, I reached into my sash, withdrew my coin purse, and fished out a silver shekel. Handing it to the old man, I said, "Thank you, my friend. I will take my prize now and be off."

He handed me the rope, looked at his wife, and said to her, "Come, dear, we have some shopping to do." He nodded at me and took his wife's arm, and they both hobbled off.

I stood there, thinking, *That is what a lifetime of love looks like. If only Rachel were alive to share the pains of age with me.*

"That was a very generous gesture for a shepherd." Turning to my right, I was almost face-to-face with the centurion Salvius. I just stood there with a range of emotions, hatred of Rome and pleasure that he had submitted to Messiah. "I am at a loss, shepherd, I do not know your name. I saw you with the rabbi earlier."

"I am Elijah ben Ezra, centurion Salvius. I am here visiting my daughter, Sarah, wife of Samuel, whom you know." I spoke a little stiffly.

"Ah yes, Samuel, a fine community leader." I was somewhat surprised at Salvius's friendly manner. "What brings you to Capernaum, Elijah ben Ezra?"

"Just a family visit," I replied with some hesitation.

"How do you know the rabbi? I—"

Before he could finish his words, a young man came rushing up to him, saying, "Master, master, Antoni is healed. Just minutes ago he sat up and asked for something to eat. He started moving in bed and hung his legs over the side. He told me to find you and tell you that he is well."

Salvius took a moment to let the news sink in and said, "Thank you. Return home, and tell Antoni I will see him later, and tell the kitchen to prepare a celebratory meal." The servant sped off.

"Elijah ben Ezra, the rabbi has healed my servant as he promised," he said with a surprised look. "This is no ordinary man, is he?"

Almost afraid to respond, I answered, "He is quite extraordinary. His faith can heal. As he said to you, authority understands how to react and behave." I was not sure I was making sense but did not know what else to say. "Before I leave to go to my daughter's home, may I offer you this prized goat to celebrate your servant's recovery and the miracle of his healing? As Yeshua said, it was faith, your faith, that did the healing."

Having said that to Salvius, I looked at him, and he was in a deep contemplative state, so deep that I had to speak and ask again, "May I offer you and your servant this goat to celebrate and seal the bond between you, centurion Salvius, and the Hebrew people of Capernaum?"

He seemed to snap out of his reverie and said to me, "Thank you, Elijah. You are a most generous and noble man," and he accepted the goat, reaching for the rope. "Tell me something, Elijah."

"Certainly," I replied, mindful of my answer.

Salvius, with an intent look on his face, asked, "Elijah, is this Yeshua your Messiah?" His question made me run cold. There I was, standing before a Roman centurion, required by Roman law to answer.

My mind raced, and without thought I asked in response, "Who do you think he is?"

Salvius remained contemplative and said, "I do not know." He looked at me again with the stare you would expect of a powerful Roman. "What do you think? Who do you think he is, Elijah ben Ezra?"

Then as if Adonai himself made my mouth move with words that I had heard before, I said, "Would our all-powerful Adonai choose a poor rabbi, a man that befriends men who fish and smell of the sea, to be the long-awaited Messiah?"

After a moment Salvius broke into a broad grin and said, "I suppose not. You have answered well. Thank you for the goat. Give my regards to your daughter and Samuel." He turned and headed home to his healed servant, leading a mangy old goat. Reeling from the encounter, I headed to Sarah's home.

Later that afternoon, when Samuel came home, Sarah was as excited as I was to tell about what we had witnessed earlier. When I told her of the encounter with Salvius in the marketplace, she started sobbing with delight. "A miracle, right here in Capernaum, and I was witness to its inception. Having a Roman, not just any Roman but a centurion, initiate and receive the blessing is almost beyond belief."

With his feet washed and garment changed, Samuel entered the common room holding a goblet of wine. He looked at me, and in a softer tone than the night before but still with a mocking, sarcastic edge, he asked, "What new information do you have about your Messiah today? Has he crumbled the colosseum in Rome, decimated their army, and minted a new coin with his likeness?"

"Enough!" yelled Sarah so loud that the children in the courtyard became quiet. "My husband, whom I love and respect, you may be a man of high standing in my eyes and those of the community in which we live, but you know nothing about this truth that my father has told you. He has taken you, us, into his confidence at the expense of your ridicule and that of Roman justice. Today I myself have witnessed something that is a miracle in and of itself."

Samuel was stunned at Sarah's rebuke and the force of her words. He stood with mouth agape, like a stone statue, holding his goblet for a few moments before he spoke.

With a most confused look on his face, Samuel asked, "What are you saying? What has happened? Of what do you speak? Why are you so vehement? Who are you talking about?" His words came tumbling out in a torrent.

Standing erect in front of of Samuel, Sarah said, "My dear husband, I am sorry if I have hurt you with my tone, but you have offended my father, and that I cannot abide. In most circumstances I submit to you, but not now, not this."

Samuel seemed at a loss as to how to react to Sarah, so I spoke up. "Let us remember that we are family bound by not only law but also love. Please, let us sit. I will get some wine, and we will talk to each other with love and respect." Both Samuel and Sarah relaxed a bit as I voiced my plea. They sat in silence until I returned with the wine and said, "Now let us talk. Samuel, something happened today that you should know about. We were there."

I poured some wine for us to taste, raised my goblet, and toasted. "L'chaim, my family!"

The children came skipping into the room from the courtyard with dirty clothes and smiles on their faces. Rebekah, doing a hora dance spin, asked, "Are we having a party?" Klutzy Saul, tripping on his own feet, fell into his father, splashing the wine on both of them.

Samuel, aghast at the last few minutes in his house, stood up with a wild look on his face, scanned the room, and then unexpectedly burst into hysterical laughter. "This family is going to drive me crazy. I may already be crazy. No, I have decided that this family is insane, and I am the craziest of the lot. So let us have a feast, right now, to celebrate insanity."

He continued to chuckle as he sat down next to Sarah and said, "Food, we need food and more wine and lots of bread. We will eat reclining on pillows, and we will celebrate our family in the old traditions."

With that Samuel kicked off his sandals, arranged two large pillows, and lowered himself to a comfortable recline. Taking a cue from her husband, Sarah did the same, leaving me standing with the children, who were more than slightly bewildered by their actions. "Eli, my father by law, please sit, make yourself comfortable, and yes, let us talk."

Samuel had indeed relaxed a bit. Sarah sat on the floor next to him, and I chose a small stool in front of him, creating a little triangle.

Sarah began. "Samuel, you are a man of faith and a man of facts," she said, reaching over, taking his hand. "Not one person I know will challenge your faith. It is fact that I believe either you are ignoring or your faith is blocking. Let me present you with a fact. Your friendly centurion Salvius asked a rabbi to heal his servant. I was there. I heard him."

"Salvius did that?" Samuel almost spilled his wine again when his head snapped up at Sarah's words.

"Yes, my son," I added, and Samuel's head swung slowly toward me. "Shortly after that happened, I was wandering in the marketplace, and Salvius came up to me to ask questions about the rabbi, and we were interrupted when one of his servants came running up to inform him that his servant was up and healed."

Silence hung in the room for some time before Samuel responded. In a quiet, subdued voice, he asked, "Who is this rabbi you speak of?"

Doing my best to be direct yet not give too much information, I answered, "I have heard him called many things: rabbi, teacher, master, Galilean. Salvius himself called him rabbi. Maybe Salvius knows more."

Samuel looked at me and said in a steady, businesslike tone, "Eli, you are being evasive. Last night you were a world of facts based on what you have seen and known over thirty years. What is his name?"

"Samuel," I replied in a stern, parental manner, "you are a brilliant young businessman, a respected Pharisee, an important man in your community, a loving husband and father, and you are my family. I caution you, be very careful with how you move forward. His name is Yeshua Ben Yosef."

"Why the caution, Eli? If I do not believe that this man is Messiah, will he smite me?"

His response angered me to a point that I aped his behavior of the previous evening by standing up, leaning in toward him, and in a low voice bubbling with anger, saying, "Son, you have a fatal flaw when you always think you are the smartest person wherever you are. I know a shepherd leader in Jerusalem that can take any of your utterings and tie them in knots so tight you would be hard-pressed to speak for a week! I am one of his elected twelve in all of Israel to select the perfect lambs for slaughter at the Passover. I speak with credentials. Now, my boy, listen carefully to what I say next.

"I have witnessed murder and injustice in my lifetime that would make your head spin. This is a dangerous world, and we live in a volatile time under the iron fist of Rome, which will crush anyone or anything that even hints of a threat. This man I speak of is Messiah, and if information that you share gets anyone injured or killed," I said, leaning closer until I was inches from his face, "his blood will be on your hands. You and your beautiful family could be in grave danger. Take care, my son."

I left the house.

CHAPTER 30

THE TABLES

I STOOD FOR a few moments looking down at the water and decided to leave for Jerusalem. Upon returning to the house, I heard Sarah and Samuel in conversation, not quite heated but louder than normal. "Excuse me," I said, interrupting them. "I have come for my things and will be leaving."

"Why now, Papa? I thought you would travel with us?" Sarah asked with a sadness in her voice.

"I need to get an early start preparing for the next class of Alephs and see to the lambs for the festival. I am sure there will be a large number of pilgrims this year, so I must be ready to assume one of many roles. Contact Shabach at the Temple Academy if you fail to find me when you get to the usual camp setting."

Looking at Samuel, I said, "Samuel, I am sorry that we have conflict, but please, my boy, keep your ears, eyes, and heart open, for there are things of this world you need to learn. Most of all, keep reign over your tongue. It is a key to a pit with an endless bottom, and I fear that you are standing on the edge. I love you all and will see you in Jerusalem." With my skyt, staff, rod, and travel bag, I took my first steps to the City of Hope.

It was a beautiful spring evening, and my spirits lifted as I headed south. Keeping a steady pace, I would be able to see the sunset at the end of the third day when I arrived at the temple training grounds. There were ten days until the fifteenth day of Nisan, the start of the Passover festival. That should give me an opportunity to find the fishermen and Yeshua before working at the academy.

As I walked I sang quietly and spoke to the memory of Rachel. How I wished she were with me to help guide me through these days and the relationships with the children and their families. As a man approaching a half century of life, I was still strong and vigorous but questioned my ability to endure the coming days.

Nearing the city on the afternoon of the third day, I looked up and said, "Oh, Jerusalem, there is none like you!" The very presence of Adonai could be felt as I neared its walls. And now Messiah was here. I felt alive and alarmed at what lay before me. My first stop would be the academy, where I had a room for my equipment and belongings. Then a quick visit with Shabach. I decided to ask the chazzen for limited duty so that I could find and be near Yeshua.

As I entered the spare little room reserved for a handful of instructors who came to the city to teach and learn, the familiar voice greeted me. "My wandering tav appears early before service requires. What brings me this great honor?" Shabach always had a stabbing yet playful tone in his voice when we spoke as friends.

"My dear and venerable chazzen, I could bear absence from the presence of this majestic place no longer. Therefore, I forsake family and friends to be here once again" was my reply as I turned to face him. "My friend, I wish to take you into my confidence about a subject that has been burdening me for many years," I said in a most concerned tone.

"This does sound serious, Eli. Join me after dimming of lights tonight. I will have wine and cakes available so we can spend as much time as needed for you to enlighten me," he responded with a look of concern.

Lightening the mood, I laughed and said, "I will see you later, after I make a quick trip to the market." Placing my gear in the room, I headed to the marketplace for some food and writing supplies.

In a short while, I purchased what I needed and headed over to Moses's stall. Over the years his little stand had grown from a temporary cart to a permanent fixture that was as wide as the larger, permanent stalls in the marketplace. In addition to dates, they had a variety of dried fruits and spices and were dealing with all the caravans that passed Jerusalem.

He and Bidi had become so successful the caravans sent their offerings of choice to their stall, saving them the need to hike to the routes. Since the first time I met them, the beautiful couple from Aksum had grown to a small tribe of eight, having added three girls and three boys. The youngest was a two-year-old girl, and she was as beautiful as the other children. The eldest, a sixteen-year-old boy, *Dani'el* (Daniel), was almost as tall as Moses and as charming as his father. It was clear that he would be taking over the business someday; he was as bright as he was handsome.

Bidi came running out of the stall and wrapped her arms around me, saying, "My favorite shepherd has come to his real home. Shalom, Eli." Her embrace was warm and welcome.

I returned her hug, saying, "Shalom, my beautiful friend."

"Release my woman, you smelly old goat!" Moses yelled from the back of the deep stall, at which we all burst into laughter. Social customs in the marketplace were much more relaxed, allowing a man and woman to embrace publicly without political or religious scorn.

"You are here earlier than usual, Eli," said Bidi with concern. "Is all well with you?"

"Yes, my sweet friend. I came to find some new friends that I made in Capernaum here for the Passover."

"After tomorrow they might be hard to find, with the throngs of pilgrims expected. There are rumors that Messiah will be revealed this season," she said, breaking into a broader smile.

"I have heard some things about Messiah. Perhaps we can talk about them soon. I am not sure how busy I will be with the academy, but I will try and get back here with my family for a visit. But for now I must go to my quarters."

I returned to my little room and put my newly purchased supplies on the spare shelving and rested until the dimming of lights. When the shofar signaled bedtime for the trainees and staff, I headed to Shabach's complex on the next level of the compound.

A guard opened the door to the chazzen's suite, let me in, and then locked it behind me. My friend was taking no chances that our discussion would fall on inappropriate ears.

"Welcome, Eli. You are looking older these days," he said with that wry smile of his, reminding me of the old chazzen. "Sit. Take some wine, eat a barley cake, and tell me what I need to hear."

While sipping and eating I told Shabach my story from the first night of nights up to the miracle in Capernaum. To my surprise his demeanor and facial expressions did not change; he remained calm and intent. He was always a rather animated and volatile personality. But age and responsibility had seasoned him into a man of wisdom. He waited a full minute, taking a little wine before he spoke.

"That he is here is no surprise, with the murmurings that are humming around the city. That wild man immersing in the country is fanning the flames of his presence. But, my friend, the big surprise for me is how this all began and that you have been able to keep silent all of these years. I understand why Adonai has chosen you for this task. There was always something special about you, and now it is revealed. You are much stronger than I ever thought, and I am proud that you are the friend that rescued me years ago. The big question is, what do we do?"

Without hesitation I said, "We remain silent until such a time that he chooses to reveal himself. We cannot make any declarations until he has come forward. Until then we are bound to just observe and be aware of truth when we see or hear it." We sat in silence for a while before I asked, "Dear friend, I officially ask for light duty as of this moment so that I may be free to explore and respond to activities regarding the possible appearance of Messiah."

Immediately Shabach stood and clapped his hands, and within minutes a scribe appeared. He dictated an edict for the shepherd brotherhood records that I be assigned special duty, free to choose time and place to serve throughout Jerusalem and the land at my own discretion.

When the scribe was finished, Shabach placed his seal on the scroll and told the scribe to duplicate the order for me to carry, making my actions official.

When the scribe left the suite, Shabach said, "My friend, I believe that Adonai has chosen you for a very special task. I am honored to be your friend and submit to you, in this quest, to be your servant." With that he bowed to me and stood tall and straight with a look of resolve.

"The honor is mine," I replied and in return bowed to him.

Shaback broke the awkward silence by saying, "I will spend the night with my family to feel the comfort of home. I shall walk with you to your quarters, then have a guard alert my family to expect my arrival."

The chazzen's family did not live in the compound. The temple provided a house for them just outside its walls. His wife and two children had resided there ever since he was elected to the position. I was grateful for him that they were so close and felt a bit lonely for myself. I went to my room and immediately fell into a deep, dreamless sleep.

I awoke before dawn and decided to spend the day at Migdal Eder. After bathing, I put on my official field uniform of roughly woven wool with adornments stitched into the fabric signifying my status as a tav. Carrying the document supplied by Shabach tucked away, I grabbed my staff and rod to start my walk. I ate dried fruit and drank fresh water from my well-used goat bladder carrier, arriving at the Tower of the Flock just as the sun was rising over Jerusalem.

The caves were filled to capacity with lambs collected and raised for the Passover sacrifice. The surrounding fields were covered with snow-white animals grazing what was left of the grass. There were scores of workers bringing carts of fresh alfalfa and greens of many types to feed the hunger of the beautiful lambs that would be slaughtered to satisfy the Passover festival and allow the throngs of pilgrims to feast. The day passed quickly. I was back in the marketplace before sundown.

"Eli, my friend and brother, you look as if you have had a long and arduous day. Come into the back of the stall, and have some tea." Hearing the rich voice of Moses was refreshment itself. I removed my turban as I sank into a huge pillow. "Bidi and the children are home. I am getting ready to close." He handed me a cup of the thick black tea that had been sitting and steeping all day. "Here, take some honey and add it, or you will not be able to take even a small sip." He was right—it was the strongest tea I had ever tasted; the honey tamed it well.

"What have you heard of Messiah in your travels?" he asked as he began putting up wood barriers to close the stall.

Cautiously I said, "There are reports of a miracle in Cana and one in Capernaum. Has that news reached Jerusalem?"

"In Cana the turning water into wine we heard about days ago but nothing of Capernaum." He paused for a few moments and asked, "Have you seen the one they call the immersing prophet? He is in the River Jordan, and it is told that he immersed the one he called Lamb of Adonai."

Moses's words both struck and confused me! "I have not been to the river, nor have I seen this one called immerser. What is this reference to 'Adonai's Lamb'? Why would he call Messiah a lamb?" I sat puzzled for a few moments then asked, "Where is this immerser now?"

"The last I heard, he was south of Jericho, about a half day from here. But he wanders about, so there is no real way of knowing day-to-day where he might be." Amusement gone from his face, Moses said, "I, too, am not understanding calling him a lamb." We sat silently for a bit.

Breaking the silence, I said, "I have light duty tomorrow, so I may be able to take a trip and locate him. I will stop by in the morning and see if you have heard anything as to the immerser's whereabouts." Struggling to get out of the giant cushion, Moses laughed, got up, and gave me a helping hand. We exchanged good nights, and I headed back to my room. I had barely gotten out of my robes when I fell onto my pallet and into another dreamless sleep.

The next morning it was well after dawn when one of Shabach's servants knocked on my door, leaving a tray with breakfast items. There was a note from the chazzen telling me to visit the sheep pool to make sure that it was properly manned and that there were enough supplies to adequately handle the thousands of sheep that would be herded through the pool beginning the next day, the first day of Passover. An official duty added to my free movement.

The sheep pool was just outside the temple wall near the *Sha'ar Keh'ves* (Sheep Gate), not far from the pool at *Beit'Zada* (Bethesda), where people came to bathe in the water constantly replenished by a fresh spring. Before sacrifice the sheep were marched through a connecting shallow pool where Levites poured water over their heads, purifying them prior to their being led to the altar for sacrifice. Other Levite servants wiped the sheep with special drying cloths on the walk.

For the inspection I wore a finely embroidered robe and matching turban and carried a staff with a small crook covered with hammered gold in the shape of a ram's head. It was not my favorite thing to wear, but the ceremonies required the appropriate attire. On the first day of the festival, one of the twelve tavs was selected to lead the first of the lambs through the pool to the altar. I was hoping that it would not be me. I had had that honor once before, and I never liked the attention given the shepherd leading the first lamb to slaughter.

The inspection went without incident, and the area appeared to be well staffed and supplied. From the pool I went to the marketplace to see if Moses had heard any more talk of the immerser's location.

Nearing the area of Solomon's Court, where I had had conflict with Shabach years ago, I heard crashing and yelling, as if there was a fight. What I saw as I neared the columns was stunning. A man was pacing back and forth with a whip chasing livestock and overturning the tables of the money changers.

Over the years the Passover festival had grown, and hundreds of thousands of Hebrew pilgrims from many countries came to Jerusalem. Local money changers set up tables to exchange foreign coins for the local shekel or Roman denarius, usually at a very high rate.

I pushed through the crowd that had gathered to observe. They separated to make way for me because I looked so official in uniform. The crashing of tables continued, and the sound of coinage hitting the stones and rolling brought gasps from the growing crowd.

I heard a familiar, anguished voice crying out to remove the tables. I came to the front of the crowd and saw Yeshua holding a whip of cords, pacing back and forth, overturning tables while the money changers scattered from him, fearing his wrath and the whip he brandished. His voice was thunder as he yelled, "Be gone! Be gone!" He was rebuking them for turning his father's house into a marketplace!

I could see many of the tables out of his reach being cleared of coins by their owners and vacated to avoid the anger of the man I knew as Messiah. Was this the beginning of his campaign to free us? *How can this work?* I wondered. *This is not the behavior of a docile lamb.*

The crashing of tables stopped. Yeshua stood at the center of the debris he created as the money changers whose tables he had overturned crawled on the stones, gathering what they could. As insane as the sight was, he looked majestic standing still for a moment. His face was ablaze with indignation, his eyes burning! In a flash the anger seemed to disappear from his face as he walked toward the crowd, toward me.

As he approached I heard the pounding of feet running to the court, the temple guards.

Yeshua stopped in front of me and with a sad look said in a soft voice, "Eli, prepare the lambs well, for the time will come when the sacrifice will be sufficient." He walked past me into the crowd. I turned to watch him leave but lost sight of him almost immediately.

The leader of the temple guards, who had arrived, called out to me, asking, "Shepherd, tav, where did he go?"

I answered truthfully, "I am afraid I have lost sight of him."

After standing there for some time, wondering about what had just happened, the crowd dispersed, the temple guards looked bewildered, and the money changers were setting up their tables again to continue their thriving business. An unexplained sadness overtook me; what did he mean?

CHAPTER 31

THE IMMERSER

THE CROWD DISPERSED, and the lines of pilgrims formed again as the money changers set up their tables under the protection of the temple guards. It was certain that the guards were not there on temple orders as I saw each one pass by the tables and receive a coin. I was disgusted witnessing the commerce of the festival and the hypocrisy of the guards.

Embarrassed at that moment to be seen in ornate garments, I rushed back to my quarters and changed into my road clothes then headed to the market. Moses, Bidi, and the children were all in the booth; what a grand-looking family they were. They were all tall, brown, and had elegant beauty and grace that was hard to ignore. Walking up to the stalls, Moses saw me and said, "Why so sad, my brother?" Anyone hearing him would wonder how we could be brothers without understanding the family of our faith.

"There was a scene at the temple I observed that has me anguished."

Bidi stopped what she was doing and joined Moses. "What grieves you, Eli, my friend?"

"There was a man disrupting the money changers, crying out that the temple is being defiled by being turned into a marketplace." My voice displayed anguish.

"It is true that the money changers and lenders should be here and not there." Moses spoke, sweeping his arm, pointing at the grand market. "They should have stalls paid for like all legal merchants. We must display our licenses to do business, but those at the temple buy off the guards to set up their tables and animal stalls." Moses stated it with a bitterness in his tone. "It does not affect us very much because of what we sell, but it still hurts the legal market."

"Something must be done, but I am not sure that whipping them and overturning their tables will solve anything. The rules and laws must be changed, but who will do this thing? Surely one man cannot make a difference. Only our Messiah can make the changes we need," Bidi added.

I changed subjects and asked, "What news of the immerser have you heard?"

"The last we heard, he still had a small encampment with his followers just north at the Jordan," Moses said.

"That is where I shall head today and be back before the eve of the festival."

"Be careful. Tensions are high all over, and the Romans are quick to react," Bidi said.

How well I knew. I left the market and headed north, hoping to see my family camp on the way to find the immerser.

I found the Capernaum camp settled near the Cana tents and discovered my family with little effort. "Papa! You are here. How wonderful!" Sweet words from my precious daughter. The children were probably off playing with long-lost friends; Samuel was there and came up to me.

"Shalom, Eli, I am glad to see you," he said with a sincere voice. "What brings you to the camp? I thought you would be busy in preparation of the sacrifices."

"I have been assigned duty to roam about by the chazzen and make sure that preparations are going well. I have already been to the caves, and things are in order. I was headed toward the Jordan to see if I could locate the one called the immerser. It is said that he has announced the coming of Messiah. Some even say he is the prophet *Eliyahu* (Elijah) returned."

"That would fit with your narrative," Samuel said without contempt. "I am scheduled to meet with Nicodemus, the council of Pharisees, and

Sanhedrin early tomorrow. Since we are settled here, may I join you on your walk?" He looked at Sarah, and she nodded assent.

"Let us be off then," I said. "I welcome your company."

Samuel ducked back into the tent for a walking stick and a full water bladder. Exiting the tent, he kissed Sarah, stepped up to me, and said, "Let us find this prophet!" Without hesitation we headed toward the River Jordan.

We cleared the camp without speaking, and I had the feeling that conversation would come as soon as we were out of anyone's hearing. Finally breaking the silence, Samuel said, "I have been weighing your words and have taken them to heart." A jolt of joy hit me hearing his comment. "But," he continued, "I am not convinced that Messiah has come. My curiosity is piqued about this immerser you speak of. That is why I wished to accompany you. Word is that he wears clothing of camel hair and lives eating only locust and honey." We walked a bit further before I responded.

"I have heard much chatter about this presumed prophet, and it is said that he has a fairly large and zealous following," I said as we walked. The day was warming quickly, and we kept a good pace. There were many pilgrims passing us, returning from the Jordan, heading back to Jerusalem.

"Tell me, Eli, what does this rabbi that you and Sarah met proclaim? According to Sarah, his looks make him to be quite ordinary."

I smiled and asked, "What do the writings tell us Adonai told Samuel when King Saul would be replaced by the child warrior David?"

Samuel thought for a moment, smiled in return, and said, "Ah, Eli, you have me. If memory serves, what I have learned is that Adonai told Samuel we people are more concerned with appearances, but he knows the heart."

"Well said," I replied, returning his smile, and we continued along silently with Samuel in a pleasant mood.

We stopped to rest and eat a short while before the Jordan came into view, and we overheard some walking past us. "Loud voice...wild hair."

We knew we were getting close. Samuel stood as we were ready to resume walking. "Eli, do you believe that a man can be reborn as another the way some believe, that this prophet we seek is Elijah returned?"

"Samuel, I believe what is written and recorded, not rumor or gossip. Whoever this man is, I do not believe he is Elijah." My words were purposeful and firmly stated.

Nodding, Samuel said, "I believe as you do. Let us view this person with a good deal of skepticism."

It was not long until we saw a crowd gathered near the banks of the river. We approached cautiously, working our way through the group, following the voice that was crying out, "Repent! The kingdom of heaven is near!" We saw him on a rise near the water. A tall thin man with bare feet holding a crooked walking stick. His hair was long and matted; he was wearing only a loincloth. As we got closer, we could see that he was all wiry muscle, his voice a rumble.

Someone from the crowd yelled, "Are you Messiah?"

The wild-appearing man looked toward the sound of the voice with blazing eyes and said, "I am not he! I am just a man, a messenger. I have said it before and say it again, I am not fit enough to even tie his sandals. Repent and be immersed! Come forward now, sinner, and be cleansed. Enter the water with me."

Samuel and I stood there while three men and one woman drifted to the edge of the river. The immerser jumped off the rise and walked quickly to the four who had come forward. We heard him say, "Join me in the water," and he walked into the river, stopping when the water was waist-high. He turned to the four and bade them come forward, and one by one he immersed them fully in the river, saying, "Your sins have been washed away. Go, fast and sin no more."

Spotting Samuel, the immerser said, "Come, Pharisee, repent and be cleansed of your sin and join me."

Samuel turned to me, and asked, "How does he know I am a Pharisee?" There was a quiver of fear in Samuel's voice.

Smiling at my son-in-law, I said, "Well, for one, maybe he recognized your shawl. Is it not the same as the one all the Pharisees wear?"

He blushed with embarrassment and shouted at the immerser, "Who are you, and from where do you hail?"

Walking out of the water, the man came toward us, speaking, "Pharisee, are you among the brood of vipers that see not, hear not, and act not according to the law? Perhaps you are not sullied yet, so I will honor your request. I am *Yochanan ben Yikrias* (John, son of Zechariah), from the north hill country."

The man seemed quite normal as he spoke, alert and intelligent. Samuel asked, "By what authority do you perform *tivihla* (baptism) and offer cleansing?"

He answered, looking up to the heavens, "My authority comes from *Ve'Lohai Avraham, Yiz'Kach, HaYa'akov* (the God of Abraham, Isaac, and Jacob), the same God that you worship, and by his authority. I descend from the tribe of Aaron, as does this man beside you. I presume you are a Levite as well."

"You cannot claim power to forgive sin. Only Adonai has that authority!" Samuel said excitedly.

"This same one that you speak of walks among us today, and we are all unworthy of his forgiveness. Yet here I stand to tell you to repent and be immersed with the same authority as I immersed Yeshua."

"That is insane! That is blasphemy!" Samuel screamed, eyes bulging, spittle coming with every word.

"The invitation of repentance is always open, my cousin," the immerser said kindly. "Now forgive me. I must return to those with open minds and hearts." He walked away back toward the river, once again yelling in a thunderous voice, "Repent and be immersed, repent and be immersed!" Samuel stood there shaking, full of rage or fear—I could not tell which from the look on his face.

"Samuel, we have accomplished what we set out to do. We have seen him. Let us return to camp." I took his arm and led him back through the crowd toward Jerusalem and our camp.

We walked in silence for a long time, and finally Samuel said, "Eli, what if I am wrong and he is who he says he is, and Messiah is among us?"

"My son, you have just uttered the words of wisdom I have longed to hear." I wrapped my arm around his shoulder for a few steps, and we walked the rest of the way to camp in silence.

CHAPTER 32

THE PASSOVER

IT WAS JUST before sundown when we reached the camp outside Jerusalem where our family of pilgrims had set up. Traditionally the campgrounds were secured year after year in the same spot with occasional disputes on boundaries. The festival site was fairly calm, even though there were quite a few more camps than usual.

We were greeted with a warm welcome from Sarah and the children when we arrived at the tents. It was pleasant to see the family awaiting our return. "Samuel, Papa, you look tired. Come in and rest and have something to eat." We both collapsed onto thin pillows and had water and dried fruit to refresh us.

With the children sitting close, Sarah asked, "What was he like, the immerser?"

Samuel responded first. "He is an unusual man, wild one moment and gentle the next. He has many followers that actually look normal. We saw him immerse several, and we even had a conversation with him." Samuel was relating the events with much less emotion than he had displayed at the time.

Saul asked, "Is he big and furry with horns and pointed teeth?"

Samuel laughed. "No, son, he is rather plain-looking except for his clothes and his hair. He is tall and thin and really tough-looking."

Sweet little Rebekah chimed in. "What language does he speak? Can you understand him?"

"Yes, sweet girl, we understand every word because he speaks just like us. Sometimes he is a little loud, but he is easy to understand," Samuel, with a little smile, said. "Children, he is very much like me and your sabba, a little rough but smart." That got a laugh out of all. I was a bit amazed that Samuel spoke so kindly of the immerser. He then added, "His name is John, like your uncle in Hazor."

Rebekah, with a worried look on her face, asked, "Did you invite him to seder? Does he have a family to celebrate with?"

Sarah took over the conversation when she answered, "Little one, a man like that probably has many places to go and many people to celebrate with this Passover. After all, he is famous."

That got a smile from Rebekah, who then declared, "I am hungry. Can we eat soon?" Another round of laughter.

We ate a simple meal, and Samuel started helping Sarah build a small firepit outside the tent so that she could begin baking the *matzah* (unleavened bread) at sunrise. I had supplied two lambs that were with Jonathan and the Cana group. The rabbi would take the animals outside the camp to slaughter early and have one of his acolytes burn the inedible remains before bringing the roasting parts back to camp.

Before I left to return to the temple compound, Samuel pulled me aside. "There is something about that man that is under my skin and in my throat. I will talk with Nicodemus about him in the morning." He looked at me squarely and said, "Thank you, Eli, for being so strong when I can be such a loudmouthed fool. I am proud to be your son-in-law."

That took me by surprise, and I reached out to him and embraced him, saying, "I have two sons to be proud of. Sleep well tonight and have a sweet Passover if I cannot be back in time for the seder." After hugs all around, I left for the city and my little room.

Sleep was not easy that night. As tired as I was, my mind was active, trying to make sense of the connection between the immerser and Yeshua. Finally I fell into a fitful sleep that had me dreaming of the wholesale slaughter of the lambs. I woke up very early, donned my fancy tav regalia, and started wandering about the city in the dark. I could hear the bleating of the sheep as they were being led to their fate.

The formal rituals that would be taking place had become a moneymaker for the temple. Way before dawn Levites of all ranks were slaughtering sheep that were being butchered and prepared for sale at tents set up near the Sheep Gate.

Levites like me were chosen for specific tasks to satisfy the needs of many thousands of pilgrims who made the journey to Jerusalem. The lambs that were bathed the day before were the first to be sacrificed. Nominal prayers were said as their throats were cut and the blood collected. The skins were stacked for transport to the tribe of scribes that would prepare them in an ancient manner. They were to be used as scrolls for sacred Torahs and sold to synagogues in villages that could afford them.

The usable meat was taken to the tent at the Sheep Gate, where pilgrims would line up to buy whatever choice pieces they could afford. The offal was collected and sold to merchants who processed the unusable parts to make meat pastes that were cooked and sold to the poor. The collected blood was stored in ox bladders and sold in small quantities for all to mark their dwellings so that the Angel of Death would pass over their households on the sacred night as dictated by *Ahyeh* (I Am) to Moses ages earlier.

The fat was collected and burned in the temple continually throughout the festival as a fragrant offering. Early that morning the smell of the burning fat would awaken everyone in the city, the aroma that signaled the start of the Passover festival. Truly a profitable enterprise for the temple and the high priest.

Fortunately my duty had not changed, so I was free to roam about. I was carrying dried fruit and water that I consumed as I walked along. The market was empty as prescribed by law, so the quiet was eerie in the place where so much activity usually took place. I sat on the steps of the temple porch, watching the sun come up over the city, which was coming to life. Footsteps in increasing numbers began to be heard as the business of the temple began.

I made my way to the Sanhedrin court, where Samuel was called to a meeting with other Pharisees. He did not know the purpose of the meeting, but I wanted to greet him before he went in with the "brood of vipers," as the immerser called them. I understood the comparison because over the years the men of law and the men of faith had become less interested in the people they represented and more concerned with their own power and wealth. Their wall of protection was the law that was always interpreted in a manner that best suited them, not the general public. Infighting and political maneuvering had become an art, and only the very best would work their way to the top and stay there.

Of course the most astute and ruthless were always the winners. This Nicodemus whom Samuel was to meet was an interesting man by all that I had heard. He was a Hebrew of Greek origins, and it was said that his family could trace their roots back to the time when *Malcha Hadassah* (Queen Esther) overcame the extinction of all followers of Adonai. He had a reputation as a brilliant and shrewd interpreter of the law and was almost impossible to beat in debate.

It was not long before I saw Samuel approaching in full Pharisee dress, including the round hat with black and white woven trailing scarf. He did look majestic for a man so young. It delighted me in a selfish way that he was married to my daughter. "*Chag Sameah* (Good Holiday), Eli," he said with a slightly worried look as he approached me.

Repeating his greeting, I added, "What is wrong, my son? You look concerned."

"This man, Nicodemus, is a legend and a bull of a man. I have seen him only once as he crushed a young student of the law into dust with his legal wit," Samuel said softly.

"As I have told you before, be quick to listen and slow to respond. What does this meeting concern?" I asked.

"There is no telling. It could be on a myriad of subjects. It is rather unusual to have called a meeting the morning of the Passover."

"Samuel, come," a voice bellowed from the steps. Walking up was a man who seemed to grow larger with every stride. He was an imposing figure, taller than me, and with the Pharisee raiment, he looked the giant that his reputation foretold.

"Sir," Samuel said, standing erect and displaying a confidence that I knew was brittle. "I would like to present my father-in-law, Elijah ben Ezra, a tav of the temple."

"Yes, I recognized the uniform. *Chag Sameah*, Elijah ben Ezra," he boomed.

I nodded and replied, "And to you as well."

Turning to Samuel, he said, "Let us not be late, even though we will probably be first to arrive." He broke into a knowing smile. With that the two of them headed to the Sanhedrin council chamber.

As early as it was, I could hear the buzz of humanity that would soon be a din of people crowding the temple area. Walking slowly to the entrance of the Hall of Hewn Stone where the Greater Sanhedrin were meeting was an old man assisted by a young servant. The young man was holding one of the old man's arms, helping his feeble steps. "Stop!" the old man creaked at his young assistant. He pointed a thin finger at me and said, "Come here, shepherd." I took two steps toward the pair, and the old man looked at me and said, "Did you ever find that boy you were looking for many years ago?"

Leaning into the man's face, I recognized beyond the ravages of time the man I had met at this very place so many years ago. "Yes, tav, it is me, Phineas ben Zev. Like you, I am amazed that I have survived so long. Did you ever find that boy for whom you were searching?"

"Indeed I did, Master Phineas. Actually he found me. He is alive and well, and he is in Jerusalem. He is the man who caused such a scene by overturning the tables of the money changers. That boy has grown into a quite a man."

Hearing that news, Phineas began to shake and whispered to me, "He is Messiah. I have lived to know he has come. Thank you, my friend. I must go to my meeting, and soon I will sleep having seen him." He nudged the young man, and they moved off. I stood there feeling both sad and happy for Phineas. He knew, all those years ago, that Yeshua was Messiah!

I wandered through the temple and the city all day, looking for Yeshua and the fishermen with no success. As the afternoon crept toward evening, I checked in with Shabach. "Go to your family and enjoy tonight's seder." I thanked him for his generosity and strode out to the Cana camp.

The smell of roasting lamb started enveloping Jerusalem, and the smoke from the pilgrim camps created a succulent cloud over the valley. My mouth was watering as I pulled back the flap of the family tent, which had blood smeared around the opening. It announced my almost unexpected arrival. "Papa! Sabba!" Happy voices greeted me as I entered.

Samuel came to me smiling and said, "Before you question me about the meeting, I will tell you it was interesting, and I did well. We can talk of it later after seder."

Samuel led me to a little stool and took my staff, turban, and outer garment, laying them aside. With little Saul's help, he washed my feet. I choked with emotion as the joy of being with family on Passover gripped me. "Since the food is ready, let us begin," Samuel announced.

There were clay pots filled with the traditional and symbolic foods and skins of wine filled to the stretching point. We all reclined on pillows surrounding the low wooden table, ready to begin the service. All eyes focused on Samuel.

As the religious leader of the family, Samuel was wearing his intricately woven tallit over his head, and he began. Holding up a small goblet of wine, he recited the blessing, and we all took a small sip. Looking at his young son, Samuel said, "Saul, do you know why we celebrate this festival?"

"Yes, Father, it is to remind us that we were slaves in Egypt and Adonai freed us."

"How did he free our people?" asked Samuel.

"By using Moses and Aaron to call down plagues on the pharaoh."

"Very good son. Now how many plagues were there?"

"Ten, Papa," said Saul proudly.

"Why did we put blood on the tent opening tonight?" asked Samuel of his handsome little boy.

"So that the Angel of Death will pass over all of Adonai's followers tonight, Papa," said Saul, smiling broadly at knowing the answers.

"That is correct, Saul. You have done well."

Samuel continued the narrative of the Passover, highlighting the plagues and the loss of the pharaoh's army after the children of Israel crossed the *Yam Suph* (Sea of Reeds). At the conclusion of the story, we began eating the lamb, matzah, bitter herbs, and a mixture of nuts and honey symbolizing the mortar that was used to construct the pyramids. It was a relaxed evening and a filling meal. Just enough was prepared so there was no waste to be burned.

At the end of the meal, I said my good nights and embraced all, ready to head back to the academy, and looked at Samuel, who nodded.

Samuel stood and said, "Abba Eli, may I speak with you a moment?" I was taken by surprise as it was rare that Samuel ever called me abba.

"Of course, my son." We stepped out of the tent and took a few steps, and we faced each other.

He seemed excited as he started to speak. "Nicodemus has asked me to be his personal assistant and wants to be my mentor. He thinks I have great potential to eventually sit on the Supreme Council." He stood there waiting for my response, stiff as a rod with anticipation of my reaction.

"That is a wonderful compliment and something you should consider very carefully." I spoke with a serious tone. "You must discuss it with Sarah as it will make significant changes in your homelife and the profitable business you run. You will be required to spend a lot of time in Jerusalem."

"Yes, I know these things, and I will speak with Sarah tonight when the children are sleeping." He was a little less rigid.

"Samuel, you have a great future no matter what path you choose. You are already a success beyond most men of your age," I said, measuring my words. "Pray to the Almighty for guidance, and weigh the words of your wife very seriously in your decision." Then I added, "Jerusalem and its politics are dangerous to all who participate. Add the danger of Rome and you have a volatile combination."

"I have another meeting with Nicodemus tomorrow to get more details of his offer. I will heed your advice and be very careful to listen more and speak less." He said that not just for my benefit but also with sincerity.

"That is all I can ask and advise, my son. Now return to your family, and have that conversation with Sarah."

"Yes, Abba Eli," he said and startled me with a quick, strong embrace before he returned to the tent.

It was a beautiful night as I headed back to my room at the academy. I was happy for Samuel that a man of such renown as Nicodemus would choose him to mentor. But I could not help but worry about the savage reality of Jerusalem and how vulnerable he and his family would be if he said yes to the offer. My mind played every possibility on the road to my bed.

CHAPTER 33

THE MENTOR

THE MORNING WAS beautiful, cool, and dry. Through the tiny window of my little room, I saw a clear sky, still dark and full of stars. Dawn would lighten the view in less than an hour. My first thought was of Samuel and his meeting with Nicodemus, the Teacher of Israel, a leading Pharisee, and a key member of the ruling council. As highly as I thought of Samuel, I was concerned that he would not be strong enough to survive in the nest with all the vipers, as the immerser called them.

I bathed, dressed in ritual garments, and met with Shabach for breakfast. "Shalom, chazzen. How did we perform during the lead up to services yesterday?" I broke a piece of unleavened bread from a flat and scooped up some soft cheese and honey.

"All reports were positive, even with the record number of lambs that were offered for sacrifice. The temple coffers are heavy with coin today. You have my permission to continue your light duty."

"Thank you, my friend," I said, bowing slightly. I told him about the offer from Nicodemus to Samuel.

"That old bear is tough but fair. He actually listens before making decisions. He will make a good mentor to young Samuel. If your son-in-law accepts the position, he will have to find living quarters here in the city," Shabach said, taking a sip of morning wine.

"He has not made the decision yet. When I left last night, Sarah did not know of it. He is meeting with Nicodemus this morning for more details of the conditions and expectations." We then spoke of a few other things, including the immerser and Messiah. Released by Shabach, I was free to leave the academy to search and learn.

My mission for the Magi was still first and foremost, so I had to try and locate Yeshua. I was not sure he was still in Jerusalem. Once again the first place I headed was the market, where news and gossip were plentiful. Morning light was brightening the city as I left the academy.

"You know, my brother, you would be noticed less if you did not wear such ornate clothing." That was Moses's greeting when he saw me near his stall. He was weighing some spice for a woman who appeared to be richly dressed. She turned, and I noticed that she was adorned with Herod's symbol of slavery: a ring through her nose and one through her left ear, which were attached with a small chain.

She was young and in a flirtatious way looked at me and said, "You are a fine-looking specimen. My master should have more sheep to tend. What is your name?"

Uncomfortable with Herod knowing anything about me, I looked down at her and answered, "I am Tav, formerly known as Eighteen."

She frowned, saying, "Impudent man!" and brushed by me, disappearing into the morning crowd of shoppers.

"I see you continue to make new friends, Eighteen." Moses laughed as he spoke.

"I am more interested in finding Messiah and his followers than having anything to do with the evil in that palace. Have you any news for me?" I asked with a smile.

"You are not the only one seeking him today."

"What do you mean? What have you heard?" I asked with concern.

"Just after dawn, as we all were preparing to open, a scribe in the employ of the very same Pharisee we were speaking of paid a visit to every stall. Nicodemus wants word out that he is interested in meeting the man some are calling Messiah."

"That is interesting. I wonder—if Messiah does get the message, will he meet with a Pharisee?"

"Ha! My friend, if he is Messiah, he already has the message!" I laughed at Moses's wit. "Where do your duties take you today, so that if I hear anything, our son Daniel can reach you?" Moses asked, as a true friend would.

"Thank you, brother. My plan is to circle in and out of the temple area all day, and with this costume I wear, I should be easy to find."

"I will dispatch him immediately if need be" was Moses's response as I turned to leave the market.

Thinking that Yeshua, fearless as he was, just might go meet Nicodemus at the Hall of Hewn Stone, I headed to the temple area. The crowds around the entire Temple Mount began to get dense, and I realized how difficult it would be to find anyone. The hall was a magnificent structure built into the north wall of the temple area. The members sat on benches carved out of marble. They were a mixture of men from different regions elected by their towns and villages to represent their people.

The hall was quiet as they did not convene during Shabbat or festivals. The crowd was thinner nearing the hall, so it might have been easier to spot Yeshua. There were knots of men gathering in small groups, but none I recognized. Strolling casually around the courtyard outside of the hall, I realized that with my official shepherd's garb, I would not be welcomed into any gathering near the hall.

My decision at that moment was to return to the academy and get into simple clothing. Passing one of the support columns, I almost ran directly into the sons of Zebedee, John and James. "Hail, Eli!" John exhorted as we all stopped short of colliding. "Well, shepherd, you look quite elegant in your temple attire," he said in a teasing manner. "Do you remember my brother James? He was there the morning the centurion came to ask our rabbi to heal his servant."

"Shalom, James." He nodded back in response. James was physically much smaller than his brother and much more reserved. He stood there, stern-looking, with his arms at his sides and his gaze at me intense. "Is the rabbi nearby?" I asked, not wanting to speak Yeshua's name for fear of bringing attention to him.

John answered, "He is wandering around the city. He loves meeting people. We are going to the meeting place of the Sanhedrin to find a man by the name of Nicodemus."

"What? Why?" I asked with concern in my voice.

"Our friend the rabbi has been asked by this man to meet," he said calmly.

"Is that wise? This Nicodemus is the lead teacher in all of Israel and is considered the greatest of the Great Sanhedrin. Could this be a trap?" I spoke, not shielding my concern.

"Eli, you do not know our leader as we do. There is no man that can trick him, no man that can trip him up. He is meeting with the Teacher of Israel tonight to teach, not be taught." The words John spoke sobered me immediately. Of course how could any man defeat Adonai in the flesh?

Looking at the brothers with a knowing smile, I said, "Yes, I understand and agree. May I attend this meeting?"

Without pause John said, "I am afraid not, my friend. This will be a private lesson. Have heart. You will have your time with our master. We must be off." The brothers left me standing alone in the middle of a crowd of pilgrims as they walked back to the hall. Somewhat dejected but not surprised, I rushed back to my room to change clothes and attempt anonymity.

Dressing in plain shepherd's clothing, I stuffed my tav insignia next to my scroll with orders from Shabach into my skyt and started back to the hall. I was hoping to see Samuel and find out about his meeting with Nicodemus.

My day was spent in vain trying to find Messiah, his followers, Samuel, or Nicodemus. I circled the temple grounds three times before going back to the market. Moses let his son Daniel go free for the afternoon to help me locate any of the men I sought. As twilight approached I returned to hear of any news. Moses and Bidi had heard nothing, and as Daniel returned to the stall, he was as frustrated as all of us.

As a thank-you to Daniel, I handed him a tin coin with the impression of a tav overlaid with a shepherd's crook. It was not currency but a token minted for the temple tavs to pass as a symbol of favor. It was essentially worthless, but Daniel accepted it gladly as a trophy of friendship.

"My friends, thank you for your diligence and help. I will go to my family camp for the evening seder and return tomorrow to continue my search," I announced to the beautiful family.

"Shalom," they all said in unison, a sweet sound as I left the market.

It was dark when I arrived at the Cana camp and the family tent. I entered to the greetings of Sarah and the children, but there was no Samuel. Noticing my glance around the tent, Sarah spoke before I could ask about his absence. "Papa, Samuel was summoned to a meeting with Nicodemus just before we began the meal." The look on her face was not one of concern but acceptance.

"Where did he go?" I asked more out of curiosity than the desire to follow him since I had already been informed by John that I was not invited.

"I do not know where. One of Nicodemus's servants arrived with a note to Samuel to accompany his man. No location was included."

"Very well then. Since the head of the household is not here, I shall take his place as the head of the family and conduct the prayers for the meal." Looking at Saul, I asked, "Why do we celebrate this night?" With that question we began the seder. The children were delighted that the festivities had begun, and Sarah looked at me with her mother's smile.

The evening progressed, and just before the children were to be sent off to sleep, Samuel returned. He stepped into the tent with a smile on his face and said, "Shalom, family!" The children squealed with delight at his appearance. After hugs and some chatter, the little ones were sent to their tent section to settle down for the night.

Samuel removed his cloak. Rachel took off his sandals and washed his feet. Settling down on one of the pillows, he told us of the evening. "I was taken to a small, isolated camp south of here, near the Mount of Olives. Papa Eli, are you familiar with the place?"

"Yes, I am," I answered. "It is quite secluded as you go up, and it is not an easy walk."

Samuel continued. "There is a small temporary camp where Yeshua and his followers have been staying during the festival. Nicodemus struggled getting up the hill, but he is so strong we did not slow the whole time as his servant led us."

"When we arrived, they washed our feet with a little water and pieces of cloth to dry them. I was really humbled by their effort to make us comfortable."

"How many of them were there?"

"I counted nine when the three of us arrived. Another thing that struck me was that they treated Nicodemus's servant as a guest, equally, as they treated us," Samuel said enthusiastically.

"That is unusual, I must admit." There was surprise in my voice.

"They offered all three of us a meal that was an abbreviated seder. There was a little wine and roasted fowl of some sort that we ate sitting on little piles of brush. There was little talk as we ate. Then an amazing conversation took place."

"How so?" asked Sarah.

"Nicodemus asked, 'Why did you have us come all the way out here to meet? We could have had a more comfortable and secluded place in or near the city.' Yeshua answered, 'Teacher of Israel, I want to protect your reputation at this time until you understand the import of what I am doing.'

"With no hesitation Nicodemus said that he believed Yeshua was a teacher from Adonai because of the miracles that have been attributed to him. Then Yeshua said something that is burned into my brain. He said that no one will be able to see the kingdom of Adonai unless they are born again."

I was not sure I had heard Samuel correctly and asked him to repeat what he had just related word for word, exactly as Yeshua had said it. With great care Samuel tried to repeat the conversation that took place next but could not. What he did say was, "Yeshua challenged Nicodemus by telling him that he only understands what he has seen and learned of things in this world, not heaven. He taught the Teacher of Israel that we cannot understand heavenly things because we have not been to heaven, only the one who has can. Then he said that the 'Son of Man' is the only one to have been to heaven because he came from heaven, and we should trust him." Samuel paused to take some deep breaths as if he could not continue, as if he had forgotten to breathe because he was talking so excitedly.

"Please go on, Samuel. Take your time. Tell us what you can," I said with a smile, in a reassuring tone. Sarah sat there quietly with tears rolling down her beautiful cheeks.

Samuel paused a few more moments then continued. "Yeshua then said that Adonai loved us so much that he sent his son to save the world, and we could get to heaven by believing in him. That was the moment I knew that he is our Messiah!"

Samuel looked at me and said, "Papa Eli, I now believe what you have told me. I believe that you were there when he was born. I am so sorry that I doubted you and had to see him before I believed." Samuel lowered his head as if to emphasize his shame for not believing my story and sobbed. He looked up at me tearfully and said, "Now I know for sure that we live in a dark world, and the Light of Heaven has appeared to us, and we are truly helpless without him."

Reaching out to Samuel, I laid my hand on his shoulder and softly asked, "What happened next?"

"I cannot really remember. After realizing I was in the presence of Messiah, it seems as if I was lost in a humming cloud as words were spoken around me. Before too long the three of us that had ventured up the mount were heading back down. It was like a dream, but I know, in my heart, it was real.

"At the bottom of the hill, Nicodemus stopped, looked at me and his servant, and said, 'Speak of this only to those whom you trust.' Looking directly at his servant, he added, 'Be very careful with your words, my boy. They can cause you grief. Now let us all go home and absorb what we have just witnessed.'"

Samuel sat quietly with a serene look on his face, and Sarah was the first to speak. "What are your plans now, my love?"

Thoughtfully he looked at his wife. "I believe that I have been called by Adonai and his son to join Nicodemus to protect and defend Messiah. I know that this will bring additional hardships to the family and business, but it is my duty to be obedient."

Sarah stood and walked over to Samuel, who rose in response, and she said, "Our people have waited long for his arrival. Yes, we must all be obedient to his call. I am with you, dear husband. I shall be the anchor at home while you fulfill your duty to Messiah and Nicodemus. I know enough about your business to be of assistance there as well."

With a broad smile on his face, Samuel said, "You could probably run the synagogue too, but we both know that the old men in the village will never listen to you. However, you now have more than enough in your charge. I will talk with my father when we return home to solidify your position with the business."

Still sitting on the pillow, I was bursting with pride at these young ones who had just made life-changing decisions with certainty and commitment. Standing up, I stepped over to the two of them, laid my hands on their shoulders, and said, "My heart is filled with joy that you are now with me, and we are on the same mission." Choking with emotion, I added, "I must return to the city and resume my tasks." I left the camp.

CHAPTER 34

THE ZEALOT

It was late when I arrived at the academy, yet I was wide awake and energized with the report from Samuel. So much had occurred in such a brief time I decided to start writing my dispatch to the Magi even though it was months before my meeting with their envoy. The writing engrossed me, and by the time I stood up to stretch, it was dawn. Lying down on my pallet for a few moments to rest, I fell into a deep sleep.

A loud pounding on my door awakened me, with an accompanying voice. "Shepherd tav, Master Eli, arise, come quickly." I scrambled up, immediately on alert, and opened the door, and a servant said, "Come quickly. Our chazzen needs you!" I grabbed my skyt and staff, still in my clothes from the night before; we ran to Shabach's office.

"That will be all," Shabach told the servant, who closed the door as he left. "Some disturbing news just arrived from Herod's palace," he said with concern in his voice.

Alarmed, I asked, "What has happened?"

"A man has been arrested outside of the palace, and they are calling him a zealot. Word is that a Roman soldier stopped a man to question, and the man attempted to run. He was captured, and during the struggle with the soldier, the zealot is accused of striking the servant of Roman authority. They are taking him before Pilate at this very moment."

With panic in my voice, I said, "Oh no! They can call anyone a zealot who does not agree with them or act swiftly enough on their commands. I must go see if it is anyone we know or even one of Messiah's followers. It would be just like Pilate to use any excuse to punish one of his followers."

"Go!" Shabach commanded. "Find out what you can, and come back with news." Without hesitation I fled the room and the compound.

It took me just a few minutes to arrive at Herod's palace at the northwest corner of the walled city. A crowd was gathered outside the praetorium adjacent to the palace where Pilate had his quarters and meted out Roman justice. To make sure the crowd did not get unruly, Herod's guards and a squad of Roman soldiers were keeping the pavement in front of the praetorium clear. I pushed through the crowd and was rewarded with vigorous elbowing in return.

Making my way to the front of the growing gathering, I saw a young man I did not recognize on his knees, head down, face dripping blood. My breath caught, followed by an anguished sigh of relief that it was not Yeshua or one of his followers. A centurion came out of the building and approached the two soldiers standing over the man. After a brief conversation, the soldiers lifted the man, who looked like no more than a ragged hill farmer, a boy really, and dragged him into the praetorium. I asked the people around me in the crowd who the man was and was met with silent stares.

I was glad that the young man was not one of Yeshua's fishermen friends but was still concerned about the punishment that Pilate would deliver. Striking a Roman soldier was serious; the young man could be scourged or worse. Before too long the centurion, soldiers, and their prisoner appeared at the top of the building at an open area of the building's parapet. The crowd immediately started chanting, "*Rachamin! Rachamin!* (Mercy! Mercy!)"

The centurion raised his hand to quiet the crowd, and except for a rumble of murmurings, quiet resulted. "This prisoner has been found guilty of sedition and has been sentenced to death." The two guards grabbed the man, whose hands had been lashed to his sides, and threw him off the top of the building. The young man screamed until he hit the pavement. The crowd gasped, moaned, then started wailing, "*Resah! Resah!* (Murder! Murder!)"

I stood there in momentary shock at the scene as the soldiers and guards started advancing toward the crowd. The throng disappeared so rapidly that I was left standing alone at the edge of the pavement and in no time was surrounded by at least a dozen armed men. One of Herod's guards stepped in front of me and shouted, "Why are you still here? Are you with the condemned man? Would you like to follow him and fly?" He kept inching toward me, his voice getting louder as he showed off his bravery to an unarmed man.

Once again I had reason to boil with rage at Rome and her so-called justice. Keeping my anger in check, I stood my ground and replied in an authoritative voice, "I am here under orders from the temple."

"Ha! You, old man? You look like an old shepherd that just rolled out of the fields. I ask again, who are you?" His tone was almost a scream; he was upset that I was not showing fear.

"I am a shepherd, a tav of the temple, here under orders from the chief chazzen. My orders are in my pouch. If you would like, I will present them to you," I said calmly.

The guard looked like he was going to strike me when a Roman soldier with obvious authority said to the guard, "Let him show his credentials." The guard backed away seething, and I slowly reached into my skyt. I presented the Roman my silver tav pin and the scroll with Shabach's seal.

"These seem to be in order. You are free to go," he said, returning my scroll and pin. The Roman looked at the guards and said, "Return to your posts immediately!" The guard was glaring as he signaled his men back to the palace. Turning back to me, the Roman asked me, "Why are you still standing here, shepherd?"

I felt the irony, but I nodded and said in a clear voice, "I want to thank you, sir." He just stood there, probably realizing that a Hebrew had never thanked him for anything. "What will become of the body?" I asked.

"It will lie there for three days as an example to all of Jerusalem that Rome will not tolerate any infraction of its rule." He turned and marched away, leaving me alone in a city that otherwise was teeming with happy pilgrims. The broken body of the young man was guarded by two Roman soldiers.

Slowly and sadly I made my way back to Shabach's quarters, exhausted from the execution and lack of sleep. Telling what I observed, he blanched and told me that he was going to draft an appeal to Pilate for the body to be buried before sundown in a pauper's grave outside the city. I asked, "Chazzen, as one of your tavs, I ask permission to act as your messenger and deliver the plea to Pilate."

He looked at me, a question etched on his sullen face, and asked, "Why would you request such lowly duty, my friend?"

"I want to look that butcher in the eye knowing that Messiah is among us, and we have no fear." I spoke with anger and disgust pouring out of me.

Shabach looked at me for a few seconds, looked down, and started writing on a scroll. Without looking up, he said, "Bathe and get into your best uniform. Return to me within the hour." As quickly as I could, I headed for the baths. On the way I told a servant to get me a fresh uniform showing all my rank and to leave it in my quarters.

In less than an hour, I was standing before the chazzen. In his office was a young Aleph dressed in a new uniform. Shabach looked at the young man then back at me, "This is Seven, our top Aleph in the current class. Since they are about to graduate, this would be a good teaching opportunity for someone that might replace me someday." I looked at the boy, who was almost as big as me, and he had a smile on his face upon hearing Shabach's compliment. "Number Seven, wipe that childish grin off your face and pay attention."

Looking back at me, he said, "Eli, he accompanies you as my eyes so that if you are seized by Pilate, I will know it immediately. If neither of you return by the sixth hour, I will assume the worst and dispatch another message to Pilate." The look on Seven's face changed to bleached stone.

"Be very careful with this snake Pilate. It would take very little, even with your rank, to have you wrapped in chains. As it is, this request will probably irritate him, so keep your tongue, my friend. It is only because you are my friend and I love you as a brother that I honor your desire to face our common enemy."

"Thank you, Shabach. I will return with his answer." I held out my hand, he gave me the scroll, and I left for the praetorium, Number Seven at my heels.

We marched in unison like military men to the praetorium, passing the two guards and the body. At the arched entrance to the building were four more fully armed guards, complete with shield, gladius, and pilum, the sleek throwing spear that could be used to stab or throttle.

Stopping in front of the guards, I announced, "I am here with a petition for Pilate from the temple chazzen."

A guard stepped forward, looked me up and down, and said scornfully, "That is very fancy dress for a shepherd. If we get the command to cut you into little pieces, I will take that gold ram's head off your stick." He smiled an evil smile and called one of the other guards over. "Wait here," he said to the three of us and disappeared into the fortress.

The guard looked as young as Seven, and I noticed sweat was pouring down his face from under the metal helmet he wore. In a calm voice, I asked, "How long must we wait?"

"I am forbidden to talk to anyone but a Roman," the boy said nervously.

I took a half step toward the young guard. "When I was your age, a soldier like you killed my best friend for no reason at all. He was unarmed and just seemed to be in the soldier's way. Would you do that, soldier of Rome?"

The boy just stood there with stiff posture, unmoving, but I saw his face change as different emotions worked their way through his mind. Face-to-face we stood for a few moments, both of us rigid, staring at each other, until he broke his gaze and looked away.

"You there, shepherd! Pilate summons you!" I turned toward a gruff voice attached to a grizzled soldier covered with battle scars standing at the mouth of the building, pointing to the inside of the structure. I led Seven and followed the warrior to a huge staircase at the right as we entered the building. He led us up to the next landing, an open area overlooking a garden in the middle of the building. I was thinking that the Romans were great architects as we were led to Pilate.

The prefect of Judea sat in a huge chair that was more of a throne than a seat. He was flanked by two well-armed guards and a slave waving a giant feather fan over the man. As he was a member of the wealthy Pontii family, I wondered how much this posting cost Pilate, or if he was being punished. Either way he was the arm of Roman law, and we were under his rule.

A scribe approached and said, "The venerable governor asks that you present him with your request." I lifted the scroll and started toward Pilate; both guards flanking him unsheathed their short swords and took a step forward to protect their ruler.

Pilate actually laughed and said, "Relax. This is a shepherd with a piece of parchment." He looked at me and said, "Give the note to the scribe." I did then stepped back.

The scribe broke the seal and handed the open scroll to Pilate. He read the short note then handed the parchment back to the scribe. Pilate stood and approached me with an amused look. "Your old leader sends a well-worn shepherd, a tav, with a note. How does it feel to be a lowly messenger after all these years of service to the temple?"

"Governor, I chose this duty to reflect the value of the life that was taken," I said as flatly as I could.

"Do you know this dead man who has stained my pavement?" His speech patterns made him sound like a feminine dandy.

Controlling my contempt for Rome, I answered, "I do not, but our custom is to bury the dead quickly, and as a father, I appeal to you for this gift of mercy." He looked at me intently for what seemed a long time before speaking.

"Very well, shepherd, you may have the body as a festival gift to the temple shepherds." Pilate nodded at the scribe, who unfolded a small table, took a stylus and ink pouch out of his carry bag, and began writing. The governor took his seat, leaving us standing there while the scribe wrote Pilate's order.

I ventured to speak and said, "Governor, on behalf of the temple and my people, I thank you for your gift."

He leaned forward and asked, "Who are you, tav?"

"I am Elijah ben Ezra of Cana, a shepherd and judge," I answered with my voice showing no pride.

"Ha! A judge no less. Shabach shows me respect. I like that. You may go. I will have a copy of the order sent to him by messenger. Take the body and make sure they clean up the mess." He stood and left the area.

Looking at Seven, I nodded and said, "We have information for our chazzen." We gladly left the praetorium.

CHAPTER 35

THE BATON

After returning to the academy and giving the update to Shabach, I went back to my quarters, took off the fancy uniform, collapsed onto my pallet, and fell asleep. The dusk shofar blast awakened me, and I realized that I was indeed an old man—an old shepherd, as Pilate called me. A jolt of fear hit me when I realized that the Romans were probably on the hunt for anyone hinting of insurrection. I had to get a warning to Yeshua and his followers about the morning's events.

Dressing quickly, I headed to the little camp at the Mount of Olives. Samuel's description of the location of the camp was perfect, and it was dark with full moonlight before I arrived at the campsite and found it deserted. The only signs that they had been there were the little piles of brush that they had sat on. Fear gripped me as I thought that they might have been captured or worse.

I stopped breathing, just stood there thinking of possibilities, when the thought of an old song we used to sing as children came to me.

> *You are the one who performs miracles.*
> *You display your power to the people.*
> *Your mighty arm redeemed the children of Jacob and Joseph.*

Calm spread through me as I hung on those words. *Of course,* I thought, *he was not captured or harmed. He must be moving about to teach and perform more miracles.*

Believing that they were safe, I decided to go to camp and see the children. On the way down the mount, a whispery voice called out, "Where are your sheep?"

I stopped moving and said, "Who are you?"

Instead of an answer, I heard a breath of a question again. "Where are your sheep?" I could not discern where the voice was coming from, so I began moving cautiously down the hill.

Keeping my staff in front of me to aid my descent, I also knew that it could be used as a defensive weapon should the need arise. Yet the calm I felt when the song came to mind persisted, and I felt no fear. Once more I heard the soft "Where are your sheep?"

My response was spontaneous, and I sang, "My sheep rest in their fields under the protection of the God of Abraham, Isaac, and Jacob!" I continued walking confidently toward the light of the camps that were twinkling from the fires at the base of the Mount of Olives.

The voice did not call out to me again; in a short while, I arrived at the camp. Standing outside the tent where Samuel and Sarah were still eating the evening meal, I announced myself so as not to startle them, and the tent flap opened. "Papa Eli, what a pleasant surprise. We were just finishing the meal, and we do have some left. Please come and eat so we do not have to place it in the fire."

Sarah had the children fetch some water and had them assist her washing my feet while Samuel set some of the remaining food on a tin platter. I reclined on one of the small pillows, observing the Passover regulations. "I am so happy to be here with you, my family. This is turning out to be a memorable Passover. Can I get a hug from my beautiful grandchildren?" Rebekah and Saul got up and came crashing into me, forcing me onto my back. What a joy it was embracing the future!

After the hugging, the children retired to the next tent area. I asked, "Samuel, any news about your position with Nicodemus? And you, Sarah, what are your thoughts about all of this?"

Sarah responded first with "Papa, I have prayed and thought of every aspect of this since it was dropped on me. This is the most important time in the history of the world, with Messiah walking among us. It would be selfish and foolish not to do everything possible, whatever is necessary to tell everyone about Messiah and what he means for all of us."

"So you would support Samuel living away from home for half of the year?" I asked.

With a laugh Sarah said, "Papa, I grew up with a father that was gone about half of the year. Why would I not follow my mother's example of a selfless marriage?" She continued looking at me with a sweet smile on her face.

Returning her smile, I said, "You state the obvious, and I was blind to see it. But now, my beautiful daughter, you delight me with your wisdom."

Samuel continued the conversation. "My father will be a little hesitant to accept the partnership of a woman. However, once he recognizes the brilliance my wife possesses, he will not only accept the change but relish the opportunity of having someone near to assist. My brother has been growing into a more seasoned ambassador and can interact with the caravans."

"Have you mentioned this to the children yet?" I asked.

"Not yet, Papa. When we get home to Capernaum and after we speak to Samuel's father and mother, that would be the best time to begin the process of change." Sarah's look was steady and her words unwavering.

Samuel added, "My parents should be solidly behind this whole idea. They love Nicodemus. My father actually believes that Nicodemus should be the king of Israel instead of that murderer Herod."

I stood, getting ready to return to the city, and said, "I wonder what he will say when you tell him that the king is here but has yet to put on his crown." They stood, we exchanged hugs, and I started back to the city. The full moon was casting a beautiful light on the camp, and my path to Jerusalem was bathed in a glow of lunar light.

I was thinking about going back home in a few days, looking forward to seeing Jonathan and telling him all that had happened, when two figures approached me from the left, coming at an angle and speed I immediately knew was trouble. "Stop! Please do not hurt me!" I yelled with ample fear in my voice while dropping my staff to the side. I raised my hands and said, "I am a poor old shepherd, but you can have everything I own. Please do not injure me so I can look after my sheep."

They slowed their approach and stopped within reaching distance. Their faces were not clearly visible in the moonlight, and the one to my left said, "Hand me your pouch now!"

I whimpered. "Of course." Lowering my hands, I feigned removing the shoulder strap with my left hand while grasping the wood baton I had kept with me for the past eighteen years.

Turning to the left, as if removing my skyt, I spun to the right, swinging the baton backhand and hitting the thief to my left, where I thought his ear would be. As soon as I made contact with the thief's head, I continued to my right in a downward motion and thrust the baton into the gut of the thief to my right. As the thief on the right doubled over, he fell on top of the other man, both landing at my feet.

It was a move I had practiced since being shown it by the old, now departed chazzen. It was the very same baton he gave me and the one I had used to train every class since given the gift. "How dare you violate anyone in such a manner," I said angrily as one lay moaning and the other retching from my blows. "I give you justice myself and save the authorities the trouble of dealing with you." I knelt and took each thief's right hand, flattened it on the hard ground, and smashed them with enough force to hear bones break. I left them screaming in pain as I recovered my staff and continued to the city.

I was thinking about the old chazzen as I walked, actually smiling about the poke in my gut all those years ago. My heart was heavy about the thieves, but they still had their hands. Herod and Rome's justice would have had them cut off in public.

The rest of my walk was uneventful as I thought about where Messiah might be headed. Sleep came easily when I finally got to my room.

CHAPTER 36

THE SON

The next three days were uneventful as the festival wound down. The last night of Passover is usually another big feast night, but this year it seemed quite subdued. I made arrangements to travel north with the children before the road to Capernaum continued northeast reaching Cana. Shabach released me until my next tour, in seventy days during the month of Sivan.

With spring blooms decorating the landscape, the trip home was a visual feast. The little ones displayed never-ending energy, Rebekah with questions about the trees and flowers and Saul wanting every detail about the zealot, Pilate, and the soldiers.

When it came time to go our separate ways, I felt a struggle leaving Sarah. She was a grown woman with a husband and two children, yet for some reason, this time was different. I realized for the first time in my adult life, I saw the woman in my daughter, not the little girl. Of course I knew from the time she and Samuel were married that she was a woman. But when I saw the mature woman she had become, it made me a little sad. I was growing up as well.

I stood watching as the contingent from Capernaum continued north until they were out of sight. Taking a deep breath, I headed home to be with the other half of my family: Jonathan, Marta, and their son, Caleb. My family was growing larger and growing up. Leaving Jonathan in charge of the household and the flocks was a big decision. Even though I did not think of myself as a man who had to be in control, it was difficult to step away from all that I had built and let my son take over, as my father had done with me.

Was I becoming a weepy old fool? I wondered. The more years I had lived, the more thoughtful about the past I had become. Perhaps that is what is called wisdom. I was hoping to have wisdom when returning to the village to see my son. An old proverb kept coming to mind, one my father had repeated to me over and over: "Trust in HaShem with all your heart and lean not on your own understanding." HaShem, the Name. And now the Name had a son; his name was Yeshua. My steps seemed to lighten.

Walking home thinking about my son Jonathan, I realized having left him in charge so abruptly might have caused problems for him. I was prepared for an interesting return. As a child he was a good student, and I believed he would have done well taking over for me. He was big and strong; plus he had the added advantage of his mother's speed and agility. Jonathan had become a formidable man.

It was late afternoon when I arrived in Cana, and I was filled with a comfort that can only come from home. Even though my world had changed so much, and the village was not the same as when I was a child, it was still home, fitting like well-worn sandals. The house where I grew up was now quite large, having expanded with the years and family. There was light and song coming from the windows, and they warmed me. I mouthed the loud bleat that was akin to a rollicking goat's, a signal we had all found amusing over the years.

Jonathan filled the doorway as he opened it to greet me. He had grown taller and stronger than I ever was, an imposing sight. "Abba! Shalom, welcome home." He took three giant strides and wrapped me in his powerful arms, lifting me off the ground. Setting me down, he took my face in his huge hands, drew me to him, and kissed my forehead. "Now come inside!" he ordered. He was doing the very same thing that I had done to him when he was younger and much smaller.

Entering the front door, the first thing I noticed was Jonathan's wife, Marta. She was standing next to their three-year-old son, Caleb, perched on a high stool dressed in a shepherd's simlah, holding a tiny sling. "What is this?" I asked with a smile.

"Sabba, I am David. Do you want to play?"

"Yes, but I do not want to be the giant Goliath. I want to be David's friend." Caleb laughed; I grabbed him and kissed his head. "I have kissed the head of the king, and now I am a hero!" They laughed at my head-kissing, my family tradition. Still holding Caleb, I said, "I am so happy to be home."

Wearing a grin, Jonathan said, "I will prepare the guest quarters for our returning hero." With a more serious look, he said, "Papa, since you left, and we did not know when you would return, I have made a few changes here in the house." Not giving me a chance to respond, he added, "We have moved into the main rooms and put your things in another section." Jonathan stood a little rigid, waiting for my response, and he looked like a little boy again, expecting a decision on punishment.

"Excellent!" I said to his relief, his smile returning. "With me planning on being away for long periods, it is the smart thing to do. I need very little room, and what I will have here is a palace compared to my quarters at the academy or my bedroll in the field."

Marta came to me, grabbed my hand, smiled, and said, "We will need more room to accommodate your next grandchild." The news of her carrying a child filled me with joy, and all I could choke out was "Wonderful!"

Jonathan grabbed my travel bag and said with a wry smile, "Come, Papa. Let me take you to your new quarters." We wove through a little warren of rooms to the back of the house, where a large area had been built while I was gone. It was perfect and complete with a fireplace, bed, table, two stools, sleeping pallet, pillows, blankets, and small supplies of everything I could possibly need. The best part was that there were two windows flanking a door. My son had added another section to our home, giving me access and freedom to come and go without disturbing anyone.

"Thank you, Jonathan. This is excellent!" I grabbed his face with my hands, pulled his head toward me, and kissed his forehead.

"Ha! Papa, you have always done that. It makes me feel like a happy child."

"I love you, son. You make me proud." He hugged me again and left me standing in my new space. It was warm, inviting and a signal that life continues, and change is constant.

I removed my outer garments down to my loincloth and walked to the wash area near the well in the field behind the house. After dousing myself with the cold water, I grabbed a block of hard soap and rubbed down vigorously to get rid of the road grime. Having rinsed myself with fresh water, I walked back to my new room. I put on a clean robe that was one of several in a stack and lay down on my pallet—the blessings of home.

"Papa, come eat." Those words jolted me awake, having fallen asleep. Like an old man, I arose groaning and followed Jonathan to the main room. Marta had set out four plates. On the table were barley bread, honey, cheese, olives, goat milk, and wine. "A feast, indeed," I said.

"Sit near me, Sabba," chirped Caleb.

"Of course I will, my little shepherd." He giggled at my words as I sat next to him.

"How long will you be staying, Papa?" asked Marta.

"For a little while, my dear girl. I will spend as much time with Jonathan as possible to make up for my quick departure. He will probably teach me how to run the family business with the changes he has made in my absence." Marta laughed, looked at Jonathan, and smiled.

After eating, Jonathan said in a more somber tone, "Papa, let us walk around. We have a little evening light remaining." We both stood, leaving Marta and Caleb in the house, as Jonathan led me to the front door.

Walking slowly toward the village square, my son began. "Abba, I love you, and you have taught me well. I make decisions with my head and my heart and want your blessings before making some changes permanent."

"My son, I love you beyond words and believe in your abilities. Please tell me your plans."

With that Jonathan seemed to stand even taller and explained his simple idea. "We can increase our sheep and wool production greatly by giving away half of our sheep."

I stopped walking and looked at my son in the fading light, and he looked even larger than he had a few moments ago. "Please, son, how do you propose to accomplish this magic?" My voice conveyed a full question without skepticism.

"We have a bit more than six hundred sheep and six hired shepherds that are loyal to us. We treat them well and provide them with extra money when we shear and market the wool. Let us give each of them fifty sheep and make them partners. They will pay us half of their profits plus a tithe each time when we all go to market, and in no time we will double our size, plus add to our income." As we stood in the darkening square, the light of the simple idea made me think that I should have turned the business over to my son years ago.

"Jonathan, that is brilliant. I approve of your plan. Actually you do not even need my approval because the business is yours completely, with me receiving a small portion each shearing for you to hold in reserve, as we had decided before I left." I reached out and grabbed his arm and said, "Son, you make a father proud."

He captured me into one of his massive hugs and said, "Let us go back home and seal this arrangement with some wine."

CHAPTER 37

THE SHAWL

THE NEXT FEW days were a delight as I spent time with my growing family. The first day Jonathan took me to the village gate, where we had to call a quorum of the required village elders to approve the official transfer of judgeship from me to my son. After the transfer of authority, Jonathan had to preside over some domestic issues as the new judge, which he handled with intelligence and poise. Then we headed to the fields to inspect the herds.

We spent the day with six shepherds who were delirious with their new roles as business owners, no longer just hired hands. Jonathan had prepared all the documents ahead of time, and we sealed the parchments to be stored in the village civil house. He brought some barley cakes and a skin of wine to bless the arrangements. It was a splendid day, and the evening was just as enjoyable with my family: food, song, and stories.

After Caleb went to bed, I asked Jonathan and Marta to sit with me so that I could tell them what had been driving me to leave so abruptly and on what mission I was engaged. They sat motionless, listening to me tell of the events from that first night of nights up until my arrival at their door. Marta was still as stone with a look on her face I could not read, tears rolling down her face. Jonathan had a wrinkled brow as he gazed off in deep thought.

I waited for some time to hear their responses; none came. Breaking the silence, I said, "Please, each of you, say something."

Jonathan snapped out of his thoughts. "Abba, that is quite a bit to absorb. Please give me a few more moments to capture what you have told us and share what I think." Saying nothing in response to my son, I turned to Marta.

She broke her silence with a loud sob and said, "Messiah, he is here! Our children will see Messiah. What a wonderful day!" Marta stood, walked over to me, dropped down on her knees, grabbed my hands, and kissed them. She looked up at me, tears still falling, this time with a smile. "My *khothen kham* (father-in-law) has met and knows Messiah. How blessed is he, to be touched by heaven."

I took her face in my hands as had her husband's days before, kissed her forehead, and said, "We are all touched by heaven now that he is among us." Marta got up and went over to her husband and sat his feet, waiting for his response.

"Papa, I am staggered by all you have told us. The only thought I have right now is that Adonai seems to use shepherds for helping and leading our people. As you, a shepherd, were telling me your story, I was thinking about the shepherds in our people's past: Abraham, Isaac, and his son, Jacob, whom Adonai renamed Israel. Moses, the prince-turned-shepherd, chosen to lead our people out of bondage. David, the shepherd who became king. I look at my father and can only imagine what he of *Shamayim* (the Heavens) has chosen for you in such a time as this."

We all stayed silent for a few moments as I was choked with pride in my family. Finally I said, "My dear children, I am humbled by your belief in me, and I will follow the leading of Adonai no matter where he takes me. I must leave soon to follow Messiah, not only to send dispatches to the Magi but also to aid and assist him however I am able."

"Where will you go next, Papa?" asked Jonathan.

Without a pause I said, "Capernaum. That is where the fishermen Messiah has befriended reside. They probably returned home after the Passover festival to resume their work. I will start my search there."

Marta, still sitting by her husband, spoke up. "What shall we tell our friends and neighbors about Messiah and what you have seen? I want to wake up the whole village and tell them all!"

"My sweet daughter, I have had some experience being excited and trying to tell of Messiah's arrival. It would be better to gently bring up the subject, telling events that have been heard of and recorded. We will start right here with Nathaniel and his daughter's wedding. I will ask questions about the wine that night and the group that arrived from Nazareth and the miracle."

"Abba Elijah," Marta said haltingly, "forgive me for contradicting you, but would it not be better for you to plant the seed here by telling the rabbi your story and have Nathaniel there as a witness to confirm what happened the night of the wedding?"

I looked at her, smiled, then said to Jonathan, "Son, you must listen to the wisdom that pours out of your beloved. You have been blessed, as I was with your mother and Samuel with your sister, by having a mate as wise and wonderful as your Marta."

Grinning at me, Jonathan said, "Papa, most of the ideas for this household and the business have come from Marta. I just work her thoughts and eventually take the credit for every success. Do not worry, I know the value of my spouse."

Returning his grin with a smile, I said, "Again, my son, you show great wisdom. Now let us sleep, for tomorrow we have a visit to make, and then I must be off to Capernaum."

After morning meal breaking the night fast, Jonathan went to fetch Nathaniel as Marta and I, with Caleb on my shoulders, headed to the synagogue. At the front double doors of the shul, I knocked and stepped inside, leaving the doors open. I called out in my loudest and most authoritative voice, "Rabbi *Yoel* (Joel), we seek counsel!"

Caleb aped my call and, in a toddler's volume, called out as well. We did not have long to wait.

"Eli, what is wrong? What brings you and Marta here during study hours?" said the aging rabbi, draped in a floor-length prayer shawl, shuffling toward us.

"We have a matter of great interest and concern to bring to you for advice, attention, and action." I said it with appropriate gravity. At the same time, Jonathan with Nathaniel in tow entered the common area of the shul.

Joel asked, "This is so important that you bring the most prominent member of the synagogue and the village to me?"

"Yes. I am about to leave on an important journey, and you are needed to play a vital role in the days to come."

At my words his annoyed look dissolved into one of concern, and the rabbi said, "Follow me." He led us to a small courtyard at the side of the building and asked all of us to sit on the benches arranged in a small circle.

The moment we were sitting, I started. "Nathaniel, thank you for coming. This is a matter that actually concerns you as a witness to a very important event." Nathaniel was about to speak; I held up my hand to silence him before he could interrupt. "Natie, remember your daughter's wedding, when you were running out of wine on the third day?"

"We did not run out, as you well know," he said defensively.

"Of course you did not. Can you explain why?" I asked in the gentlest voice I could muster.

Nathaniel sputtered and said, "The steward told me that he found a great supply of wine, really very good wine."

I paused a moment and asked Nathaniel, "Did he ever explain where the wine came from?"

Hesitating again, he said, "All he said was there was as special provision brought by a guest."

Holding up my hand again, I said, "Natie, take a deep breath and listen to what I say, and please do not interrupt, as much as you may want to." Turning to the rabbi, I said, "Joel, I must ask the same of you. Say nothing until I am finished."

Looking at their questioning faces, I began. "Thirty years ago I saw an angel from Adonai who told me and several others that Messiah was born. The angel told us where he was near Bethlehem, and we saw him. He is alive today and performing miracles. You saw him at the wedding with his mother and friends. His name is Yeshua ben Yosef." Pausing for a moment, I looked directly at Nathaniel. "The night of your daughter's wedding, I saw him change water into the delicious wine you spoke of."

Joel gasped and started to speak. I held up my hand again, bore my gaze into the rabbi, and said, "With a word he healed a dying man. My daughter, Sarah, can verify that miracle. He is among us. He is teaching and healing, and I am going to follow him."

Jonathan shattered the silence that seemed to have taken the air out of the garden by saying, "Do any of you doubt my father's honesty?" Both men were silent.

I began again. "The day he was born was the day Jacob was slain by the Roman soldier on the road. We were on our way here to tell you the good news of his birth. I said nothing at the time because I was crushed with grief and, in the seven days of my isolation for being unclean, realized the time was not right to come forward."

Little Caleb was playing with a small wood carving of a sheep I had made his father years ago; this was the only movement in the courtyard. "My Rachel was the only other person in this village I had told of his birth, until now."

Like a child, Nathaniel meekly raised his hand, and I nodded with a smile, giving him permission to speak. "I have never in my life tasted such wonderful wine. I remember the man, his mother, and his friends." Hesitating for a moment, Nathaniel, hand still raised, continued. "He is Messiah? My distant cousin from Nazareth?"

"Yes, my friend, he is the one we have been waiting for." I quickly summarized thirty years in minutes.

Looking at my friend, the rabbi, who was sitting there in the little yard wide-eyed, I asked, "Joel, do you have anything to say?"

"Eli, my mind is racing through writings trying to remember prophecy that would confirm your words. I must study." He stood abruptly, signaling the end of our meeting, and we all stood. The rabbi looked at me. "Eli, you are a man of courage, and I have never known you to lie. If what you have told us is true, then the world has changed and will change from now until…until…time ends! I must go to my scrolls." He took a step and looked at me with a questioning face and said, "I do not doubt what you believe, but I am a man who lives by what has been written. I must study the scrolls."

The village rabbi, a man I had grown up knowing, was shaken with my account and went to seek solace in words of the past so that he could accept the present. Facing Nathaniel, I said, "Natie, how are you doing?"

With a glazed expression and a faint smile, he said, "Messiah was at my daughter's wedding, and we have tasted his abundance. I must go home." With those words he moved in a trancelike fashion to exit the synagogue grounds.

"Well then," I said, "the message begins here now." Jonathan gathered up Caleb, and we went back to the house. Jonathan was bouncing up and down on the way, and Caleb had such an infectious giggle that by the time we were at the front door, we were laughing like children being tickled. The cool of the house settled us, and I headed to my room to retrieve my travel gear.

When I got back to the large common room, both Jonathan and Marta had serious looks on their faces. "Abba, please be safe and cautious as you travel. We need more time to spend in each other's company." Jonathan's brow knitted with worry as he spoke.

Sincerely I said, "I have learned much in my years, and recently it seems that my education has been accelerated as I have been living the mission to which I was sworn."

"Papa Eli"—the sweet voice of Marta drew my attention—"I stitched this some time ago, waiting for an appropriate time to present it to you." She was holding a fine linen object that looked like a folded prayer shawl. "My father used to recite this old writing to me and my brothers over and over. He used to start many Shabbat evenings with these words." She unfolded one of the most beautiful prayer shawls I had ever seen. The multicolored, fine stitching was as exquisite as any I had seen the Kohen HaGadol wearing in the temple.

I held it up, and it read, "Whoever sits in the refuge of El Shaddai shall dwell in the shade of Adonai." With tears in my eyes, I took it, kissed each corner of the shawl, and draped it over my head. Stepping forward, I placed a hand on each forehead and recited the *Shema*. Gathering them into a common embrace, I was able to say "I love you as life itself and pray that I return to you soon!"

The three of us were weeping in one another's arms when we heard Caleb crying painfully. We disentangled to see the poor little man gushing bitter tears with arms upstretched to his mother. Marta said, "Darling, we are fine." She bent to pick him up, and he quieted immediately.

I carefully folded the shawl, kissed it again, and put it in a corner of my skyt. Looking at the handsome family, I said, "Shalom. Pray for me daily as I seek HaShem!" I walked out of the house I knew as a child, where I raised my own, wondering if I would ever see it again.

CHAPTER 38

THE MADMAN

As I headed to Capernaum, I kept thinking about the shawl that Marta had made, relishing the intelligence and substance of the women in my family. Rachel, Sarah, now Marta had such depth and abilities it made my skills seem small by comparison. These women should have been the heads of most of the villages in Galilee instead of some of the puffed-up bullies that pushed their way into leadership. Thankfully Cana had men like Joel, Nathaniel, and Jonathan to maintain wisdom and stability.

In my youth the walk to Capernaum would have taken me little more than half a day. But the road to Sarah and Samuel reminded me that my body needed a slower pace and more rest. My hopes were to get to their house before sunset and celebrate Shabbat with them then worship at the synagogue in the morning. The days were getting warmer, my waterskin was full, and I felt a freedom that I had never before experienced.

As I walked along, the words on the shawl were like fuel for my soul and comfort for my mind; I knew that I was seeking the one that the sages had predicted. I was still a shepherd, but I felt like a lamb seeking the comfort of the flock and the Shepherd. King David's words were a constant song on my lips as I strode toward the light of the morning sun. "My shepherd is Adonai…" I kept singing, and others on the road heard me and joined, singing the most famous song of our people.

Before I realized it, I was in the outskirts of Capernaum; it was well before sundown, and I was not the least bit tired. How strange and wonderful. Minutes later I was chirping my goat song to let Sarah know I was near. By the time I arrived at the front door of the house, the family was lined up and waiting. Joy was mine.

A smiling Samuel said, "We knew it would not be a long wait for your return. Sarah had a place prepared for you long before she heard your signal. Shalom, Papa Eli." Rebekah and Saul ran to me, crashing into my legs.

"Do you have a crumb of bread and a sip of wine for an old traveler?" I asked, entering the fine home.

"We might be able to scrape something together for a weary pilgrim," Sarah answered before her strong embrace. Saul led me to the room that was already prepared with a fresh bowl of water and towels to wash. One of my old robes was freshly laundered and folded on my sleeping pallet.

When I entered the dining area wearing the prayer shawl that Marta had fashioned, Sarah lit up. "What a beautiful tallit, Papa. Where did you get it?"

"Marta" was my simple reply.

"She is so gifted. Her needlework is perfect," Sarah said admiringly.

"I am blessed to have such talented children. Sarah, will you begin the meal with your candle lighting and prayer, please?" My voice echoed in the room with appropriate solemnity for the beginning of Shabbat.

Sarah had Rebekah light the two candles, pulled a shawl over her head, drew the breath of the flames toward her face trice, and began the blessing. "Baruch atah Adonai..."

The meal was simple, the chatter was light, and soon the children were off to sleep. "Eli, I have some very interesting news," Samuel said with a grin on his face so large I could barely see his ears.

Sitting after the meal, feeling tired but content to be with my family, I lazily looked at Samuel, wondering what could be so exciting. "Yeshua has been invited to teach in the shul tomorrow morning."

"What? How?" I sputtered, feeling immediately energized.

"He returned with the fishermen during the week, and the head rabbi asked him to speak, having heard reports about his teachings and healing. That is not all. I received a dispatch from Nicodemus to give our synagogue leader. As the Teacher of Israel, Nicodemus reminded us that since the *golah* (exile), rabbis that roam the land have been invited to speak. It has been a longstanding tradition in Capernaum. So when we heard that he and his followers were back, the rabbi walked down to the water to speak to Yeshua."

The news was doubly exciting because he was here, and he was going to teach in the synagogue. "That is wonderful news. I hope I can sleep tonight with all of the thoughts bounding around in my head." Having said that, I realized how tired I was, bade them a good night, and barely made it to my pallet before I was asleep.

I was awake long before sunrise and bathed and dressed in a clean garment that Sarah had provided. Sarah had prepared a huge breakfast of boiled eggs, olives, bread, cheese, grapes, pomegranate, and figs. Fresh goat milk and strong tea washed everything down. We all left the house at the second hour and arrived at the synagogue early, but the crowd was already forming. With Samuel being a Pharisee and a representative of Nicodemus, the three of us were able to sit on a bench just to the right of the *bema* (raised altar). Rebekah and Saul had been left outside under the care of female servants, nurses who worked for the shul.

Inside the three of us stood and greeted those we knew. Samuel being a center of attention, everyone in the village wanted to greet him. After a few minutes of fellowshipping, the rabbi mounted the altar to begin the morning service. We sang a few songs we all knew, starting the service. The village rabbi had a huge scroll Torah locked in a wooden cabinet behind the podium. As tradition dictated, every week the rabbi would choose a man from the village to give an *aliyah* (honor) to rise up the bema and join the ceremony. This week he asked Samuel, the newly appointed assistant to Nicodemus, to receive the honor. To my delight Samuel was humble in his agreement to withdraw the Torah from the ark.

The place of the Torah was not just a plain two-door cabinet. It was hand carved from thick beams of Lebanese cedar. Each door had five symbols raised on it, numerals representing the commandments given Moses on the mountaintop. The symbols were hammered with gold, indicating the value of the scrolls stored within.

Samuel lifted the Torah and set it on the lectern, opening the scroll for the rabbi, and was allowed to read a portion dedicated to the story of *Yiftah* (Jephthah), a judge who presided over a portion of Israel for six years before the nation had kings. It was a sad story. Samuel chanted it with appropriate vigor and sorrow. He had a beautiful, rich voice; the reading was well received.

At the end of Samuel's reading, he tightened the scroll, placed it back in the ark, and took his seat again next to Sarah. It was then the rabbi introduced the guest speaker as Yeshua ben Yosef *HaNatziret* (of Nazareth). The entire gathering turned as Yeshua walked briskly down the aisle, mounted the bema as the rabbi stepped to the side.

Looking out at his audience, he nodded at me with a solemn face and began. "Why did Jephthah sacrifice his daughter? Was his agreement with Adonai made in haste? Is there a lesson to be learned for all of us from Jephthah's sacrifice?" Yeshua's voice was gentle but commanding as he made point after point about the story Samuel chanted. Sounds of approval from the gathering kept emphasizing each aspect of the story.

Suddenly an ear piercing shriek came from behind us. Everyone stood in alarm, seeking the source of the horrible sound. A well-dressed man was twisting in the aisle, his body and face contorting unnaturally. It was obvious the man was possessed by a spirit of evil. In a thunderous voice that sounded like it came from the depths of *Sheol*, the man bellowed at Yeshua, asking what he wanted of "them." Was he there to destroy "them"? The possessed madman called Yeshua the Holy One of Adonai!

I had seen men and women who were said to be possessed, but this was louder and more terrifying than anything I had ever witnessed. Samuel and Sarah were white-faced staring at the man. Yeshua stepped calmly down from the bema, slowly walking forward. In a loud, stern voice, he said, "Be silent! Leave him!" Immediately invisible hands threw the man down on the floor. All eyes in the shul were glued to the scene. The man became calm and stood, surprisingly uninjured, never once taking his eyes off Yeshua. He then brushed himself off and took a seat, as if just entering the building.

The synagogue buzzed with amazement until Yeshua retook the bema and finished his teaching. The presiding rabbi, still shaken, stepped forward and intoned a short prayer, ending the service.

Yeshua came down from the bema, and as he walked by me to exit the building, he said, "Shalom, Eli," then left through the front doors. I looked at Sarah and Samuel, whose color had returned, and said, "Another miracle—he casts out demons!"

The rabbi came walking quickly to the three of us and asked, "You know this man, this teacher?"

Samuel answered, "Yes, rabbi, we have all met him before. My father-in-law has known him all of his life. He was there the night this wonderful teacher was born."

The rabbi looked at me and asked, "This is true?"

Being used to disbelief, I looked at the head rabbi of Capernaum and said, "You have just hosted the Chosen One!"

Though never at a loss for words, the rabbi was silent as we walked out of the building to find Rebekah and Saul.

CHAPTER 39

THE MOTHER-IN-LAW

OUTSIDE THE BUILDING, we were looking for Yeshua, but he was nowhere in sight. I had to smile at the thought that he was able to avoid being spotted when leaving a gathering. Thinking that he might head toward the fishing area where his friends worked, I told Sarah and Samuel I would be back at the house later and headed toward the shore.

It was a short walk to the fishing houses as the synagogue was near the center of the village, with the boats close to the central market. There was a small crowd near one of the houses, among which I saw familiar faces. They were the same men who had congregated when the centurion Salvius had asked Yeshua to heal his servant. As I neared them, the surly fisherman with wild orange hair spotted me, raised a hand, and shouted, "Shalom, Eli!"

Even though I was surprised by his greeting, I responded politely, "Shalom, Simon." John and Simon's brother, *Aryeh* (Andrew), were there with several others, and I continued toward them.

"Eli, welcome back to *Kephar Nahum* (Capernaum)," John said, using the ancient name of the city, named after the prophet Nahum. "What brings you back so soon?"

Stopping face-to-face with the fishermen, I responded, "Well, family, of course, and I am taking the long route to Jerusalem, where I am scheduled to teach for a month."

"Teach? Where? What?" The sincerity in his questions told me that he really did not know the importance of Levitical shepherds. John spoke with intelligence, but his knowledge of the structure and functions housed in Jerusalem were not part of his education.

"I am a shepherd that works my flocks and trains shepherds at the academy in Jerusalem. What I teach is timeless. I add experience, having been born into a family of shepherds." John had an astonished look on his face, so I said, "My friend, you have a lifetime of work and experience as a fisherman. You could teach young men how to read tides, find schools of fish, all the things that make you successful with your catches."

He thought for a moment; his face brightened. "Oh I see." With that he broke into uproarious laughter so infectious that everyone in his little group started laughing with him.

When they calmed down, I asked, "Is Yeshua nearby? I have a question for him."

"No, he is not," Simon said softly in a tone that seemed unnatural for him. "He has left to find an isolated place to pray."

How odd, I thought, *that the Messiah would pray.* "Thank you. I will just go back to my daughter's house."

Before I could leave, John said, "Eli, stay a while. Come, it is Shabbat, have some wine and a piece of bread while we say a blessing." The invitation was so sincere I just stood there. Simon handed me a small wooden cup, Andrew produced a loaf of bread, and John was holding a skin of wine.

John poured the wine, Andrew broke the bread into pieces, and Simon recited the ancient blessings, adding, "Our teacher would be proud that we practice this fellowship on Shabbat."

I asked Simon, "Does he do this often, go off by himself?"

"Almost daily. Sometimes he is gone for days. His teaching is not always received well."

"What do you mean?" I asked, confused by his remark.

Simon's face darkened, as did his mood, and he told me that Yeshua was rejected by his people in Nazareth.

"I do not understand what you are saying—rejected?"

Simon continued in a somber voice. "He went to the synagogue on Shabbat and read a portion of a prophet's words. It was then he declared that he was fulfilling prophesy! They became furious at his teachings and were going to throw him off a cliff outside of the village. But he just walked through the angry mob and left. His own people, where he grew up, were going to kill him for teaching the truth." I stood there, dazed at Simon's words.

He added, "We are going to meet him three days from now." My heart sank upon hearing that it would be a while before I would see him again. Then he asked, "Eli, would you like to join me and share our noon meal? My wife's mother has been cooking everything she can find after Yeshua healed her fever with a touch. There is more food than we all can eat."

"Certainly, it would be my honor."

Throwing an arm around my shoulders, he boomed, "Come, friends, let us nourish." With that he started guiding us to his home near the large port area.

On the way I asked, "I am curious, how did you come to meet Yeshua?"

He smiled. "We had been fishing all night and were coming in empty. John and James spotted a small crowd where we were going to dock. The other boatmen were cleaning their nets, listening to this man teach. When we got close to shore, this teacher was the man my brother Andrew called Messiah. We pulled up to the shore, and Yeshua asked if he could come into the boat and teach from there because the crowd was growing. He sat down with us on the boat and taught the crowd on shore.

"When he was finished teaching, he looked at me and said, 'Go out to deep water, and let down the nets.' I was thinking, this is not a fisherman who speaks. Why should I listen? But since Andrew claimed he was Messiah, I obeyed."

Simon stopped walking, grabbed my arm, turning me toward him, and with tears welling up said, "We caught so many fish the nets began to break. We had to have others on shore come out to help us with the catch. The boat was so full it began to sink. I knew then that Andrew spoke truth. I fell to my knees at Yeshua's feet, telling him I was a sinner and not worthy of his presence. He lifted me up and told me that from that moment I would be a fisher of men." Simon's tears turned to a smile. "Eli, my friend, you know this man I speak of is the Chosen One, do you not?"

Returning his smile, I said, "I have known this for over thirty years." The group had circled around us, and the only thing I could think to say was "I am hungry. Please feed me!"

Simon broke into laughter, slapped me on the shoulder, and said, "This way!" pointing forward.

Simon's home was larger than most but typical for a fishing family, with netting, oars, and spare masts piled by the side of the house. We all entered the large common room, which looked like an inn dining area. Rows of tables with benches filled the room. The aroma of baking bread and roasting fish beckoned. I was swallowing with anticipation; the sound of women singing was a delight. It was a feast for my senses!

"Mothers," Simon bellowed, "come meet the rabbi's shepherd friend!" Three smiling women—one young, two older—came from behind a waist-high preparation table toward us. "Eli, this is my beautiful wife, my mother, and mother-in law," he said with a sweeping gesture of his arm.

"Shalom," they sang in harmony. The oldest of the trio came forward and said, "Welcome, Eli, we have heard much about you." I was surprised that any word of me had been spoken. "We are glad you are here. Please sit. The food will be ready shortly."

"Is that your mother-in-law, healed by a touch of the hand of Yeshua?" I asked Simon.

"Yes, that is our Bekka! She was delirious, and we were afraid that the fever was so high she would not last the night. Yeshua walked into her room, kneeled at her bed, and reached for her. The moment he touched her face, she relaxed, and her normal color returned. He took a cloth, wiped her brow, and she opened her eyes. Then she smiled at him. We all fell on our knees, sobbing with relief."

"The hand of HaShem," I whispered.

"Let us eat," Simon commanded, and we ate a wonderful meal. In Cana fresh fish was uncommon; mostly we ate dried fish. The meal in Simon's house was so fresh and delicious it was memorable. At its end the three ladies serenaded us with local songs. At an appropriate time, I excused myself and headed back to Samuel and Sarah's house.

"Papa, where have you been all afternoon? We were about to worry." She had a dubious look. "Fortunately I remember the times you would be gone longer than expected." She ended her short reprimand with a smile.

"I was invited to have lunch with Yeshua's friends and met some family. By the way, the roasted fish was terrific. They should open a public house." My smile was broader than my daughter's when I announced, "Tomorrow I will leave for Jerusalem." Another questioning look appeared on Sarah's face.

"Why so soon? I thought you might be here for another Shabbat."

"Sarah, Messiah has a practice of going off and being by himself for days at a time. I was planning on taking a long, wandering trail to the Holy City, perhaps to run into him again. He does like to teach in Jerusalem."

"Do you really think a chance meeting will occur while you are wandering around the countryside? When he disappeared as a child, he was near the temple for three days, and he had to find you!" Her little girl giggle emphasized her tease.

Smiling, I said, "You are exactly right. I am hoping he will find me on the road." I desired to get to the academy early to do some writing for my upcoming meeting with the Magi's courier. "I will leave in the morning, but for now where are the children? I would like to see them and tell them wild stories."

Sarah laughed. "If they are not in the courtyard, they are probably running in the field behind the house."

Off I went.

CHAPTER 40

THE INNKEEPER

THE NEXT MORNING, when the children were with their tutors and Samuel was instructing Sarah on some business transactions, I said my goodbyes. After crushing hugs from Sarah and a warm embrace from Samuel, I headed south along a well-worn path that paralleled a caravan route. The day was hot, my skyt was heavy with dried food, my water bag full, and I was determined to camp that night with Mount Tabor on the horizon.

Making good time, I was able to tent at the foot of a palm tree just before sunset. The evening was calm and comfortable as I looked at the sun setting behind the historic mountain. Recalling two women from ancient writings, *Div'orah* (Deborah) and *Ya'el* (Jael), I was thinking about two courageous women in my life, my beloved Rachel and our daughter, Sarah. Such strong, accomplished women, so taken for granted by some of the men around them. I thought that perhaps someday women would be treated as equal to men. Perhaps.

The Valley of Jezreel lay between me and the mountain, the flat land dotted with campfires. Comfortable in the field, I was being lulled to sleep with the faraway sounds of sheep and goats and the occasional snort of a camel. All my years living under the stars had taught me to be vigilant, with one hand always on a defensive weapon. As I was drifting off to sleep, I heard a voice. "Where are my sheep?" An uneventful night found me waking with the lightening sky. It did not take long before I was up and moving with the wisp of the voice hanging in my head.

Hunger gnawed at me, but instead of reaching for some dried meat, I spotted a roadside *malon* (inn) with smoke rising from it, hinting a hot meal. I noticed an ox and an old horse attached to posts near the field behind it; there were guests. The ox reminded me of the old man's animal that had been slaughtered by the Roman soldiers. The horse prompted the thought of getting one, to spare my aging legs going to and from Jerusalem. All these years of walking and now a horse? I laughed at myself for the thought.

Entering the two-story building, I was hit with the smell of roasting lamb, old wine, and melted wax. All around the entryway and common room were beams covered with the remains of many candles. In the early morning, the candles were still the main source of light for the room. A giant of a man, the innkeeper, stood next to a long table where two men sat facing each other.

"He was dead and wrapped for burial." The man speaking was young but weathered-looking dressed like a farmer, talking to a man in dusty city garb.

"It is impossible to bring back the dead. Even the pharaohs, with all their wealth and magicians, could not do this thing you speak of," said the man wearing a familiar-looking scarf.

Looking at the city stranger, the innkeeper said, "I, too, was there. The entire village of *Nahen* (Nain) passed right by my main door. I know the young man who died. He worked here from time to time when the roads were choked with pilgrims for festivals. His father died years ago. He has been supporting his widowed mother by farming and working here. This man, a stranger from Galilee with a band of followers, walked up to the widow and told her not to cry." The innkeeper spoke with a voice that sounded like it came from a young girl. Remembering a Levite shepherd who came through training who had suffered an injury from a blow to the neck, I realized the innkeeper's voice was nothing to laugh at. Plus the fact he was a mountain of muscle probably kept people quiet.

"Not cry? How dare he!" said the man with an arrogant attitude, sounding like a man of the law.

The young farmer said, "Just wait. The man had followers that called him rabbi. He walked over to the litter, laid a hand on the wrapped body, and said, 'Young man, I say to you, arise!'"

"Blasphemy! The man speaking as if he was divine! Making statements like that in front of the dead man's mother?" The stranger seemed agitated and attempted to stand.

With odd gentleness, the innkeeper laid a huge hand on the stranger's shoulder. "Friend, listen to the rest of the story before you get upset." The stranger sat, not that he had a choice.

Improbably the innkeeper's voice got even higher as he became excited telling the rest of what he had observed. "As soon as the rabbi touched the chest of the figure on the litter, the dead man moved! He sat up and started shaking off the funeral wrappings then spoke. The crowd was amazed. I was amazed! The rabbi helped the dead man who was now alive up from the litter and led him back to his mother."

"I do not believe this tale you tell. It is a joke." The city man seemed to relax and even started laughing at the innkeeper.

The big man removed his hand from the stranger and in a calmer voice said, "Believe what you will. I saw it, as did the whole village. They stared, cheering and calling the man prophet, shouting, 'Adonai has come to help his people!' Some young men from the crowd started running to other villages to tell what had happened."

Sarcastically the stranger added, "What then? Did they carry this 'prophet' on their shoulders and have a feast of thanksgiving?"

"No," the young farmer said. "The crowd took the widow and her son back home, and the prophet, without staying for praise, headed east with his followers." I was delirious hearing this news.

The stranger sat there shaking his head, then I stepped up to the table, full of excitement, and said to the stranger, "Believe what they tell you. I know the man they speak of. His name is Yeshua."

The stranger's head snapped toward me, but he remained silent. I said to the giant man with the high voice, "I am hungry for a hot meal."

"Sit, my friend, and I will serve you," the innkeeper said with a smile.

"You know this man who makes these claims?" asked the stranger, whom I recognized as a Pharisee wearing his official scarf.

"Yes, my friend, I have known this man since his birth, and I can tell you with certainty he is Messiah!" My tone was factual and my gaze intent.

"Blasphemer!" the man screamed, stood, and grabbed his possessions. "I will hear no more of this nonsense!"

As he was leaving, I stepped in front of him and calmly stated, "When you go to Jerusalem, talk to Nicodemus. Tell him Eli, the shepherd, said to report what you have heard."

The Pharisee stopped, looked at me puzzled, and asked, "You know the Teacher of Israel?"

"Yes, friend, this lowly shepherd has family working with your leader. Have a safe journey." I stepped aside, and the Pharisee seemed to deflate as he walked by me into the cool morning.

"Now, friends, will you join me with a morning blessing of wine? My treat!"

CHAPTER 41

THE CURSE

BACK ON THE road to Jerusalem, I was wanting a horse or a mule, even an ox. I was finally feeling the years and distance on my old shepherd legs. But for the time, my comfortable sandals would have to do. There were plenty of memories to keep me company on the road and at night. Before I realized it, the walled city of Jerusalem was looming in front of me. The last three days since passing through Nain were uneventful and surprisingly dull. The first person I thought of to tell recent events was Moses, so I headed to the market.

It always surprised me that you could smell the market from far away and identify some of the items for sale by sniffing the air. That hot summer afternoon, the air was heavy with the smell of baking bread. How different was the fragrance of yeast-filled bread compared with the flat smell of unleavened bread, the bread of haste, the Passover matzah. That day it felt like the market and the city itself were a bakery, with loaves rising from the hot cobblestones.

Bidi spotted me first as I neared the stall of my friends. Her usual happy countenance was marred with a look of sadness. Alarm jolted me and quickened my walk. "What is wrong?" I asked, concern heavy in my voice.

"Our Daniel has been injured," Bidi moaned.

"Where? How?" Fear was filling my gut.

"He was coming back from delivering some ground spices to a wealthy customer. He loves to run after making deliveries. A Roman soldier thought he was a thief fleeing a robbery and tripped him with a pilum then beat him before Daniel could explain himself."

Hatred boiled over my fear as I thought, *A Roman soldier again!*

"Where is Daniel?" I asked, worried that he had been taken prisoner.

"There, in the back. Moses is seeing to him." Bidi sobbed.

I stepped around the front counter and made my way to Moses, who was seated next to an improvised pallet. The other children were huddled in a corner of the stall as I approached.

Moses looked at me with a pained face. "Shalom, Eli. You come at a sad time."

"May I see Daniel?" I asked, thinking that I might help with what little medical knowledge I had.

Moses slid back across the floor, making room for me to kneel beside the injured boy. "Shalom, Daniel," I whispered and swallowed my words when I saw the extent of the boy's injuries.

Daniel turned his head slowly toward the sound of my voice. Only one eye was visible as the left side of his head was raw with wounds and swollen so much his left eye was closed. The boy's left arm was lying across his chest with an unnatural bulge in his forearm. Through puffed lips he could only press out, "Shhhchh." I touched his head, and my alarm grew upon feeling his fever.

"We must get him a doctor quickly!" I snapped to Moses.

"We have tried. No one will come to the market to help." Moses's anguish was clear.

Daniel was moaning lightly when I told his father, "Get the largest blanket you have and some rope." Moses reacted quickly. I then turned to his twelve-year-old daughter, who was standing in a corner whimpering. "Layla, please go and find the longest, heaviest stick that looks like this and bring it to me." I was pointing to my staff; the beautiful young girl nodded and scampered away.

Moses returned with a blanket and a ball of twine. We unrolled the blanket, and Layla returned with a long wood rod she had found at the front of the stall that was used to keep sheets covering product inside the stall. "Excellent, Layla." Using my flint knife, I cut long pieces of twine and, with Moses's help, made a sling to carry Daniel. I carefully moved the groaning boy, and I noticed that his left ankle had swelled to twice its normal size. As I was swearing in my mind against all things Roman, we hoisted Daniel, and I said, loud enough for Bidi and the children to hear, "We are taking him to the temple physicians!"

"But...," Bidi uttered.

I did not wait for anyone to object. "We will go as fast as we can!" The authority in my voice brought no contradiction. We exited the stall and started toward the temple. I shouted for all in the market, "A reward to anyone that helps us with a cart!"

To my surprise several nearby merchants responded, "Here!" The closest was a young couple selling baskets woven out of dried palm fronds.

The young man turned, started unloading the baskets, and said to his mate, "I will return as soon as possible." The cart was large enough to hold Daniel, whom we laid down gently. The young man put on a harness and started pulling the cart, with me and Moses pushing from the rear.

"I am Abijah," the man said, grunting as he pulled.

"Thank you, Abijah! Enter the south gate, and head to the shepherd's compound." The young man continued to pull, we pushed, and Daniel groaned. It took about a quarter of an hour before we were at the entrance to the academy. Two guards were positioned at the gate, and I yelled ahead, "Get the chazzen, all the available doctors! Do it, and *do it now*!" My voice was rising with each word. The guards looked at each other; one nodded and the other started running to the inside of the structure.

We continued forward within the columns, and before we reached the area used as an infirmary, two young doctors came rushing up to us. We slowed down and stopped as the physicians approached. The older of the two uncovered Daniel and asked, "When did this beating occur?"

We were all breathing heavily; the trip had been mostly uphill, but Moses was able to respond. "Two days past, in the afternoon."

"He has broken bones that are causing the fever. We must take him to a pool, bathe him, and straighten his broken limbs."

Looking at me, the younger physician said, "The chazzen told us to prepare a bed for this young man in the infirmary and treat him as an injured Aleph." We followed the young doctors to the room I had been in every time I was injured during training. There were empty pallets raised to waist height near tables laden with small and large metal tools that looked terrifying. Tables were piled with clean linen sheets and strips of cloth, reminding me of that cave so long ago.

Two other older physicians were in the room. The oldest, white bearded and bent, shuffled over to Daniel, who had been transferred to a tall pallet. "Remove his garments," he said to nobody in particular. The young physicians started slicing off Daniel's garments with curved blades. The old doctor leaned close to Daniel, smiled, and said, "Son, I am doctor Pelez, and I will take care of you. Can you swallow?" Daniel nodded weakly. The doctor produced a small vial with a reed straw, held it to the boy's mouth, and said, "Drink." Daniel accepted the straw, drew in, swallowed, and grimaced. "It tastes terrible but should ease your pain." The old physician spoke in a calming voice.

Never taking his eyes from Daniel's face, the old man said, "These young doctors are going to clean your wounds and bathe you. I will return in a little while to help them tend to your injuries." Leaning closer to Daniel, Pelez placed a bony hand on the top of Daniel's head. "My boy, close your eyes, and think of the most fun place you have ever been, and let us take care of you. You do that, and we will fix everything." His voice was soothing and reassuring. Pelez nodded at the young doctors, who draped a clean blanket over Daniel and started moving him out of the room on the pallet, which had wheels I had not noticed before.

The old physician turned to the three of us, who were just standing and watching the smoothness of how the medical men moved, and stepped over to Moses. "You are the boy's father, I presume?"

In a moment of levity that would have otherwise seemed inappropriate, Moses looked at me then Abijah, nodded, and said, "How did you come to that conclusion?" We all looked at the tall ebony man, and the tension broke with our laughter.

The old doctor nodded, smiled, turned serious, and said, "Your son is gravely ill. The broken bones should have been attended to sooner. We will do the best we can for your son, but you must be prepared for the worst outcome." Moses inhaled as if struck. "The fever is advanced. We will bathe him in cool water to calm him then straighten the broken limbs. He will be in pain, and if he lives through this ordeal, he may have limited use of his damaged limbs."

We stood silently for a few moments. I turned to Abijah and said, "Thank you for your help. It made a difficult task much easier. Return to your stall. I will visit with you later." Abijah bowed and wordlessly left with his cart.

"How can a father lose a son? This cannot be. He is but a child. He must live." Moses's shoulders slumped as he spoke.

All I could say, with a seething voice, was "Romans."

Straightening up, Moses said, "I must stay here with my son. Please tell Bidi we are fine for now."

Taking my cue to leave without him, I said, "After a quick meeting with the chazzen, I will return to the market and offer words of comfort to your family. If only Messiah were here to lay a hand on your son." I nodded to Moses and headed toward Shabach, who was standing behind us at the doorway.

"How long have you been here?" I asked.

"Long enough to see that the boy is in trouble. I know you love this family, so I will do everything to help." Shabach looked sad, appropriate to the occasion.

"Thank you, my friend. I will bear any expense so that the kohen will not object. Speaking of finance, do you have any idea how much a horse would cost?" The thought just popped into my head at that moment, and we both laughed, again easing the tension of the event.

Smiling, my friend said, "I cannot imagine you on a horse—a donkey perhaps, but not a horse." We walked in silence toward his quarters, leaving Moses alone in the medical theater. When we reached his office, he handed me a cup of wine and said, "Here, refresh."

I took a deep draught and blurted, "I saw Messiah cast out a demon in Capernaum and heard that he raised the dead in Nain."

He froze for a moment and said, "Miracle upon miracle comes drifting into the city about him. Apparently everywhere he goes he teaches and heals. News and rumors abound. I welcome the day he rids us of Rome. He may have a bigger problem right now with Herod, the Pharisees, and Sanhedrin."

"Yes" was the only response I could muster.

"Your training for the next month is necessary, so we need you to be prepared after the next Shabbat," my friend said with little enthusiasm.

Having been reminded of my obligation to the temple and my Levite heritage, I answered, "I will be here and ready. I will move into my room tonight after I return from the market and speak with Bidi. Please prepare a place for Moses to stay while he comforts his son."

"Side-by-side pallets will be set up in a room next to yours. Now go!" Shabach said, adopting an imperious manner. Over the course of our friendship, I never resented being dismissed by him. I left the temple grounds as evening was settling over Jerusalem.

It was getting dark as I arrived at the market, which was quiet and void of most vendors. Bidi and the children had packed up the goods for sale, and the door was firmly shut. A faint flickering light was seeping out of the large front door, so I knew that Moses's family was waiting for us to return. I knocked gently and called out my name; the door opened. In hushed tones I told Bidi what I knew and had observed. She nodded and said grimly to the children, "Come, we will go home tonight and return in the morning and do what we must do." The children came swiftly to her side as Layla blew out the two candles that were the source of light.

"I will walk with you then return to the academy to tell Moses that you are safely home."

At their house I told them news would come to them in the morning. I hurried back to the temple compound and my quarters. Moses was in the room next to mine; I heard him weeping quietly. I tapped on the door frame and asked him if I could enter.

"Come, my friend, and speak words of comfort to me." He was sitting on the floor, and I joined him.

"Words of comfort at this time cannot come from me but only from writings of the sages," said Shabach, entering the room wearing a simple shepherd's robe. The chazzen sat down on the floor with us. He looked at our friend and said, "Moses, I am aggrieved with you and pray that Adonai will bring your son back to full health. I have sent out word to all of the best physicians in Jerusalem to come and assist our medical people."

Wiping his tears, Moses said, "Thank you, chazzen. It is my prayer that the Messiah will reveal himself and finally rid us of the Roman bondage. I feel the curse of my ancestors."

Puzzled by Moses's statement, I asked, "Curse—what curse do you speak of, my friend?"

"You, Eli, more than most should know of Jacob's curse upon the tribes we both came from." That became a moment of clarity about an aspect of my heritage that I had forgotten.

"Moses, are you a descendant of Simeon?" I asked haltingly.

"Yes, my brother of ancient blood. Our ancestor Jacob, whom Adonai renamed Israel, cursed his sons, our tribes, for the slaughter at *Sichem* (Shechem)." Moses's statement reminded me of the lessons I heard as a child, which had been reinforced by the teachings in the temple. *Lehvee* (Levi) and *Shimohen* (Simeon) avenged the abduction of their sister *Deenah* (Dena) by the prince of Shechem when they entered the city and killed all the males after they were circumcised. A sin-filled tragedy.

"Why do you think Daniel's beating is a result of a curse?" I asked with a cracked voice.

Looking at me through sad, red eyes, he said, "Almost every generation of my people has lost their firstborn sons in a tragic way. Now I fear my firstborn son will succumb to the ancient curse. His screams as they were working on him will never leave me."

Leaning into him, I said, "My brother, Messiah walks among us. Take heart!"

"Yes," Shabach added, "history is about to change, and we are in the center of it all."

We sat silently, and Shabach finally broke the mood, saying, "Some wine and some sleep will freshen us for a better day tomorrow." We agreed, had some wine, and then went to our separate rooms for the night.

Sleep was not easy, my thoughts flipping back and forth about the pain Daniel was suffering to the fact that I, a Levite, and Moses, a Simeonite, were brothers bonded together by ancient blood—and tragedy.

CHAPTER 42

THE HONOR

AT SOME POINT I drifted off to a fitful sleep and was awake before dawn with the vague memory of a voice saying, "Where are your sheep?" Dressing quickly, I looked at an empty room next door, thinking Moses was with Daniel in the infirmary. Heading there, I ran into Shabach, who was wearing his most formal attire.

"Have I missed a special meeting?" I asked.

"In response to my request, Herod has sent his personal physicians. I will greet them formally." Glancing at me, he smiled and said, "You may accompany me. They expect shepherds."

Entering the infirmary, we encountered a large entourage of richly attired men each wearing the elaborate symbol of Herod. "Shalom, my friends. Who honors us today?" Shabach said with his full-throated, commanding voice.

The visitor wearing the fanciest costume nodded at Shabach and said, "I am Evilah, master physician to Herod. We are here, I believe, at your request, chazzen." His tone was dripping sarcasm.

"Thank you. Please tell us, what have you found?" Shabach responded politely.

"We see an injured slave that has no place here," the arrogant physician stated. I stepped forward; Moses stood more rigidly.

Shabach's hand grabbed my garment, holding me back, and he replied with appropriate sternness, "This young man is one of my special students, not a slave. I suggest you offer, and provide, your supreme skills, or leave if it is beneath your dignity to care for a servant of the temple." Shabach's word had enough of an edge to make his point, and he added, "I am sure that Herod would not be pleased to receive my word that you refused his order." The physicians huddled for a moment then surrounded Daniel.

I approached Moses, who was standing near the foot of the table that held Daniel. Muted conversation floated over the young man, giving me an opportunity to look at him. Except for a loincloth and bandages, Daniel was naked, with the men pushing and poking, getting groans in response. The academy physician in charge of Daniel was on the sidelines, watching and apparently having had enough. "Stop! Desist! Let him be! He needs rest, not annoyance. You have done nothing but a superficial assessment."

The group leader fumed. "How dare you—a doctor of sheep speaking to the king's own physicians in such a manner. We are finished here." Following the lead of the pompous doctor, they left Daniel's side and breezed past Shabach without a word.

The chazzen turned as they walked by him and said, "You have all shown that your intent was not to help but rather to imitate concern. Herod's health is in danger with you tending to him." Spinning about, he came to Daniel's side, the anger melting from his face; bent down; and said, "You are safe here. They will not bother you again. Our physicians are the best, and you will receive care fit for a king." Daniel looked at Shabach with a weak smile.

Three of the temple medical men started wiping Daniel with wet towels. The senior physician, Pelez, came over to Moses, telling him that the young man was not out of danger yet but seemed more comfortable with baths and towel applications, which kept his fever down. Satisfied that his son was in good hands, I spoke a few words to Moses and Shabach then left the infirmary to bathe and change clothes.

Having done that quickly, I went to the market to update Bidi and the children and give them some encouragement. The basket merchant Abijah was delighted with the gift of a denarius for assisting us with his cart.

Daniel's fever persisted for three more days, and Moses never left his side. Shabbat came and went, and my month of teaching began. Every day for that month, at midday, I went to the market to check on Bidi and the children. After classes in the evening, I would take meals to Moses's room, and we would feed Daniel, who was recovering and getting stronger by the day.

Although my teaching was acceptable, my heart was not in it, and Shabach noticed my lack of enthusiasm. My mind was on my families in Cana, in Capernaum, and now here in Jerusalem. I could not shake the statements made by Moses about ancient brotherhood and Jacob's curse of his sons. How could we be cursed? And if we were under curse, how could the curse be broken?

Over and over the nights were turmoil for me until I realized that Messiah had a plan, and I was part of that plan. The comfort of that realization came full circle toward the end of my tour at the academy. Messiah's plan for me would be revealed in his time, not mine. Finally, three days before the end of my teaching regimen, I was able to sleep well, and Daniel was able to return home.

The boy had recovered from the fever but had lost much weight, and sadly his hand was unable to function and had begun to curl. His foot never straightened, forcing him to walk with an awkward limp, and he lost sight in one of his eyes. However, it was a joyous day for the whole family when on the evening of Shabbat, we were able to walk Daniel to his home. We had a wonderful meal, a warm welcome home for the injured young man.

At the end of my required stay, Shabach asked me to join him for a meal in his quarters before leaving Jerusalem. Agreeing was easy; meals with the chazzen were always a treat. To my surprise, the kohen, *Yosef ben Calfai* (Joseph, son of Caiaphas), was seated at the table with Shabach when I arrived. Apprehension had me a bit wary.

"Please, sit and join us," the kohen said pleasantly. Never before had any of the Caiaphas brothers been pleasant to me in all the years I had served the temple. Shabach just sat quietly with a crack of a smile on his face.

Without ceremony the kohen stated, "Elijah ben Ezra, tav of the Levite Brotherhood of Shepherds, by my authority you have been elevated to tav *leshe'avar* (Emeritus)." He stood, signaling both me and Shabach to stand with him. He presented me with a parchment scroll and a gold tav pin. He added, "For your outstanding achievements and service to the Levite Brotherhood, you are free to serve the temple in any manner you see fit. An office and sleeping quarters are hereby provided for use as you choose to serve." With that the kohen bowed and embraced me. To our astonishment he kissed my cheeks and said, "You are a man of integrity, and I am proud to call you my brother." The kohen released me and left the room.

I looked at Shabach, who was still standing at the table with a grin on his face, and he started clapping his hands. I could feel my face flush with embarrassment and excitement at the honor that had just been given. "Did you know this, you vermin?" I said with a smile.

"Of course, you donkey. Where do you think the idea came from? You are close enough to mandatory end of service. Now is a fine time for your freedom. Move about, and do what you need to assist Messiah. You now have a secure place to prepare your correspondence with the Magi." The moment continued to be unreal as I read the commission.

Shabach came over to me and slapped my shoulder in a brotherly gesture. "Thank you for refraining from an embrace and a kiss," I said, laughing out the words.

"Let us sit, drink, eat, and plan, my friend." We drank more than a bit of wine and ate a wonderfully prepared meal. We chatted about the bygone years, and the mood turned a little solemn.

Shabach looked at me intently. "I hated you when we first met because you had confidence and a heritage that I never knew. My tribe is unknown, my childhood a mess, and I survived by being a thief. I became an Aleph as a result of a bribe. Being a shepherd was my escape." I was at a loss for words.

He continued. "That day on the court grounds, you saved my life, and from that moment on, I considered you a brother. And now I have a position of authority, a family, and a brotherhood." He stood, raised his cup of wine, and said, "To everlasting brotherhood!"

Standing, I responded, my with cup raised, "To my brother, a true Levite. Now and forever, we are a tribe." We drank more wine until we both decided bed was appropriate. He showed me to my new quarters, which were a mirror image of his. What an unexpected honor this day had brought.

CHAPTER 43

THE AIDE

THE NEXT MORNING brought me a freedom I had never realized and a headache that reminded me I had had too much to drink. My body sent me reminders that it had nearly fifty years of wear. Rising slowly, I began to inspect my new quarters and was delighted to find a table with a stack of papyri, ink, and several Roman styluses. Sitting on top of the papyri was my coin purse, a roll of red wax, and a brass stamp fashioned to look like a tav with a staff—my own seal! I allowed myself a moment to feel puffed up before heading to bathe.

When I returned to my quarters, a young former student named *Aysah* (Asa) was standing rigidly at my door. He was wearing Aleph attire. "Tav, I have brought you a morning meal. It is on your table," the lad said in a deferential tone, making me feel even older.

"Asa, call me Eli, and relax. I am just like you, only worn out with years. How did the chazzen describe your duties?"

Loosening just a bit, Asa said, "I am to bring you your meals, clean your quarters, take your laundry, remain at your door, serve at your request, and learn."

My own personal servant—how had I become so elite overnight? I was not going to bask in any glory; I was going to work. "Asa, go to the market and do three things." The lad nodded. Reaching for my coins, I said, "Purchase six oranges, and pick up my supplies from Moses."

Asa waited a few moments and sheepishly said, "Tav, that is only two orders."

Smiling, I said, "Call me Eli, or I will throttle you. The third thing to do is locate a *cha'mohr* seller. Find out the price of a mature animal, male or female." Asa had a confused look, and I asked, "Do you understand your tasks, young man?"

"Y-Yes, Tav—er, Eli." I handed him a small purse of coins. Hesitating briefly, Asa did an about-face and ran off, leaving me laughing at the innocence of youth.

I sat down at the table, took a piece of papyrus and a stylus, and started writing my next Magi dispatch. Hours passed before I finished many pages to seal in clay. Asa returned with the items I had requested and a meal. I nodded at the young man and asked him to sit and eat with me. He seemed uncomfortable with the invitation, so I pointed to a stool at the table.

Asa reluctantly sat. I took the food he brought and shared it with him. Sitting erect and uncomfortable, the young man picked at the morsels of bread and cheese in front of him.

"Asa, are you a Levite?" I asked while chewing a piece of salted lamb.

"Yes, T—Eli, all Alephs are Levites." His nervous stammer was easing.

"Well, then, we are family, cousins, so you need to relax and enjoy this opportunity the chazzen has given you."

Asa relaxed a bit and said, "Yes, but I have been instructed to call you tav by the chazzen."

Amused, I followed with "Very well, but you now work for me. Let us go forward with you addressing me as tav except when you feel like discussing something personal, like family."

"Yes, sir, or should I call you uncle?" We both started laughing. "Eli, thank you for making me feel so comfortable. There was one more thing you asked of me."

"Yes, Asa, did you find a donkey seller?" I asked, drinking the last of my goat milk.

"There is a man in the market who represents several livestock owners. The nearest donkey breeder is in *Beit'Anyeh* (Bethany), a short walk from here, north of the Mount of Olives," Asa reported proudly, a student getting his answers correct.

"Very good, thank you," I said, not knowing what duties he should perform next.

Asa stood, gathered the plates, and cleaned the table. "Eli, I am not sure how I am to fill my time serving you. It will be very difficult for me to stand outside your door all day waiting for instructions." Asa was obviously hesitant to express his concern.

"I am not at all sure that there is that much for you to do around here. But while my friend Moses's son Daniel is recovering from severe injuries, perhaps you can help them in the market each afternoon, unless there is something pressing I need from you here."

"After all my training as a shepherd, you want me to sell dried fruit and spices in a market stall?" His face had a look of disbelief.

Seeing that the young man was upset at the notion, I added, "Actually my purpose is more than just aiding a friend. I need ears in the heart of the city to get news of the one they are calling Messiah." He stood there puzzled, so I continued. "The Romans have an expression, 'sub-rosa,' meaning 'done in secret.' I have a mission that I cannot talk to you about right now. Just trust your tav."

At my remark Asa straightened his slumping posture and snapped, "Yes, tav!"

I smiled at the lad. "All you need to do is bring me the news that Moses gives you and pay attention to what is going on. Take this note to him, spend the afternoon, and return at dinnertime."

Taking the note with my seal, Asa set off for the market, and I continued writing. From that afternoon of sitting and writing, I developed a great appreciation for scribes. I found that being bent over a desk all day was hard work, and I wanted no part of it. I was standing and stretching my aching back when Shabach came to my door.

"What do you think of young Asa, my friend?"

"He reminds me of me thirty years ago," I said while shaking my head.

"Then you deserve him!" the chazzen said, laughing. "What now, Eli?"

"It is time to finish my writing, leave Jerusalem, and find Messiah." My answer was full of determination, then I added, "What of Asa? Does he stay here, or are you expecting me to take him with me?"

"That is your choice, my friend. He goes with you or goes home. I have no place for him here. His support was to come out of the funds I have stored for you here." Shabach's statement put an interesting twist on my decision moving forward. Did I see Asa as a burden or as an aide while I traveled? I certainly could afford to provide for him between my accumulated funds here in Jerusalem and my fortune in Cana. "I will let you know my decision in the morning, my friend. Either way I will be leaving tomorrow."

Shabach nodded and said, "A cup of wine and a prayer before your departure—seek me out." He nodded and almost bumped into Asa as he was leaving.

The young man was startled by the chazzen and almost dropped a parcel he was carrying. "Be wise, young Aleph," Shabach said as he walked by the lad, who again wore a puzzled look on his face.

"Eli, this is from Moses and Bidi," he said, handing me a large basket holding the leather pouch he was carrying.

"Thank you, Asa. Please sit for a moment." I set the pouch on the table, unloading its contents. On top was a large cloth filled with a dark tea I had become fond of. Underneath were three rolled leather maps that detailed strange-looking lands, dried figs, almonds, and, on the bottom, an odd package. I set all the things on the table, took a stool, and sat facing my young assistant, who had been in my charge for less than a day.

"Asa, tomorrow I will be leaving the city to try and find the one they call Messiah. I do not know where it will lead me or how long I will be on the road. You may come with me or return home. The choice is yours." Seeing the young man was about to blurt out a response, I added, "Say nothing just yet. Think about it and ask Adonai for guidance. Let me know your decision in the morning. Meanwhile go to the baths, refresh, then return with dinner, and I will answer any questions you may have." The boy stood with a determined look for a moment then left my quarters.

I returned to the table and the odd-looking parcel that was in the bottom of the pouch. It was two pieces of hard leather about the size of my open hand laced together with pieces of aging twine up one side. On the hide of one piece, tapped into the leather, was spelled out "Adonai is my shepherd." Held in between the leather were old pieces of papyrus with very small writings on each page. A closer look showed that each sheet of papyrus had exquisitely written songs of King David on them. I had never before seen such a prize. I sat reading each one until Asa came through the door with the evening meal.

"Did Moses or Bidi say anything about this?" I asked, pointing to the parcel as Asa was setting the food on the smaller table.

"No, Uncle Eli, not a word," he said with a smile, just standing by the table.

"Speak!" I said, mirroring his smile.

Snapping to attention, Asa spoke from the heart. "As you said, we are family, and I shall go where you go."

"Very well. Tomorrow after morning meal, we will pack what we need and be off." We sat and ate silently.

At the meal's end, Asa stood, cleared the table, and leaving the room, said, "Shalom." I went back to the parcel of songs, read for a while, and sang some of the songs of my youth. I packed my skyt and travel bag, making sure that I had everything ready for our departure. Drifting off to sleep, I heard that now familiar voice in my head, asking, "Where are your sheep?"

CHAPTER 44

THE GUEST

MOST OF MY life I never had vivid dreams. After Jacob's murder I had a few nightmares, but since then, no real dreams, until that night before leaving Jerusalem with Asa.

I was riding on an animal of some kind, alone on a flat desert except for a huge herd of sheep walking away from me. I spurred my mount to go faster and faster, but no matter how fast we went, the sheep never got closer; I was losing them. Just when I thought the flock would disappear over the horizon, a giant flaming double-edged sword came slashing out of the sky and sliced into the sand in front of me, exploding into a fireball of light that blinded me. I was lying on my back on the hot sand and opened my eyes looking up at the faces of sheep surrounding me.

I blinked at the sight, and when my eyes opened, I was awake. It was dawn, and the face I was looking at was Asa's; he was standing at the door, dressed and ready to leave. The young man made me smile. He was a vision of an excited adventurer.

"Shalom," he said happily.

I said, "Good morning."

He laid his staff, rod, and skyt off to the side of the room and left, his voice trailing after him. "Getting the morning meal." I rolled off my pallet and headed to the baths.

The chazzen and Asa were waiting when I returned, the wine already poured. Shabach recited the blessings over the bread and wine, and we started eating. "News of Messiah comes from all parts of Judah and Galilee, inflaming the Sanhedrin and Pharisees. They say he is a false prophet and are disturbed by the reports of miracle healings and amazing teachings. I say these things for you to be very wary and cautious on the road. Be prepared for Herod's men or representatives of our Hebrew leaders to disrupt everything he does."

"Why would they do that?" Asa asked, alarm in the boy's manner.

"Fear, selfish fear. They do not want their status to change. If we have a new, divinely appointed king, Herod will be usurped, Rome overthrown, and the leadership of Israel changed forever." Shabach's manner was as serious as I had ever seen it. "If they feel threatened by Messiah and his followers, they will do everything they can to destroy all who oppose them."

I sat quietly, but Asa said, "But if we have a true Messiah, will he not vanquish his foes?"

Answering the lad, I said, "We do not know the time or manner that he will choose. Therefore, the chazzen's words are spoken wisely. We must be wary at all times and never slacken our vigilance. It is the same principle you have been taught here at the academy—protect yourself and your sheep, whatever the cost." He sat thinking and nodding his understanding.

"The time has come for us to be off." We all stood. "Thank you, my good friend." Shabach and I embraced. He handed me my staff as Asa followed me out the door.

The walk to Bethany was quiet and uneventful. By noontime we were ready for a meal, so we stopped at a roadside inn, a good place to hear news. The innkeeper had no news of Yeshua but told us where to find the stable and pastures of the donkey merchant. We headed there after a light meal.

In Bethany we looked at the stock with the merchant, and to my pleasant surprise, Asa knew a great deal about donkeys. On his advice I purchased a she-ass for myself and her three-year-old male offspring for two gold shekels. The price included leather bridles, blankets, and a double-sided storage bag for each animal. Each donkey had a name—the mother was Rose, and her son was Sand. The merchant named them after colors in their coats.

We chose to continue walking with the animals for a while so they would get to know us. After feeding them some small oatcakes as a treat, we continued north on a wide, well-used caravan route. Not too far from the inn was a roadside market, where we purchased some carrots and apples to feed our new mounts later in the day and other stores for our meals.

Both Rose and Sand were accustomed to being ridden, but we decided to wait until morning to ride them, after camping with them overnight. We headed north from Bethany toward Jericho, thinking that eventually Messiah would go back to Capernaum for some rest among his friends. I was selfishly thinking about another visit with Sarah and perhaps some news from Samuel. We camped within sight of a large caravansary on the outskirts of Jericho.

It was a beautiful summer evening when we set up a little fire and ate from our supplies, which Shabach had provided, and some vegetables we had purchased. Our new donkeys were hitched together to our staffs, which we planted in the ground near our bedrolls. The animals settled comfortably while I took first watch—the road was famous for thieves and robbers.

As the fire turned to embers, Asa was sound asleep. I sat remembering a night like this so long ago, and pangs of loss hit me when I saw Jacob's face on the young man camped near me. It was no wonder I had taken such a liking to the boy.

When morning came Asa had already fed mama and son, packed them, and was sitting on Sand. "We have walked around camp a few times. Rose is ready for you." I packed my roll, tied my staff to the bags, then gently sat on Rose, and we headed toward the inn for a meal and some news.

The inn was a small building just south of the huge caravansary up the road. The front of the structure was open, allowing a full view of the tie posts in front. We secured the animals and took a seat at the large table in the center of the room. There was only one other patron sitting at the other end of the table, bent over a small plate. The top of his head and one of his hands were bandaged, and he looked up at the innkeeper who was bringing him a cup.

After setting the cup in front of his guest, the innkeeper walked over to us and said, "We have salted fish, hot barley stew, and morning beer for a copper." Asa nodded; I took two coppers out of my small belt purse and handed them to the innkeeper. He walked off, and I spoke to the other patron. "Looks as if you had a nasty fall, friend."

The man looked at us and replied, "Bandits. Beat me, left me for dead, and took everything I had, including my clothes."

I looked at Asa and said, "This is a rough road we are on. We must be always on the alert." Looking back at the man, I said, "At least you were able to get here for help and shelter."

The innkeeper brought our food, shaking his head. "He was practically dead when he got here. A *Shomron* (Samaritan) had him on his donkey, carried him in here, and paid me two silver coins to put him up until he returned. He said he would pay me whatever it cost to shelter and feed him. That was five days ago." The innkeeper set the plates down and said, "A Samaritan doing that for a Hebrew, I never heard such a thing."

The injured man looked at us and said, "If it were not for that man, my family would be sitting shiva today. I was asleep for two days before the inn owner here woke me to eat something."

Asa asked, "Did you say a Samaritan did this good thing for you?"

"Yes," the innkeeper said, setting our drinks down. "The man is a Samaritan. I expect him back any day. It makes me think a little differently about Samaritans."

The injured man added, "He acted like family or a good neighbor. I hope I would have acted as kindly to a Samaritan as he did to me, a Hebrew merchant." We all nodded in agreement.

CHAPTER 45

THE BLESSINGS

AFTER OUR MEAL we fed our mounts, determined to get to Capernaum before Shabbat in four days. On the third day, the number of travelers heading north increased. We settled for the night under a walnut tree south of *Ginosar* (Gennesaret). Our routine with Rose and Sand of alternating between walking and riding was paying off; we were ahead of our scheduled arrival in the village of Nahum. I was looking forward to the comfort of shelter and family.

In the cool of the evening, camping under a huge fig tree, I had a memory of my father and his reading from a scroll in synagogue. "My soul finds rest only in Adonai. From him I receive salvation." Pulling out the odd package from Moses, I turned the individual sheets of papyrus and found the song I was remembering. I felt a peace that had been eluding me for a while now that I was seeking the Son of the Most High.

Looking at Asa preparing the fire for our evening meal, I felt a deep kinship with the boy; it was a good feeling.

Early the next morning, we were awakened by the chatter on the road. "Is this road always so crowded?" Asa asked. The string of young and old on the road stretched longer than a caravan.

"I do not believe it is. We can ask when we get up and join them on the road." My answer seemed to be more of a question; possibilities swirled in my head.

We fed and watered our mounts, ate quickly, then led them to the road. Pulling up near a young couple, I said, "Shalom, friends. We are going to Capernaum to see family. Is that where you are headed?"

"Shalom, shepherd. We are going past Capernaum to hear the prophet speak on Shabbat." Again I was hit with a jolt of excitement thinking that it must be Yeshua!

"Where will he be teaching?" I asked.

"He is camped on *Har Korazin* (Mount Chorazin). We will camp there and be near when he begins."

"Very well, then perhaps we will see you there," I said, not hiding my excitement.

I told Asa that we needed to get to Sarah and Samuel's house quickly, so we mounted the donkeys and quickened our pace. Arriving later that morning, we found Sarah and the children at home; Samuel was in the synagogue at a meeting.

After I introduced Asa to Sarah and the children, Saul attached himself to my young aide, leaving me with Sarah and Rebekah for the moment. I bent to kiss my granddaughter's head, then Sarah told her to go to the neighbor's house to play. "Papa, I see you finally relented and do not have to walk everywhere. Did you make a deal that included Asa?" she said with a smile.

I filled Sarah in on the past weeks, including the fact that "the prophet" was going to teach not far from here on the mountain we could see from the back of her house.

"It could be none other than Yeshua. He has been back here for a few days. I pray that he is well received. Word is getting around that he is spouting revolutionary anthems." Her brow wrinkled with concern as she spoke.

"Nothing could be further from the truth. Anyone who hears him understands that his message is only truth, peace, and love."

"Samuel should be home soon. We can have a Shabbat meal, arise early in the morning, and walk to the slope of the mountain to listen to his lesson."

I agreed and left the house, finding Asa and Saul tending to Rose and Sand. Saul was sitting on Sand, stroking his neck. My grandson looked as happy as I had ever seen him.

"Shalom, Eli!" Samuel called in a loud voice from the house.

I told Asa and his new playmate to finish with the animals, wash, and get ready for the evening meal. "It is too early to eat, Sabba!" Saul shouted.

"Not if you are hungry!" I yelled, drawing laughter from the boys.

Having returned to the house, Samuel had poured wine and handed me a cup. "L'chaim, Papa Eli." Samuel was still in his official Pharisee garb and said, "We will wash, change, and talk in a little bit. Your young friend can use the guest room across from yours." He left me, giving time for all of us to prepare for the evening meal.

Asa came in with Saul, who was excited to have a new guest and playmate. Before long we were at the table celebrating Shabbat.

"It has been quiet here at home regarding Messiah until recently." Samuel began the serious part of our dinner conversation. "Upon my return from Jerusalem some days ago, all was normal except that Sarah is now running our family business much better than I ever was able," he said sheepishly. "I thought that merchants and suppliers would be disdainful with a woman in charge. It seems that her intelligence and charm won them over immediately, and business is better than ever."

I smiled and said, "I never doubted her success. She is her mother's daughter. What of Yeshua?" I asked.

"In Jerusalem the leadership is mostly irritated by him. They consider reports of miracles just rumors from the inflated expectations of the people. The biggest concern right now is Herod, who always thinks the slightest news is a threat to his throne." Samuel himself seemed irritated as he spoke.

"What of Nicodemus?" I asked.

"My mentor speaks well of Yeshua but is careful not to confront his peers. The Sanhedrin are basically amused by the news at this point in time."

"We shall see if they remain amused as Messiah's influence spreads and grows." Changing subjects, I offered, "Let us leave for the mountain before sunrise. The crowd will be fairly large."

At Samuel's words of good night, we all stood and left for our rooms.

On the way to his room, Asa said, "You have a great family. Perhaps you could adopt me." I looked at Asa; his face was a picture of longing.

"In the days you have been with me, I have never asked where you are from or about your family."

His features turned solemn. "I am not proud of my past or family."

"Tell me now," I said gently but with firmness.

Asa's shoulders sagged, and he faced the floor. "I do not remember my parents or family, other than Shabach. For as long as I remember, I lived on the streets, begging and stealing until I tried snatching something from an old man near the market."

Asa looked up, anguished. "My hand was on his purse when he grabbed me by the collar and lifted me off the ground. I thought he was going to kill me right there on the street." Asa paused to breathe.

"How old were you when that happened?" My heart was melting at his story.

"I do not know my age then or now. I can only guess." I nodded for him to continue. "He lowered me to the ground, took my thieving hand, and said, 'You are coming with me.' He was not angry. That surprised me." Asa lifted his head and looked at me.

"Where did he take you?" I asked as gently as I could.

The young man recited blandly, "He took me to the academy, cleaned me up, then brought me to the kitchen. He said that I needed to learn how to live under the law. I needed to work, not steal. He put me to work in the kitchens and gave me a pallet in the shepherd barracks." Asa stopped his narrative, his gaze drifting off.

"How long were you there?" I asked.

"A few years. Each month he paid me some coppers and allowed me to go to the market and buy, not steal. One day he became ill and sent me to the new chazzen, Shabach."

As he spoke I realized that he was talking about my first teacher at the academy, the old chazzen. He had saved the boy's life and kept him safe in the academy.

I smiled and said, "I know the old man you speak of. The first chazzen I knew. He also taught me how to be a man." Putting my hand on Asa's shoulder, I said, "Son, you have a family. You are a shepherd and have been adopted by the brotherhood."

Asa smiled weakly and said, "Yes, Eli, I do have a family of sorts. What I do not have is a name."

We stood in silence for a moment, then he said, "I will see you in the morning." He turned and went into his room, leaving me alone in the hallway. His words disturbed my sleep.

It was well before dawn when Saul came jumping onto my pallet. "Sabba, get up. We have to leave." I grabbed the little man and started tickling him until his laughter became infectious enough to wake up the rest of the house. Samuel came and rescued Saul to bathe and dress him. We met in the kitchen for a light meal. Sarah had prepared enough food for all of us to carry so that each of us had two meals. Well before sunrise the six of us left the house for the mountain.

We were surprised by the numbers of people on the road heading toward the mountain. Shortly after the sunrise, we had to leave the road to walk on well-trodden grass. There were hundreds of people sitting halfway up the slope of the mountain. We settled at the outer edge of the crowd to sit and wait.

After a little while, there was a distant murmuring working its way toward us from higher up the mount. When I stood, I could see Yeshua at the top of the throng. Sitting near him were some of his followers: Simon, John, and Andrew. Yeshua raised a hand; the air grew still. He sat and started speaking to his close friends. From a distance that was equal to the length of the temple grounds, Messiah's voice carried so that he sounded as if he were standing near and speaking to each of us directly.

The rabbi spoke for most of the day, stopping occasionally to sit, quietly facing his followers. It was as if he was speaking to them exclusively but wanted all of us to hear his words. The most stunning thing of all was the silence that settled the moment he started teaching. The quiet continued until he arose to walk down the mountain.

The entire crowd stood and parted for Yeshua and his little group as they started downhill toward Capernaum. Their path came straight at me and my family. Samuel picked up Saul and put him on his shoulders, and I hoisted Rebekah so that she could watch the procession. As they moved, the gap behind them closed, and the listeners followed behind them. It became a great parade.

The throng parted, and Messiah walked up to Samuel and stopped. "How are you and Nicodemus getting along these days, Samuel?"

Saul jumped in, his voice full of awe. "You know my father?"

Yeshua looked up at Saul and said, "Your abba is a very important man. He is learning a lot from our friend Nicodemus, and he will teach you many important lessons." Looking around at Sarah, Asa, then at me, he said, "And who is this lovely girl, Eli? Is she your *nechda* (granddaughter)?"

Not giving me an opportunity to reply, with a loud, proud voice, Rebekah yelled, "Yes, Rabbi, he is my sabba!"

Yeshua laughed heartily, looked at me, and said, "Where are your sheep?" My jaw dropped open as he slapped me on the shoulder. "We will be at Simon's house for a few days. Come visit."

As Yeshua started walking, John came to me and said, "Come for breakfast tomorrow."

Simon, looking at Sarah, said, "Bring the family." Andrew nodded at me as they moved further down, the crowd following.

As we were walking down the hill, Samuel said, "Papa Eli, this teaching that the poor, the mourning, the meek, the peacemakers are blessed is confusing but makes sense when you think of all he has taught today."

"Yes, my son. His words may be new, but they are divinely spoken." I set Rebekah down, looked at Asa, and said to my little family, "Let us go home and talk about his words."

CHAPTER 46

THE BREAKFAST

THE SUN WAS setting as we arrived back at the house. Sarah and Rebekah went to the kitchen to prepare a meal, Asa went to care for the animals, Samuel took Saul to bathe, and I joined them.

Samuel had a worried look. "Eli, what did Yeshua mean when he said that we would be blessed when people insult, persecute, or bear false witness against us? He said that he has come to fulfill the law and the prophets. I do not understand these teachings."

"We need to digest these words and look at the old writings, like Rabbi Joel in Cana. I must admit that when he said we should love our enemies, I thought about Herod and Rome. I confess that loving them seems impossible. This is something I must pray to Adonai about. Let us bathe, eat, and sleep on what we heard today."

The evening meal was quiet except for the children. "That big man with the wild orange hair looked at me and smiled when you were talking to the teacher," Rebekah said with a grin.

Saul added with wide eyes, "He was carrying a big knife in his belt. It looked like a sword."

I looked at Saul and said, "*Neched* (grandson), he is a fisherman. He uses that knife as a tool for many purposes. Tomorrow we will go to his house, and he will tell you what he does with that sword you saw." The meal concluded, and the fatigue that follows a long day set in. We all helped clean up the kitchen then headed to our rooms.

Asa stopped me outside his room and asked, "Eli, what do you make of these teachings? I have never heard such words before."

"My boy, what you heard today is new to all of us. We must consider everything in light of what we know and study words that have been passed down to us. I have known this man for a very long time, and even as a child, he seemed to know all of the Torah. Go to sleep. We will see him in the morning."

Sleep was difficult despite my fatigue. Messiah's message kept repeating in my head—so much to try and understand. But it was his question "Where are your sheep?" that had me tossing and turning. Was it his voice that I had been hearing? Had he been speaking to me all along? Soon it was dawn; the family started stirring. I arose, anxious to go to Simon's house, not for the food but to see Yeshua and his followers.

Morning meal for those who caught fish for a living was a hearty affair. As we gathered together for the walk down to the shore and Simon's house, Asa was still grooming Rose and Sand. "Come along, Asa!" I yelled to the field where the animals were kept.

As I spoke Asa was running toward us. Another stunning image came to me as Jacob's face seemed to be on Asa's body. A chill of remembrance of Jacob's slaughter was replaced by love for the friend I had lost. "I am here, Uncle Eli," the lad said, laughing and slightly breathless. We all started walking down the hill to the docks in a merry mood.

As we got closer to the houses and boats, Samuel noticed there were many more people than usual clotting the streets. "I have never seen so many strangers in town, except for important weddings."

Sarah agreed. "Yesterday's crowd wants more from the rabbi."

We worked our way through the clusters gathering around Simon's house; Yeshua came out with Simon to greet all. Just as he looked at us and smiled, a loud voice from the back of the crowd yelled, "*Tumah! Tumah!* (Unclean! Unclean!)" People started running away from the voice, creating a wide opening. There, limping toward us, was a man with *tzara'at* (leprosy).

"*Tumah!* Stay away!" People were screaming as they ran from the man. Messiah turned toward the leper as he waddled nearer. The man fell to his knees a few feet from Yeshua. We were standing behind him as the man looked up with one eye exposed from dirty wrappings and said in a wailing voice, "Prophet, if you are willing, you can cleanse me."

Yeshua started raising his hand, and someone yelled from the crowd, "If you touch him, you will be defiled!" He raised his other hand to quiet the crowd then approached the leper. He reached out his right hand and touched the man. "I am willing." With his hand on the top of the ragged man's head, Messiah said, "Be clean!"

To the astonishment of every witness, the man stood and unwrapped his head and hands, showing that he was immediately cured of his disease. Yeshua leaned into the man, his hand still on the now clean leper, and said something we could not hear. The man nodded, turned, and walked quickly back through the crowd, which had been silenced by what we had all observed. The now clean man was singing and jumping every few steps as he left the village.

Rebekah looked up at her parents and excitedly asked, "Abba, Eema, was that a miracle?"

Samuel and Sarah bent to hug their children, and Sarah said, "Yes, my loves, what you just saw was a miracle from Adonai, and this man is his messenger." She was looking at Yeshua.

Simon stepped up to us, acting as if this were an everyday occurrence, and said, "My mother and wife prepared a wonderful breakfast. Please, it is time to come in and join us." Simon kneeled in front of Rebekah and Saul. "You are my new friends and must be hungry." He held out his giant, rough hands to the children. They willingly accepted his offer and walked with him into the house.

Asa was standing like a statue, with a blank look on his face. I gently wrapped my hand around his arm and said, "Come. I know this is hard to take in, but you need to get used to the idea of miracles when you are near Messiah." I led him into the house, and the aroma of roasting fish and baking bread broke him out of his trance. There was room at the large table for us, and we sat as a family. For me the moment was filled with joy.

"Shalom, shalom. Come. Eat. Drink," Simon's mother said as she walked around the table setting freshly baked golden loaves of bread in front of us. Simon's wife was busy at the fire stirring a huge pot. With the six of my family, we were twelve at the table.

Yeshua was sitting at the head of the table with Simon at his right and a young man to his left whom I did not recognize. Andrew was next to the young man, and there were two empty spaces for Simon's wife and mother.

Yeshua spoke. "Shalom, my friends. This is my brother *Ya'acov* (James), who is visiting from Nazareth."

Ya'acov looked at us, nodded, and said, "I am the quiet, practical brother." Yeshua laughed, picked up a loaf of bread, and recited the blessing. "Blessed are you, Adonai, sovereign of all, who brings forth bread from the earth." He tore the bread into twelve pieces and passed them around the table.

I put my arm around Asa. "Welcome to the family." The meal was delicious as expected. At one point Saul called out to Simon, "Where is your sword?"

Simon laughed, leaned back, and grabbed his knife from the top of a cabinet. He held it up and said, "With your father's permission, I will show it to you." Saul looked at Samuel, who nodded, then scrambled over to Simon. "This is a very important tool for men who fish. We use it to cut rope and bait and clean the fish that we eat. It is kept very sharp, but you may touch the grip if you like." Saul wrapped his tiny hand around the leather-covered handle, smiled, then scrambled back to Sarah.

There was talk around the table about Jerusalem, Herod, Rome, Pilate, the temple—typical talk of no consequence among people at a large table. Rebekah sat through the entire meal soaking everything in, not saying a word. Samuel could no longer contain himself and said, "Rabbi, what did you mean when you said you have come to fulfill what was said by the prophets?"

Messiah looked at Samuel, smiled, and answered with a question. "What does it say in the scrolls that you read in the synagogue?"

Samuel's brow wrinkled, and he responded, "There are so many writings and so many prophets. Which ones do you mean?"

Still smiling, Yeshua asked, "Have you read and studied all that has been written?"

Samuel burst into laughter and said, "I suppose you will answer every one of my questions with a question, so I will yield and tell you that I will read and study them again."

The rabbi nodded and closed the conversation with "As you say." Everyone at the table started laughing.

Simon stood, saying, "There are men and fish waiting. We must be off."

We all rose; Yeshua came over to our group, embraced Asa, and said to him while looking at me, "You are worthy to be this man's son." I knew in that instant what he meant. "Shalom," Messiah said, and he walked out of the house with his brother and friends. We thanked Simon's wife and mother and started for home.

Walking up the hill, I came up to Samuel and Sarah while the children walked ahead holding Asa's hands. I said, "I would like to make arrangements to adopt this young man Asa into our family and give him a name." Sarah and Samuel stopped and looked at me with puzzled faces. Before they had a chance to ask any questions, I told them Asa's story.

Samuel nodded and said, "I understand. You are a good man, Eli, and I am proud to be your son. It appears that I will soon have a new brother-in-law." Sarah grabbed me, just like her mother used to, and squeezed me with her agreement.

CHAPTER 47

THE SANDALS

THE CHILDREN WERE learning how to care for the gentle donkeys Rose and Sand under the guidance of Asa. The young man had fit into the role of uncle even though he had no idea of my thoughts to officially bring him into the family. I needed to have a conversation with Jonathan since the plan would affect his inheritance. That evening, after dinner, Samuel explained the ritual of *Amatz*, the legal model for adopting a child. It was rather simple but needed to be done according to tradition. The next step was going to Cana and visiting with Jonathan.

When Asa returned to the house with Rebekah and Saul, I announced that we would be leaving in the morning for Cana to meet with Jonathan to check on the flocks. "What about Messiah?" Asa asked. "Were we not going to follow him?" His concern was evident.

I answered, "Have we not found him before? We are not his *talmadim* (disciples), his most intimate group of followers. We are friends and students who have the luxury of being able to trail him and learn as much as we can before he claims his title. We have other work to do. I will explain as events lead us."

"Very well, Uncle. I will have everything ready for our departure in the morning." Both Sarah and Samuel had knowing smiles on their faces when Asa called me uncle.

Rebekah chimed in. "Why are you are leaving so soon? You can stay here."

Saul added, "We have a lot of room."

Looking at Asa, I said, "The children seem to be attaching themselves to Rose and Sand. Perhaps we should leave them here for Saul and Rebekah to care for while we are gone."

"Yes!" They both jumped up and ran to me with smothering hugs. "Thank you, Sabba," Saul said in a voice that made him sound older. Then they both ran to Asa, who looked first surprised then delighted with their affection.

Asa said to them, "Only if you agree to take good care of them! They need to be fed, watered, and groomed every day. And you must ride them as well."

"Yes! Yes!" was their chorus of replies.

Then I added, "Very well, it is settled. They will remain here in your care until we return. Of course you will have to pay me for every day you care for them." The children stopped hugging Asa and stood silently with puzzled looks on their adorable faces. "Oh wait, I may have said that in reverse. I will give each of you a copper for every day you care for our big-eared friends."

"Yes! Yes!" they repeated with hugs, and everyone in the room laughed at the children's reaction to our bargain.

With little further conversation, we were all off to bed in a fine mood, and dawn came quickly, as it seemed to every day. In the morning, after we broke the night fast, Asa was preparing our skyts, and I told him to dress in his Aleph garb, that I would take the morning walk to Cana wearing my tav work clothes as well. After Asa checked on the children's care of Rose and Sand, we started for Cana.

It was a beautiful summer day that promised to be hot, but at a good pace, we would be in Cana before sundown. It did not take long before Asa asked, "Eli, please tell me again why we are going to your home."

Walking a little further, I answered, "Asa, you know me as a tav, an instructor, and an important man in our brotherhood. What you do not know is who I really am."

We continued in silence before the young man could stand it no longer. "Uncle, cousin, tav, Eli, will you tell me, or am I to guess?"

I stopped, laid my gear on the ground, and faced him, taking his shoulders in my hands. "Look me in the eyes and swear an oath that you will repeat nothing of what I tell you to any living soul unless I give you permission or I am dead."

The lad got rigid, expecting something ominous. After a slight pause, he said, "I promise."

"You understand that you are making a vow. Do you remember what the chazzen read to you from the writings of King *Shlomoh* (Solomon)?" The boy stood silent for a few moments, and I could see his mind working to recall what he was taught.

Squeezing him with my hands to raise the importance of the words, I said, "'It is better not to vow than to make one and not honor it.'"

Asa stood even more erect, his eyes not wavering or flinching, and in a solemn voice repeated, "I promise."

After gathering my equipment, we started out again, and for the remainder of our walk to Cana, I told Asa my story. By the time we reached the outskirts of my home village, the young man knew the details of my life, with an emphasis on the night of nights and my covenant with the Magi. He had few questions along the way. Just before we entered the village, he stopped, laid down his gear, faced me, bowed his head slightly, and with his with eyes on mine, said, "I am honored to be serving you." The boy's sincerity brought me a newfound joy.

"Come," I said, "let us find Sarah's brother, Jonathan."

It did not take long before we saw my son at the village gate in conversation with two men. He saw us, smiled, nodded, then reengaged with the men. I said to Asa, "We will go home. He will join us as soon as he is able. There is no argument to settle, so he should not be long. My son has *chochmah* (wisdom), the ability to get to the heart of a matter quickly and make a decision." Jonathan was becoming an excellent judge. Silently I thanked Adonai that our son had his mother's good sense. We were at the family home in a few minutes.

I made the shrill goat sound that always announced my arrival home, but sadly there was no response. At the front door, there was a beautiful new mezuzah on the frame. I touched it and kissed my hand then knocked on the door. Moments later an unfamiliar young lady opened the door and said, "Shalom. May I help you?"

I smiled and said, "I am Eli, and this is Asa. I live in this house, and this young man is my guest."

Her brow furrowed for a moment, then she noticed my tav, smiled, and said, "Of course do come in." She opened the door to allow us in and added, "Thank you for knocking. You would have been a fright since we have not met before. Forgive my manners. I am Yodi, Caleb's teacher. Marta is in the garden. I will announce your arrival." She left us standing at the door. I looked at Asa, who seemed delighted at the sight of the lovely young lady.

"Sabba!" Caleb crooned as we entered the house.

"Shalom, Caleb," I said, lifting the boy and nuzzling my beard into his neck, raising cheerful laughter. I set him down and told him to go with Yodi. He ran to his new teacher, and she took him to another part of the house.

"Come with me to clean up. Then I will introduce you to the other half of my family." I led Asa to the addition Jonathan had built, which was large enough to house the two of us comfortably, grand compared to the tiny rooms at the academy. Stepping out back, we used the well water for washing. From that vantage point, I was able to see sheep grazing and felt that all was well.

When we returned to the main portion of the house, Marta greeted us and warmed immediately to the friendly Asa. "When did you acquire a teacher for Caleb?" I asked.

Marta was fixing tea; she said, "With the demands of the new partnerships and Jonathan's judging responsibilities, I needed help with our son." Marta turned, wearing a large smile, adding, "With a growing family, Yodi was a gift from Adonai."

I approached Marta with a happy face and embraced her. "Good news, my child." A great homecoming! I hoped the conversation with Jonathan would be as smooth.

I took Asa around the village and the surrounding areas, introducing him to a few of the partners who had added to the growth of the flocks. Asa was wide-eyed at the number of sheep and the size of the flocks. "Eli, these sheep are perfect! How do you do it?"

"I do not do it at all. These beautiful creatures are a gift from Adonai, he who provides all. My boy, we are merely custodians of his gifts to us."

Asa thought for a moment then asked, "Will these flocks be taken to Migdal Eder?"

"Many of them, yes, when the timing is correct. The lambs of the right age and without defect will be taken. If we are in Cana at the herding time, we shall be the shepherds making the journey with them."

The young man looked so sad. "The little ones are so innocent and beautiful. I hate to see them slaughtered."

I laid my hand on Asa's shoulder. "The ancient writings of the prophet Moses tell us, 'The animals you choose must be year-old males without defect.'" I paused to let the words sink in. "For over a thousand years, Levites have been entrusted to provide the lambs, and now you are part of that tribe. Come, the evening meal will be waiting for us."

Back at the house, the aroma drew us to the table after we bathed and changed into clean garments. The meal was wholesome and delicious. All the time at the table, Caleb could not take his eyes from Asa. Just like Rebekah and Saul, he was drawn to the young man.

"Jonathan, you have done a wonderful work with these flocks," I said admiringly.

"Abba, it is our partners that have made the difference. Making them owners has inspired them. The harmony on the hillside is delightful. These men trust us and each other so that their work is not toil." Jonathan's words were spoken without arrogance or pride.

At the end of the meal, I asked Asa to take Caleb for a little walk so that I could have a little time with Jonathan and Marta. Caleb ran to Asa, who picked the boy up and set him on his shoulders. "We will return after we make sure the flock is safe," Asa said jovially as he carried Caleb to the garden.

"Children, I have a family decision to make that will not take place without your approval and consent." My tone was as solemn and appropriate as the occasion deserved.

"Tell us, Abba," Jonathan said, looking at me then Marta.

I reached across the table to take their hands in mine. "Jonathan, your mother and I were to have another son to be a brother to you, but sadly they were both taken too soon. I believe this young man Asa is a gift from Adonai to honor their memory and be a part of this family. I ask for your guidance and permission to adopt Asa and give the boy a name." Silence followed.

I told them Asa's story and asked them to not speak of it to him until they had considered all the aspects of what I proposed. Marta and Jonathan sat with studied faces, and I concluded. "Please, talk with each other, and let me know what you decide. We will be here through Shabbat then return to Capernaum. From there, we will follow Yeshua. I bid you good night, my loves, and will see you in the morning." I left them at the table to find Asa and Caleb.

The boys were sitting in the garden. Asa was telling Caleb a story, so I sat with them until Marta called for her son. Few words were spoken before we all went to our rooms for the night. Before falling into a peaceful sleep, I heard Asa humming some of the songs we sang on the road.

I woke the next dawn with a smile on my face, looking forward to taking Asa to the wool gathering sheds. At the breakfast table, Jonathan was wearing his judge robe; he would be at the village gate all day. He asked if we could join him in the afternoon so that Asa could observe how judicial affairs were conducted in a small village as opposed to the business dealings in Jerusalem. We said we would be delighted and accepted his invitation.

The shearing sheds were busy when we arrived; the sheep produced great wool. Our flocks needed shearing twice in a year, and it was a prime season. Asa was fascinated with the work, taking part in the hot, sweaty shearing. As the men cut, there were women, young and old, gathering the wool for washing and baling. It was a well-run operation; the chief shearer was an old friend, a wise and able man. "Shalom, Eli. Another good year. Your young friend here seems naturally able. The sheep are calm in his care."

"Yes, my friend, he is a gifted shepherd. I must take him now since we have a meeting to attend." Asa joined me, and I said to him, "Son, you need a bath!" He laughed, and we headed back to the house.

Jonathan had already gone back to the village gate when we arrived at the house for the midday meal. Caleb awakened from a nap. The meal was a simple affair. We ate, and with Caleb on Asa's shoulders, we headed toward the judge area just inside the main gate to Cana.

Over the years the gate had grown in size with the village and was a fairly imposing structure of cedarwood. The nominal wall attached to the gate that surrounded the main area of Cana was combination of stone and wood. As we neared the gate, there were at least a dozen men clustered near Jonathan. I asked Marta, "Is it always so busy on *Erev* (Eve of) Shabbat?"

She answered with a little smile, "Sometimes yes, sometimes no."

Jonathan saw us approaching and said in his official-sounding voice, "Shalom, Abba, Marta, Caleb, and Asa. Welcome to our official gathering." Looking at the group of men, Jonathan added, "Friends, allow me to introduce a guest in our home." He looked at Asa and said, "Asa, please come forward."

Asa looked at me questioningly. I shrugged and said, "Give Caleb to Marta. I will go with you."

Marta took Caleb, smiled at me, and said, "Go, you two."

Jonathan announced in his best judicial voice, "Men of Cana, this young man is Asa, visiting from Jerusalem. Asa is an Aleph shepherd trained at the academy, as was my father. We are here today to welcome this man into our family."

Jonathan reached into an ornate leather bag at his feet and took out a pair of my worn sandals. He looked at Asa, who wore a puzzled look, and said, "Today you are given the name Asa ben Elijah, and it is my official duty as judge of Cana in the region of Galilee to pronounce you, according to the law and tradition of Amatz, my brother and son of my father, Elijah ben Ezra. Now and forever your name is in the records as Asa ben Elijah." With those words spoken, Jonathan handed Asa my worn sandals, and Asa became my son.

Jonathan and Marta's answer to my question was a public affirmation that Asa was welcome into the family. Asa looked at me with a broad smile and tears running down his face. Through my own wet eyes, I stepped forward and embraced my newfound son and whispered, "You can no longer call me Eli, uncle, or tav. You are no longer nameless, Asa ben Elijah." Jonathan wrapped his arms around the two of us, and Marta, still holding Caleb, entered his embrace.

As we stood there as a newly formed family, the minyan chanted in unison, "Amen! Amen!"

We unwound our hug; Jonathan picked up his bag, took out a parchment, handed it to Asa, and said, "This is yours, my brother. Let us go home and celebrate."

Asa took Caleb from a smiling Marta, put him on his shoulders again, and started toward our family home.

CHAPTER 48

THE ROOF

SHABBAT WAS A time of delight for the family. Yodi had prepared some baked sweets cakes that I had never seen before. Her family was originally from *Tzidon* (Sidon) but was dispersed during the time of the prophet Daniel. They eventually moved back to a small country camp north of Cana that was now considered part of the village.

She was an interesting young lady. Another rare, highly educated woman who had come to Marta's attention through the synagogue during a festival celebrating our beloved Queen Esther. Women from all around Cana came to the synagogue once monthly to learn news and share information. The village rabbi would speak briefly to encourage the women. Widows were helped with food and other provisions. A practice I remembered as a child—my mother was always helpful to ladies who were less fortunate. It was a mandate from Adonai and a tradition that Marta embraced as an active participant.

After Shabbat, during the morning meal, I told the family that it would probably be months before we could be together again. After going to back to Capernaum, we would work our way to Jerusalem to complete the dispatch for the Magi in time for the festival of Sukkot, celebrating the Feast of Tabernacles. At the table Asa said, "This is now my home, and I hate to leave it so soon. But I am pledged to our father. Calling anyone abba is strange coming from me. However, I will get used to it." Asa was grinning in a way that I had not seen.

We said shalom with embraces and started out, looking like a shepherd teacher with his student son. It was a wonderful feeling walking the road with a newfound child; my steps were easy. I told Asa stories of our family, of those who had passed, so he could have memories based on our history. It seemed but minutes before we were on the outskirts of Capernaum. "This is really beautiful El—I—Help me. I am sorry that it is difficult for me to call you abba. My entire life I never had the luxury of calling anyone by that title."

"Asa, call me Eli for now, and let 'abba' come naturally." He nodded, and we headed to the home of Samuel and Sarah.

We made the trip in good time. Walking with Asa filled an aching that had emerged after losing Rachel and our son. The late summer sun made the day hot. By the time we reached Samuel and Sarah's home, we were exhausted and immediately went to the well at the rear of the house, drenching ourselves with cold water.

Sand and Rose looked as if they had been cared for very well. Asa went into the house, coming out with carrots to treat our mounts. They both nuzzled us; we patted them and talked to them a bit before going to the garden to sit and dry our wet garments. Sitting in the garden as our clothing dried rejuvenated us just in time for Sarah's arrival home.

"Shalom, Papa and Asa, welcome back," she said, looking first at Asa then at me. I smiled and nodded to Sarah. She looked back at Asa, who stood sheepishly. Sarah rushed to the young man and embraced him, saying, "Now I have two younger brothers I can boss around and irritate." Asa was tentative at first about returning Sarah's embrace. Yet another new experience to which my son had to respond. "You are a wet puppy!" she yelled, releasing him. "Go, take your father, change garments, then come to the kitchen. I have news."

Minutes later we were sitting in the dining area eating fresh pomegranate wedges. Sarah began excitedly, "There is news of Yeshua! Travelers have been talking about the young rabbi teaching and healing all around Galilee. Stories he heals many ailments, those in pain and possessed by destructive *shedim* (spirits). They talk of his amazing teaching. Many are coming to believe that he is Messiah."

Looking at Asa, she said, "My dear brother, you have witnessed the beginning of a wonderful time for our people!"

Asa responded, "I feel as if my life has just begun now that I have family. I did not know what the word 'joy' meant until now."

Sarah went to him, took his face, and kissed both cheeks. She turned to me. "I must go get the children and bring them home from their studies at the synagogue. They will be so happy to see their uncle Asa."

We went to our rooms to rest, but Sarah was back with the children before long. They greeted me and ran to Asa, dragging him out to play with Rose and Sand. Sarah peeked in my room and said, "We will tell the children at evening meal about Asa. Rest until then."

After she left, I dozed to the echo in my head. "Where are your sheep?" I smiled, thinking that I had found one that was missing.

The children woke me as the sun was setting for the evening meal. At the table they were informed that Asa was truly their uncle; they were overjoyed with the news. Samuel spoke of talk in the synagogue that the young rabbi was indeed creating quite a following throughout Galilee, except in his home village of Nazareth. Despite his teachings and words of miraculous healing, the people in his home village did not believe that the son of a local builder could be the long-awaited Messiah.

Other than conversation at the table, the evening was quiet and relaxing, with Asa playing his flute and the children singing songs. We retired for the night. I planned to take Asa and introduce him to the fishermen's family the next morning. Once again sleep came easily.

In the morning Samuel took the children to the synagogue for lessons while Sarah went to visit merchants and take orders for expected passing caravans. Asa was eager to see Capernaum and the fishing area I had spoken so much about. We took a leisurely walk to the shore, heading toward the boats.

It was very quiet all along the shoreline, with boats pulled up away from the water. A few fishermen were sitting near their crafts working on net repair. At Simon's house the boarding was down so that the air would flow through with any breeze available. Simon's mother was working over a tub at the side of the house, so I called to her. "Shalom."

She looked up and smiled while holding a wet cloth that might have been a garment and returned my greeting with "Shalom, shepherd. Who is this young man?"

Pausing for a moment, I laid my hand on Asa's shoulder and said, "This is my son Asa."

Raising his hand in greeting, Asa said, "Shalom. I hear you are a wonderful cook."

Simon's mother laughed and replied, "Today I am a wonderful launderer." She set the wet item down on the edge of the tub and added, "Simon and the others have been gone for some days but should be back one day soon."

"We shall be here then leave after Shabbat with hopes of seeing them before we go to Jerusalem."

She waved and went back to scrubbing.

For the next two days, we wandered through the hills around Capernaum and marveled at the old village that was really an ancient city. I shared what I knew with Asa. "Many of the original streets were cobbled with stones that were in place for a thousand years. It is said the prophet Nahum was born here and the village was renamed when he died."

When we returned, Samuel was as excited as I could ever recall. Putting the animals up for the night, he brought the children to help and said, "Yeshua has returned. I asked him and his friends to come for a midday meal. He has agreed to speak in the evening tomorrow with the synagogue leaders and other prominent citizens."

What wonderful news, I thought and turned to Asa. "My boy, never think that all things just happen. I believe that this meeting is part of a divine plan." Asa nodded and remained pensive for a few moments, then I asked Samuel, "What can we do to assist you and Sarah?"

"Let us ask Sarah as she is the better planner in this family." Samuel said it with no hesitation or embarrassment. I smiled to myself, thinking that this was a man gaining wisdom.

That night and the next morning, the house was a flurry of activity. After breaking the night fast, we carried the large table under the roofed area near the garden. Sarah decided to use the garden area, which was large enough to gather many. She left us to organize as much seating as was available. Sarah, Rebekah, and a young man from one of the markets carried enough bread, cheese, olives, fruit, and wine to the house for most of the village. The table was set, the food laid out just in time for the guests to arrive.

At midday Yeshua came walking up the hill. He was trailed by Simon, Andrew, John, and two others I had not met. With a smile on his face, Yeshua came to the front door, touched the mezuzah, kissed his hand, and said, "Shalom, my friends."

Rebekah and Saul stood with mouths agape at the crew of rugged men about to enter their home. "Shalom, and welcome to our home," Samuel said with Sarah at his side leading the visitors to the table set up in the garden.

With twelve of us standing around the table, Samuel lifted a small wine goblet to recite the blessing for the meal. All hands raised drinks as the blessing was chanted, then we sipped. Still standing, Samuel introduced all in our family, and Yeshua responded, introducing his friends. The new arrivals we had not met before were *Pali'ef* (Philip) and *Natana'el* (Nathanael), two Yeshua had added to his flock when he taught in *Beit'Tzaida* (Bethsaida).

The meal was casual, and the children were delighted with the gentle nature of the tough- looking group, who paid attention to them. After the leisurely meal, we moved the table back to the kitchen area and gathered in the garden.

Spotting the donkeys, Yeshua asked Sarah and Saul, "Who are they?"

Sarah answered, "The mama is named Rose, and her baby is Sand."

Saul took Messiah's hand, pulled him, and said, "Come. Let me show you to them."

Samuel seemed upset with Saul, but before he could say anything, Messiah looked at him with a smile and said, "Saul, I love hardworking donkeys. Lead me to them."

As Saul led his new friend, Asa stood with Samuel and Yeshua's followers talking about the teaching on the mountain and the leper he had healed. Sarah and Rebekah were cleaning up; I just remained in place and marveled at the time with my family and the closeness to Adonai's anointed one.

Some village elders came to the house, followed by prominent citizens, Pharisees and scribes. The door to the house remained open as the crowd grew larger, spilling into the street. Everywhere I looked there were people of all shapes and sizes. Yeshua stood under the roof covering a portion of the living area hanging over the entrance to the garden.

Messiah held up his hands, and the crowd quieted. He welcomed everyone and started teaching from the ancient writings. Shortly after he said, "It is written," a piece of the roof fell at his feet. Yeshua looked up and took a step back. Other large pieces of the roof came tumbling down, and Samuel raced over to Messiah in alarm. Yeshua whispered something to Samuel; they both looked up and smiled.

To our amazement a man was being lowered from the hole in the roof. He was lying on a simple mat supported by ropes. When the man was on the floor in front of Yeshua, four heads of men appeared at the roof opening; the men were looking down. One of the men said, "Rabbi, our friend is paralyzed. Please help him. Master Samuel, please forgive us for hurting your roof. We could not get close because of the crowd. We will fix it. Please, teacher, help him."

Yeshua, with a serious look on his face, looked down at the man and said, "Your sins are forgiven." A great buzz of comments arose from the crowd. Yeshua looked out at them and claimed his authority to forgive sin! *This is it,* I thought. *He has said it! The world will never be the same!*

Tears burst from my eyes. I looked up to the heavens and said, "Praise Adonai!"

As I said my praise, Yeshua, in a commanding voice, said to the man lying at his feet, "Stand, take your mat, and go home." The sounds of gasping came from all the people in the garden. The house and the street filled with chatter lasting long minutes.

After watching the man get up, gather his mat, and walk out through the parting crowd, Yeshua was circled by many questioning him. Here and there I heard angry voices saying only Adonai could forgive sins.

Nathanael went over to Samuel and said, "Perhaps we should leave and give you back your home." He worked his way through the crowd, forming a wedge with Simon and Philip, leading Messiah out of the house and down the street.

The people slowly drifted out, and one of the village elders addressed Samuel. "You, a Pharisee, condone such speech? How can you allow such a thing?" He angrily left the house.

Samuel just shrugged and looked at me. "I suppose he did not witness this miracle."

Ruach HaKodesh—Holy Spirit

CHAPTER 49

THE FOOL

IT WAS A very busy two years after Messiah healed the paralyzed man at Samuel and Sarah's house in Capernaum. Although Asa and I were not part of Yeshua's disciples, we did witness many miracles in that time. With our regular trips to Cana and visits to Capernaum, we did not witness all his teachings and miracles. However, we were able to speak with many who were at the scenes of extraordinary events.

One miraculous occurrence took place not far from Sara and Samuel's house, and they were there! Samuel noticed a large crowd gathering on a hillside at the other side of the village. Hearing Yeshua was going to speak, he took Sarah and the children to witness and listen. Nicodemus had asked Samuel to be at as many events as possible so that he could prepare reports for the Sanhedrin. At that time Asa and I were in Jerusalem assisting Shabach for the upcoming Passover festival.

The crowd was so large they sat at a place at the edge of the gathering. As they waited the audience grew behind them. The crowd continued to grow; Yeshua began speaking. He taught on many things, and as the day wore on, Rebekah and Saul grew hungry. All that was left from what they had carried was a skin of water. Very few around them had brought enough provisions to last the full day.

Rebekah saw Yeshua wave and beckon to a boy about her age, who approached the rabbi with a small basket and set it at his feet. Yeshua had everyone sit. He reached into the basket, withdrew a small barley loaf, broke it, and said a blessing.

Then to everyone's astonishment, Yeshua had his disciples reach into the same basket and distributed barley bread to everyone in the huge crowd. He repeated the miracle with dried fish. Everyone who was gathered had enough to eat, and there was much left over. All from that small basket the boy had laid at Messiah's feet.

Samuel sought out the boy who had presented the basket to Messiah. With Rebekah's help recognizing the child, they approached the boy with his family as they were walking down the hill. When they asked how much food was in the basket, they were told two loves of barley bread and five small fish.

At home Samuel prepared a dispatch describing the event for Nicodemus. A miracle of feeding a multitude—having not witnessed it, I was envious.

Asa had become a very capable scribe, building on his academy training. He was with me in Jerusalem at two dispatch exchanges with representatives of the Magi. Each year it was a different man at the meetings after Arsham stopped coming to Jerusalem. The couriers were always tough, experienced scouts disguised as pilgrims visiting for the festivals. Another Passover was just a few months away; Asa helped me prepare the next dispatch, which had grown to five sealed cylinders.

My young son had aided me with writing down many of the events and was adept at properly sealing the dispatches. Though he had never trained as a carpenter, Asa was very talented working with wood. He built the tables we worked on and a sturdy cabinet to store our sealed documents. My son had abilities that came so naturally, gifts from Adonai.

During one trip to Cana, with Jonathan's help, we built a small addition to my quarters so the two of us could sit and write comfortably. We often laughed to each other, thinking that we looked like old and young ink-stained shepherd scribes.

Another of his gifts was *habinah* (great discernment). Asa was able to recognize acts and words as part of a pattern. He could predict events as they followed logical paths. Early in our travels together, he said to me, "Abba, the immerser is going to be arrested and killed."

I asked, "Why do you say that, my son?"

"The authorities he rails against cannot abide the growth of his following. They will do anything to silence him." Then with a heaviness in his voice, he added, "I fear the same for Messiah." From that moment on, there was always a fear surrounding Yeshua's miracles and teachings.

We heard of Yeshua stopping at a well near *Shi'kher* (Sychar) in Samaria on the way back to the region of Galilee. He paused to ask a Samaritan woman for a drink of water, an action forbidden by tradition. Yeshua used that opportunity to teach, and many Samaritans became his followers. Samaritans and *goyim* (gentiles) added greatly to his numbers.

Asa recorded many of the events that became part of the dispatch to the Magi. There was excited talk about miracles of walking on water, calming storms, casting out demons that reached us. We were able to interview witnesses of these events, and all facts had been gathered, recorded, and sealed.

One incident of healing in Jerusalem was very personal. Moses and Bidi's son Daniel, beaten by a Roman soldier, blind in one eye, had a shriveled hand and a deformed foot from the assault. Daniel told us of the day he was bathing in the Bethesda pool near the Sheep Gate, where I had taken him when he was able to walk after his injuries. The young man made it a habit to limp to the pool three times each week to be refreshed. He believed that the waters made him feel better every time he entered the pool and claimed that someday he would be completely healed.

It was before dawn on a Shabbat during a festival that Daniel awakened feeling very poorly, so he decided to make an extra trip to the pool before going to synagogue. The pool was crowded with visiting pilgrims and the usual lame, blind, and sick. After he was in the pool for a while, the sun was rising, and it was getting light, time to leave for the synagogue.

When Daniel started getting out of the pool, he noticed a man who was there, day after day, lying on a mat near one of the columns talking to someone. The man, Ga'len, always asked for help getting into the pool. Most of the time he was ignored, as if he was invisible. That morning a stranger standing with his back to the pool was talking to him. As the boy told it, the paralyzed man who could never move himself incredibly stood up, lifted his mat, and left the pool.

The man to whom Ga'len was talking still had his back to Daniel; he was turned, looking down at the pool. The man walked over, put a hand in the water, then stirred it in a circle, splashing water at Daniel. When the young man wiped the water from his face, the man was gone, and to his joy, he was able see out of both eyes. When he looked at his left hand, it was no longer shriveled. Then instead of limping out of the water, he was able to climb the stairs and run home to his family. All were overjoyed at the miracle of Daniel's healing and knew that the man stirring the water was either an angel or Messiah.

News of Yeshua had been steadily spreading, and his followers grew in numbers each day. There were many instances when he referred to himself as a shepherd, and the followers who knew his voice were his sheep. To our amazement and fear, there were times when some actually wanted to stone Messiah, but his ability to remain untouched was reassuring. The immerser had already been executed by beheading, the work of the family of Herod. Tension and underlying fear had become ever present throughout the land. Rome was not the only authority bringing death.

CHAPTER 50

THE SLEEP

My position at the academy in Jerusalem, though requiring limited work, still entailed occasional service and visits with Shabach. Flocks of snow-white lambs continued to pour into Migdal Eder, and as tav emeritus, I had ceremonial duties to perform. With Passover two months away, we headed to Jerusalem for a graduation ceremony I was required to attend and at which I was to make a speech.

Since acquiring our pack animals, Rose and Sand, we would leave them in Bethany, where they were purchased. There was ample livery space to house them before going into Jerusalem; there was no room for them at the academy.

On one occasion Ta'oma, the merchant, was not there. His mother, Y'oyas, said he was visiting with a grieving family of a friend who had died from an illness and been buried days before. The deceased man, *Eleazar* (Lazarus), was a dear friend of Yeshua, who was on his way to visit the family.

As soon as we heard the news, we headed for the home of Lazarus, hoping to meet with Yeshua. The large house appeared empty, but we still went to the door and knocked. The family should have been at home observing the seven-day mourning ritual. The door opened; a servant holding a broom answered.

"Shalom," I said, smiling at the woman. "We were told that the family of Lazarus was here mourning."

"They were here but left to go to the burial site. The rabbi wanted to see his friend's tomb." Pointing the broom handle, she added, "They all went to the graveyard at the edge of the village." She shook her head in disapproval and closed the door. Asa and I looked at each other and started walking quickly in the direction in which the servant had pointed.

On a small hillside, we spotted a group of men and women standing outside a family burial cave. As we drew close, we saw the large stone covering the entrance of the cave had been moved, leaving the burial chamber wide open. Asa said, "This man Lazarus must have been a man of means. Look at the size of the chamber and the large crowd."

We were close enough to see Yeshua, who had tears on his face. He nodded at us, looked at the opened tomb, took a step, and in a loud voice, said, "Lazarus, come forth!"

Everyone gasped at his words, which were followed by silence and stillness. It was as if sound and motion had stopped. I cannot recall how long we stood without moving or speaking before a woman started sobbing as a shadow had appeared at the mouth of the cave.

Then slowly the figure of a man wrapped in strips of burial linen took small steps forward. Yeshua instructed the man's sisters to remove the cloth strips, and they rushed forward. Chatter and praise erupted from the gathered group as the women unwrapped their brother's face and arms.

Two men stepped up to Lazarus, whose face was now clear of wrappings, looking as if he had been asleep. They lifted him onto their shoulders with urgings and cheers from the crowd.

It was a procession none had ever witnessed before as they headed back toward Bethany. The man who had been dead and entombed for days showed no sign of decay as they carried him back to his home. We had witnessed an unprecedented miracle. Others Yeshua had called back to life had not been dead long. This man Lazarus had been dead for days!

Asa and I followed the boisterous group back to the house. Messiah was in the center of the crowd, led by the two men carrying their living and breathing friend. All along the way, villagers stopped and stared at their neighbor they had been grieving, now back among them. Outside the house Yeshua paused then turned toward me and Asa while the others rushed inside.

With a smile Yeshua asked Asa, "Is your father teaching you well?"

Asa laughed in reply. "I believe he is trying to cram knowledge into me every waking moment. I must sleep just to escape the constant barrage of facts and reasonings." I smiled at my son's exaggeration.

Yeshua said, "Come inside and join us. We will celebrate Lazarus's awakening and return." We followed him into the home of his friend and rejoiced with his family. It was a while before Lazarus joined us, having bathed and donned fresh clothing.

I was sitting next to the fisherman John, who handed me a small cup of wine and said, "We were not that far from here when *he* was told of the death, but the rabbi waited three days before coming to call out his friend." Puzzled, I was looking at John when Lazarus entered the room, and everyone cheered.

The first question shouted at Lazarus was "What was it like to be dead?"

The house got quiet; after a moment the response came. "It was a dreamless sleep, until I heard Yeshua's voice telling me to come."

CHAPTER 51

THE DIVIDE

ASA AND I spent a week in Jerusalem after my speech at the academy, graduating another class of Aleph shepherds. The young men were in awe of Asa, who had become a legend. Not just because he was an orphan ward of the school but also because he was now considered a success traveling throughout the land with the tav emeritus, who had become his adoptive father. Shabach used the story of Asa as a teaching tool, giving more strength to the fact that shepherds were not just honorable workers but also had a future worth pursuing.

We spent one full day in the market, visiting with Moses and his family, marveling at Daniel's recovery. He was strong, agile, and happy spirited. Daniel had begged his parents to let him follow Yeshua. They prevailed and promised that he could at some time in the future. Meanwhile he had become a valuable part of the merchant family while keeping up with his studies. He was so bright he was accepted as a student of the famed Sanhedrin Pharisee *Gamliy'el ben Haly'el* (Gamaliel, son of Hillel).

One of Daniel's young instructors visited the booth to buy some dates. He was an arrogant little fellow who introduced himself as *Sha'ul HaTarsi* (Saul from Tarsus). He and Daniel got into a spirited discussion about Yeshua and his teachings. Daniel was eloquent in claiming that Yeshua was Messiah. The wiry Pharisee instructor was vehement in his argument against him. They parried back and forth, each convinced the other was wrong. Even though the disagreement was strong, they parted friends and looked forward to their study together. Daniel displayed an aptitude for arguing both sides of the law. He could make a formidable Sanhedrin in the future. Saul left the market convinced he had won his point with Daniel. Asa said, "What an odd fellow."

Daniel replied, "He debates every day with the Great Gamaliel, who gets frustrated with the exchanges."

"He should be careful of being expelled, what with the anger he displays," Asa said.

"Actually I think Gamaliel likes the verbal battles since we all learn how to present our points of view," Daniel added before he hoisted some boxes to be delivered. "As an instructor he argues with the revered rabbi then turns around to the students and presents the same side he was just against. He is a brilliant Pharisee!"

With concern I said, "What we witnessed is a great divide with our people. Despite the many who are following and believing in Yeshua, there seems to be just as many against him. I wonder, what will he do to bring all of our people, our nation, together?"

We left the market with Moses and his family and had a wonderful meal at their home. After a spirited talk about Messiah and some music presented by Asa and the girls, we headed to the academy for the night.

Shabach greeted us at my quarters with alarming news. "Apparently the Kohen HaGadol Caiaphas has hatched a plot. To me, it sounds like he wants to have Yeshua killed."

"What? You have heard such a thing?" I said, my voice shrill with alarm.

"No, my friend. I did not hear this thing directly, but one of my scribes was outside the temple when he overheard some chatter. He came rushing to tell me this evening."

"What else did he say?" I asked, gaining control of my emotions.

"The only thing directly attributed to Caiaphas was something akin to 'Yeshua will die for the Hebrew nation.'"

"Perhaps he was only speaking of Messiah's fervor," I said without much conviction.

Mirroring my original alarm, Asa said, "We must get word to Yeshua! Does anyone know where he is?"

As soon as Asa's words were spoken, a feeling of peace overcame me. Taking a deep breath, I looked at Asa, put a hand on his shoulder, and said, "He is Messiah. There is nothing man can do that he cannot overcome. We need not worry." Pausing, I added, "We need to focus on his followers and make sure they are protected. We are shepherds. What do we do?"

Shabach's immediate response was "You are right, my friend. We have spent our lives caring for and protecting our flocks. What we must do now is be shepherds to the flock that follows Messiah."

"How do we do that?" asked Asa. "We cannot protect them from Herod or the Romans. They have armies. We have rods and staffs."

Shabach looked at Asa. "During your academy training, what were you taught about protecting your flock from predators?"

Asa's rapid response was "'Fight, feint, flee, guard, move.'"

"Exactly!" the chazzen said. "In the morning let us put on our finest garments and spend the day walking around the temple, any area where leadership meet or congregate. Eli, walk around with Asa and speak to him as the teacher you are. I will drift about as well to learn. Let us meet midday at Moses's stall and share information." Agreed, we set off for a night of sleep.

After an early morning meal with Shabach in his quarters, we left the academy. He started his wanderings in the main temple area close to Caiaphas's core contingents. As a constant presence in the temple, he would not stand out. Asa and I went to be near the Hall of Hewn Stones, where the Sanhedrin meet. I was carrying a short, sealed note for Nicodemus, advising him of the rumored threats.

We stopped to listen to the young Levite cantors chanting the writings of David on the steps of the Nicanor Gate. They had beautiful, natural harmony; it was one of the pleasures I enjoyed while taking breaks from attending classes as a student. We stood for a while after they were done as some lingered in groups to chat.

Walking over to one of the groups, Asa said, "Shalom, cantors. Your songs were beautiful."

"Thank you, shepherd. Your ear is keen. You probably play an instrument for your flock." The cantor bowed, saying, "Compliment well received."

Asa nodded in return. "I have been traveling with my tav and am out of touch with news here in the City of Peace. What of the one called Messiah?"

One of the older singers said loudly, "He should be stoned for blasphemy and sedition!"

A younger singer came to Yeshua's defense. "He performs miracles as no one else in our history. He should be lifted up and replace Herod as king!"

The zeal of the young man's response had me tell him, "Please, friend. For your sake and the sake of those in your circle, speak not those words. Your safety and that of all those around you depends on wisdom. If any temple guard or Herod's spies heard you, you can only guess the penalty."

He calmed and answered quickly. "Yes, tav, you are correct. Even though I love my friend here, I do not agree with him, and my outrage can get the best of me." He then walked over to the older man, offering an embrace that was accepted.

Walking away from the steps, heading toward the hall, I said to Asa, "My son, I have never seen such divide. We must follow our own advice and take care with each word."

When Asa said, "Yes, Abba," joy washed away my concern. He had called me father for the first time! There I was, walking on sacred ground with my son, who had filled such an ache of longing of so many years. Moments later we were at the entrance to the grand hall where the Sanhedrin would meet.

To my additional joy, Samuel was standing near an entry column with several other men. I called out to him, "Samuel, shalom."

He turned toward me and Asa. "Good morning, tav," nodding in a very businesslike manner.

Sensing his coldness was a signal, I said, "Samuel, allow me to introduce my son Asa." Turning to Asa, I said, "My son, this is Samuel, a Pharisee from Capernaum. I have known his family for years."

Asa's discernment was obvious when he immediately nodded to Samuel and said, "Shalom, Samuel, gentlemen," while looking at the others.

Samuel excused himself from the other men and came over to us, walking away from the hall. In a low voice, as he steered us away from the others, Samuel said, "These men sit in judgment in the great hall, and they are saying terrible things about Yeshua. They are not the only ones, but there are those who are excited about the prospect of the long-awaited one."

We stopped walking well away from anyone. "What of you? Have you told them what you have witnessed and that you know him?"

Looking straight at me, Samuel responded, "I have only told them that I have met the man and he is wise, kind, and poses no threat, that he preaches love. When the time comes, I will declare in front of the entire Sanhedrin body that I believe he is Messiah."

"What of Nicodemus? What is his position?" I asked.

"The Teacher of Israel is torn. He wants to believe Messiah has come, and he truly likes Yeshua the man. But he is not ready to declare his position. I am following his lead in the hall, but when approached I shall declare for Messiah completely." Samuel said his words firmly. Then he added, "My great concern is Rome and Herod. If Herod takes this to Pilate and demands a Roman trial, his sway will not be good for Yeshua."

"You are correct, but we all must remember that the power that raised the dead cannot be defeated. Take heart. His time to act is fast approaching."

Samuel told us that he had been summoned by Nicodemus to bolster moderate voices in the chamber. I handed him the note to Nicodemus. Samuel agreed to deliver it and started back to the hall. With Asa at my side, we continued to wander about the temple grounds to get a feeling from the rest of the people.

Except for the Levite singers and the small group standing with Samuel, there was no tension in the air—other than the resentment of Rome. At midday we went to meet Shabach.

CHAPTER 52

THE BREEZE

It was a cool early spring day but warmer by midday meal. We purchased some cheese, bread, and two roasted chickens from a tent at the edge of the market and brought enough for all at Moses's booth to eat. When we arrived, business was brisk, with a fresh shipment of dates, figs, and spices, one of which I had never before seen or tasted. It was causing a sensation at the sales table.

"What is this?" I asked behind several people finishing transactions with Bidi.

She looked up at me with a radiant smile and said, "It is called *zenghevil* (ginger). It is a root plant we have heard of that has a wonderful fragrance and is quite strong. Wait a moment, and I will let you have a taste. It has recently arrived from a southern caravan."

Layla, the eldest daughter, had grown as tall as Asa. She handed us small slivers of yellow with a brown edge. "Be very careful. Take only a tiny piece in your mouth, and do not touch your eyes after handling it."

I put the piece on my tongue and felt a mild sting and inhaled a clean fragrance. As I removed the spice from my mouth, Asa shrugged his shoulders and put the whole slice in his mouth. He chewed twice then spit out, coughing and gasping, tears welling in his eyes. Layla laughed. "I told you to take care. You have just wasted two coppers' worth of this fine spice. You can pay me when you get to the table." Shaking her head and still laughing, she returned to assist her mother.

Moses came from the back of the stall with Daniel after loading and storing the new shipment of exotics from the caravan. "Shalom, friends," he boomed.

Asa and I rounded the sales table and brought the food we carried, putting the items on a small sorting stand near the supplies. Shabach came, and we began sharing the food and relating what we had observed. After telling what we had experienced at the hall with Samuel, Shabach had a much different story.

"There was not one mention of Yeshua or his presence anywhere in the temple proper. Very strange. Then I went to the pools, and the people were teeming with praise for him and expect that he will soon take a crown over Herod and Rome. They spoke without fear of being heard or any retribution even though temple guards were near. The guards ignored them as if they were speaking nonsense."

Moses chimed in. "There was a time in the history of Aksum the people were expecting a savior to come and release them from the tyrant that ruled. It happened one day, and the outcome was not what the people wanted or expected."

"What happened?" Asa asked.

"The people rose up, declared a new king, and on the day of his coronation, an invading army came thundering in. They impaled the ruling family, enslaved the army, and became the new tyrants in control of our people."

Asa stood silent then said, "Rome is too strong for an invasion. Only a miracle from Adonai can free us."

Layla walked up to the table, took a piece of roasted chicken, and said, "We do have a miracle maker among us." She looked at Asa, shook her head, smiled, then walked back to the sales table.

Asa nodded at her remark then looked at Moses. "Maybe she should study with Gamaliel."

Moses laughed. "True, but she is much too valuable here. Since she started working, our sales have increased. People love talking to her. She might be smarter than all of us combined."

Shabach smiled and said, "If it was allowed, I would bring her to the academy. She would make a great chazzen." We all snorted at the irony of the statement. Shabach more than anyone knew the absurdity of the comment because of politics and tradition.

Our mood had lifted, but the fact remained that there was a plot against Yeshua. Bidi came to the little table and said, "Caiaphas's lackeys are wandering about the market asking questions." Looking at Asa, she asked, "Would you care for another piece of ginger?" She grinned at my son, tore a small piece of cheese off the chunk on the table, handed it to Asa, and said, "Here, this will take the sting away."

Asa just smiled with his head down and said, "Moses, this family of yours is relentless." We all laughed good naturedly at Asa's discomfort.

I patted my son on the back. "Let us find these errand boys of the kohen and see what kind of questions they are asking." The three of us left the stall and went in different directions. Returning after an hour passed, Asa was the first to speak.

"The two I had conversations with are scribes from a class at the academy who now work in the temple library. They were friendly enough but were a little uneasy talking about Caiaphas. They did ask me if I knew anything about Yeshua or where he might be. I did not have to feign ignorance as I have no idea where he might be at this moment."

Shabach showed us a beautiful carved box of a rare wood. "I had to purchase something since I encountered the temple bursar at a rare gift stall. He, too, was asking if I or any of my staff had heard of the whereabouts of the one who now has the following of the immerser's disciples. No doubt there is great concern over his growing flock."

All shepherds sense dangers; as we care for our flock, it becomes our nature. Just when that thought entered my mind, I felt a breeze carrying the words "Where are your sheep?" I had finally come to realize completely that Messiah was speaking to me and that someday, perhaps soon, I would know where to look.

CHAPTER 53

THE WELL

WITH THE PURPOSE of getting as much information as possible, we continued walking the streets of Jerusalem. When we returned to the market at dusk, we shared what we had heard. There was information that Messiah was headed in every direction, every road out of Jerusalem. None we met and spoke with had a clear indication where Yeshua had gone.

With a few weeks before the Passover, I decided to go home to Cana, then Capernaum, before returning to Jerusalem a week before the festival. Even though I was not expected to perform regular duties, it was necessary to be available and prepared. Asa, on the other hand, was required to be at the temple for the sacrifices, as were all Alephs. We said our goodbyes to Moses and his family, returned to the academy with Shabach, and retired early.

The next morning Asa and I left at dawn for Bethany to get Rose and Sand. Our sweet animals seemed happy to see us, and we headed to Cana. Having been around sheep all my life, I knew that every animal had a personality, though most people thought they were all just dumb walking, unroasted meals. My father taught me every living creature was created with and for a purpose. When holding a newborn lamb, I was always in awe of Adonai's power and love. Those sweet, gentle creatures were born for sacrifice. Our Rose and Sand were created and born for hard labor.

They knew us when we arrived at Ta'oma's stable and seemed to smile at our presence. We petted them, spoke to them, gave them treats, and walked them for a bit before mounting them to start our way to Cana. It was another beautiful spring day.

Everywhere on the road, there was talk of Yeshua—mostly good, some bad. We kept to ourselves on the trip and arrived early afternoon on the third day. Approaching the house, I kept up my tradition of goat calling. To my delight I heard Caleb yell, "Sabba!" from the inside. The door opened, and the five-year-old ran directly to Asa, hugging him and saying, "Shalom, *Dohd* (Uncle) Asa!" Caleb looked at me and added, "Shalom, Sabba." Releasing Asa, who was wearing a teasing grin that said, "He likes me better than you," Caleb went to Sand and Rose to pet their muzzles.

We heard another shalom from the doorway, and Yodi was standing there looking at Asa with a smile. I knew at that moment that the family would continue to grow; Asa lit up looking at Caleb's teacher. "Welcome home you two," she said, finally looking at me.

Returning her smile, I said, "We are delighted to be here as always. Blessed is the home of the righteous. We will take Rose and Sand out back, wash, and meet you in the kitchen. If you and Caleb would be kind enough to fix us something." Yodi smiled and called to Caleb, and we went to the wash.

We had a chance to bathe and dress in clean garments. Yodi was waiting at the table with Caleb, who was writing on a slate with soft sandstone. "He is practicing his letters. Come look, he is very good."

I looked over Caleb's shoulder, touched his head, and said, "You will be a judge someday, just like your father." Asa and Yodi continued to gaze at each other. Yodi broke the moment. "Please, sit. I have some tea and honey cakes to refresh you."

Caleb broke in. "Look, Sabba, I wrote you!" On the slate board was a neat rendering of my name.

"You could teach other children to write. You are so good," I said, kissing his head.

After a short respite, Asa said, "Abba, I am going to write about that glow we saw on Mount Tabor that evening, even though we heard nothing about a fire on the mountain. There was something about the color of the glow, how white it was. It was probably nothing, but it should be recorded."

I nodded agreement and said, "I will take Caleb for a walk around the village." Yodi agreed, saying it was the end of the lessons for the afternoon, and she would start preparing dinner since we had arrived unexpectedly.

During the past two years, Yodi had become more a family member than just a teacher. I left with Caleb, and since he was a little more than five, he did not think it proper to hold my hand.

I did not have to introduce my grandson to anyone. He took the responsibility of introducing me to the merchants and passersby. Jonathan was not at the village gate; I presumed he was visiting our flock partners. When we returned to the house, Marta was there with Addassah, my beautiful toddling granddaughter, the only child in our family with flaming red hair. She waddled over, calling me "Ba." I scooped her up and kissed the top of her head. Adda giggled, yanked my beard, and kept repeating, "Ba, Ba." I loved my new name.

Marta greeted me with a hug, took the sweet redhead for a nap, and returned to the kitchen to help Yodi prepare the evening meal. I joined Asa in our quarters, where he was engrossed in writing.

Stopping, he looked up at me and said, "I am convinced Yeshua was on that mountaintop and was the source of that light. He is like a light when he teaches, and to me, he radiates the light of love wherever he goes."

"Yes, my son, he is brightness in this world, but what you are writing cannot be part of the dispatch to the Magi. What we send them must be fact and confirmed by two according to the laws passed down by the sages."

Asa thought for a moment. "Abba, I would like to keep a record of my thoughts and observations apart from the dispatches we send. May I do this on my time when the thoughts come upon me?"

"Of course you may! We will seal your writings and keep them separate and store them. Perhaps someday you will be a renowned scholar whose writings will be passed from generation to generation."

Asa laughed heartily and said, "No doubt a shepherd will garner the attention of the world in the future!" He shook his head, still smiling, and went back to his stylus.

Jonathan came home excited about the number of lambs to be delivered to Migdal Eder for the upcoming Passover. "Papa, we have never before been blessed with such a yield of perfect-looking lambs. We will need many shepherds to move our flocks this year."

How blessed we had become since that first trip I took and the night of Yeshua's birth, I thought. "We are blessed indeed, my son. Well done."

Dinner was a delight, and Asa asked permission to escort Yodi for her walk home at the north end of the village, which I granted. Both Jonathan and Marta agreed that we should be prepared for a ritual *erusin* (betrothal). "I will ask Asa upon his return this evening if I should present my offering to Yodi's parents." Marta put the children to sleep, and the house was quiet when Asa returned.

At the table, with small cups of wine, I asked Asa if tomorrow would be a good time to present my betrothal offer to Yodi's parents. "Is it that obvious?" He was surprised that we all had noticed his constant gaze at her every move and hers in return. When we all laughed, he just smiled and nodded his head. Looking at me, Asa said with a little boy look on his face, "Tomorrow would not be soon enough for either of us."

"Very well. In the morning you will take me to her home." Jonathan and Marta patted the table with their approval, and Jonathan nodded at me.

I looked at Asa and said, "Son, join me and Jonathan."

We stood, Jonathan kissed Marta, and we walked to the back of the house. We exited the family home and went to the workshop that had replaced the small shed when we acquired Rose and Sand. We now had four birthing stalls for the lambs and a shearing area. The location of the original stall where we built the storage and shearing stands was where we were headed. It had been purposely constructed over a dry well by my father's father for a dual purpose. Stories were passed down of roving hoards terrorizing small villages. With calculated caution one of our ancestors used an old dry well to hide and store food, crude weapons, and bags of coins. Over the years the well was enlarged; many years later it became a huge room with oil lamps to provide light deep underground, a large storage area for family survival and wealth. It had an escape exit at the far end.

Jonathan moved a table, revealing the old, dry well artfully concealed under a fake floor. It was black as coal looking down when Jonathan lowered himself on a wooden ladder the height of three men. We could hear the scraping of flint before a faint light appeared. I told Asa to descend, and when he reached bottom, I stepped on the ladder, pulled the wood floor over the opening, and went down.

Asa stood stunned by the sight. Jonathan lit four lamps, revealing walls of cobbled stones. There were wooden shelves with sealed clay water jugs, linen sacks of dried meat, fruits, and vegetables on one wall. The opposite wall had a stack of bedrolls and blankets. On the wall above, there were shelves filled with neat piles of clothing. Farther down, a wooden table was braced against a wall with a stack of stools underneath. Farther down still was a large chest filled with weapons: swords, knives, and many slings and a huge supply of stones.

Jonathan spoke first. "Asa, you have just entered the family treasure room. It was created many years ago for safety and escape but has become the secret housing of our family wealth."

I placed my hand on Asa's shoulder. "My son, you have just cut covenant with the rest of the family. We are down here to show you this for the future, should you ever need to hide and escape. However, tonight there is another reason. As I am father of the groom, we are here to prepare an offering for Yodi to become your wife."

Jonathan went to the wall opposite the table and wiggled out two stones about chest high. Setting the stones aside, he lifted what appeared to be the entire wall below the stone opening, a wood slab covered with pieces of flat stone. "Come," I said, leading Asa to the space. Jonathan held a lamp in front of the opening, revealing shelves loaded with stacks of gold and silver coins, wealth accumulated over generations. Tucked in a corner of the space was the clay-encased scroll that had been given to me by the Magi many years before. "What I am about to do is gather a fair price to give Yodi's father for losing a lifetime of service from his daughter. It is a custom as old as our people, the betrothal price."

Asa stood silent, absorbing this information about his new family. I filled two large leather pouches. "You will help me carry this price, equivalent to your future bride's presumed weight, and we will present it to her father. We shall seal the written agreement should he accept." While I was loading the coins, Jonathan prepared the betrothal document.

The two bags were ready, and Jonathan showed Asa how to properly cover the opening and replace the stones so that it looked like a solid wall again. We walked him to the end of the long room, to the foot of another ladder, the escape end. There was enough covering at both ends of the room to fool most eyes yet allow enough air in and out. With that done we extinguished the lamps, climbed out of the room, replaced all the coverings, and returned to the house.

Marta was waiting for us with four small cups of wine so that we could toast the future.

CHAPTER 54

THE SCROLLS

YODI'S FATHER, *DAV'ED* (David), was much older looking than I had expected. My future daughter-in-law said her father married her mother after her natural father died, when he hit his head from a fatal fall. Her new father was the unmarried elder brother who followed the law and tradition of *geu'lah* (kinsman redeemer). Yodi's mother, *Sadyah* (Sadie), was young, vibrant, and smart. When Asa and I arrived at their modest home, I was not surprised to find it neat, clean, and full of life. What did surprise me was a wall of scrolls. From floor to ceiling, there was a wall filled with parchments, except for a window in the center allowing in morning light. It was the home of scholars.

We were greeted warmly, sat drinking tea and munching on flat bread and honey. At what I perceived to be the appropriate moment, I began. "I am here to present my son and my offer for your lovely daughter. Removing her from your home will be a loss. The offer of my son and some coins is agreement that a date will be set for all to witness the vows, creating a new family." I nodded at Asa, who exited the house. He had to make two trips, bringing in the sacks of coins carried on the back of Rose.

"David, this gift I ask you to accept will not replace the loss of your daughter in this household but is an offer of fair compensation. Should you say yes, we will begin to enlarge our family home to receive the new couple on the agreed upon date of *kiddushin* (sanctification) when they become one."

As was custom, Yodi and her mother sat apart from the table, remaining silent. I could see that Sadie's face reflected surprise at the size of the offering. David sat still, his eyes locked on mine, his face expressionless.

As the silence grew, I could feel Asa's tension behind me. I knew that he and Yodi were looking at each other expectantly. Without blinking or moving a muscle, David sat silent until his mouth began smiling. "Do you expect me to believe that these bags of lifeless coinage will replace the radiance of the life removed from these walls?"

Keeping his gaze, I said, "I do not. What I do expect is that these mere coins will enable you to acquire assistance and comfort as needed for your home and body. What you do not see is the fellowship of a growing family into which you and your wife will be grafted. The joy of kinship and children's laughter will help fill a void that can never be fully replaced."

Silence.

Sadie shifted uncomfortably behind her husband. Yodi's face was a mask of uncertainty. We all waited.

"I agree, my friend. Our family and yours will be woven into an eternal tapestry." When he raised a gnarled hand to offer acceptance, I could hear the other souls in the room exhale with relief.

Adding my hand to his, I said, "It is I who am honored to receive distinguished minds as part of our mutual inheritance." I stood, and Asa handed me the parchment scrolls of the contract, which I laid in front of David. He stood, his wife and daughter stood with him, and they all embraced.

I looked at Asa and said, "My son, you are now legally betrothed and will follow all customs and rituals of our people."

To Yodi and her parents, I said, "Please join us this evening for a meal to celebrate." With a chorus of acceptance, plans were made. Asa remained behind to talk with his new family members. I left with Rose and went home.

Marta prepared a wonderful evening meal for the combined family. The food was wonderful and the company a delight. David was a fountain of knowledge, telling stories of famous men, their triumphs and failures. Sadie matched her husband's knowledge, comparing the gallant men he spoke of with women who had been lauded throughout history. She had a way of bringing humor into every story she told and had a lovely singing voice.

Asa played his flute, and Sadie sang songs of the kings. It was a lovely evening of celebration. We stayed in Cana through the following Shabbat to work with Jonathan, the flocks, and our partners. It allowed Asa time to spend with Yodi in the evenings. The morning after Shabbat, we left for Capernaum.

Our family in the village of Nahum were delighted with the news of Asa's betrothal. We stayed with them through the following Shabbat. It was a time rich with family togetherness. Asa was happy to be with the children, taking them for long rides on Rose and Sand. I was able to visit Simon's wife and mother. Neither one knew exactly where Yeshua was roaming and teaching.

Evening meals were enjoyable, with Samuel having lots of stories about arguments in the great hall. Nicodemus had Samuel studying ancient scrolls and writings prophesying the advent of Messiah. Samuel claimed the more they studied, the closer Nicodemus came to the decision that Yeshua was indeed Messiah. However, he had not made declaration to anyone. There was one writing Nicodemus kept discussing with Samuel, from the writings of the prophet *Yesha'yahu* (Isaiah).

One evening Samuel said, "Abba, Eli. Nicodemus keeps going back to one scroll and one particular passage. The parchment talks about a man of sorrows, one who was despised." Samuel was quiet for a moment. "I have read the words over and over, and I, too, have come to a point of deep concern."

"What is it, my son?" I asked.

Tears welled up in his eyes, and Samuel looked at me with pain on his face. In a soft voice, almost a whisper, he quoted the scroll. "'Through his wounds we are healed.' My heart breaks every time I read those words."

Projecting hope, I said, "We must believe that Messiah will prevail. We already know there is great opposition to him, plots to deny, even kill him. But the prophet whose writings you speak has a name we can trust."

Samuel's face lightened a bit; he cracked a small smile and said, "Abba, I am constantly amazed at the wisdom of a shepherd."

We slept well that night, and in the morning, Asa and I left for Jerusalem

CHAPTER 55

THE BEGGAR

THE ROUTES TO the big city were not crowded as we made our way from Capernaum. The road was becoming familiar to Asa as he had made many trips with me, giving us an opportunity to create memories. He had progressed in his training at the academy to a dalet shepherd and was determined to eventually become a tav. My son wanted to follow in my footsteps! I missed him the months he was in Jerusalem for training. But the time was good for him, and the increased stipend earned would help with his future needs.

Much of our conversation on that trip was about marriage, the wedding, and building on to the family home. "Abba, should we add on to your side of the house or the side with Jonathan?" His question made me realize that my time with him would grow less as he built his own life and family. I was grateful for the road trips having given us concentrated time together, something I had very little of with my father. At times they made me melancholy thinking of my Rachel.

The route we took was through Jericho on the way to Bethany to put up Rose and Sand while we were in Jerusalem. We had become friendly with the innkeeper near the caravansary where the Samaritan had rescued the Hebrew merchant and made it a practice to take meals there each trip on that route. We never met the Samaritan but were told he had paid the innkeeper for the entire time the merchant took to recover.

It was a chilly late afternoon when we tied up in front of the inn. "Shalom, Eli, Asa. I have a hot stew loaded with vegetables, fresh-baked bread, and new beer, three coppers each."

Without hesitation Asa said, "Lorah, bring us all of it and a beer for yourself. Since we are the only ones here, join us."

The big man laughed and said, "Eli, you are teaching your son well!" It was but a minute before he returned with a large tray, carrying all that we had ordered plus a huge flagon for himself. Asa and I looked at each other with knowing smiles.

Lorah sat after setting the tray down, took a swallow of beer, and said, "You have missed two miracles just up the road yesterday." With our mouths full of food, Lorah milked the moment, waiting for us to chew and swallow.

"What happened?" I asked, still chewing.

Taking another drink, the innkeeper put his flagon down, wiped his mouth with the back of his hand, and said, "There is this local tax collector, a nasty runt of a man who has gotten rich off the backs of all of us that are squeezed paying taxes to Rome. He climbs this tree to get a better look at the one they call prophet coming through town. The rabbi calls to him by name and invites himself to the miserable man's house."

Lorah paused, smiling, rocking his head up and down. "Many of the people around here were furious that the prophet would meet with a man so despised."

Asa asked, "Why would he meet a tax collector?"

The innkeeper looked at Asa, still smiling, and said, "The next thing that caused such a stir was the little man running out of his house telling everyone that he was giving half his fortune away and would be paying back anyone he had cheated fourfold. Then the rabbi comes out of the house and tells the crowd the tax collector is a son of Abraham, and salvation had come to his house."

"Think of it," I said, "a few minutes with the prophet and the man changes his ways. Yes, my friend, that is a miracle. What of the other?" I asked, taking another mouthful of the delicious food.

"It was wonderful! For as long as I can remember, there has been this blind beggar, *Bar'Timai* (Bartimaeus), sitting on a blanket between here and the caravansary, pleading for alms. Some mornings I would bring him parcels of my leftover food and give him a copper."

The grizzled innkeeper lowered his voice. "I heard this shouting from a crowd telling someone to be quiet. So I go out the door and see Bartimaeus on his knees yelling at the top of his voice, 'Son of David, have mercy on me!' over and over, even louder than the crowd trying to quiet him. I started walking over there, getting angry at them, ready to protect this poor beggar that I had finally realized was my friend." Lorah stopped to take a breath. "Then I heard the rabbi's voice over everyone saying, 'Call him.'"

Another pause and Lorah's eyes began to water. "The crowd called to Bartimaeus. He jumped up and ran, his hands outstretched, and stopped in front of the rabbi Yeshua. He asked my blind beggar friend what he wanted, and Bartimaeus pleaded, 'Rabbi, I want to see.'" Lorah stopped his story, took a rag from his apron, wiped his face, and took another sip of beer. He took a deep breath and, looking at us with the face of a man who had witnessed a miracle, said, "The rabbi said, 'Go, your faith has healed you.' What do you think Bartimaeus did?" We sat there with our mouths open.

"He left his cloak lying on the road and joined the group that follows Yeshua. When Bartimaeus walked by me, he smiled looking at me with clear eyes. And this man who could not see is now walking with the rabbi."

Asa beat me to the words "Where were they going?"

"They were heading toward Bethany." We gulped down our food, paid, and as we were walking out the door, Lorah said, "If only I had the courage to follow."

I turned to the sorrowful-looking innkeeper and said, "Take heart, my friend. Perhaps someday you will." We gathered Rose and Sand and left for Bethany.

CHAPTER 56

THE PERFUME

THE ROAD FROM Jericho to Bethany on the way to Jerusalem was hilly and famous for robbers, so we camped on a ridge that night. It was a cold evening that early part of Nisan, especially on that open hill. To make things worse, Shabbat started at sundown, so tradition and law forbade us to make and keep a fire. We ate cold food with a strong wine then sat talking about what the future might bring. There was a half-moon, giving us enough light to see anyone approaching. Plus Rose and Sand were excellent lookouts. They would natter if a stranger neared, so we were able to sleep without incident. The extra gear we had packed for the festival came in handy in keeping us warm without a fire. The breeze on that hilltop whispered as I was falling asleep, "Where are your sheep?"

We were off to a predawn start the next morning, walking briskly without mounting our beloved animals; riding was forbidden until sundown. The day was off to a cold start but warmed up nicely, and we were on the outskirts of Bethany on a beautiful late afternoon. We had to pass the home of Lazarus, the man Messiah called out of the tomb back to life. "Abba, let us see how he and his family are doing, being so close. We can get Rose and Sand to Ta'oma at dusk." I nodded in assent, and we went to the house where the awakened man lived with his sisters.

Traditionally families would gather for a meal just after sundown, but the house was dark as we approached. "I pray that he is well. The house looks so desolate," Asa said, looking at the quiet home.

"He is at a dinner up the way," boomed the voice of Simon. Asa and I turned quickly even as Rose and Sand spun at the sound of the large man's voice. As Simon walked toward us, we could hear him laughing at having startled us. "I am sorry, my friends, for frightening you." If we did not know the man, we would have been taken aback by the sight of him approaching us with the sun at his back. His orange mane with the setting sun behind him made Simon look as if his hair was fire, a silhouette enveloped in a radiant glow.

"What are you doing here?" I asked.

"We are on the way to Jerusalem for the Passover, of course. Would you think our teacher would miss the festival?" he asked in a joking manner. "Come with me and join us. We are about to have a meal at the home of a Pharisee that bears the same name as me. He is somewhat renowned having been cured of leprosy. His son *Yehuda* (Judas) is with us and carries the purse for the group. Yeshua will be delighted to see you."

We followed Simon to a large house that was aglow and buzzing with chatter. Asa took Rose and Sand to the side of the house, took off their packs, and fed them while Simon waited at the door. We entered the house and were hit with the fragrance of a very expensive perfume. The room was silent, eyes were on us, and we saw Yeshua sitting near Lazarus. There was a woman at the rabbi's feet. Yeshua smiled at us. "Shalom, shepherd friends."

A younger man who appeared angry or frustrated walked right past the three of us at the door and left the house without saying a word. "That is Judas, the son of this house, the follower I just mentioned," Simon offered.

As he was speaking, Marta, the sister of Lazarus, said, "Shalom. Please join us." She led us to a place at the table. The perfumed air was coming from Yeshua, who had the sweet-smelling oil on his hair and feet.

We sat, and the sound of voices drifted in from the street. A crowd had gathered to get a glimpse of the rabbi and the man he had called back to life. Blessings were said, a meal was served, food was eaten, and talk filled the room.

At meal's end I asked Simon, owner of the house, if Asa and I would be permitted to camp beside his home. Being a gracious host, he said, "Of course! Had we a room available, you would be welcome to stay. Certainly, camp here. Also, feel free to join us for the morning meal."

We said our thanks and good night to all and set up camp near the side of the house. The crowd disappeared, the house got quiet, and we went to sleep with the fragrance of perfume heavy in the air.

CHAPTER 57

THE COLT

THE SKY WAS lightening, the smell of baking bread the new perfume in the morning mist.

"*Boker tov* (Good morning), friends." I looked up at the man whose home we were camped beside.

"Shalom." I said; Asa stirred. Rose and Sand were eating out of two buckets.

"I took the liberty of feeding your good-natured mounts. You must have been exhausted to have slept so soundly." The man named Simon was smiling as I stood. He bowed his head and said, "Please forgive my son Judas who passed by and did not even acknowledge you last night. He was angry after a disagreement with the rabbi and some of his followers just before you entered. Please come into my home again and break the night's fast." Asa stood and brushed himself, and I accepted the invitation.

Simon was about my age and wore a simple wool garment and a plain knitted *yarmulke* (skullcap). "One of my servants will water and groom your animals while you are inside." He left us to groom ourselves as best we could.

"I am very hungry, Abba." Asa growled the obvious with his cracking morning voice.

"Pin on your dalet. I will wear my tav. After all, we will be eating with a powerful Pharisee and a friend of Messiah." As we headed to the front door, a servant carrying water rounded the back of the house to Rose and Sand. Our mounts seemed as grateful for the attention as we were.

We entered as the sun was rising. The room looked quite different than it had the previous evening. It was spare, with only a large table and four chairs. Our host was seated when we entered but stood as we neared the table. He said, "My friends, please sit," pointing at chairs to his right. "I am not sure my son will be joining us."

Two servants brought hot bread, boiled eggs, olives, and figs to the table, with goblets of warm morning wine. Our host said the appropriate blessings and tore a loaf, handing each of us a piece. "The rabbi and his followers left very early. They were quiet so they would not awaken you."

Taking a sip of wine, I said, "Thank you for your hospitality. We are on the way to Jerusalem. Is that where they are going?"

Simon's demeanor changed. With a concerned look, he said, "I hope not. There is a terrible split in the leadership over Yeshua. I am afraid there are those who would do him harm. It has been reported to me there are some who would kill Lazarus because Yeshua brought him back to life and the rabbi's following has grown so large so fast." His words alarmed me more for Lazarus, a man, not Messiah. He continued. "Some in powerful positions are outraged that any living man would call himself 'Lord of Shabbat.'"

Lowering and shaking his head, our host confessed, "I regret I did not show the rabbi proper respect last night. He cured me of leprosy. I believe he is Messiah. I did not greet him with a kiss or anoint him. Instead his friend *Maryam* (Mary), a follower from Magdala, gave him that honor. Perhaps my behavior is more closely reflected in my son than I care to admit."

When he looked up, a pained look etched on his face, I said, "We are just men, and we are all subject to errors of omission."

Simon nodded somberly. "His followers are planning a great announcement and entrance into Jerusalem. They are proclaiming he is Messiah and that they have witnessed untold miracles."

Asa asked, "When are they planning this revelation?"

"Very soon, I expect. Certainly, with the city crowded with pilgrims, it may even occur today." Looking at me, he asked, "You are the shepherd Yeshua has spoken of, the one that was there the night he was born, are you not?"

"I am."

"There has always been the wisp of a notion that there were shepherds at his birth. I am happy to know that it is true. You honor my home with your presence."

"Your words humble me, my friend. Someday, perhaps soon, I will share the details of that night. But for now our Levitical shepherd duty beckons. We must prepare the sheep."

Silence filled the room. Our host leaned forward, looked at Asa then at me, and said, "His enemies, those plotting against him, may make you a target as well. Please, be very cautious, my friend. You never know how close you are to one who would do you great harm." Sitting up straight again, he added, "You are always welcome in my home, and again, I am sorry my son misbehaved. Hopefully you will see him soon and know that he is a fine young man."

Standing, I nodded to our new friend. "Thank you, Simon, for your hospitality." He nodded in return, and we left the house to gather Rose and Sand before going to Jerusalem.

On the way Asa asked, "Abba, do you think we are in danger?"

"No, my son. If there is any danger, it will be to those who have been walking with him, the close group of followers, Simon, John, and Yeshua's other disciples."

Asa remained quiet until we arrived at the building and stalls of the donkey merchant. Ta'oma was standing with his mother, Yoyas. She held hands with her grandson *Baruch* while Ta'oma carried her other grandson *Noach*. "Shalom, Eli and Asa. I was expecting you," Ta'oma said, rocking the little boy.

"Are you putting the little man to work already?" I asked jokingly.

"He is strong and can get a good grip on the short hairs of any mount. He will be riding before he can walk," Ta'oma said, tickling the boy, eliciting a giggle.

Asa asked, "Since your hands are busy, where would you like me to put Rose and Sand?"

Ta'oma answered Asa but was looking at me. "Just tie them to the post in front of the house. Noah's father will be out shortly to take them back to their stalls. Eli, your young friends, the students of the rabbi, were here earlier to borrow a donkey and her colt. It was very odd."

"Borrow them? What do you mean?" Asa asked.

"It was barely light. I brought the animals to the posts to attract buyers. Two of the rabbi's men were here, and one of them asked for the colt. He said, '*Ha Adon* (The Lord) needs it and another. They will be returned shortly.'"

"What did you do?" I asked excitedly.

"I allowed them to borrow the mounts. They knew exactly what was needed, a mother and her unridden colt. When they referred to the rabbi as 'Lord,' I knew the colt would be back after a special event."

While clasping Ta'oma's arm, I said excitedly, "My friend, you are an important part of a day that will be remembered. I believe the rabbi will ride your colt into the city as foretold in an ancient scroll: 'The king comes riding a colt.'"

I turned to Asa and said in a voice charged with excitement, "Son, grab our gear. We must get to Jerusalem quickly!"

I turned back to Ta'oma, grabbed him by the shoulders, and kissed him on each cheek. "Thank you, my friend, thank you. We will be back after the festival."

I released Ta'oma and looked at Asa. "We must make haste to observe what is about to unfold!" We walked briskly toward Jerusalem.

CHAPTER 58

THE RIDE

As we neared Jerusalem, we heard a great uproar of many voices chanting, but the words were not clear. As we passed the Mount of Olives, following the sounds, there was a path of palm fronds leading to the city. They were crushed, telling us that many feet had passed over them. As we got nearer the throng, the words "*Hoshia na! Hoshia na!* (Deliver us! Deliver us!)" were the chants. The closer we got, the denser the crowd, the louder the words. Near the Temple Mount, there were more branches on the ground, with garments trampled on top.

The crowd entered the temple compound through the *Sha'ar Harachamim* (Gate of Mercy) on the northeast corner near the academy. I said to Asa, "Let us bring our gear to the rooms so we can move about more swiftly." We veered off to our quarters.

Not a soul was at the academy. We dropped off our loads and ran to the wall that overlooked the city. Shabach and several others were gazing at the mass now filling the streets. We went to the edge and witnessed a truly wonderful sight.

Yeshua was riding the borrowed colt, followed by Simon, who led the other donkey and many of his followers. The crowd parted as he approached, laying down their cloaks and palm fronds, creating his path. Many in the streets were jumping up and down, shouting, "Blessed is he who comes in the name of Adonai. Blessed is the king of Israel." It was a scene never before witnessed, a frenzy of joy!

"Enough of this!" All on the parapet were startled by the loud exclamation. "We must put an end to this madness!" It was Caiaphas, who had turned and was striding back toward the temple center. The look on his face was a twist of madness, as if he had been suddenly possessed by a demon of destructive fury.

Shabach came over to us as he watched the departing Caiaphas with his toadies. "I have never seen the kohen in such a state. There is a storm coming." Turning back to the two of us, Shabach said, "I am glad the both of you are here. You are a comfort, my family. These are strange times. It is as if the world is splitting in two. I have never been so unsettled." Looking directly at me, he asked, "Brother, I know your family will be camping nearby, but can you stay near the temple and the academy during the next few days? I may need your assistance."

I nodded. Asa asked, "Chazzen, how may we help?"

My friend looked at my son. "Asa, you and Eli together are a strong team. Being near to me is all I ask. Stay with each other, and celebrate with your family in camp." With a surprising look of sadness for a man who was always quick with a smile, he said, "I will be happy when this festival is over, when the city empties of pilgrims and celebrants!" He perked up and said, "But for now let us go look at the happy madness in the streets." We returned to the wall and watched the procession wind through the streets.

When Messiah and his followers were out of sight, I turned to Asa. "Let us bathe, put on our official garments, then go observe." Asa nodded; we went to clean and change clothing while Shabach went to the temple to gauge the intensity and intent of the kohen.

The baths felt good after a couple of days on the road. With each passing year, I gained greater appreciation for warmer nights, softer pallets, and clean clothes. After dressing, I called out to Asa, and we met in the corridor of the sleeping quarters. My son looked very official and proper in his dalet uniform, asking, "Where to first, Abba?"

"The center of the city near the market. There is bound to be activity and information there."

The temple grounds were quiet, as were the streets. We walked to Herod's compound then to the market as the early spring sun was casting long shadows. What should have been a bustling area days before the Passover festival was eerily serene. Moses and his family were sitting inside their stall having not one customer to serve. Bidi was the first to greet us. "Shalom, wandering Hebrews!" she said with her usual joyous voice and beaming smile. The rest of the family came out to greet us.

A grinning Daniel said, "We saw him! He was like a beam of light sitting on that donkey. I waved the garment I wore the day water was splashed water on my face, and he smiled at me!"

Layla was the next to speak. "He looked sad to me. He should have been smiling all the time, but it looked like he had been crying. It is strange that two of us could look at him at the same time and see him differently." Layla looked so sad as she spoke; her brother still wore a smile.

Moses put an arm around each of his older children, saying, "Life is like the products we sell—a mixture of sweet, salty, tangy, and bitter. Each day we have a chance to taste what life has to offer."

Bidi produced a small woven sack and said, "Today we taste sweets." She opened the little bag and produced a cluster of amber crystals, handing each one of us a small rock. "Put this on your tongue, and let it melt to sweeten the day." I put the candy in my mouth; it was indeed sweet—crystalized honey.

As we enjoyed the treat, the noise of a crowd grew near the temple. Looking at Asa, I said, "Let us go observe."

Daniel looked at his parents and asked, "Mother, Father, may I go with them?" Moses nodded, and Bidi rubbed her son's cheek, saying, "Return as soon as you get a good look at him." The three of us left the market for the temple.

We were standing on the north porch of the temple compound as Yeshua led the crowd still astride the colt. At the base of the temple wall, he dismounted and silently started walking around, just looking. Simon and the others stayed with the donkeys. The crowd followed Messiah, chanting, "Hoshia na! Hoshia na!"

Yeshua turned to the crowd and held up a hand for silence. He stood there looking at them for a moment then turned to us and said, "It is time to prepare for the sacrifice." He smiled at each one of us, touched Daniel's cheek where his mother had, returned to the colt, and left the city back toward Bethany.

CHAPTER 59

THE TENT

We took our evening meal with the chazzen in his quarters. The common dining room was filled with shepherds from all corners of Judea returned to the academy to earn their stipends. Shabach said, "There are a great many more pilgrims this year, much earlier than usual. Camps are springing up everywhere. The roads into Jerusalem are clotted with travelers."

I looked at Asa. "Tomorrow morning we must go to our family campsite and see that there is enough room for them to set up." Asa nodded.

Shabach said to Asa, "I will need you available tomorrow to go to the cave at the Tower of the Flock and get a count of the sheep ready for the sacrifice."

"I will go with him," I said. "It will be good to see familiar faces and feel useful as a shepherd."

Shabach laughed at my suggestion. "My friend, you have the bloodline of a Levite. I expected no other response."

Well before dawn we left for the fields below the Tower of the Flock and the caves. The sun was breaking on the horizon as we walked through the fields covered with snow-white lambs and dew sparkling on the grass. We were greeted as honored guests, and Asa went off with one of the shepherds for a tally to bring Shabach while I met with the newly ordained chief of Migdal Eder. "Shalom, Tevyeh!" I said to the short, powerful mound of muscle that was now in charge of the most important flock of sheep in all of Judea. We had remained friends from Aleph training.

"Shalom, Eli. This year there are way too many sheep and not enough shepherds." The man was a fierce fighter, as many academy mates had found out when they had chosen to bully him because of his height. He grew to be the perfect man for the tough job of maintaining the chosen flock.

"How can I be of service, my brother?" I asked.

With a twinkle in his eye, he replied, "Sweep the Romans out of our land, and replace Herod with a man who understands the *Shema*!"

I returned his wry smile and said, "I believe change is coming soon."

He nodded, pointed his staff, and said, "Follow me." Tevyeh led me into the largest cave at the foot of the tower, the grotto where Messiah was born. My heart was beating faster as we entered. It looked as if nothing had changed since that night of nights, even though I had been back to this very place many times. This Passover I felt an excitement as never before.

"Eli, look at these." Tevyeh took me to the largest pen in the cave, housing the most perfect lambs. "These are all from your flocks. Your partners arrived with them last evening. Your son Jonathan was the lead shepherd."

I smiled. "My son the judge still knows how to lead a flock. Thank you, my friend. That means he is setting up camp with the family." Bowing, I said, "I will take my leave to help him and visit with my growing family. When Asa has finished his task, please tell him to meet us at the campsite after reporting to the chazzen."

Tevyeh clasped my arm, saying, "I shall. Shalom, my brother, until we see each other again." It seemed as if my brother shepherd was saying a final farewell.

I left the cave and walked to the area at the foot of the Mount of Olives where our family had camped for generations. Tents were springing up throughout the valley. I saw our family banner surrounded by many other tents. As I neared the flag, it was easy to spot Jonathan, standing so much taller than those around him. "Shalom, my son. I see you have been busy!"

One tent was erected; the area of our little camp was staked out with pegs bearing our colors. "Abba!" Jonathan came lumbering and picked me off the ground in a familiar bear hug. "We are all here, all but Samuel. He has gone into Jerusalem to meet with Nicodemus and deliver some documents. Yodi insisted on coming to celebrate with Asa, so we will need two tents, one for men, the other for women. Propriety must be maintained. After all, we have the noted Samuel, student of the Teacher of Israel, in the family. We must not sully his reputation with a betrothed couple in the same tent." At first I thought my son was joking but realized he was correct.

Squeals of delight interrupted our conversation when the grandchildren poured out of the tent, followed by their mothers and Yodi. Three of them wrapped themselves around me as Sarah glided over; Marta carried Addassah, followed by Yodi. "Shalom, Papa. Shalom, Sabba." Words that were a melody to me.

"I am so happy to see all of you here and glad you decided to arrive early," I said with glee, kissing every head.

"The nights were cold, but with all of us bundled on different sides in the same tent, it was comfortable," Jonathan said. "I will go into the city and find another tent."

"Son, since I must go to the academy, I will find a tent. You stay with the family."

Sarah, always the tactful one, said, "Papa, I am sure you can find a suitable tent for us."

"If ever there was an opportunity to find one in Jerusalem, this would be the time. Craftsmen have probably been working long days to make enough to sell at the festival. It is their most profitable time of the year," I said as I hugged my daughter. Looking at Yodi, I added, "Asa should be here later, perhaps for the midday meal." My comment was greeted with a broad grin.

"Having said that, I must go back to the city and file a report with the chazzen." Looking at Jonathan, I added, "We should be here for evening meal. Are there any supplies you need?"

Yodi was the one to respond. "Yes, please bring Asa." That got everyone laughing. I untangled from the hugs of Sarah and the little ones and headed to the academy to present my unofficial report on the flocks.

Just outside the wall of the city, near the Sheep Gate, I spotted Asa. I used my goat call; he stopped, looked around, saw me, and smiled. We met to speak with Shabach.

The chazzen received Asa's written tally, and I reported what I had seen. "It appears that this Passover will be one to remember," he mused, looking at the parchment Asa had presented.

"I must head to the market to find another tent for our camp," I said to excuse myself.

Looking at Asa, the chazzen said, "You may as well go with him. He is too old to carry such a burden by himself." Shabach smiled, nodded at the two of us, then flicked his hand as a signal of dismissal. We all laughed then headed to the market.

As expected, the days before Passover, the market was teeming with people. We worked our way over to Moses's stall and were surprised to see an added item, tents. What a convenient coincidence, or was it?

Daniel was at the edge of the stall, standing next to a mound of unusual-looking tents with a stack of bundled wood poles. Next to Daniel stood his instructor, Saul. Bidi and the girls were busy with customers when Moses came from the back of the stall with a large box filled with yellow fruit. "Shalom, shepherds."

"What have we there?" I asked Daniel, pointing at the tents.

His instructor friend answered, "These were made from old clothing then rubbed with oil to protect the fabric from rain. I used beeswax where I had sewn each piece together to seal the stitching." The wiry little Saul smiled as he spoke.

"Very clever," I said. "Where did you learn such craft?"

Saul replied, "At home. My family has been making tents for generations. My father and grandfather taught me the finer details when I was a child."

I smiled at the young man, walked to the pile, and lifted a corner of one of the larger tents, looking at the handwork closely. "Well done," I said. "I would like to purchase a large one."

Daniel spoke up. "Eli, we will find the largest and best one for you." Leaving Asa with them to choose, I walked back to Moses and asked, "When did you start selling these things?"

Moses broke into one of his big smiles and said, "My son's friend must pay his way to stay and study with Gamaliel, even as an instructor. Daniel convinced me to take these to sell and help him earn. Daniel receives a small amount as a commission for each tent sold. It works well for all of us."

"That sounds like a fine arrangement. What of his friend's position on Yeshua? Has it changed at all since we first met him?" I asked.

"Not at all," said Bidi as she came over to the two of us. "The more we hear and talk about the rabbi, the more rabid he becomes. He will fit in with all those narrow-minded Pharisees." Bidi nodded in the direction of the tents. "It appears they have settled on the one you will carry back to camp."

The three young men were approaching when it struck me how different they appeared—Daniel: tall, thin, ebony skinned; Asa: shorter, broad shouldered; and Saul: small, wiry. They carried the bundle and poles to the counting table.

Moses, Daniel, and Saul rolled the tent around the poles in a tight bundle. Asa picked up one end, with me on the other. We made our way back to camp. Memories of carrying Jacob's body home filled me with sadness and a sense of foreboding.

CHAPTER 60

THE CHILDREN

WITH JONATHAN'S HELP the new tent was set up quickly. It was a colorful thing with squares and strips of different cloth stitched together with great craftsmanship. Rebekah was the first to shout that it must be for the women as she ran into it. "It is not an ordinary-looking thing," Sarah said a running her fingers over the stitching. "It does look like great care was used in its making."

"It looks like a giant flower," Caleb said. He added, "I am glad I will sleep in the men's tent," drawing a laugh from the adults.

Looking at Jonathan, I said, "It is nearing evening mealtime. Asa and I will stay and help finish the campsite and wait for Samuel." We busied ourselves with the details of camp while Asa built a sturdy roasting pit for the paschal lamb, teaching little Caleb and Saul how to assist.

As dusk approached Samuel came into the camp, excitedly proclaiming, "He did it again! He did it again!" Surrounding him, we asked what he was talking about. "I have a story to tell, so let us sit. I must catch my breath and drink. I almost ran all the way to be here." Sarah brought her husband a skin of wine and a pillow to sit on. The entire family sat at his feet, waiting.

After a few moments, my son-in-law took a deep breath and began. "I had my meeting with Nicodemus. He told me that the Sanhedrin had been arguing all morning about Yeshua, his teachings, and followers. Many are overjoyed with the possibilities of his appearance, but there are just as many who fear and are enraged by him."

Sarah asked, "What of Nicodemus? What is his position?"

Samuel shrugged his shoulders. "My mentor is a bit of a puzzle. He fiercely defends the teachings but does not argue that Yeshua is the long-awaited Messiah." Samuel shook his head. "I think Nicodemus believes he is Messiah but cannot argue enough facts to satisfy the Sanhedrin."

Asa asked, "What did you mean when you said, 'He did it again'?"

There was another pause before Samuel continued. "I left the meeting and was walking on the porch when Yeshua started overturning tables and benches of the money changers and the dove sellers outside the Court of the Women, exclaiming, 'My house is to be a house of prayer, but it is being made into a place of thieves!'" Smiling, Samuel continued. "Then after the tables were overturned, he walked calmly to the steps and sat down. Many blind, lame, and sick came to him, and right there, in full view of the priests and rabbis, he healed them all!"

I asked, "What did they do, the priests and teachers?"

Samuel, still smiling, said, "Nothing at first. They just stood there and watched. Occasionally they would put their heads together and argue. I just stood at the edge of the crowd and observed. It was then, after the healings, that children came flocking to Yeshua, shouting praises, calling him 'Son of David.'"

Rebekah excitedly asked, "Children came to him? What did he do?"

Samuel looked at his daughter and said, "He did what any good teacher would do—he spoke to them about what was written. Then the best part happened."

Samuel sat and waited patiently until Rebekah, almost at a yell, asked, "Abba, what happened?"

Samuel smiled. "The priests were indignant, questioning Yeshua about the children's praises. He then calmly stood and asked those that questioned him, 'Have you never read from the lips of children and infants that you have ordained praise?'"

Samuel stood; walked over to each of us, who were seated, helping all to our feet; then said, "Yeshua stood and walked toward me in the silence. He smiled and nodded then began walking back toward Bethany. I walked with him and his disciples until I reached the path to camp."

Yodi, who had been quiet all the time Samuel was talking, asked, "Did you speak with him as you walked?"

"Yes, we spoke of what has been written. Then when we were parting, he said to me, 'Teach the children.'"

CHAPTER 61

THE TEACHING

THE EVENING MEAL was a simple affair of dried fruit, cheese, barley cakes, and wine. The children sang songs, with Yodi leading and teaching new tunes. Marta played her small harp, Asa played the flute, and I reclined, watching my family, relishing every moment. Asa and I had to returning to the academy to receive instructions for the coming day. We made our way by moonlight around the other camps to the temple grounds.

Thankfully it was a quiet night. Asa's charge for the next morning was to prepare the path for the sheep to the altar. I had had that duty in the past, but it was my son's first time to take the trek from the field through the pool into the temple. He would be a very tired shepherd by the day's end. My note from Shabach bade me to rest well and dress well for the day. My fancy tav uniform was clean and hanging, waiting for morning. I laid my weary bones down and enjoyed the blessing of a solid, dreamless sleep.

The sky was lightening when Asa knocked on my door and leaned into my quarters. "Abba, I will see you this evening, and we can walk to the camp together. Shalom." He closed the door. I arose and went to the baths. On my return a note sat on my bed asking me to join Shabach for morning meal. Dressed in my sparkling white garments, I took my ornamental staff, rod, and skyt to eat with my friend.

Boiled eggs, dried grapes, and wheat cakes were on the table. The chazzen smiled. "My old friend, it seems as if we are well prepared for this Passover festival."

Grabbing a sweet cake, I said, "Very well. Then why am I dressed so formally?" I chomped down.

The chazzen's smile disappeared. "It is a requirement of our false friend Yosef ben Caiaphas to be in the courts if Yeshua comes to teach today. He wants as many priests and officials as possible present to listen and challenge his teachings."

At those words my mouth got very dry, and the cake was no longer appealing. Taking some morning wine, I was able to swallow and asked, "What do you think he is planning?"

"I can only guess, but having priests and officials challenge him might be the play to dispute his teachings and declare him a blasphemer in front of a crowd."

Coughing at the remaining cake in my throat, I said, "They have tried that before and failed."

"Nevertheless, we must be in attendance should that occur," Shabach said sourly.

Taking some more wine, with growing confidence, I said, "Messiah cannot be trapped with words. He will make fools out of all those who challenge him. Even when he was a child, he would turn their questions around and speak brilliantly of the writings. I look forward to my duty at your side today." Feeling much better, I ate heartily, stood, and said, "Let us pick a place with a wide view of the courts." Shabach stood, drank some wine, and nodded, and we left the academy for the court area.

With the official start of the festival nearing, people of every description were crowding the streets. As far as observable from the wall of the temple, tents and smoking fires were seen on every hill and in every valley surrounding Jerusalem. We made our way to the steps of the Nicanor Gate, where the cantors were singing the songs of King David. It was still too early for a large gathering; we stood near one of the treasury columns and waited.

Slowly priests, Pharisees, Sadducees, Sanhedrin, and regular celebrants began to gather. A voice startled the two of us when, in a low tone, almost a growl, it said, "I see no sheep here. Are you lost?" We turned to face Simon, wearing a sly grin, standing next to Yeshua.

"Shalom, my friends," Messiah said, smiling. "I am here to teach those who will listen." Looking straight into my eyes and into my soul, Messiah said, "Eli, find my sheep. They will know my voice." He touched my hand holding the ornate staff, turned, and walked toward the steps.

"Eli, what did he mean?" asked Shabach.

"I do not know, at least at this moment. His words have a way of digging into your mind and heart until you understand." I took a deep breath.

We watched as many gathered. Visitors to the temple were listening to the gifted rabbi as he walked. Yeshua climbed the first step where the cantors had been singing earlier and began teaching. It was not long before one of Caiaphas's underlings, in a knot of his peers, asked Messiah who gave him the authority to teach. Just as I had told Shabach earlier, Yeshua answered the kohen's question with a question of his own. I had to smile.

He was frustrating the temple leaders who were there to trick him. The crowd loved the way he taught. Off to one side of the gathering, I saw Pharisees arguing with one another. It was then I saw Caiaphas talking to Judas, the son of the man Simon, who was healed of leprosy. The young man was watching Yeshua but listening to the kohen. Caiaphas leaned closer to the son of Simon, said something, then left the temple area.

I looked back at Yeshua as he told parable after parable, obviously intended for those who came to dishonor him. Out of a clutch of Herod's men came a voice, a question about taxes. Again, Yeshua answered with a question, asking the man whose face was on a Roman coin. When the response was Caesar, he told the questioner to pay Caesar his due. Question after question was answered; Shabach laughed quietly.

A teacher of the law I had seen talking with Nicodemus at the Hall of Hewn Stone asked Yeshua which was the most important commandment. Still teaching, he recited the *Shema* then said, "Love your neighbor as yourself. There are no greater commandments." He asked the

Pharisees who they thought Messiah was. Their answers were turned around to the point they became silent. The spectators were delighted.

Having enough of the questioning, Yeshua called the Pharisees and teachers of the law hypocrites time and time again. He gave them examples of their hypocrisy and finished by telling them that a poor widow offers greater sacrifice than any of them. Ending his teaching, he left the temple. As the crowd dissolved, I saw Nicodemus across the court, looking as if he was crying.

Shabach and I left the courtyard.

CHAPTER 62

THE COURTYARD

As we neared the academy, I heard Samuel's voice. "Papa Eli, wait!" He was coming toward us at a near run. He stopped in front of us. "Shalom, chazzen." Shabach greeted him in return. "You saw him, did you not?" asked Samuel, who looked like he had been crying, just like Nicodemus.

"What is wrong?" I asked.

"Why, nothing is wrong. It is going to be wonderful! My mentor is now convinced that Yeshua is Messiah and will stand for him at the meetings to come."

"Why did he look as if he was crying when Yeshua left the courtyard?" I asked Samuel, who was smiling, looking like a little boy.

"Nicodemus was upset because he realized that he had wasted so much time in doubt. He knew Yeshua was correct when he called all of us hypocrites. When Yeshua said that the Son of Man was going to be like a shepherd and separate the sheep from the goats, the words stabbed Nicodemus in the heart. That is when my mentor turned to me and said, 'It is he!' Pappa Eli, it is going to be a wonderful Passover!"

Samuel's enthusiasm was infectious. We stood smiling for a moment, then Shabach said, "Eli, go spend time with your family at the camp. If I need you, I will send a runner."

Nodding to the chazzen, I turned to Samuel. "I will go to the market to see Moses before camp."

Samuel, still smiling, said, "Abba, I will walk with you."

The market was a frenzy of people buying goods at every booth and stall. Moses, Bidi, and the children were busy, so we headed for the camp. As we neared the edge of the market, Daniel came running up to us with a little parcel. "Shalom, Eli. This is for you and your family." The young man handed me a fist-sized linen bag and said, "It is a fresh order of herbs for your lamb. Mama says to rub these on the meat to make a fragrant offering." With those words said, Daniel raced back to the stall to help his family.

We spent the evening relaxing, making sure all supplies were ready. Asa was able to join us for supper and then drifted off to walk with Yodi around the camp. It was always a time of melancholy for me as I was thinking of my Rachel. I retired early to get a predawn start for the academy. The last thing I remembered was Yeshua saying, "Find my sheep."

It seemed like only moments passed before the tent flap sprang open and four grandchildren were jumping on me to a chorus of "Wake up!" They playfully tugged at my beard. What joy it brought me, the gift of Rachel's blood in these little ones. "Enough!" I yelled in a gruff, playful voice and started tickling each of them to tears.

Sarah looked in and said, "You must have been exhausted to sleep so late. Come, there is hot tea with honey for you." The children left so that I could dress properly. I wore the most comfortable clean simlah and sat with the family to break the night fast.

Yodi brought more tea and said, "My sweet Asa left for the temple grounds before dawn. He told me last night that he has been given the honor to serve at the altar today to prepare for the sacrifice tomorrow." Her voice was brimming with pride and love.

"That truly is an honor for someone so young. It will be a painfully long and arduous day. He will sleep soundly tonight," I said, smiling at my beautiful daughter-in-law-to-be. "I should be going to the temple grounds myself to see if Yeshua will be teaching today."

With that I rose to gather my gear, when Sarah said, "Samuel left early as well, to meet Nicodemus and monitor the teachings."

I nodded. "Your husband is well placed to become a leading Sanhedrin someday should he choose. For me, I would rather talk to the sheep." Sarah, Marta, and Yodi laughed heartily.

As I was leaving, I asked Marta, "Where is Jonathan this morning?"

"He left to go to the Tower of the Flock to see how many of our stock will be used tomorrow in the temple. It will be a great honor for our sheep to be presented as a first offering," Marta said with some excitement.

"It would be an honor indeed to have one of our lambs chosen as perfect." I kissed the grandchildren's heads and left for the academy.

In my quarters hung a pair of brand-new uniforms each bearing a patch over the heart embroidered with the *Shema* in purple thread surrounding beautiful, hammered gold tav pins. A short note asked me to meet Shabach at the same place we had been the previous day. The expression of friendship and love from a man who so long ago hated me filled me with the joy of a bond that was rare in my life. I bathed, dressed, and went to the temple grounds.

The chazzen was standing in the exact same spot as the day before. "Shalom, my friend," I said.

"Good morning, Eli. Let us see what the day will bring. I have assigned all of my duties to assistants, so I am free to observe and enjoy." Shabach removed a small skin of wine from his cloak, took a sip, handed it to me, and said, "L'chaim!" I laughed, took a sip of a wonderful sweet wine, and repeated his blessing to life. We stood and watched as the courtyards slowly filled.

Clusters of foreigners, Pharisees, Sadducees, priests, and Herod's men gathered at different parts of the courtyard. Samuel and Nicodemus stood together; they looked at us and nodded. The murmuring was a din until a hush settled over the open area when Yeshua entered from the south near the treasury. Only a few of his followers were with him as he walked to the center of the crowd.

He stood quietly for a few moments then began reciting and teaching from the prophet Isaiah. Again, there were many questions put to him, which proved many still disbelieved. There were also many leaders who smiled, nodding approval to the teachings, bolstering the fact that they believed in him.

He stunned everyone to silence when he said that he had come into the dark world as light. I gasped when he said, "I did not come to judge the world but to save it." Yeshua concluded, telling all assembled that he was speaking the words of the Father who sent him and whose commands lead to eternal life. In the following absolute silence, he left the courtyard.

It took minutes before the gathering stirred, and amid hushed tones the courtyard started to empty. Samuel and Nicodemus came toward us, and we met them in the middle of the courtyard. The Teacher of Israel greeted us excitedly, saying, "Shalom. Today we have witnessed teachings from the anointed of Adonai. I must leave you all to go and share the good news with my family." Nicodemus clasped Samuel on the shoulders and said, "My boy, I have chosen well. Thank you for leading me to Messiah." Nicodemus teared up, kissed Samuel on both cheeks, and left.

Shabach put his hand on my shoulder. "Eli, go tell your family what you heard here today. I must go back to the academy and record what I have witnessed."

We were alone in an empty courtyard except for the sweet familiar smell of perfume in the air.

CHAPTER 63

THE PET

BEFORE GOING TO camp, we decided to look at the altar site where the next day's main sacrifices would be taking place. At the Nicanor Gate, temple guards were posted in front of the huge ornate closures leading to the Altar Court. Holding the parchment with the chazzen's seal, the guards not only stepped aside but also opened the gate without a word spoken.

In the past I had served at the altar the first night of the festival. With magnificent banners and all those officiating resplendent in their finest ceremonial garb, it was always an inspiring sight. Rehearsal was in progress; I immediately spotted Asa standing rigidly at the entrance to the *Kadosh HaKodashim* (Holy of Holies). He was supporting a pole twice his height that held a huge banner representing the kohen's breastplate. It was an honor given few of his age and level of experience.

Across from Asa was an older shepherd I recognized from years past, bracing a similar banner. Behind them was the enormous woven veil covering the entrance to the Holy of Holies. There were twelve shepherds at the base of the altar representing the tribes of Israel. Caiaphas stood atop explaining the order of service to be held the following afternoon. I waved at Asa, who nodded slightly in return. Satisfied all was well, Samuel and I left for camp.

The rest of the day was spent relaxing and enjoying the family. Asa returned for the evening meal. Plans were made for Jonathan and Samuel to secure the lamb for our sacrifice while the women cleaned camp and prepared the roasting pit. Asa and I left after sundown for the academy.

Beyond the edge of camp, I noticed a glow on the Mount of Olives and told Asa that was where I believed Yeshua and his followers stayed. Many times, on the road, we spoke of the night when Samuel and Nicodemus met with Yeshua and later when I found the empty site.

The academy was quiet except for the sound of sleeping shepherds. Before long the morning shofar blast signaled the first day of sacrifice. After bathing, Asa put on a special uniform; I wore my finest tav garment. We ate in the common hall with the brotherhood of ceremonial shepherds. That very night blood of the sacrifice would be spread on doorposts and tent flaps throughout the land.

Shabach made the announcement for places to be taken and recited a prayer before dismissing all to assume their duties of the day. When the dining hall was empty, the chazzen came to me and said, "Enjoy your freedom today. I must assume my position on the altar with Caiaphas to present him with a ceremonial dagger. He never gets close enough to a lamb unless it is roasted meat on a fancy platter. I am happy that you can spend this day with your family. Mine will have to wait until late tonight for our meal." Shabach slapped me on the shoulder. "Shalom, my friend."

The day was busy, with the women baking the ceremonial bread of haste, matzah, and vegetables to accompany the lamb. Jonathan and Samuel took Saul and Caleb to select the lamb for our feast. I removed my ceremonial garb and put on simple clothing, making sure that I had a sash to tuck into my garment as a symbol of haste for the meal. Pillows were arranged around the firepit, and I began preparing the fire with wood and stones.

Before long the little group of men returned with a lamb that had not been slaughtered and two crying children. "What is wrong? What is going on?" I asked as the boys ran to their mothers, begging them not to slaughter the lamb. Sarah held Saul, and Marta embraced Caleb, who was inconsolable. "Please do not kill the lamb. Please do not kill the lamb," he repeated over and over. Saul joined the pleading, along with Rebekah. Little redheaded Addassah just sat crying along with the other children.

Samuel and Jonathan were as frustrated as I had ever seen them. They both agreed it was a mistake to take the boys for the ritual slaughter. "We had already selected the lamb, but the children never made the connection between the food and the live animal!" Jonathan said, relaxing a bit. He understood the power of the moment when the children understood the link between the sacrifice and the meal.

Samuel added, "One of us will be taking a lamb home for a pet. What should we do now?"

I stepped forward. "As leader of this family, I will get prepared chickens to roast for the meal. It will be good for us to celebrate as those less fortunate." I went to a tent market at the edge of camp and returned with enough meat to avoid a catastrophe. With a small flask of ceremonial blood for the tents, we were ready for the first seder.

We waited for Asa to return. It was well after dark when he came marching into our camp. "That was an honor that I hope never to receive again," he said as he hugged Yodi then plopped down on a pillow, reaching for a skin of wine. We all laughed and began the celebration, with the adult men painting the blood of the sacrifice on the tent flaps, reciting the ritual prayer.

It was a wonderful time with my family, recounting the story of Moses, Aaron, and Joshua leading the slaves of Israel out of bondage, a celebration Adonai declared for the ages. The bitter herbs were eaten, the roasted birds were delicious with the mixture of Bidi's spices, and the wine was the perfect beverage for the feast.

The perfect lamb that would become a family pet lay quietly, tethered to a wagon.

CHAPTER 64

THE DARKNESS

I STOOD OUTSIDE the tent looking at the dying embers of all the fires in the valley. Looking to the Mount of Olives, I saw only darkness and wondered where Yeshua was celebrating the Passover with his close followers. I crawled into my bedroll, thinking about what he meant by saying, "Find my sheep." As tired as I was, my night was unusually restless.

"Papa, Papa, wake up! Hurry!" It was Sarah's voice, accompanied by her slapping on the tent wall.

"Abba, get up now!" Jonathan said with alarm as he opened the tent flap. A surge of fear gripped me, thinking that something had happened to one of the children.

"What is wrong?" I asked in a voice cracking with emotion.

"We do not know for sure. There is a messenger from the chazzen holding a sealed note. He ran all the way from the city to deliver it."

Wearing only my linen sleep cloth, I exited the tent; the family gathered around the young messenger. "Where is Asa?" I asked, panic making my voice quiver.

"He left early for his post at the temple for his day of service," said Yodi. I nodded and took the note from the shaking hand of the young man, who had steam rising from his sweat-drenched body in the morning chill. The women were gripping the children, Marta had an arm around Yodi.

Breaking the wax seal, I saw that Shabach's hand said Yeshua had been arrested, that I needed to come at once. Anger flared in me as questions whirled through my head. *Who would dare? Where was he? Was Herod or Pilate responsible? They both had the ability to order execution!* I dressed quickly in my most ornate garment, knowing I might be standing before officials of some import. Samuel stood beside me. "I am going with you. I must find Nicodemus. He will know details." We strode at a quick walk behind the courier back to Jerusalem.

At the academy door stood another runner who told us that Shabach had gone to the Hall of Hewn Stone. Samuel and I made our way to the hall, passing through the temple grounds, where we could hear the beginnings of the formal service. Asa would be at his post in front of the Holy of Holies. My emotions bounced from hot rage to icy fear back to molten anger.

The hall and corridors near the Sanhedrin's court were empty and silent except for two temple guards standing by the closed doors. "Where is he?" I asked in a cold, commanding tone. Standing at attention, facing forward, they had a one-word, emotionless answer: "Pilate."

In anguish Samuel groaned, "Oh, no! Eli, this is terrible!" as he started toward the praetorium.

Rounding a column, we nearly tripped over a huddled form on the top step. "Teacher?" Samuel asked as he stepped down below to the man, who was indeed Nicodemus.

The Teacher of Israel looked up at us with red eyes and a tear-stained face and spoke in a wretched voice. "They would not listen. They feared him so much they have successfully plotted to have him killed."

In an icy voice, cutting through my hot anger, I asked, "Who is responsible for this abomination of justice?"

Nicodemus burst into pitiful sobbing. "It is I! I could not convince them that he is divine."

In a soothing voice, Samuel said, "It was not you that plotted. It was Caiaphas, was it not?"

Nodding his head, unable to speak, Samuel's mentor finally said, "Yes. He has been plotting with many others for a long time and finally bribed one of Yeshua's followers to betray him."

"Who?" I asked, my word a rumbling of hatred.

Nicodemus's face changed in an instant from grief to stone. "The son of a fellow Pharisee, Simon, the one Yeshua wiped clean of leprosy."

My blood raced when I remembered the young man who had walked by me the night Messiah was anointed with fragrant oil by the woman *Maryam HaMagdala* (Mary Magdalene). Also, I remembered watching *Yehuda* listen to Caiaphas in the temple court while Yeshua was teaching. "We must try to save him!" I said firmly. With Samuel's help, the Teacher of Israel stood even as the sound of singing from the temple was floating in the air.

As we made our way through the crowded streets of the city, Samuel was moaning, "No, no, no."

Through a group of gawkers, we saw Mary, Yeshua's follower from Magdala, on her knees at the base of the scourging post in front of the praetorium. She was sobbing as she used a garment to soak up the blood on the stones. I knelt beside her; she looked at me with anguish, her eyes red, face wet with tears. "He is being crucified!" she wailed.

Her words were like a knife in my belly. Tears sprung from my eyes, and a roar of anguish erupted from my lips. "Adonai, why, why?" I screamed to the sky.

Samuel, whose composure had returned, gently placed a hand on my shoulder and in a subdued voice said, "Abba, we must go with her."

Mary continued to capture his blood from the pavement and the post. She stood and started walking unsteadily past Herod's palace, stopping every few steps to gather the blood, for by custom our people must be buried with all parts of the body; it is all *kadosh* (sacred).

Samuel and I walked behind her, Nicodemus trailing. Every now and then, one of us would have to catch her from stumbling or help her stand after capturing more blood. "They beat him, they spit on him, they mocked him," she chanted. Every few feet she would scream, "Noooo!"

People stood silently weeping as we followed her through the city while others were yelling, "*Letzlov! Letzlov!* (Crucify! Crucify!)" We wove our way up through the crowded streets toward the city wall. I was finding it hard to breathe. The air was still; I felt as though it had weight and was slowly crushing me. Samuel was pushing ahead with Mary, and I had to pause to give Nicodemus courage to go forward, courage I did not have.

With each step I had a memory: the baby in the cave, the toddler in the house, the visitors, the gifts, the boy teaching in the temple, the man he had become, the teachings, the miracles. I could not understand why the power of Adonai was not being unleashed to protect Yeshua and vanquish those who would destroy him. The stones beneath my feet felt like hot coals, and my legs were heavy as we trod upward.

Samuel and Mary disappeared into the crowd ahead, which funneled through the gate to the outside of the walled city. I turned back to Nicodemus, who looked as if he had aged with every step. He was pulling at his beard and pounding his chest as tears poured from his eyes.

Words came to me without thought as I said, "My friend, the story is not over. We must see what Adonai will do. A wind dried up the sea, the sound of voices and shofars collapsed Jericho, three hundred conquered an army, the voice of a young girl saved our people. Let us take heart and see what is next." An unexpected calm washed over me as I turned and walked through the gate. Music from the temple was rolling in the air as we slowly pushed our way through the crowd to the top of the hill.

There, with the backdrop of a darkening sky, was the silhouette of three men hanging on Roman crosses. Anguish speared through me at the sight; I could not breathe. I wondered, *Who are the other two?*

At the foot of the middle post was young Mary collecting blood trickling down the wood. Samuel was standing behind her. A Roman soldier stepped up, pushed him aside, grabbed Mary by the hair, and yanked the garment from her hand.

Samuel moved toward the soldier, who dropped Mary and the garment and drew his sword. I screamed, "Cease!" in my most commanding voice, and the soldier froze. I walked calmly toward the soldier; he turned toward me.

Nicodemus walked beside me and asked the soldier, "Do you know who I am?"

Before the soldier had a chance to speak, the officer in charge said, "I do. You are the Teacher of Israel. Why are you here?"

In a steady voice, Nicodemus replied, "I am a member of the body that convinced Pilate to crucify one of the men you spiked. It is my duty to see that he is treated according to the laws of our people, to be buried before sundown as required." The officer nodded and had the angry soldier sheath his sword and step back. Nicodemus picked up the garment and handed it to Mary, who went back to collecting the blood. I looked up and saw Yeshua on the middle cross between two strangers. I could not breathe.

The voice of Shabach forced me to inhale, and I turned away from the gruesome sight. He stepped out of the crowd and walked up to the officer between me and Nicodemus, affirming our authority. "As the temple chazzen, I am here to make certain every rule of the law is followed." Looking at Nicodemus, Shabach added, "Proceed and be precise. I will report everything to the high priest." My old friend had placed himself in a position of peril with his words.

Slowly I raised my eyes again and saw the bloody, battered face of Yeshua, who looked at me wordlessly. I lowered my head, my body shaking with rage and sorrow. Raising my eyes, all I could see was the face of the toddler I held the day I became the Magi's Man. The vision faded, and the battered face of the man nailed to the middle post crossbeam, arms outstretched as in supplication, smiled at me through swollen, split, bloodied lips.

At that moment I seemed to go into a trance and felt as if I were being carried by the wind. Images of places I had never been passed before my eyes: mountains covered with snow, lush green valleys, dunes of a desert, a purple sea. Still standing, I heard an anguished voice in the distance that cried, "*Salach* (Forgive)," and I was swallowed in darkness.

There was a rumbling beneath my feet, the ground shook, lightning flashed, the crash of thunder startled me alert. I knew it was still daytime, yet it was dark as night. Looking at the form of the man I loved as my own son hanging on a cross, I knew that life from him was gone. I grabbed the gold tav pin over my heart and tore it downward, letting the rent piece hang. Grief sucked the air out of my lungs as I sobbed.

I recognized Nicodemus as he stepped in front of me. "Eli, we have work to do." The Teacher of Israel touched my arm and said, "Come with me." The elaborate garment he wore was also torn over his heart.

Torches were being lit around the hilltop. I heard voices to my right and looked at a finely dressed man handing a parchment to the Roman officer. He broke the seal, read the document, and shouted orders to his men. I watched as a soldier brought a tall ladder to the back of the cross. At the same time, four men dressed in loincloths and carrying small ladders approached the middle cross, placing the ladders on each side of the heavy wood post. While two of the near naked men climbed, the others positioned themselves in front of the hanging, lifeless Yeshua. The soldier on the tall ladder hammered the nail from the back of each wrist; another soldier did the same to the spike through his feet. The two loinclothed men on the short ladders linked their wrists in front of the beloved rabbi.

When the spikes through the wrists were removed and the rope holding the dead Messiah's forearms dropped, his body folded over the arms of the men in front of him. They, in turn, lowered Yeshua to others at the foot of the cross.

The two on ladders came down, and the four men gently carried the body of Yeshua to a wheeled litter next to the finely dressed man. They laid him on the litter, covered him with a white linen sheet, and with one on each corner, started walking down the hill in the dark.

CHAPTER 65

THE PATH

I WATCHED THE Roman soldiers unceremoniously remove the remaining two crucified bodies. With their broken legs, the dead men looked small and wrecked as they dropped to the ground. They would be carted to a pit on the other side of the hill named *Gulgoleth* (Skull), dropped in, and covered with lye.

Shabach called as he and Samuel started following the litter with Yeshua. "Eli, we must see what they will do with him."

I turned to my friend's voice and saw a spectacular sight. As I looked down from the hill, I saw that Jerusalem and the valley were speckled with torches in the daytime darkness, the temple ablaze with burning menorahs. There was a small group following the litter, and I recognized Simon, John, and Mary from Magdala holding on to Yeshua's mother.

I did not remember seeing Mary near the cross, but she was there. Crushing sadness made me dizzy to think about witnessing the torture and execution of a child. I had to stop, turn around, and catch my breath.

The soldiers started a fire for more light, and when I turned, all I could see were three bloodstained crosses. Shabach implored, "Please, Eli, we must continue, or the dark will make it impossible to walk safely."

I turned, and another miraculous sight was evident. There was a soft light surrounding the litter carrying Yeshua, and a beam from heaven cut through the dark sky, illuminating a path that wound through the valley to a distant hill on the other side of Jerusalem. Once more I felt peaceful assurance seeing the divine illumination. The glow was surely leading us to a place of importance. I joined Samuel and Shabach as the tail of the cortege.

Slowly we made our way to a new burial cave on the opposite hillside. Standing on each side of the huge, elaborate stone that covered the cave were eight men dressed in fine white linen robes. I walked up to Nicodemus in the dim illumination. "What is this place?" I asked.

"Eli, this is my friend *Yosef HaRamatayim* (Joseph of Arimathea)." I looked at the finely dressed man I had first seen at the crosses. "This is his burial tomb. He has presented it as a gift for Yeshua to be laid to rest so he may be interred before sundown. I am not sure the position of the sun at the moment. It should be high, providing light."

As Nicodemus was speaking, the four men in loincloths lifted the body of Yeshua and carried it into the tomb. When they came out, each man gathered jars and bundles from the lower portion of the litter and returned to the chamber.

"They are *kavranim* (burial servants)." The man speaking was Joseph. "I am a follower of Yeshua. I petitioned Pilate, and he permitted us to carry him here for burial. Those who lowered the rabbi are now preparing him properly before the tomb is sealed by the men standing at the stone."

I bowed to the man. "Thank you. It is a wonderful gift." I looked at Messiah's earthly mother sitting near the stone, huddled with Mary from Magdala. Samuel and Shabach echoed appreciation to Yosef. I did not see Simon or any of the other disciples. We all stood silently while those preparing the beloved Yeshua worked. I do not recall how long we stood and waited, but with each passing moment the sky lightened.

At last the men exited the cave, and the others in white robes worked the huge stone, completely covering the opening. When it fell into place, it made a dull thumping sound as it sealed the tomb. Daylight reappeared brightly in the sky. From the position of the sun, it was probably the ninth hour. The men in loincloths and white robes left with the litter.

The two Marys stood and approached. "We will return to the city to prepare for Shabbat and mourning." Nicodemus and Yosef accompanied them. Samuel said he would go back to camp; Shabach and I headed for the temple compound. Roman soldiers neared the tomb and stood guard.

CHAPTER 66

THE CURTAIN

"WHOM ARE WE serving?" I asked as we walked.

"I have been wondering the same thing, my friend. If it is true that Caiaphas orchestrated the execution of Yeshua, how is that service to Adonai?" His question was more of an answer.

As we neared the wall of the temple, there was no music when there should have been singing and trumpet sounding as the sacred night of Passover and Shabbat overlapped. Instead there were sounds of shouting, running, and marching. We looked at each other and walked quickly through the south gate and entered the temple grounds.

The sound of one voice carried over all other noises, Caiaphas's. His words were not clear until we reached the altar area. "I demand an explanation!" he bellowed. There were men lined up in front of the Holy of Holies as Caiaphas paced back and forth in front of them. One of them was my son Asa. I felt a combination of anxiety and anger walking toward the ranting priest.

I stopped cold, as did Shabach, when we saw the obvious subject of Caiaphas's wrath. The magnificently embroidered giant curtain in front of the Holy of Holies was ripped in two, from top to bottom. It was hanging limply in the late afternoon light. Only a stone table with a Torah standing on top stood in the middle of the revered enclosure. The walls were covered with cedar planks engraved to look like huge tablets that would have been in the ark. It was a stunning sight to behold, a huge room that only the high priest was ever allowed to enter.

Everyone in the altar area faced away from the Holy of Holies that was exposed, its veil torn. Asa glanced at me and Shabach, drawing Caiaphas's attention.

The kohen spun around, screaming, "What are you two doing here? Out, out!" His face was flushed and contorted, resembling a mad cur. "You cannot be here! This is the place of those chosen only by me!" Calmly we stepped toward Caiaphas, who pointed and yelled, "Guards, seize them!"

Shabach and I were still dressed formally. Before any of the guards were able to move, the chazzen, with his boldest command voice, yelled, "Stand firm!" The guards did not move.

We stepped closer to Caiaphas, whose head was snapping back and forth as he looked at us and the stationary guards. I asked, "Are you responsible for the crucifixion of the rabbi Yeshua?" The color drained from the kohen's face, and everyone within earshot gasped.

Asa stepped forward, asking, "Abba, is this thing true? The rabbi has been nailed to a Roman cross?" Confusion and pain were evident on my son's face.

"Yes, my son. He has already been entombed." Wailing rose up from men all around the altar area. Many of them dropped their banners, while some actually smiled and nodded.

Emboldened again, Caiaphas screamed, "Leave this place at once!"

I tore the tav pin hanging from my chest and threw it at the kohen's feet. "You have brought a curse upon yourself and those who assisted you." My voice was a rumble of contempt.

Caiaphas smiled venomously. "You are just a lowly shepherd. Go, be with your sheep. I have the power to command sacrifice. I have, and I will."

Asa walked past the kohen. "This son of a shepherd prefers the company of sheep as well."

As we were leaving the altar area, Shabach said something to Caiaphas, called for us to wait, then joined us. We went to the chazzen's office. "Asa, tell us what happened," Shabach said in a quiet, concerned voice.

"Everything was going as planned until the sky darkened. The ceremony stopped while all the menorahs were lit. The singing and trumpeting continued, but you could tell that everyone was nervous and concerned. At some point there was a rumbling; everything began to shake. Caiaphas cowered on the altar, fell facedown, and pulled his turban over his ears. There was a thundering sound like the roaring of a giant lion. Then an ear-shattering wail came from above the temple, and the curtain started ripping slowly from the top. It was as if heaven were rending its own garment in mourning." Asa paused and took a deep breath.

"When the curtain was completely torn, the shaking and sound stopped. We stood silently, waiting for Caiaphas to get up and continue the service. It was a while before he peeked through his hands to see that all was quiet. His actions prove he is a coward!"

"He is worse than that." I seethed. "He convinced the Sanhedrin to have the matter put before Pilate for the crucifixion of our beloved rabbi and friend." When I said those words, Asa slumped and started weeping quietly. In a calm and reassuring voice, I said, "His story is not over yet." I told Asa of the light in the darkness that led to his tomb and the daylight that returned when the cave was sealed. Shabach nodded confirmation.

"What does this mean, Abba?" Asa said, looking at me for assurance.

"We shall see," was my only answer.

The chazzen spoke. "We must make plans to have you out of the temple area while Caiaphas is busy with ceremonies to repair the curtain and rededicate the Holy of Holies. His wrath and reach are formidable." I agreed; Asa and I left for the family camp while Shabach started pulling doors open in his office.

CHAPTER 67

THE SILENCE

IT WAS FULLY dusk when we arrived at camp. The news of the day traveled fast, and ours was a somber group. Many campsites in the valley were ablaze with fires, singing, and laughter. They either had not heard the news or cared about a Roman crucifixion as many followers of Adonai had been nailed to crosses in the past. If one was labeled an insurrectionist, crucifixion was the sentence.

The family was gathered around a small fire, waiting for me and Asa to arrive. "There will be no sacrifice for this meal tonight," I said in a quiet voice. "The sacrifice of the innocent rabbi is enough to cover all of us this Passover." I finally understood why he was called a lamb!

We agreed meat would not be eaten at the meal. The women made the bread of haste, and we all sat silently eating roasted vegetables and drinking weak wine.

Jonathan told the story of our people exiting Egypt, leaving out parts so the children could ask questions. The men took turns answering the children, and the women chanted sad songs of King David and recited poetry passed down through the ages. Asa played haunting melodies on his shepherd's flute; Marta accompanied him with her harp. Yodi's beautiful voice led the children in songs she had taught them. The adopted lamb lay quietly with his head on Rebekah's lap.

Finally, before bedtime, I announced, "We shall spend Shabbat in camp, but at sunrise we will break camp and return home. Tomorrow we will make plans for our departure." Good nights with sincere hugs were shared, and we went to our proper tents. The night was silent.

Sleep was not easy. Visions of Yeshua on that cross unsettled me until I remembered his smile. Peace settled over me, and I slept dreaming of strange, beautiful places. I awoke before dawn, rested and at ease. I left the tent and stood in the dark chill of predawn morning. Looking up to the black sky dotted with countless stars, it looked like a giant map. The brighter stars here and there pointing to important locations. I felt a gentle nudge on my leg and looked down at the beautiful snow-white lamb the children had rescued. I picked him up and held him as I would a child of my own.

In the quiet, as the eastern horizon lightened, Sarah's was the first voice I heard. "Good morning, Papa. I see you have taken to our new pet." I looked at my daughter in the dim light and saw a vision of her mother.

"Shalom, my sweet girl. He is a peaceful little fellow. We shall call him *Lebad* (By Himself)."

"What shall we do today?" she asked with sadness. I touched her cheek and smiled as she stroked the lamb.

"We will wake the men, call a minyan, and have a Shabbat service here in camp. Rabbi Joel will lead."

I set the lamb down in an improvised pen. Then I gently woke Jonathan, Samuel, and Asa. Sarah went to the women's tent. We gathered in the morning chill as the sun was rising and ate the preprepared Shabbat food. Jonathan went to arrange the morning service in a clearing at the center of the northern camps. The rabbi had already prepared a table with a small scroll of writings from Torah.

Many of the villagers from Cana and Capernaum gathered to hear the reading of Abraham's test on the Mountain of Heaven's Provision. As Rabbi Joel chanted, I could not but wonder if the cruel Roman crosses were at the same spot where Abraham had been able to sacrifice the ram Adonai provided in place of his son. I looked at the hill, and in the glow of morning, it looked like an altar that might have been made by Abraham. I closed my eyes and looked again, and there were three crosses bathed in dim light. The middle cross glowed red.

When morning service concluded, we returned to our tented area. There was an eerie silence in the valley. It was as if nobody wanted to talk. The children played while we planned our departure the following morning. Asa and I would go to Bethany to retrieve Rose and Sand then to the academy for our personal belongings. The rest of the family would pack the tents and gear on carts to head north together. Asa and I would try to catch up with them in two days.

The second full day of the festival was when I usually met the messenger at the pool. The scrolls I had prepared were in my quarters at the academy; I had to go there early, retrieve them, and get to the pool. The plans made, we spent the rest of the morning relaxing. After a spare midday meal, I decided to go into Jerusalem and observe the effects of the crucifixions.

Jonathan, Samuel, and Asa went with me. Dressed in plain, simple clothing, we walked to the center of the city in the warm afternoon sun. We talked about the previous day, and Jonathan was aghast at our recounting of events. In the middle of the deserted market, we realized that on the road and in the city, we had not seen a single soul. I led our little party to Moses's house and knocked on the large wood door.

"Who is there?" When I answered, the door opened, and the smiling merchant said, "Shalom, friends. Come in." We entered and were greeted warmly by the family.

"Where are all the people?" I asked, looking around the room at the beautiful family.

Bidi was the first to respond. "Fear of Rome has gripped everyone."

Daniel spoke up. "I believe the hearts of Yeshua's followers were torn out yesterday. Like me. It is not fear but loss that has me at home mourning." The boy's words hung in the still air.

"Our families will not be staying for the full festival. Tomorrow we break camp and leave. Asa and I have torn our relationships with the academy and the temple."

"Oh, my friend, I am sad for you. You have worked so hard and long as part of the Levite Brotherhood," Moses said with great sorrow.

I smiled at him. "We are shepherds without sheep for sacrifice. We will go home to reacquaint ourselves with our missions. No longer will we bring sheep for slaughter. What happened yesterday shows that the temple has lost its way. The innocent was slaughtered but not in the temple. I no longer believe the way sacrifice is offered follows the will of Adonai." The silence in the room was heavy.

Jonathan broke the moment. "My abba needs time away from the temple. From now on we are only wool merchants."

Looking at the family of friends, I said, "I do not know when I will return to Jerusalem. I love you all. Shalom!"

We all embraced and returned to camp through the deserted streets and road.

CHAPTER 68

THE EVICTION

THE REST OF the day was quiet in camp. Evening meal was salted fish, bread of haste, dried fruit, and wine. Everything that could be packed was bundled and stowed for an early departure the next morning. After sundown we built a fire, and Yodi surprised us all by baking some wonderful, sweet fig-filled treats. They brightened our spirits before bedtime.

At dawn our camp was a beehive of activity. Caleb jumped on top of me, pulling my beard, saying, "Sabba, get up. We are going home." I tickled him until fun tears ran down his face. Jonathan and Samuel brought the carts and donkeys into our camp. As soon as I was out of the tent, Jonathan collapsed it, then folded it for the wagon.

A quick morning meal and we were ready to leave. Asa and I planned to meet the family camped on the outskirts of Nain on the second day after my exchange with the representative of the Magi. Jonathan and Samuel went north with the women and children while Asa and I went east to Bethany for Rose and Sand.

Our animals looked well and seemed to relish our arrival. Ta'oma and Y'oyas were glad to see us but carried a pall of sorrow over the death of Yeshua, whom they believed divine. We paid their charge, leaving them to tend the mounts that Yeshua had ridden victoriously into Jerusalem just days ago.

We walked on roads that were still barren until we reached the outer wall of the temple. Asa had very little to retrieve from his room. I entered the academy while he remained with the mounts.

The only items we truly needed to collect were my reports for the Magi. My quarters were stripped bare! Hoping Shabach had taken my scrolls, I quickly made my way to his quarters. There was an armed guard posted at the door. I told him I was there to see the chazzen, and he informed me that the new chazzen had not been approved by the Levite Council yet.

I fought through the wrench in my gut and said, "Shabach was holding some of my personal belongings. May I enter and retrieve them?"

The guard was an old, rugged man who had been in the temple service for years. "No one is permitted," he said in a loud voice. He looked at me and quietly said, "Tav Eli, Shabach was pulled out of the academy early this morning and escorted home. Everything here was taken to Caiaphas and sealed in his chambers."

I stood silently, anger building, until I realized the guard at the door was the same man who had spared Shabach's life years ago on Solomon's Porch. I looked at him and said, "You showed great kindness to a lost boy that became a great man. For that I will always be grateful."

He let out a sigh and said, "You best go help that man. The guards that dragged him home are evicting him and his family from the chazzen's house."

Less concerned about my possessions than about my friend and his family, I said a hasty thank-you to the old guard and ran to Asa. We left the compound and were minutes away from the house the temple provided the chazzen.

Out on the street were Shabach, his wife, their two children, and a mound of their belongings. Two guards were lounging at the door of the house while an unknown number were inside hauling the remaining goods to the pile. Shabach's wife, *Channah* (Hannah), was clutching their two girls while all three wept. The discarded chazzen stood rigidly beside one of the guards, talking to him in a low voice. When my friend saw us approaching, he smiled wearily, pointed to the pile of belongings on the street, and said, "Shalom, Eli. Welcome to our new home."

Handing Asa Rose's reins, I walked over and, mimicking Shabach's humor, said, "At least he just locked you out and did not have you locked up!"

Stepping away from the guard, Shabach pointed at Rose and Sand and said to his wife, "Hannah, take the children to pet the donkeys." Even though Shabach and I were about the same age, he had waited until late in life to marry and have children. The two, still hanging on their mother, walked over to Asa.

The chazzen looked painfully at me. "What am I to do now? This is the only life I have known."

Without hesitation I said, "Come to Cana with us. There are needs for shepherds and friends."

He looked at me for a moment, and his grave face cracked into a smile, "You are an answer to prayer, my brother." Turning to his wife, he said, "Hannah, select only what we need. We are leaving Jerusalem."

Asa brought Rose and Sand over to Shabach's mound of possessions; together we packed items Hannah had selected. Suddenly we were all startled by the voice of a man running to the guards. "To posts, to posts!"

The guard at the door snapped erect. "What for?" he demanded.

"The tomb of the crucified rabbi is unsealed! His body is gone! We are summoned for new orders!" Three soldiers exited the house, and all started running to the temple, leaving it unattended. We all stood bewildered by the news.

Shabach grabbed my arm. "Follow me!" He led me into an office where small items were scattered on the floor. The room was stripped of furniture; all the shelves were bare. My friend went to a wall, motioning me over. "You see this little scratch?" He pointed to a slight mar. I nodded. Shabach hammered with his elbow, and the board split in two. He grasped the broken wood and pulled a panel from the wall, revealing an opening.

Reaching in, he retrieved a large leather pouch.

"This is yours. Over the years I kept a portion of your stipend saved." The pouch was the size of a large melon and was heavy. Cradling it, I opened it and looked in; it was full of silver and gold coins. "The old chazzen allowed me to save a portion for you, and this is the result of all the years."

My mouth fell open at Shabach's remarks and the treasure. Handing it back to him, I said, "Thank you, my friend." I took a few coins, handed the pouch back, and said, "Please hold on to it for me. I must go to meet the Magi's courier at the pool. Take Rose and Sand, put as many of your possessions on them as you can, and go toward Cana. Find a safe place to camp before sunset. Use our tents. Tomorrow continue north. If we do not catch up to you by the time you reach the split for Capernaum, camp again, then go on to Cana the next day."

With his free arm, the former chazzen embraced me. "Shalom, brother! Be careful!" He walked to his family.

Asa came to me, and we headed to the Pool of Siloam.

CHAPTER 69

THE NEWS

"ABBA, WHAT DO you think happened at the tomb?" Asa asked with great concern.

"I do not know. I pray we will find answers." We quick-walked toward the pool, passing the large house of Caiaphas at the edge of the city. It was quiet. Closer to the gate, on the other side of the street, was a house with a cluster of men and women in excited conversation. Recognizing some of them, we approached.

"Eli! Asa! Come quickly!" It was Simon, the big fisherman. We neared the group, and Mary from Magdala came rushing toward us.

Tears wet on her face, eyes wide and red, she wore a radiant smile. "He is alive! I saw him! He spoke to me! The rabbi lives!"

Her words made me take a deep breath; my heart raced. "When? Where?" Asa grabbed my arm.

Simon and the others from the gathering rushed to us. "It is true, what she says. The tomb is empty!" The fisherman with the flaming red hair was ecstatic recounting what he saw. "When she came running to the upper room where we have been hiding from the Romans, I had to see for myself." Pointing to John, he added, "We ran to the burial site, and the huge stone had been moved."

"I saw two angels, gleaming, dressed in white, and I was told that he who had been crucified has risen. Then I was told to come here and tell his followers to go to Galilee where they will see him." Mary was breathless and started gasping as she spoke.

I was exuberant with the news and was just standing there, on fire with excitement. "He has done it!" I whispered.

"Do you believe me? That I saw angels? And that the rabbi spoke to me?" She remained wide-eyed with her fists clenched against her chest, awaiting my answer.

I was able to speak as calm washed over me. "Yes, I believe you. I have seen angels before. At Yeshua's birth. How fitting that angels appeared today at his tomb, announcing that he lives again."

Simon spoke. "He left these behind." The fisherman held up strips of linen clenched in his huge fist. When he showed me the cloth that were stained with blood and oil, the air was filled with the sweet smell of perfume. It was the same intoxicating aroma that I had experienced in the house of Simon the Pharisee the night Mary anointed Yeshua.

My voice crackled with excitement. "We must share this news with everyone. I must meet someone at the Pool of Siloam and tell him that Messiah lives!"

I turned to my son, handing him the pouch with the star signal to the Magi's messenger. "Asa, go to the pool and wait. I will be there shortly." He took the leather bag and started running to the pool. Turning back to Simon, Mary, and the others, I said, "You must leave the city for Galilee. Surely Yeshua will meet you there. I will catch up with my family, who left for home early this morning, and tell them what you have witnessed!" I was delirious with joy!

Looking directly at Mary, I said, "Your love and trust that Yeshua is Messiah is why he chose you to announce his return to life. You are an example of true faith. You anointed our sovereign! Go with the others to share the news that he is alive!" I grabbed Simon in an embrace and said, "You have much work to do, my friend. Shalom!" I left for the pool.

Asa was sitting on a bench at the outer edge of the completely deserted enclosure. Even though it was still the Passover festival week, bathing was allowed. It was unnatural to see the water so empty. "Abba, where are all the people?"

I sat down next to my son. "I do not know. What I do know is that the long-awaited Messiah has come. He is a man who taught. He is a man who stood up to the injustice of power, for which he was beaten and executed. He is a man who died and now lives."

"What does it all mean, Abba?" Asa asked in wonder.

The thought struck me, and I said it aloud, "He is proof that there is life everlasting. He has shown us that there is eternal reward to following him. Surely his close followers know the answers. We must share the good news that he lives." We sat silently for a long time.

"Are you Elijah ben Ezra?" A soft child's voice startled us.

"Yes, child. I am."

A young boy in tattered clothing approached us sheepishly. He held out his hand, which contained a rough piece of papyrus. "A foreigner gave me a copper to find you." I looked around, and the pool was still empty except for the three of us.

"Thank you, young man," I said, reaching for the note. The boy turned to leave. "Wait!" I said. Fear stiffened the child.

"I mean you no harm. Please stay for a moment while I read this." The boy remained as I read the hastily written note.

> The man you report on is dead. I must tell my king.

"When did you get this?" I asked gently, alarmed that I had missed the courier.

"Early this morning. He saw me hiding in that corner," the boy said, nervously pointing.

"What is your name, child?" I asked softly.

Backing a step, wariness written on his dirty face, he said, "Jacob."

At the mention of his name, I choked up, and my head dropped forward, tears rolling down my cheeks. Asa spoke. "Jacob, do you live on the street?" The boy looked around for escape, then Asa said, "I used to live on the street until a shepherd saved me. I am now a shepherd and this man's son. We are shepherds. We are going home to Cana. Would you like to come with us?" The boy stood silent.

I looked up at the frightened child, asking, "Jacob, did you know the rabbi that was crucified?"

The boy's shoulders slumped, and he sobbed. "Yes, he was my friend. Every time he came to the city, I would follow him. He once put his hand on my head and told me to follow the shepherd. Is it you?"

I smiled and held out my hand. "I am," I said. "The rabbi is my friend. Did you know that he is alive?" The boy's eyes widened.

Still holding out my hand, with excitement in my voice, I said, "Jacob, I believe the rabbi we both know is Messiah. We are going to see him and tell everyone we know the good news—that he is alive."

Jacob calmly took my hand; the three of us left the pool.

CHAPTER 70

THE SMILE

WITHOUT ROSE AND Sand to mount, and no supplies, we took the Damascus route to the giant caravansary north of Jersualem. The city was still quiet, but life had started pulsing again. The few people we saw on the streets were wary; the three of us looked rough, especially with little Jacob in tatters.

The little man dropped my hand on the outskirts of the city and drifted closer to Asa. My son took it as a signal and started talking to the boy. "When I was your age, I was living on the street and had to steal everything just to live from day to day." Interested in a fellow street urchin, Jacob asked how he had become a shepherd. Asa told the story of being caught stealing and how the temple chazzen saved him from the streets.

The wariness returned, and the boy stopped, looking like he was ready to bolt back to the slums of Jerusalem. "Why are you doing this? Why are you helping me?"

Asa and I looked at Jacob. I crouched down to be eye to eye with him and said, "Yeshua taught us to feed the hungry, give drink to the thirsty, give our own clothes to the poor. We are doing his will." I reached into my skyt, pulled out the shawl Marta had made, and handed it to Jacob.

The child looked at the beautiful stitching then back at me. "You may have this if you like. My daughter-in-law made it for me, but it is yours as a gift. It will keep you warm on a cold night." Jacob reached, grabbed the shawl, and stuffed it into his torn upper garment. I stood and said, "I am hungry. Up the road is a place we can get some food. Would you like to eat with us shepherds?" Jacob relaxed and started walking.

Just over the next hill was one of the largest caravansaries in all of Judea. In a short while, we were eating roasted chicken and bean paste at a stall near the merchant tents. Jacob ate like a hungry puppy and was delighted with a sweet honey cake to finish the meal. He was half-asleep when I said, "I need a bath and clean clothing. Come."

We entered the main building. Jacob was wide-eyed at the rows of booths selling everything imaginable. It was a huge indoor market. I purposely walked over to the clothing section and chose a plain wool tunic. Asa asked Jacob if he wanted new garments and sandals, surprising the little boy. Asa picked a fancy tunic for himself and showed a similar one to Jacob, who simply nodded excitedly. I grabbed a handful of garments for the boy and two pair of sandals and said, "Time to bathe!"

The caravansary was built over a large stream, which ran near the back of the building.

Having lived on the streets near the Pool of Siloam, Jacob was used to a bath setting. He admitted stealing clothing and leftover food from some of the bathers. Baths and fresh clothing have a wonderful effect on mood. The lad's demeanor greatly improved; he wore his new tunic, trousers, and sandals. Wearing similar garments, Jacob and Asa looked like brothers.

To the north were barns and animal enclosures. As we walked past the donkey pen, I looked at Asa, who knowingly smiled and nodded. After a few minutes of haggling, we had secured a mature she-ass Jacob named Flower because of a marking on her neck. I used two gold coins taken from the cache Shabach had saved for me. With Flower and three blankets as part of the purchase, we placed our belongings on the docile donkey and started in earnest to meet our family on the road.

We walked in silence, giving us a chance to think about the events of the past few days. Yeshua, beloved rabbi, my friend, was plotted against, beaten, crucified, died, and now walked among us again. What did it all mean? How could Adonai have let this happen? How could Yeshua have let this happen? Could this possibly be part of a divine plan? My heart was beating so fast that I had to stop walking.

"Abba, what is wrong?" Asa asked. He handed the reins to little Jacob and came rushing to my side.

"I am fine, my son. I suppose the events of the last week have taken a bit out of me. Let us sit for a while and rest." We went to the side of the road and let Flower nibble some grass as we sat. I looked at Jacob and said, "Do you know my name?"

The boy looked surprised at my question. "You are Elijah ben Ezra. He is your son Asa."

I laughed and said, "You are correct. But you may call me Eli."

The boy nodded and said, "That is much easier to say." Asa and I burst into laughter, and Jacob smiled.

"Well then. Now that we know who we are, let us be off again."

Asa handed us each the water bag. After drinking, I asked Jacob, "Would you like to ride for a while?"

The boy's face lit up with a beautiful smile. "Really?" I smiled back at him and nodded at Asa, who lifted the boy and set him on top of the packs on Flower's back. Our walk continued.

Without a word Jacob reached into his new garment, removed the shawl I had given him, and handed it to me. The smile remained on his face all afternoon.

CHAPTER 71

THE FIRE

It was just like any other spring day. I had to remind myself that only hours earlier we had heard the news that the tomb of Messiah was empty, and he was alive again. So much had happened in three days it was hard to keep it all in perspective. It was as if the world had been in balance then turned upside down with the murder of Yeshua. The next day it was as if life had been sucked out of everything, creating stillness and silence. Then on the third day, the news that death and the tomb could not hold the Messiah! *Of course not,* I thought.

Jacob almost fell off Flower several times before we had him walk to keep him awake. At dusk we stopped to camp. Before Asa lit a fire, Jacob was sound asleep. The night was cool, so we bundled the boy up with the blankets from the pack, fed Flower, ate some dry food, and slept.

Morning came; we were up and moving before sunrise. Sleep had invigorated Jacob. All morning we were peppered with questions about sheep, the temple, traditions, and Yeshua. The boy's energy was boundless. Asa was able to keep pace with the constant chatter, and their exchanges kept me going. I felt a challenge and enthusiasm that had been buried for many years. But there was an unanswered question just out of my mind's reach. The Magi's messenger would only bring them information of Yeshua's execution. It gnawed away at me. How could I ever get them the good news?

We kept a solid pace all day, each of us riding Flower for a bit to meet our family between Cana and Capernaum before sundown the following day. An early camp, a night of sleep, and we were off again. Jacob was comfortable with us.

I asked the child, "How old are you?"

Jacob held his fingers in front of him as he walked, hesitated, then said, "I am nine." I smiled at the little man.

"How did you come to live on the street?" I asked in a casual manner.

His face changed to a somber look; I could see tears well up in his eyes. "My mama got sick last year and died. After that my father left one morning and never came back. The man who owned the room we stayed in made me leave. He chased me with a whip, but I was fast. He never could hit me." He smiled proudly.

At midday mealtime, Asa, who had been walking ahead, said, "Abba, I see Shabach and his family." We sped up and within minutes were walking beside the former chazzen, his family, and Rose and Sand. Hannah and the two girls looked tired and bewildered. Shabach was happy to see us.

"Who is the new recruit?" he asked, looking at Jacob.

"Another lost to be saved," I answered. "By sundown we should be at the road split, where the rest my family should be camped." I said that as much for the benefit of Jacob, to prepare him for the little crowd he would encounter. I asked Shabach how his family was doing, and his response was predictable.

"They are sad and confused. The life they knew was taken from them."

"Perhaps they will find peace with the simple life in Cana. But first we have news." Asa and I told them about our encounter with Mary, Simon, and the others. Shabach was as happy as I had ever seen him, Hannah was excited, but the girls were too young to really understand. We stopped for a quick meal of dried food and water.

By midafternoon we were nearing the road split when I saw Jonathan and Caleb in the distance sitting on a little grass knoll playing *shesh-besh* (six-five) on papyrus. Asa called out, and Caleb came running. He jumped into Asa's arms then reached over to grab me. Noticing Jacob standing next to Flower, Caleb just stared at them.

I said, "This is Jacob and Flower. Jacob was lost, then we found Flower and decided to bring both of them home."

Asa lowered Caleb, who walked over to Jacob and said, "Would you like to play *shesh-besh* with me?"

Jacob's shoulders slumped. "I do not know games."

Caleb started walking toward the little knoll, turned, and said, "Come, I will teach you."

Jacob ran after my smart little grandson as Jonathan came up to us. "Shalom, all you weary travelers."

Shabach's daughters huddled with Hannah as the chazzen greeted Jonathan. He then looked at Hannah and the girls. "We have a camp set up over there," he said, pointing to three tents on the knoll. Bending to the girls, he continued. "There are some young ladies you should meet. Come and join us." Taking the cue, we left the road and followed Jonathan. Everyone was happy to see us, but a pall hung over the encampment. Asa and Yodi were the only ones sharing broad smiles.

"Gather around me now. I have important news!" When I shared that Yeshua was alive, they all shouted with joy and badgered us with questions, many of which we could not answer.

"Let us build a fire, have a meal, and we can give you every detail." Samuel was so excited he reminded me of Jonathan as a child; he would get delirious with joy at hearing good news.

The men gathered wood; the women parceled together a meal. We ate at dusk at a sizable fire built with plenty of scrub branches found around the camp.

I recounted the morning they left Jerusalem and our walk to the pool. Tears of joy flowed when I described the conversation with Mary and Simon. The anticipation of seeing Yeshua again had the children jumping up and down, led by Jacob, the most excited of all.

I had them settle down to explain Jacob's presence with us. All the children gathered around him to form a protective barrier. When I told my family that I was planning on going to Capernaum first to wait for Yeshua's disciples, a voice from the developing darkness said, "I see you have found your shepherd." With those words the fire grew intense, enveloping us in a bright glow. Yeshua stepped into the circle near the children and touched Jacob's head.

Stunning silence followed his words. Messiah was dressed in a simple, spotless white linen garment. He looked at every radiant face. Yeshua placed his hand on my chest and said, "Shepherd, find my sheep." I gasped at the raw wound on his wrist, but at his touch, a warm calm filled me. My path became clear.

Messiah turned again to each one around the fire and said, "Shalom." He disappeared after three steps into the dark night.

CHAPTER 72

THE CYLINDER

WE ALL SAT in awe and wonder that Messiah had come to visit our camp. Rebekah announced, "We are his friends." She took Saul's hand, walked over to a silent Jacob, touched his arm, and said, "Welcome to the family." Caleb and Shabach's girls, Chaya and Emma, rushed over to Jacob and jumped up and down, chanting, "Shalom! Shalom!"

Sarah came to me, laid her head on my chest where Yeshua had touched, and said, "You are a very special shepherd. I know you will find Messiah's sheep."

When she spoke, I was drawn to Cana and the old clay cylinder I had been holding more than thirty years. The time had come to open it and reveal its contents. I spoke solemnly. "Since the birth of Yeshua, I have been on a mission for visitors that arrived from foreign lands. The answer to the question of which sheep Messiah has commanded me to find may be revealed in that old clay package waiting for me at home. I believe everyone gathered around this fire needs to come to Cana with me and see what this appointed shepherd must do next."

My family nodded in assent; Shabach agreed. Jacob wrapped his arms around me, looked up with concern in his eyes, and asked, "May I come with you?"

Lifting him up, I kissed his cheek and said, "You are the first lamb Yeshua told me to find." He hugged me with the strength of a lion cub.

We prepared sleeping places for all and settled down for the night. Once again I dreamed of strange places: dunes of a desert, a field of yellow flowers, a sea of purple water. Morning came—a quick cold meal and the appearance of a caravan of believers, followers of Yeshua with their animals, headed to Cana.

It was a beautiful spring day when we arrived at our family home. The hired caretaker was surprised to see us earlier than expected. He greeted us and left with the two village donkeys. Asa took Rose, Sand, and Flower, accompanied by all the children, to the stable behind the house while the rest of us entered to decide where everyone would sleep.

I announced, "Tonight we will discover what the Magi's message contains."

After cleaning up from road grime, we enjoyed a simple meal of bread, cheese, wine, olives, and dried fruit. Once again Yodi delighted us with the sweet treats she baked. We talked about the visit with the living Yeshua and wondered who would believe us. I told them of how excited we four young shepherds were after his birth and how nobody believed what we had witnessed in the cave at Migdal Eder.

Shabach and his family were comfortable as we accepted them into our home. My family knew him from stories and visits to Jerusalem. The children were put to bed for the evening. Jonathan took Samuel and Shabach to my little work area to talk business. We had already discussed having the former chazzen become overseer of the flocks and the shepherd partners.

After the bloody sacrifices in Jerusalem, Jonathan was excited with the prospect of concentrating on wool rather than breeding lambs for the temple. Also, he needed to devote more time to being a judge and administrator of Cana. Samuel and Sarah agreed to partner with Jonathan to expand the wool market in Capernaum, utilizing their access to caravans. Marta and Yodi were talking with Hannah about teaching and weaving while Asa and I went to the old well to retrieve the clay cylinder.

Before long there were nine of us gathered around the table in the center room. Alive with anticipation, they sat while I stood holding the cylinder reverently. "For over thirty years, I have been a faithful servant of the temple as a shepherd and leader. At the same time, I have been devoted to a mission starting with the visit of strange, wise, powerful men who traveled almost two years to honor the birth of Messiah."

I took a deep breath and recounted the blinding light, the sounds, the angels, the grotto, how I had found Yeshua with Joseph and Mary in Bethlehem, the surprise visitors presenting their gifts. I told how the couple fled to Egypt while the men of wisdom returned to their lands, knowing Herod had murder on his mind. I spoke of Arsham, the first messenger, and our meetings at the Pool of Siloam. And the contract with the men called Magi to keep them apprised of Yeshua as he grew into his kingdom.

"Now is the moment for which I was told to be patient. This is the right time." I laid the cylinder on the table, took a heavy wood rolling pin, and smashed one end of the parcel. It shattered easily and revealed the obvious contents—scrolls. Samuel helped me gently remove the parchment rolls. Sarah and Yodi took away the remaining cylinder and broken shards. The time had come to solve a mystery and answer thirty-year-old questions.

The air in the room was tingling with anticipation as I took the largest of the skins, carefully unrolling it.

CHAPTER 73

THE PARCHMENTS

THE PARCHMENT WAS like no other skin I had ever seen. After all the years, it was still soft and pliable. The scholarly Samuel stood to my left and with deft motions helped unroll the document while I held it on the right. It was like a fine Torah scroll, and the text was written in the same careful script. My heart beat faster as I started reading aloud from the top.

> To the Chosen Elijah ben Ezra of Cana,
>
> We, the followers of the God of Abraham, Isaac, and Jacob, have come far to bow down and worship the one sent as Messiah. It has been over twenty-five generations since our people were scattered in exile. We are five of the tribes that escaped to settle in other lands. We never met before the star appeared in each of our countries. We were beckoned to gather in Sousa for the last part of our journey to worship Messiah, present ourselves and gifts.

You, Elijah ben Ezra, were ordained by Adonai to witness his arrival. You were present with Messiah, the one named Yeshua, when we bowed down before him, our king, the son of the One True God. You have been elected for duty to chronicle the life of the one who was sent as the ancients prophesied.

We are five of the tribes lost–Il Gadsparim, descendent of Gad. Balthea del Salazar, descendent of Zebulun. Heshben Nebo, descendent of Benjamin. Tizra Ebal, descendent of Manasseh. And I, the leader and scribe of this group, am called Melech.

When I read the name "Melech," thoughts swirled in my head. I remembered the night those strange men came to the house in Bethlehem. Mary, in a quiet, respectful voice, looked at the leader and asked, "Who are you, sir?" I closed my eyes and could even smell the fragrance of his gift.

"Papa, are you all right?" Sara asked, jolting me out of my memories. "Yes, I am fine. I was thinking of the sweet aroma rising from the gift presented to Yeshua that night."

Samuel touched my hand and said, "Eli, we smell that aroma. It is embedded in the scroll."

I smiled. "Of course." I continued reading.

My name means "king." I am not a king in the royal sense, as in ancient times when kingdoms were defined by wealth, armies, land, power, and family. It is true that I come from an old line. Some call me powerful. I own much land and retain many servants. The many who guard my family and property are said to be an army. I am quite wealthy. I will elaborate.

Many generations ago, too many to count, my family was called a tribe. We have prospered here in a land far from the countryside our ancestors inherited. We were a small part of a large nation established by Adonai when he favored our patriarch Abraham. Through his seed came Isaac, who sired Jacob, who begat many sons. One was named Yissachar. It is from him I am branched.

Names mean much in our culture. Yissachar means reward. Our family survived many struggles, yet today we live in abundance. We are truly blessed, having come from a long line of shepherds beginning with Abraham. Yissachar, a son of Israel, found joy in herding. He was a tough, rawboned man who knew how to work hard and shoulder burdens. His tribe succeeded by inheriting his toughness, understanding the times, and knowing what to do.

There was a time when all followers of Abraham were enslaved in the Land of Egypt. They survived more than four hundred years in bondage as a nation before being led into the desert by the beloved prophet Moses. The pain of our ancestors continued; they wandered forty years until they entered the land Adonai had promised.

Yissachar's tribe was given territory in the north. It was a good place with small mountains and a fertile valley near the Sea of Kinnereth, feeder of the River Jordan. While they raised sheep in that fruitful area, they learned of many uses for the fats of animals. Creating salves and unguents became an art that was the foundation of making incense.

Living at the foot of Mount Tabor many years, they prospered, using the river as a trade route for their fragrant creations. Local flowers and spices were the basis of many aromas. A favorite comes from a small yellow bloom I have named Leah's Smile after my daughter. The first time she looked at me, I was delighted, and so named the blossom. They are harvested yearly and carried by a merchant caravan to our coastal village by the Purple Sea.

We maintain our prosperity by creating and selling fragrances. What started as a simple lotion from the fat of sheep became our trade and the secret of financial success. Our most treasured scent comes from a local tree. It is a scrawny thing we have learned to cultivate. Every spring these trees produce the most wondrous blooms, with an orange center surrounded by six dainty yellow petals. They look like jeweled stars in the same shape that called us to Bethlehem. The aroma is faint but delightful, the secret, its sap.

Our climate near the sea provides enough moisture for our beloved trees to flourish. Small but strong, they take root even though fresh water was not plentiful. Scores have voluntarily taken root in the rocks near shore at the edge of our orchard. The endless supply of water from the sea is the source of salt used in the drying process of the sweet sap. We harvest and dry it. Tears form at the stripping of limbs that are captured and placed on salt covered planks of cedar. It crystalizes into precious fragrant nuggets.

For generations our people served as suppliers of incense to the temple in Jerusalem until assassins forced us from our homes. The old, wise fathers followed trade routes looking for ingredients used in the making of fragrant offerings. They became nomads, living in tents, tending their sheep while gathering materials to make and sell salves, perfumes, and incense. At each stop along the way, craftsmen learned new techniques. They settled in a land many years in finding. Today, in our village named Chiore, we labor to create and bring to market the gifts from our wonderful trees.

We have a well-secured stone hut in the center of our compound that houses formulas and methods of producing each scent. Through the years scribes recorded every secret formula. So valuable are these parchments they are kept in the same structure as our blessed Torah and ancient writings.

Being so close to the sea, we store important documents in clay enclosures sealed every time they are opened. On Shabbos our rabbi arrives early and is escorted to the enclosure to retrieve scrolls for the service. The prophet Moses wrote of a star and scepter rising out of Israel. Micah declared an everlasting ruler would come out of Bethlehem. Solomon, the wisest of all, wrote that kings from distant shores would bring gifts and bow down to the Messiah. These are the reasons my brothers and I traveled so far. We are those kings.

The gift from my people is the very blend Adonai declared holy, to be burned for him alone. Therefore, I presented Yeshua, our Messiah, the very same most sacred and precious incense.

I write these words camped near Bethlehem, not knowing how many years will pass before you, Elijah ben Ezra, will read these words. We escape by a different route for our homelands, lest we be captured by Herod.

You are entrusted with a mighty task. Keep us informed. May Adonai protect you and keep you. May his face shine upon you, giving you peace, safety, and prosperity.

Faithfully I affix my seal,

Melech ben Yisscachiore

I was astonished to learn that the Magi who had come to honor Yeshua were long-lost tribes, descendants of Israel! I looked around the table at other stunned faces. Samuel said excitedly, "This is an extraordinary document! We must take it to Jerusalem. It is proof that Yeshua is the one prophesied!"

Shabach agreed, "We should take it to Nicodemus to present to the Sanhedrin. They will have Caiaphas in chains or, worse, for his plotting."

After remaining quiet for a few moments, I said, "Let us finish reading and then calmly talk." There were smaller scrolls to read.

Again, a memory came, confirming what I was reading. These written words were almost the same that were spoken by the one named Melech that night. I recalled Mary's and Joseph's eyes riveted on the regal man as he spoke. His accented Hebrew was different but understandable. He spoke softly but in a manner that bespoke authority, that of a ruler. His garments were simple and strange yet splendid. I went back to the scrolls.

I sat with a breaking heart for my next duty.

CHAPTER 74

THE DECISION

WE SAT QUIETLY, attempting to absorb what we had just learned. Shabach, the wise chazzen, was first to speak. "I can tell by the look on your face, my friend, that you have something to tell us."

I looked at my friend, smiled, pointed at the scroll, and said, "This changes the story of our people. The birth of Messiah fulfilled and children of Israel long lost now found."

Yodi stood up. "This is wonderful! We can teach the children about Yeshua and these humble men whom Adonai chose to bow before him as their king." Her smile radiated excitement.

Asa looked at his bride-to-be. "Yes, my love, we can teach everyone what we have learned, but there is pain in the cost." He looked around the table. "Our Abba Eli has been ordained and must fulfill his mission."

Silence settled heavily in the room. Slowly I looked into every pair of eyes around the table. "Asa is correct. The men who traveled so far may not be living today. But their children, their tribes must know that Messiah lives. They must know the truth." I paused, stood, laid my hand on my chest over my heart where Yeshua had touched me, and said, "I must find his sheep!" I put my hands on the scrolls and declared, "These are his sheep."

Sarah had a stricken look on her face at my announcement. "Papa, what do you mean?" She knew my answer before I spoke, and tears poured from her eyes.

"I must find this Melech, the leader of the men who know Yeshua is Messiah. The messenger at the pool will bring word only of his crucifixion. What they will not know is that Messiah lives! They must know the truth!" The determination in my voice ended any opposition to my mission.

Asa stood. "Abba, this journey will take years!" His statement was more of a question as I stayed silent and resolved.

Yodi came around the table and took Asa's hand. "We will go with you!"

Asa looked at his bride-to-be, nodded, looked at me smiling, and said, "Yes!"

Jonathan, still seated, said, "Wait, we have no idea where this king, this Melech, makes his home. You cannot just wander to the east in hopes of finding him."

Samuel answered my son without words as he turned the scroll over, revealing a map. Tracing his finger over the parchment, going from left to right, Samuel's finger stopped; he looked up and said, "Here is where you will find Melech and his people. There is no mystery. This map leads east and south to a body of water."

Silence again in the room. Samuel looked at me. "With your permission I will make copies of these documents, front and back. I will present them to Nicodemus." I nodded in agreement.

Jonathan asked, "Papa, how will we know if you find the ones you are looking for?"

Walking over to my son, I put my hand on his shoulder. "We will tell you all about it upon our return. Now let us read the other scrolls."

The remaining parchments were in Melech's hand and told short stories of each visitor paying tribute to Yeshua. Just like the largest parchment, each had a map on the reverse. Samuel was excited to copy each to gift the Teacher of Israel. Everyone around the table had a chance to look at the scrolls and maps.

I announced it was time for sleep; the next day we would detail our plans to prepare the family for the journey. Carefully lifting the old skins, I took them to my room, set them on my desk, and went to my pallet for a peaceful night of sleep.

CHAPTER 75

THE PREPARATION

WEEKS OF PREPARATION started the moment I woke up the following morning. Marta, Sarah, and Hannah arranged wedding plans for Asa and Yodi. Jonathan was successful in placing Shabach as leader of the shepherds prior to the start of spring shearing. He brought the shepherds to our house, and in one day the frame for Asa's addition was completed. Within the week it was finished.

Yodi and Asa's visit with her parents went as well as possible. They were concerned about the travel and time away but looked forward to her return. The wedding took place a week after Rabbi Joel and the rest of the Cana pilgrims returned from Jerusalem. Samuel completed the reproduction of the scrolls and, along with the rabbi, added their certification to the authenticity and origin of the documents.

Caleb and Jacob became very close. Jacob was so loved Marta and Jonathan adopted him! Jacob delighted everyone with his quick mind and willingness to learn. He devised a plan to hide coins in the rugged wagon we had bought and modified for the journey, a trick he learned on the streets, hiding the coins he begged.

Rose, Sand, and Flower would be our mounts for the journey, but we needed at least one other that was trained to pull a cart, so we purchased one from the village. The more I thought about traveling with Asa and Yodi, the lighter the burden of the venture became. I thought about Abraham, who lived seventy-five years before leaving his home for foreign lands. I laughed realizing I was a child by comparison.

How quickly the days passed. Shabach took full charge of the flocks, the shepherds yielding quickly to his authority. Jonathan staked out an area to build a home for the chazzen and his family. Hannah and the girls loved the simple life in the hills of Galilee. With her credentials Hannah became a teacher and member of the synagogue ladies. Sarah and Samuel returned to Capernaum and prepared to add more wool trade to their business.

Shavuot (Festival of Weeks) was approaching, and the plan for the trip was clear. We would go to Capernaum first to bring a shipment of freshly shorn wool as samples for Sarah. Samuel would accompany us to Jerusalem and present the scrolls to Nicodemus. Then our journey to find Melech and his tribe would begin.

Word of my history with Yeshua rallied the village, and a party was planned for our departure. There was a feast in the village square with food, wine, dancing, and speeches. Many speeches. My favorite and most poignant was delivered by Jonathan. He talked about life with me being gone so much as a child and about knowing there would be a day I would return to Cana. There were many hugs and tears before the evening was over, and the next morning the three of us were off to Capernaum.

We arrived early afternoon on another beautiful spring day. Saul spotted us climbing the hill and came running to greet us. He was delighted with the new donkey, named *Shimshon* (Samson) by Caleb for his size and strength. Saul wasted no time climbing the wagon onto the bales of newly shorn wool, bouncing up and down.

Sarah was excited to see us, especially Yodi, whom she so admired for her courage to make the journey. The women went into the house while we moved the wagon to the back and tended to the animals. The evening meal was prepared, and we dined early. When the table was cleared, Samuel showed us the reproductions of the scrolls, which were precisely done. Before dark Asa took Sarah and Saul riding on Samson's back; the children went to bed happy. We planned to spend at least three nights in Capernaum with the family before leaving for Jerusalem.

The morning after our arrival, the whole family walked to the fishing area to show Yodi the shore and meet Yeshua's followers, but none were there. Simon's mother-in-law informed us that they were in Jerusalem for the upcoming Shavuot festival. Yodi had never seen such a big body of water and stood in awe of the expanse. We were all looking at the water when a voice called out from behind us. "Elijah ben Ezra, the man I have been looking for." Turning in unison, we all faced the Roman centurion Salvius.

To our surprise, the tough Roman officer greeted us with "Shalom!" I smiled at the soldier as Yodi grabbed Asa's arm with a look of fright on her face.

Looking at my daughter-in-law, Salvius said, "Please do not be alarmed. Your family knows me. I pose no threat." Samuel had an amused smile on his face as the centurion continued. "Eli, I have been talking to Samuel, and he has informed me that you are about to embark on a journey to a land that you know nothing of."

I nodded, and Salvius continued. "I am retiring after twenty-five years in service to Rome. I would like to accompany you on your quest to find the man you met at the home of Yeshua when he was a child." His request was stunning. "You see, the day he healed my servant without a word or a touch, I knew he was divine. I have my documents from Rome and the requested payment of gold rather than land. I offer you my service as a guide and guard."

I was speechless, Sarah and Samuel were grinning, Rebekah and Saul ran over to the soldier, and Asa and Yodi stood silent with me. "There is something else," Salvius said in a manner that had a note of humor. "My entire household staff and six of my men, all of whom believe that Yeshua is the Messiah of your people, will be coming if you accept our service."

Samuel looked at me, still smiling. "This Roman centurion has been studying with me for two years. He can read and write Hebrew. He has been studying Torah."

Immediately I knew this was the hand of Messiah at work. Instead of three travelers alone, we would have the protection of seven experienced soldiers. I was still silent and struck by the news, but the centurion had one more thing to add.

"If you honor us as your escort, we will be traveling with added protection under the banner of Rome." Yet another twist in the planning of my journey, the authority of the Roman Empire.

I simply smiled, nodded, and said, "Yes!"

Salvius left us, saying he would be ready to depart the morning after Shabbat.

CHAPTER 76

THE BEGINNING

We walked to the house of Simon, which was empty except for his mother-in-law, Bekka, who was kneading precious challah dough, the crusty egg bread with the soft, fragrant insides. "My lady," I called to her in a jolly tone, "every time we meet, you are pounding something. The last time it was laundry. Today it is flour and eggs."

Jovially she replied, "This bread is mine to enjoy. When it is at its delicious best, I will tear off a piece and soak it with sweet wine—a party of one. If you are looking for Simon, his brother, and friends, they are in Jerusalem to pray and celebrate Shavuot with the other followers of the one who arose, blessed be his name."

"We hope to see him there. We leave for the city of David after Shabbat." I waved and walked back to the house; Yodi turned every few steps to look again at the water.

Samuel and I decided that the original scrolls should be presented to Nicodemus for study and placed in the Sanhedrin library. They were packaged carefully for presentation. One set of copies would remain with Samuel, and I would carry a copy to present to Melech and his people. Extra maps were made for the journey.

Shabbat was a pleasant time of relaxation. Everything was prepared for loading onto the wagon the morning of our departure. Sarah was excited for our adventure but sad at the length of time we would be gone. She did not dwell on the dangers now that we had the addition of Salvius and his men.

The morning came to leave Capernaum and meet up with the former centurion on the road south of town. It was an incredible sight to behold: a total of thirty-six men and women and eight mule-drawn wagons. And what wagons indeed! Grandly restored from retired pieces of the Roman Army. One wagon was a rolling kitchen complete with food supplies. The others were piled high with all manner of goods and covered with heavy, tightly woven wool blankets tied down with thick roping.

Standing in military-style formation with Salvius at the head were all who were joining our quest. As we neared them, at a signal from their leader, they kneeled. The seasoned centurion looked up at me and in firm voice said, "Elijah ben Ezra, the one chosen by Messiah to tell the story of his birth, we pledge our fealty to you as our leader. We submit to your authority in our quest to reach the king who honored Yeshua." Salvius stood, approached me, and offered his right arm as his sign of loyalty.

Grasping the Roman's arm, I said, "I accept your offer, citizen of Rome. You are a man of many surprises, my friend."

Then there was another surprise as the man who had been the representative of my sworn enemy for so many years pulled me into a strong embrace. "Shall we be off?" he asked. I nodded, and our little caravan made for Jerusalem.

We arrived at the north of the city and struck camp on the fourth evening out of Capernaum. The hills were crowded with tents of all types, sizes, shapes, and colors. We had left our tent of many colors at home for the more sturdy, military kind. It was a treat to see how quickly the soldiers and Salvius's household set up. Night after night we had witnessed the precision exercise of the men and women who had become our extended family.

Before dawn on the morning of Shavuot, Samuel and I set off for the home of Nicodemus while the others broke camp. We were going to meet them all at the foot of the road to Jericho near the Sheep Gate and Bethesda pool. Nicodemus was about to leave his home when we arrived.

Samuel greeted him. "Shalom, Teacher of Israel."

Nicodemus looked as if he had aged years in the last fifty days. His sad eyes matched his voice. "I am *Nachdemon ben Guryon* (Nicodemus, son of Gurion), a simple Pharisee, no longer considered a teacher. Please come in."

He told us that since the day of the crucifixion, when he and Yosef had taken Yeshua's body, he had been rejected by the Sanhedrin and shunned. Even though there had been many reports of seeing Messiah, his resurrection was called a hoax.

In a buoyant voice, Samuel said, "Take heart, my friend. We bring you proof of his divine birth!"

My son-in-law laid out the scrolls, and Nicodemus seemed to regain energy and youth as he read. "These are wonderful documents. What will you do with them?"

I answered, "They are a gift to you from me. We are leaving today to find Melech ben Yissachiore and tell him that Yeshua lives!"

With joy in his voice, Nicodemus said, "This is what I need to present to that body of mockers and nonbelievers! Thank you, my friends." He stood and hugged the two of us. We told him about our little caravan. He said he would walk with us to meet them.

The city was jammed with thousands of pilgrims from all over. Strange looks and strange languages were seen and heard as we made our way toward the Sheep Gate. At the edge of the crowd were Asa, Yodi, and Salvius standing with Moses and his family. We made our way to them.

In his booming voice, Moses bellowed, "Shalom, my brother!" I received my second crushing embrace of the morning. "I am so happy to see you again." His beautiful family huddled around him.

"Asa has told us about your journey. We have been discussing the possibility of returning to Aksum to share the news of Yeshua." It was at that moment I realized I would probably never see my friend and brother of heritage again.

Before I had a chance to say a word, a powerful wind came straight down from heaven as if Adonai's breath were upon us. I looked at the faces of those around me; they all glowed as if each were a candle and above each head was a flame. Through the din every voice I heard I was able to understand, even though different languages were being spoken. When I spoke, strangers from other lands were able to understand my words. Another miracle from Adonai!

As we all stood in amazement, a voice louder than any other rang out from the top step of the porch. It was that of the huge redheaded fisherman Simon surrounded by Yeshua's followers, his disciples. He spoke the words of the prophet Joel and King David, telling all assembled that we had been visited by the *Ruach HaKodesh* (Holy Spirit) and that the crucified Yeshua was Messiah.

Each one of us felt filled with the breath of heaven, and Simon invited all gathered to the pool to be immersed. Not to my surprise, it was Salvius who advanced and was the first into the pool, followed by his men and his entire household. I looked at Asa, Samuel, and Nicodemus and said, "We must be immersed as well!" Moses and his family followed us.

We all stayed in the pool and helped immerse everyone who came forward. By noon there were thousands who had come through the water. Finally, when there were none left to be immersed, we exited the pool to our wagons.

Waiting for us was a wet Samuel with an equally drenched Moses and his family. I looked at Moses and said, "I love you, my brother. Go in safety and peace."

I embraced Samuel and said, "You are my son. Take care of my daughter and grandchildren. Be close to your brother Jonathan."

With tears in his eyes, Samuel said, "I shall! I love you, Abba!"

Nicodemus embraced me once again and kissed my cheeks. "Return to us, my friend."

I, Elijah ben Ezra, the Magi's Man, nodded, turned, and began leading my little family caravan of believers on our mission to find Melech, his people, and the lost tribes of Israel, to tell them Yeshua is alive!

NAMES

Aaron—brother of Moses, first high priest during the Exodus
Abel ben Tashi—old man with his wife in a Capernaum market
Addassah—Eli's granddaughter
Anna—Jacob's grieving mother
Antoni—servant of Salvius, centurion of Rome
Aryeh—Andrew
Avraham—Abraham
Avram—Abram, shepherd from Cana
Aysah—Asa, former Aleph
Balthea del Salazar—Magi, descendant of Zebulon
Bar'Timai—Bartimaeus
Baruch—Y'oyas' grandson
Bekka—Simon's mother-in-law
Benji—nickname of Benjamin, shepherd friend of Eli
Binyamin—Benjamin
Bidi—merchant, wife of Moses, friend of Eli
Caleb—Jonathan and Marta's son
Dani'el—Daniel, son of Moses and Bidi
Dav'ed—David, Yodi's father
Div'orah—Deborah
Eleazar—Lazarus
Eli / Eliyahu ben Ezra—Elijah, son of Ezra; shepherd born in Cana
Eliyahu—Elijah
Emma—Shabach's daughter
Ga'alen—disabled man at pool
Gamliy'el—Gamaliel
Gavri'el—Gabriel
Golyat—Goliath

Hannah—wife of Shabach
Havilah ben Paran—old man on the road whose ox was slaughtered by Romans
Heshben Nebo—Magi, descendant of Benjamin
Hordes—Herod (Note: Herod the Great was king of Judea from 72 BC to AD 4)
Il Gadsparim—Magi, descendant of Gad
Ira—Eli's cousin
Jacob—Eli's childhood friend
Jacob—Street urchin saved by Eli and Asa
Jonathan ben Elijah—Eli's son
Ka'lev—Caleb, Eli's grandson
Layla—eldest daughter of Moses and Bidi
Lorah—innkeeper near Jericho
Mal'akhi—Malachi, last of the recorded Hebrew prophets
Marta—wife of Jonathan
Marta—sister of Eleazar (Lazarus)
Maryam bas Yoachim—Mary, daughter of Joachim
Mattityah—Matthias, Jacob's grieving father
Melech Dav'ed—King David
Melech bin Yissachiore—Magi, descendant of Issachar
Moshe—Moses, the Prophet
Moses—merchant, friend of Eli, named after the prophet Moses
Nachdemon ben Guryon—Nicodemus, son of Gurion
Natana'el—Nathanael, follower of Yeshua
Natan'el/Nathaniel/Natie—elder of Cana, father of the bride when Yeshua changed water to wine
Noach—Noah, grandson of Ta'oma, great-grandson of Y'oyas
Pali'ef—Phillip
Peleg—shepherd who took Joseph and Mary to Migdal Eder
Pelez—doctor at the Shepherd Academy
Phineas ben Zev—Greater Sanhedrin
Rahel—Rachel, wife of Eli
Rivkah—Rebekah, Eli's granddaughter

Sadyah—Sadie, Yodi's mother
Salvius—centurion in Capernaum
Sarah—Eli's daughter, wife to Samuel
Sha'ul—Saul, Eli's Grandson
Sha'ul HaTarsi—Saul of Tarsus
Shabach—Number Eleven, Chazzen of the Temple Shepherd Academy
Shannah—old lady, wife of Abel ben Tashi in Capernaum market
Simcha—Eli's cousin, Ira's wife
Shi'mon ben Yonah—Simon, son of Jonah
Shimshon—Samson
Shimyon—Simeon
Shlomoh—Solomon
Shmu'el ben Zev— Samuel, son of Wolf, Sarah's husband, Eli's son-in-law
Sylva—servant of Shabach in the academy
Tamar—childhood friend of Sarah
Tepaysh—Herod's master physician (*tepaysh* in Hebrew means "fool")
Tevyeh—Aleph, friend of Eli, master shepherd at Migdal Eder
Tizra Ebali—Magi, descendant of Manasseh
Tobis—ox taken from Havilah ben Paran and slaughtered
Ta'oma—Thomas, donkey breeder
Ya'acov—James, earthly brother of Yeshua
Ya'akov ben Mattityah—Jacob, son of Matthias; Eli's friend, murdered by a Roman
Ya'el—Yael
Yehuda—Judas
Yeshua—Jesus, Yeshua ben Yosef (Jesus, son of Joseph)
Yesha'yahu—Isaiah
Yiftah—Jephthah
Yiz'kach—Isaac
Yochanan ben Zekria—John, son of Zecheria
Yochanan ben Zavadai—John, son of Zebedee
Yodi—Caleb's teacher
Yoel—Joel, chief rabbi of Cana
Yosef ben Calfai—Joseph, son of Caiaphas

Yosef ben Heli—Joseph, son of Heli, earthly father of Yeshua, Messiah
Yosef HaRamatayim—Joseph of Arimathea
Y'oyas—mother of Ta'oma
Zvadyah—Zebedee

GLOSSARY

abba—father
Adonai—Lord
"Adon Olom"—"Eternal Master"
Aksum—a region in North Ethiopia
Aleph—*A*, (א) the first letter of the Hebrew alphabet; name plus number given to a new class of students at the Shepherd Academy
aliyah—honor
amatz—adoption ritual
ark—wood cabinet housing the Torah
bar mitzvah—son of the commandment
baruch atah—blessed are you
barucha—blessing
Beit'Anyeh—Bethany
Beit'Lehem—Bethlehem
Beit'Zada—Bethesda
Beit'Tzaida—Bethsaida
bema—altar, podium
boker tov—good morning
centuria—one hundred soldiers
Chag Sameah—Good Holiday
cha'mohr(s)—donkey(s)
chazzen—servant of the temple, primary leader of the academy
cherev—flint knife
Chiore—town on the coast of the Purple Sea
chochmah—great wisdom
chuppah—wedding canopy
Dalet (ד)—*D*, fourth letter of the Hebrew alphabet assigned to noncommissioned officer in the Shepherd Academy; sergeant

davening—praying while rocking back and forth
dohd—uncle
El Shaddai—the Lord Almighty
eema—mother
ephah—large basket
erev—eve of
erusin—betrothal
Ezrat HaGoyim—Court of Gentiles
Ezrat HaNashim—Court of Women
Ezrat HaKohanim—Court of Priests
Geu'lah—Kinsman Redeemer
Ginosar—Gennesaret
goyim—gentiles
Ha Adon—the Lord
habinah—discernment
Hagafen—blessing of the wine
HaMakabi—the Hammer
Hamotzi—blessing of the bread
HaNatziret—of Nazareth
Har Korazin—Mount Chorazin
Har Ta'avar—Mount Tabor
HaShem—the Name
hoshia na—deliver us
isha—wife
Kadosh HaKodashim—Holy of Holies
kashrut—Hebrew dietary law; kosher
kavranim—burial servants
Kephar Nahum—Capernaum
ketubah(s)—marriage certificate(s), ornate contract(s)
khothen kham—father-in-law
khozeh—contract
kiddushin—sanctification
kohanim—priests
Kohen Hagadol—high priest

korbanot—sacrificial animals
l'chaim—to life
leshe'avar—emeritus
lepton—small copper Roman coin; mite
letzlov—crucify
Lishkat HaGazit—the Hall of Hewn Stones
Malech HaMovet—the Angel of Death
malon—inn
Mashiach—Messiah
matzah—unleavened bread
mazel tov—good fortune has occurred
menorah(s)—lampstand(s)
meyaladet—midwife
mezuzah—prayer scroll encased in a small container mounted on a door post, inscribed with Deuteronomy 6:4–9, 11:13–31
mikvah—water purification ritual
minyan—ten men, a quorum consisting of mature men
Natziret—Nazareth
neched—grandson
nechda—granddaughter
Pesach—Passover
pilum—spear, javelin
P'rushim—Pharisees
rachamin—mercy
resah—murder
Rosh Hashanah—Feast of Trumpets
sabba—grandfather
safta—grandmother
saftim—grandmothers
salach—forgive
seder—ceremonial meal
Shavuot—Feast of Weeks, Pentecost
Shema—Hear, the first word of Deuteronomy 6:4–9, most reverent prayer

Sheol—land of the dead
shesh-besh—six-five
Shi'kher—Sychar
shiva—mourning
Sichem—Shechem
Sifrei Torah—Holy Scrolls
simlah—shepherd's outer garment
Sivan—third month of the Hebrew calendar
Sha'ar Harachamim—Mercy Gate
Sha'ar Nikanor—Nicanor Gate
Sha'ar Kevesh—Sheep Gate
Sha'ar YaFar—Beautiful Gate
Shavout—Feast of Weeks, celebrated fifty days after Passover, Pentecost
shedims—spirits
Shomron—Samaria
Shomroni—Samaritan
shul—synagogue
skyt—shepherd bag
Sukkot—Feast of Tabernacles
sukkots—temporary dwellings made of wood walls and palm fronds as a roof
tallit—prayer shawl
talmadim—disciples
tefillin—phylacteries
tivihla—baptism
Todah, Adonai!—Thank you, Lord!
Torah—Five Books of Moses, the Pentateuch
Tav (ת)—*T*, last letter of the Hebrew alphabet
tumah—unclean
Tz'dukim—Sadducees
tzara'at—leprosy
Ve'Lohai Ha—the God of
yarmulke—skullcap
Yitzra'el—Jezreel

Yom Kippur—Day of Atonement

ACKNOWLEDGEMENTS

Mark Cardona gave me his notes and I ran with them. Writing a book is impossible without the support of family and friends. My wife Joyce was there every minute we were locked in our home during the pandemic of '20-'21 prompting me to rest when necessary and was my daily editor. Early conversations with Tommy Earl and Tim Cobb kept me motivated. The very first iteration was sent to Dawn Steinker who told me to fix the dialogue making the manuscript readable. Then the formidable LaRose Coffey gave me lessons on the phone that helped me hone the work. Thanks to my Beta Readers: Betty Burrus, Scott Greer, Danny Hutcheson, Carolyn Palmer and Dr. Michael Smith. Justin Achelpohl took my raw sketches and created beautiful art and Chase Wall turned an image into an actual coin. Finally, my daughter Jody with her 3rd degree blackbelt in Tae Kwan Do, grit and humor inspired me to get this book published.

Made in the USA
Coppell, TX
02 October 2023